# Chertsey Park

G J Bellamy

ISBN: 9798850345327

This publication is a work of fiction. All names, characters and events in this publication, other than those clearly in the public domain, are fictitious and any resemblance to real persons, living or dead, or actual events is purely coincidental.

Copyright © 2023 by G J Bellamy. All rights reserved.

The moral right of the author has been asserted.

No part of this publication may be reproduced, stored in a retrieval system, or transmitted in any form or by any means, without the prior express written permission of the publisher.

G J Bellamy

gjbellamy.com

# Contents

| | |
|---|---|
| Cast of Characters | V |
| 1. An evening's entertainment | 1 |
| 2. Paper! Paper! | 17 |
| 3. Going to the dogs | 29 |
| 4. Repairing to Rotten Row | 41 |
| 5. A network of intrigue | 55 |
| 6. Dinner at Lyall Place | 69 |
| 7. Chasing an idea | 86 |
| 8. Dear old Fleet Street | 98 |
| 9. Important arrangements | 113 |
| 10. Wildlife | 124 |
| 11. Red Fist and blackmail | 139 |
| 12. Planning stage | 152 |
| 13. The dormitory | 163 |
| 14. A bear in its den, and a lion in the hall | 178 |
| 15. Head counts and speeches | 192 |

| | | |
|---|---|---|
| 16. | Hunting grounds | 205 |
| 17. | Shoot | 220 |
| 18. | A strange dance | 231 |
| 19. | Plans large and small | 244 |
| 20. | A stop on the stairs | 257 |
| 21. | Pull | 271 |
| 22. | Watching and whispering | 285 |
| 23. | Probing attacks | 298 |
| 24. | Everything stops for tea | 310 |
| 25. | Courses | 324 |
| 26. | Time to leave | 336 |
| 27. | The best laid plans of mice and maids... | 347 |
| 28. | Running with the hare & hunting with the hounds | 358 |
| 29. | Sunningdale | 367 |
| 30. | Enemy at the gates | 378 |
| 31. | The Grand Salon | 390 |
| 32. | Reunion | 404 |
| 33. | Aftermath | 422 |
| 34. | Epilogue | 436 |
| Also By | | 449 |

# Cast of Characters

**Family & Friends**
Sophie Burgoyne / Phoebe King
Henry Burgoyne, vicar - Sophie's father
Lady Shelling (Elizabeth Burgoyne) - Auntie Bessie
Ada McMahon / Nancy Carmichael - Sophie's friend
Flora Dane / Gladys Walton - Sophie's long-time friend
Archie Drysdale - Sophie's second cousin

**The Agency**
Miss Jones, typist and office manageress
Elizabeth Banks, researcher and office helper
Nick, errand boy
Fern / Dora Datchet, maid with a photographic memory
Alfie Tanner, footman
Douglas Broadbent-Wicks / Dan Ely, footman

**White Lyon Yard**
Hawkins, butler
Mary Roberts, maid
Marsden, footman

**Lyall Place, Belgravia**
Georgiana, Countess Stokely
Mr Dalgleish, butler

Miss Beech, maid

**Chertsey Park**
Lord Stokely, Roderick Fielding
Uncle Teddy, Edward Fielding, Roderick's uncle
Mrs Newnham, housekeeper
Bertha, maid
Mrs Potter, cook
Kemp, estate manager
John, one of Kemp's men
Miller, another of Kemp's men
Agnes at the Gardeners Arms

**Lord Stokely's entourage**
Vincent Cobden, Secretary.
Lester Dawkins, executive officer
Morris Wilberforce, financial officer.
Aides, bodyguards, drivers, and a photographer.

**Newspapers and others**
Jack Long, editor-in-chief London Mercury
Jeremy Rushton Editor-in-chief Albion News
Auckland of the Times
Nigel Johnston, M.P. for Walthamstow North

**Scotland Yard and Government Departments**
Superintendent of Special Duties (Inspector) Penrose
Inspector Morton, CID
Sergeant Gowers, CID
Ralph 'Sinjin' Yardley, Foreign Office agent
Len Feather, Yardley's chauffeur, Foreign Office agent
Lord Sidney Laneford, Home Office
Charlotte Terrence, professional gambler and recruited spy.

# Chapter 1

# An evening's entertainment

Britons drive on the left. This is a well-known fact. However, when approaching the entrance of the Savoy, the law of the land has been set aside. Turning off the Strand and onto Savoy Court, which is private property, all vehicles must drive on the right. This regulation-ousting convention, undergirded by a Special Act of Parliament, was born out of the economical habits of bygone hackney carriage drivers. Instead of getting down and doing a proper job of opening the door for his passengers, the cabbie, remaining seated on his perch, reached back for the handle and, without inconveniencing himself any more than strictly necessary, unlatched the right-hand door.

A motorized cab turned onto Savoy Court and, at the halfway point of the tight turning circle, it came to a stop. The doorman opened the passenger's door. Sophie alighted, immediately followed by Sinjin Yardley who, quick to join her, was wearing a long, immaculate black coat, with a white silk scarf and a faultless topper.

Sophie stood on the pavement and gazed, awestruck, taking in the distinguished entrance to the legendary establishment. So many famous and celebrated people had stayed at the hotel or dined in its restaurant that it fired her imagination — making her not only think of things she had read about but also wonder who she might see there tonight.

Yardley had a glimpse of Sophie's profile in that attitude. He thought her beautiful — fresh-faced and, in that second, very young-looking and charming in her unguarded moment. Her cap was a soft, dark brown velvet with a long tassel, and looked like an artist's oversized beret. Her long, sweeping, mid-brown woollen coat hid a dark blue evening gown, created by Mrs Green, the Burgoyne Agency's preferred couturier. When Sophie had tried it on in the Spartan dressing rooms in Brick Lane, Mrs Green said it was as if she had designed the gown with Sophie in mind, so well did it suit and become her.

By some process, which Sophie could only assume included divination, Flora and Ada had guessed that Sophie was to meet Mr Yardley and had then extracted from her that she was going to dinner with him at the Savoy. This had occurred because he had diverged from their agreed-upon agenda by telephoning Sophie at her office instead of writing. Yardley had furthered his outrageous behaviour by suggesting they have a quiet dinner together instead of the originally proposed meeting in a general setting with others present. Sophie, for once forgetting to upbraid him, had surprisingly said yes.

Once they learned of the dinner, Ada and Flora decided they should be involved, too. In the afternoon at White Lyon Yard, Sophie's long brown hair was first brushed, and then clasped into place by Flora, who used her very pretty silver and turquoise comb shaped like a resplendent crown. Use of the hair comb was possible because Flora's jewels had yet to be returned to her pawnbroker for safekeeping.

Ada had ensured that Sophie was turned out to the highest standard possible, while giving pointers to Mary, Sophie's maid courtesy of Aunt Bessie, as she did so. The matter of make-up was a joint decision by the agents. The result — comprising a light application of powder, a dark pink lipstick, faintly pencilled eyebrows, the merest suggestion of kohl, and a faint blush of rouge on Sophie's cheeks — met with approval of all three.

At the time of Sophie's final inspection, Aunt Bessie approved of everything, and lent Sophie a triple string of pearls, and a small black beaded evening bag to complete her ensemble. Turning to practical matters when her niece was ready, Aunt Bessie said that Sophie should find out what income Yardley had at present and what he would have when he became Viscount Ranemore. A sharp interchange between niece and aunt followed, but was thankfully cut short by the arrival of the taxi. After Aunt Bessie had met the well-mannered and confident Mr Yardley, her opinion of him founded itself upon a surer and brighter footing. After the taxi drove away, she said as much to Flora, who agreed with her.

"You look radiant and fabulous," said Sinjin, as he and Sophie sat together at a quiet table in the Savoy Grill.

Unused to such compliments, Sophie felt it was absurd for him to say these things and came close to laughing. Instead, she smiled and replied,

"That's very nice of you... We both look rather different tonight than at our prior meetings."

"True. The maid and the gardener, what? They wouldn't have let me in, of course, but you I think they would."

"There were other outfits of yours, too... I notice that there is quite a relaxed standard of both dress and conduct here. There's a woman I can see who is still wearing her overcoat while eating, and another woman is smoking."

"I believe it has been like that from the start. The Grill is popular with several quite different sets of people. The wealthy clientele staying at the hotel come from many nations; artists and writers frequent the place at lunchtime;

actors and actresses arrive late at night; then there's the theatre crowd rush. Also, politicians and business men of every type drop in at all hours. So, all those various groups have shaped the standards set by the management."

"Yes, I can see they would."

Sophie looked around the room. Sinjin noticed a puzzled look appear on her face.

"Is there anything the matter?"

"Well, this type of place is all rather new to me, but what I notice in particular is that many of the women have their hair cut short."

"Isn't that the latest fashion?" he asked.

"It is, but I hadn't realized until now how prevalent it's become."

"Are you thinking of bobbing your hair?"

"No... I don't think I will. I've never really followed fashions... Couldn't afford to." She laughed. "Besides, some, not many, but some ladies who hire servants stipulate no bobbed hair."

"Do they, indeed? Short hair is very practical. Everyone in the services has their hair bobbed."

They both smiled.

"Not like those old photographs from the last century," said Sophie, "when men had such long hair and beards — even some officers."

"And going back further, don't forget wigs and braids. I couldn't sport the long-haired look." He touched his thick, wavy, pale hair. "My thatch becomes quite unruly over a certain length, so it has to be kept short."

Sophie watched him make the careless action, and then noticed, or rather noticed again, the scar along his jaw. She had seen it before, of course, and now wondered how he had come by it. She also remembered he had walked with a bit of a limp when she first met him, but had not seen him do so since. Behind him, she saw a figure bearing down upon their table.

"The waiter's coming," whispered Sophie, repressing an unexpected mild panic over how to order dinner in such a restaurant.

"What would you like?" asked Sinjin. "I can recommend the chateaubriand."

While waiting for their dinner, they talked about their respective families.

"The title of Viscount Ranemore was created in 1690," began Yardley, "after Colonel John Yardley deserted James the Second in favour of William, Prince of Orange. Hardly a reputable basis for a title, I know. He went on to perform a few notable exploits and provide indispensable services for the new king and queen, for which he received a large estate with a ruined house along with the title. Fortunately, John Yardley had some money and built a rather rambling but altogether comfortable manor house north of Worthing. We're absolutely buried in the country."

"It sounds lovely. Lord John did choose the winning side and rightly so," said Sophie. "It was one thing to be Catholic or Protestant, but for King James to suspend parliament for three years and rule by decree was reprehensible. In my opinion, he made a short-sighted step backwards."

"Yes, he did, and it would gratify Colonel John to hear you say so." Sinjin paused, and looked uncomfortable before resuming. "I mentioned to mother that I was meeting you tonight... This is rather awkward, and I attach no importance to it myself, yet I confess to being curious. She asked about your family. And, for my part, where does Lady Shelling fit into the scheme of things? She is your aunt?"

"Yes, she is. The Burgoyne family has a long history." Sophie explained her immediate family and then its connection to ancient French kings and the dukes of Burgundy.

"Quite fascinating. Then, by rights and had you escaped the French Revolution, you would either be a princess or the daughter of a duke... That should buck mother up no end."

"Mr Yardley...? Sinjin... is not the cart before the horse?"

"My apologies, and it is most definitely so. Mother is very concerned about the title. For her, family is of the utmost importance. She asked me to ask you. Please excuse my impertinence."

Sophie did not like to say what was of utmost importance to Aunt Bessie. "What would she have said if my family had been otherwise?"

"She would be put out, but it makes no difference to me."

"And your father?"

"You only need discuss potatoes with father and he will become your friend for life."

Sophie laughed. "Is he really so devoted to agriculture?"

"Yes, he is. When the weather is more pleasant, you must come down and meet him to find out in person."

"I could further ingratiate myself with Lord Ranemore with a little family history."

"Oh, can you? Tell me about it." He looked relaxed and interested.

"Yes. We had a barony once, but lost it. Lord Giles Burgoyne had an estate in the Buddlesgate Hundred near Winchester. I saw the house years ago, and I've always thought to get it back one day... A childhood fancy, and only that. He built it in 1620 and by 1636, there was only a small mortgage remaining. Unfortunately, that was when he became enamoured of tulips and sought to improve the family's fortunes. He re-mortgaged the property to its fullest extent upon ruinous terms. Then he visited Holland twice to buy tulip bulb contracts. He went for the second time in February 1637, and that was his undoing.

"Lord Giles stayed at a tavern outside Haarlem because, as he discovered upon landing, the city was shut up with an outbreak of the plague. Having fortified himself with copious amounts of jenever — Dutch gin — against the cold and against the plague, he set off for a nearby tulip bulb auction he had seen advertised in the tavern.

"Because of the plague, he more or less had the sale to himself, and spent everything he had in buying up good quality stock and many prize specimens for pennies in the pound. Poor thing, from his diaries it is apparent he had convinced himself on the homeward voyage that he was now the richest man in England, because he had filled his pockets and cases with bulb contracts.

"However, word of the tulip bulb price collapse had preceded his return to England, and by the time he reached home, he knew he was bankrupt. Tulip mania was over and all the frenzied speculation had ended. Realizing he needed to act quickly and before the creditors closed in, he sold off the furniture locally for what he could, and then removed his family to Brittany, where he purchased a farmhouse near the village of Colombel. There, he took delivery of a large quantity of the best Dutch tulip bulbs and went to work. He did well over the years in supplying bulbs to notable Parisian gardens. Later on, he branched out into cheese-making and lived to a good old age. The abandoned barony, however, became extinct, and the estate went to the creditors."

"I'm sorry it fell out that way for Lord Giles," said Sinjin, "although Father will greatly appreciate the story. I'm sure the Bretons cherished the colourful sight of Lord Giles' tulip fields."

"I suppose they did." Sophie laughed.

"Quite remarkable. It's marvellous listening to you... Do you have any more stories like that?"

"A few... Continuing in the same vein, we Burgoynes are very good at losing titles. After Giles re-established the family's fortunes in France, his son, Sebastien Burgoyne, was made a viscomte and received lands in Normandy. He then married into a noble Guyenne family. At the end of the century, Sebastien's grandson, Arnaud, inherited the title of the Marquis de Mimazan. Of course, we lost both those titles and estates during the revolution. That disaster the Burgoynes avoided by emigrating to England in 1789... before things got *really* bad."

"I'm heartily glad that your family did so. May I relay a little of this information to my mother? I won't steal your thunder and repeat your stories because, should you get to tell her them yourself, you will have her spellbound."

"Of course, you may. I'm well aware of the importance placed by many people upon one's heritage... It shouldn't really matter, though, should it?"

"Ah... no, I don't think it should, either." Sinjin smiled. "The fact is, it does in our circle. However, as the influence of the aristocracy diminishes, it is quite apparent that the influence of celebrities, for example, is in the ascendant, and filling in the void."

"That immediately makes me think of a certain person who manages to be both an aristocrat and a celebrity."

Sinjin stared at her. "We should try to avoid talking shop or we'll be here until sunrise and accomplish little."

"I quite agree. I only pointed him out as one who has transitioned into new areas of influence."

"Yes, that's true. And heaven help us should Stokely ever make a move into radio broadcasting when it matures. We'll have to put up with the sound of his wretched voice in addition to him grinning and posturing in photographs."

"Miss Carmichael refers to him as the Big Boat-race — that's cockney rhyme for face."

"It is a very apt expression... She's quite a friend of yours, I think."

"She is... And Len?" With a certain archness in her tone, Sophie was referring to Yardley's chauffeur.

"Oh, yes... Unfortunately, I cannot satisfy your curiosity as to *why* I have a chauffeur who insists on being called by his given name... Here comes the food."

"You do not get off that easily," said Sophie. "I *will* find out."

Sinjin smiled.

After they had finished their dinner, they were on the point of adjourning to the Lancaster Ballroom to dance. A new ensemble had just started its tenure on the first day of the new year, and already, by the fifth of January, the Savoy Havana Band was being mentioned in glowing terms.

Sophie was an indifferent dancer. Even after having been coached by Flora, and practising with Ada, she had only reached the heights of minimal adequacy. She thoroughly hoped that Sinjin was a poorer dancer than she was. However, Sophie did not get the chance to find out. A note was delivered in a sealed envelope to Yardley as they sat at the table. She could tell it was important by his studious look as he read the missive. At last, he looked up.

"I am so dreadfully sorry..."

"A mission?"

"Yet again, I'm afraid it is, Sophie." He sighed heavily.

"Can't be helped," she said, disappointed, but with some relief at not having to dance.

"I'll have to make amends for this somehow."

They both then noticed a second waiter approaching the table, bearing another envelope on a silver tray.

"Perhaps the orders have been countermanded," said Yardley.

He was nonplussed when the man approached Sophie instead.

"Are you Miss King?" asked the waiter.

"I am she." Sophie tried to hide her surprise.

He held out the tray, and she picked up the envelope. When the waiter had gone, she opened it.

"Oh. It seems I've been called away, too... Care to swap notes?"

"We can't. Standing orders and all that."

"But supposing it's the same mission? We could discuss it."

"Absolutely not."

"Spoil-sport... Sinjin, thank you *very* much for such a lovely dinner. I enjoyed our talk, and the food was simply superb."

"I'm so pleased. Dining with you has been most interesting

and a thorough delight. It's such a pity that outside forces should bring the evening to such an abrupt end. Excuse me a moment."

He turned away to summon a waiter.

---

It was Archie who had summoned Sophie from the Savoy. He was awaiting her return in the drawing room at White Lyon Yard. He and Aunt Bessie were sitting comfortably, chatting and drinking sherry, when Sophie entered the room. Archie got up.

"My abject apologies for interferin' with your evening," he said.

"Rest assured, you were not the only interferer," replied Sophie. "Sinjin received a note, too. Is it the same business?"

Archie hesitated. "Possibly... I wonder, Bessie, if you would excuse us for a moment. It's rather important."

"Out of the question. I wish to observe these cloak and dagger proceedings and I forbid you to use another room."

"We're trapped," said Sophie, who sat down. "Say what you can... but do let Auntie hear a juicy bit, for goodness' sake."

"I happen to be still in the room, Sophie," said Aunt Bessie with mock indignation. "However, she's perfectly correct. Make it good and juicy, Archibald."

He sighed. "Very well, but this must go no further than these walls." He sat down and smiled at her. Aunt Bessie smiled back.

"Through information received, it is becoming apparent that Lord Stokely is planning something on a large scale and is presently putting in the necessary groundwork. I can't go into all the details, even if you were not present, Bessie, but the upshot of his activities seems to be this: he wants to foment a general strike.

"His mode of operation is to supply cash to union representatives and, in essence, convert them into being his agents. The half a dozen union agents so far identified hold a wide range of political opinion, from far left to the right of the trade union movement. Yes?" Sophie had put her hand up.

"I have two questions," she said. "If you don't answer one of them, I probably won't understand what you're saying."

"Go ahead."

"What do you mean by 'to the right of the trade union movement'?"

"Ah, yes. These are men who are very much invested in improving working conditions and wages for their union members, but desire few or only limited changes in the governance and laws of the country. The far left, by contrast, wishes to install an entirely new regime and jettison everything else."

"Oh, I see. Improve the current system versus a new system. Please, continue."

"What was your other question?"

"Well, I was just wondering how you and the Foreign Office are involved. Isn't this a *Home* Office matter?"

"Naturally, it is. If I may, I'll answer how the FO came to be involved in just a few moments, and why I sent for you with such urgency."

"Thank you."

"Look, Archibald. I'm on the very edge of my seat here," said Aunt Bessie, "so get on with it."

Archie ignored her comment. "Stokely's union agents are not particularly interesting because of their politics. What is of interest is that these agents are in certain key industries. Two of them belong to the Miners' Federation of Great Britain, and one each in the National Union of Railwaymen, the Associated Society of Locomotive Engineers and Firemen...," Archie tapped his forehead in remembering the names, "the National Union of Dock Labourers, and the

National Union of Printing and Paper Workers."

"*That*," said Aunt Bessie, "is the most depressing assortment of words I have ever heard uttered in a drawing room. Do you require a headache powder or a stiff drink?"

"I'll survive, thank you... If his agents are being primed to act in concert, it will be seen that there is the potential to cause another railway strike, close the mines, hold up imports and exports, and selectively control what gets printed in the newspapers.

"Now, a few individuals in his pay are unlikely to have much effect. However, if and as Stokely recruits more agents, we might have a better understanding of what his intentions are."

Sophie's hand went up again.

"Yes?"

"How do you know they are Stokely agents, and how did you find out?"

"Good questions. This work comes from another department upon whose activities I cannot comment, even if I were familiar with them. My guess is that they have noticed the union agents being in possession of some *extra* money. Whether it was made evident by a change in their habits or by their paying money to others, I do not know. The sources, I'm told, are reliable, and the money traces back to a Stokely associate.

"Now, Bessie, here comes the juicy part, which may tie in with the recruiting of union agents. We were alerted at the FO when an ordinary individual named Arthur Brooke, age 31, entered the country two days ago. The reason he drew our attention is that, although he is a British subject, he has been working in Italy as a freelance journalist for the last six months, during which time he has maintained close associations with the Fasci Italiani di Combattimento. Roughly translated, it means the League of Italian Fighting Bands, which, I'm sad to say, is an apposite description of the league's activities. The targets for their violence are competing political parties and any detractors of their movement.

"Several of Brooke's reports from Italy have been printed in Stokely's newspapers. They were favourable to the fascisti and downplay any violence and illegal dealings. I know he has minimized those elements for a fact, because it so happens I have a mild curiosity in Italy at present." Archie smiled briefly.

"Had that been all, we would have no further interest in Brooke. However, the gentleman dropped a clanger. Brooke mentioned conversationally to someone who was taking more than a passing interest in him, shall we say, that he was going to attend Lord Stokely's birthday party in Belgravia next week."

Aunt Bessie put up her hand this time.

"He's more important than he looks, isn't he?" she asked.

"We believe so, but we're not sure how."

"But if Brooke is invited to Countess Stokely's party for her son," said Sophie, "then either *she* knows Brooke directly and the party could still be a surprise one, or Stokely knows all about the celebration and had Brooke deliberately included in the list."

Archie shook his head. "It is almost inconceivable that she knows Arthur Brooke unless she is directly involved in Stokely's schemes."

"Oh, no, she's not," said Aunt Bessie. "She's not the type. The Countess is that brainless, doting type of mother who believes her foul son to be a gift from the gods. If any family member is involved in Stokely's schemes, it's his uncle, Edward Fielding. Stokely calls him Uncle Teddy, sees him at least once a week, and is always sending him stamps for his collection."

Sophie and Archie stared at Aunt Bessie.

"Um, how did you acquire such information?" asked Archie.

"You have your agents. Sophie has hers. And I have mine. I'm not going to divulge any of their names. There are too many of them, anyway."

Sophie stifled a laugh.

"Come on, Bessie," said Archie. "You needn't give away your

sources, but how do you come to know? Is it friends of friends? That sort of thing?"

"I'm not tellin', but any information I advance shall be as trustworthy as the Bank of England."

"I'm not dismissing or belittling what you say."

"No, you're not, because I shan't give you the chance. You're a busy fellow and I like you, but I can find out things your agents, who can only show a passing interest, will miss entirely. You have no conception of the vast reservoir of information about titled families I can tap into. Now, it is not encyclopaedic and, of course, some families are extraordinarily private, but not the Stokelys."

"Then, Auntie," asked Sophie, "what is your opinion upon Mr Brooke's inclusion in the party guest list?"

"Thank you, my dear. I would say Stokely is aware of the party and asked his mother to include this Brooke fellow, simply because Stokely wishes to show favouritism to the man for a job well done."

Aunt Bessie and Sophie looked at Archie.

"That is an entirely plausible scenario," he said. "It also agrees with the estimate of Brooke's character. His reported candour and overall friendly tone means he does not think of himself as an agent and, by all accounts, seemed not to be concealing anything. Also, if Brooke was bringing vital news, Stokely would not delay seeing him until the party. He would see him immediately." Archie stood up and began to pace. "The urgency, Sophie, is that we need a list of the guests. Obtaining it beforehand has become a must with this odd inclusion of Mr Brooke. Our idea is that Stokely may also invite some of his current inner circle. Should he do so, it would be rather a coup to get their names ahead of time. We can start our investigations much earlier, you see. Do you think you can manage it?"

"Let me see... I would need a good reason to ask for a list of names from the butler... Dietary considerations and preferences might do it. I'll say I need the list to mark in such information for each guest."

"I like that," said Aunt Bessie.

"Yes, that sounds like a reasonable request," agreed Archie.

"His name's Dalgleish," said Sophie. "Although we haven't spoken, I shall telephone him first thing in the morning to ask."

"Excellent. Don't mention any of this to..." Archie paused, giving Aunt Bessie a narrow look, and then he spoke slowly and quietly. "I would wager that you already know the name I was about to mention." He glanced at Sophie and then returned his gaze to Aunt Bessie.

"To whom are you referring?" asked Sophie.

"Miss Terrence — who *should* be a closely kept secret."

"And who is this person, Archibald?" asked Aunt Bessie innocently.

"On this one, you *cannot* pull the wool over my eyes. You are both looking far, far too virtuously guiltless."

"Well, I am surprised at you," said Aunt Bessie. "What a thing to say."

"How very dreadful of me to be suspicious... Anyway, Sophie, we can verify some of what Miss Terrence tells us and that is to the good. I think that's all for the present, and I thank you both for your time and contributions." He stood up. "I'll bid you good night. Thank you for the sherry, Bessie. It was excellent, as always. And Sophie, once more, I sincerely regret spoiling your evening."

After saying good night to him, and upon hearing the front door close, the two ladies burst out laughing.

"Archibald is *such* a lovely fellow," said Aunt Bessie, looking very pleased. "Of course, I know about Charlotte Terrence! Anyway, I must tell you this. While you were returning from the Savoy, I tried getting him to talk about Victoria Redfern, but he refused to say much. Touchy on the subject, I think. You see what *you* can do. Otherwise, how are we to help him...? I honestly believe that, should they marry, the lack of money will make it tremendously difficult for them to succeed. Her father must be made to change his mind about a settlement."

"Oh, I know, Auntie. It's an absolutely dreadful situation. She has everything money can buy, and Archie earns a civil servant's wage. How can she give up the life she knows?"

"I wouldn't do it, but I suppose it *is* possible." She paused. "Now, tell me about your evening with the more than acceptable Mr Yardley."

# Chapter 2

# Paper! Paper!

It was Thursday morning, the 6th of January, 1921. Inspector Morton sat back in his chair and gingerly touched his cheekbone. His face had almost healed completely since the rough and tumble of his last major arrest. Across the desk from him sat Inspector Bygrave, who was writing at that moment. Without looking up, he said,

"This is the second peculiar burglary report I've received this week."

"Peculiar in what way?" asked Morton.

"Two London MPs, both Liberal, had their homes burgled during the night. Entry was through a ground-floor window in both instances. That's to be expected, but the unusual thing in each case is the thief, or thieves, only stole private papers from desks — plus a few trinkets that were within reach and easily pocketed."

"Then he, or they, had to be after the papers," said Morton. "I can see why it landed on your desk. Blackmail, I suppose."

Bygrave looked up. "It's a very strong possibility, I believe... Your face is almost back to normal, by the way."

"Finally, and thank goodness. Do you have their names?" Morton dipped a pen in an inkwell.

"Yes. First, on Monday night, was Frank Briant, MP for Lambeth North. Then, last night, it was the Minister of Labour, Thomas Macnamara."

"Indeed? Any cabinet documents missing?"

"He says not. Most of the papers taken were personal letters, rough notes for speeches, receipts — run-of-the-mill stuff taken from drawers, except for address books and Briant's 1920 diary. He's very put out about that, as he'd only just finished up the year. The thieves took nothing of any real marketable value. What do you make of it?"

"I don't really know... Although, aren't most of the Liberal seats outside of London?"

"Now *that's* a good point," said Bygrave. "I'll put out a few feelers to see if any MPs' residences have been burgled in other cities or rural ridings."

"Let me know if you find anything," said Morton.

"So you can add more grist to the Penrose mill?"

"I have to keep the Superintendent busy somehow."

---

Burgoyne's Agency had become busier than it had ever been. The stream of typing assignments had increased to the point where there were always three and often as many as six typists working. Regular placements for domestic servants continued at a steady pace, but the largest area of growth was for temporary domestic staff. The London Season was beginning. It was as if a singular thought suddenly seized High Society:- *The Season! How could I forget I need extra servants!? Ones that don't spill soup!* In a determined rush, butlers, housekeepers, gentlemen's gentlemen, and sometimes even the lady of the house herself besieged the various employment agencies for experienced staff to serve at table. As more and more festive dates were pencilled in on calendars, the demand for staff burgeoned. The sudden press of orders made Burgoyne's feel it was managing a church jumble sale when the doors are first opened and it's all elbows and an '*I saw that first!*' attitude. Lady Bermondsey, a former landlady who married her lodger and then pushed him to do great things for the nation, was the possessor of a formidable pair of elbows. In the process of her 'pushing', her husband earned such an indecent amount of money he had to be knighted.

"Now see here, Miss Burgoyne," said Lady Bermondsey, ensconced in Sophie's office and demanding her rights. "I've come down here expressly to meet you to get this terrible situation settled. I've been told your agency is as good as it gets by people I respect. Now, like I said, I must have four maids for the twelfth of January. It's a very important dinner and there are no ifs, ands, or buts about it. I'll pay extra if I have to; just tell me how much. So, then, is it a go?"

Sophie felt skewered. Reluctant to turn business away, yet with the twelfth already booked, she had no other choice.

"I'm terribly sorry, Lady Bermondsey. Burgoyne's has already fully committed to another large engagement for that evening."

"Cancel it, and I'll pay double."

"As generous as that offer is, Burgoyne's does not break its word once given."

"What a *waste* of my time. There's no proper staff to be found *anywhere*."

"Could you not change the date? I still have a few open evenings at the end of January. Also, the thirteenth is open."

"The thirteenth! Heavens *above*, the very idea of it."

"It falls on a Thursday, not a Friday, Lady Bermondsey."

"That hardly makes it any less unlucky, does it?"

"May I ask why the twelfth is so important?"

"I don't mind telling you. It was the day my husband proposed to me. That was twenty-two years ago." She smiled with satisfaction. "I like to do something special every year so that he doesn't forget. Men can be very forgetful about anniversaries sometimes, but I make sure he *never* forgets. I tell you no lie. His marrying me was the making of him. Oh, yes. There, Miss Burgoyne, you bear that in mind for when you get married. Don't let your husband forget a single thing or he'll be off looking for greener pastures." She nodded in agreement with herself.

After a moment to digest this unusual wisdom, Sophie ventured a suggestion. "The twenty-sixth is still open. If your husband is as forgetful of anniversaries as you say, why not pretend he proposed to you on the twenty-sixth?"

"I can't do that. It's not true."

"No, it isn't. But would it really matter if you went first to a fine restaurant on the twelfth for your own secret peace of mind? Then you could have the planned dinner on the twenty-sixth. I can charge the regular rate, less ten per cent. Four maids, wasn't it?"

"Yes, it was four." Lady Bermondsey rapidly calculated the benefits of the suggestion. "But what if he notices it's the wrong date and says something?"

"Then just make a fuss of him for being so observant."

"I suppose I could... Ten per cent off, you say? All right, we'll do it your way."

"Excellent, Lady Bermondsey. You've given me the menu and all the other details. Everything appears straightforward enough. My staff will arrive two hours before dinner to help prepare the dining room."

"I'll leave all that to you. It's such a relief to come to terms and have the matter settled. Perhaps I'll sleep properly tonight." She stared at Sophie for several seconds as a thought crossed her mind. "Now afterwards, I'll be looking for a permanent maid. Would the ten per cent discount still apply to your fee for that?"

"I'm afraid not. The discount was a special accommodation for you and your husband under the most exceptional circumstances. Burgoyne's normal rates are already very competitive and, with our guarantee of satisfaction, you are paying for what you get, which is excellent staff and nothing to worry about."

"Well, there is that, I suppose. I believe that's everything for now, so I'll say goodbye."

In a spare moment after Lady Bermondsey had gone, Sophie once more considered the night of the twelfth of January. It worried her for several reasons because, at that important dinner, she would meet not only Lord Stokely's family but also the earl himself. To be more precise, she was unlikely actually to meet him, but she would serve dinner in his presence. She would take every opportunity to study the most popular man in Britain and, also, its worst enemy.

She had corresponded with the butler, John Dalgleish, the major-domo at Georgiana, Countess of Stokely's London house in Lyall Place. The exchange of letters had proved satisfactory, and the references Burgoyne's had supplied had convinced the butler to hire the agency to serve at the dinner on the condition there was a trial run on Monday, the tenth of January. Therein lay Sophie's chief worry. The complement to be sent was to be composed of five maids and two footmen. As recently as Friday, a footman had announced he was emigrating to Australia immediately, which had Sophie scrambling to find a replacement for him. Of all the people in the world that could be a footman, the only one that Burgoyne's had available on its books was Douglas Broadbent-Wicks, who was obviously a gentleman, and that would in itself require explanation.

Beyond his being tall enough for a footman and his having good manners, there were several pros and cons about Mr B-W when considering him for the position of servant-cum-spy. Pro, he was probably open-minded about spying and had the right sort of spirit and energy for the job; he had performed some work tantamount to spying in the recent past; and he already had half an idea that Sophie herself was a spy. Con, Sophie doubted he was good at keeping secrets, his being somewhat naïve; he was altogether too friendly and talkative; and he had never worked as a servant in the past. Sophie's trouble was, there was no one else she could get at such short notice for the trial run — assuming Broadbent-Wicks would come in and submit to being trained immediately. Her alternative was for either the Foreign Office or Scotland Yard to send someone. Having already discussed the matter with Archie Drysdale and Superintendent Penrose, she feared who they would send. Neither man seemed fully to grasp the potential hazards of a) sending a Scotland Yard man who looked like a policeman, or b1) the Foreign Office supplying a bewildered clerk, or b2) an independently minded diplomat or b3) an intense-looking agent. Compared to these likely outcomes, Mr Broadbent-Wicks did not seem half so bad. Sophie stared at his card, waved it like a fan, came to her decision, and then wrote two notes.

"Nick." She summoned the office boy from her doorway.

"Yes, miss," he replied, putting down the book he was reading, and going into Sophie's office.

Once the door was closed, she said,

"Deliver this to 22 Cabbell Street, flat E. Try to find out where Mr Broadbent-Wicks is today. Should he be at work, track him down, if you can, and put this copy of the note into his hands. Tell him to come at once... the nation needs his help."

"Nation!? Streuth! What's going on, miss?"

"I need another footman for Countess Stokely's dinner."

"Oh, the big one, eh?"

"I'll tell you something, Nick. If you were four years older, you'd be going as a footman."

"You'd hire me for that?" Nick smiled. "All right, I'll tell him... Is he simple or something?"

"No, he's not! I believe he just has a vivid imagination."

"A what...? Whereabouts is Cabbell Street?"

"Marylebone, close to the Edgware Road tube station."

"Up there, eh? I'll find it on the map. It'll be about an hour before I get back *if* I don't have to go looking for..." Nick stared at the double-barrelled name. "Mr Wicks."

"Please, call him Broadbent-Wicks when you meet him."

"It's a bit of an 'andle, though, ain't it? What happens if he works outside Central London?"

"Then just come back."

"Right you are, miss," he said, already on his way.

When he had left, Sophie assembled three sheets of paper and two of carbon to type out in triplicate the guest list for Lord Stokely's birthday party. The seemingly pleasant Mr John Dalgleish had raised no objections to providing the list — even welcomed Burgoyne's dedication to service — and had taken the time to supply all the names, accompanied by several observations concerning known gastronomic likes and dislikes for a few individuals. There was only one Stokely-related tidbit she learnt. The Countess preferred her dinners to be served by *silver service,* where the waiters serve food onto each plate by dexterous, single-handed manipulation of spoon and fork. Mr Dalgleish said that Lord Stokely, despite his mother's wishes, always insisted on serving himself from a salver held by a footman. As she typed the notation, she thought to herself, *So that he can take the best pieces.* She found the fact most irritating.

---

195 Fleet Street housed the offices of The London Mercury, the National Chronicle, and The Country Times — Lord Stokely-controlled papers. He had other papers, provincial ones, that concerned him less. The Mercury appealed to the intellectual, the university-educated, and those with political interests, The National Chronicle had a broader appeal, while The Country Times was squarely aimed at Britain's upper

classes and those of the middle class who had unilaterally elevated themselves a notch or two in the class structure. The political orientation of these papers was difficult to identify, as none of them seemed markedly Liberal or Conservative. They were, however, staunchly pro-Stokely. Occasionally, the earl wrote an article but, usually, the mild Stokely sycophancy contained in these newspapers was left to his editors and writers to impart. Photographs of Stokely at his most genial or looking particularly statesman-like frequently adorned the pages. The readership did not seem to mind because, after all, he was really quite handsome and had Britain's best interests at heart.

Jack Long was fifty-five. Fleet Street had been his life for forty-one years, starting when he had sold newspapers as a boy. Later, he became a reporter, then was an editor, until he became the current Editor-in-chief of the London Mercury. Stokely had wooed him away from a larger newspaper and had offered a more than attractive salary. Although it was early January, he stood by the side of a chemist's shop window, smoking a small cigar. In the warmer months, he often spent time lounging about or walking along Fleet Street solely to gossip with other newspapermen. In this way, he gleaned a lot of inside information. Today was not a day for lounging. Instead, Long waited for a particular man to exit a building on the other side of Fleet Street.

While he smoked, endless streams of vehicles passed in either direction. Long reflected that, if he had a penny for every Pears Soap bus advertisement that had caught his eye in recent times, he would be quite a wealthy man.

Finally, the man for whom Jack Long was waiting appeared. They saw one another. Jack Long nodded, and they each began a separate walk. Their destination was The Baynard Castle, a public house on Queen Victoria Street, which lay outside the journalistic lunchtime catchment area. A quarter of an hour later, they had met and were settling themselves with their drinks and pies at the quiet end of a moderately full saloon bar.

"I don't recognize anyone," said Long, speaking in a low voice.

"No. In the public bar, they look like warehousemen from around Puddle Dock," said Jeremy Rushton, a forty-five-year-old senior editor for a large newspaper. "So what's this surreptitious meeting about?"

"We're both busy men, so I'll come to the point. This is all in the strictest confidence, mind you, so neither of us will breathe a word of this discussion. Agreed?"

"Agreed," said Jeremy Rushton.

"Lord Stokely wants to expand his newspaper interests." Jack Long paused to allow a response.

"That's not exactly a surprise. There's been speculation he would do something for quite a while."

"Well, now it's going to happen. He wants to launch a new national paper with you as editor-in-chief."

"Does he?" Rushton sipped his drink. "I'm quite settled where I am."

"I should imagine you are. But seeing as they passed you over for the top editor's job on your paper four months ago, you might wait ten years for another chance."

"Unfortunately, that is all too true."

"Are you interested?"

"Naturally, I'd like to hear about it. What type of paper are we talking about?"

"He wants a popular paper with a large circulation — the larger, the better. He wants to beat the Chronicle, the News, the Mail, and the Express."

"Hmm, doesn't want much, does he? But then that's the type of fellow he is."

"That's right," said Long.

"What is the political slant to be? I'm a Liberal, as I'm sure you're aware."

"Pro the people, pro change, and let us not forget, pro Stokely."

25

"Ah, I see. He's after the popular vote."

"Could be, although I've never heard him express a desire to run in an election."

"You may be aware of this, Long, I don't know, but they say he's bought your soul."

"Yes, I know that, and they might be right. He's offering you fifteen hundred for each year of a four-year contract."

"Goodness... That's a great deal, even for the top job."

"That isn't all. Maintain a circulation of five hundred thousand and you get a five hundred pound bonus. One million and it's a thousand pounds. When you hit two million, it's five thousand."

"So much money... What happens after four years, or do I need to ask?"

"You don't. If you succeed, the contract will be renewed, if you don't, it won't be. He expects you to succeed. Your job is to make sure the paper has the right mixture of objective news and interesting features to achieve that circulation. The news can't just be from Whitehall. We want good regional representation and plenty of foreign correspondent reports included. The paper has to appeal to working men and women, have something for the children, the sportsman, the vicar, and the publican — everyone. A majority of the public.

"Within reason, there will be money for competitions, stunts, cartoons, and the paper will have the best sports event reporting the nation has ever seen. The project's under way and it needs a man at the helm to steer it properly. There are three editors still to find and, for the interim, I'll be your managing editor. We'll work together to see who we need. Stokely wants the best, so we'll get them wherever we find them."

There was a long silence as the men drank and studied the plush surroundings or the other patrons.

"Does he interfere much?"

"Not often. If he wants something done a certain way, one

has to make sure it happens or have a very good reason why it isn't possible. Other than that, he'll leave you alone. You'd be the man in charge."

"I've heard a few rumours." Rushton sounded hesitant.

"That's right. We've all heard them. Either they're true, or it's unlucky to oppose him."

"What do you think?"

"I've never seen a scrap of evidence, so I honestly don't have an opinion either way. Perhaps I don't want one. Aside from that, I do my work and my conscience is clear. But here's the thing, just name me one owner who doesn't meddle in his newspaper's editorial opinion... For people like you and me with just a grammar school education, Stokely has given us the chance we would never have otherwise seen. He's a gift to us. I'd say you're one of the best newspapermen on the Street. But you won't go any further up the ladder. We both know that. It was true for me, too, which is why I joined the Mercury."

"Yes... This is the moment when I should talk about my principles... I can't say I'm against Stokely, particularly. What bothers me about him is I can't see what it is he wants to do. One day he supports the government, the next day he's almost rabidly against them. It's as though he's waiting for something disastrous to happen." He was quiet for a moment. "But then what?"

"I don't know if he's waiting for anything. His position on the government, though — isn't that how it should be? No government is going to get it right all the time, but it should be called to account when making poor decisions, whether one is for or against the party."

They were silent again until Rushton said,

"When do you want my answer?"

"In two days, but please don't repeat anything we've discussed."

"I gave my word... Does this newspaper have a name?"

"The Albion News."

"How typical of Lord Stokely to appeal to the past in championing his *New* Britain. I'm probably going to say yes, but I wish to inform my wife first. Afterwards, I must give the obligatory two weeks' notice."

"Then give me your decision as soon as you can, and I'll arrange everything... This pie's not bad. How's yours?"

# Chapter 3

# Going to the dogs

On a triangular strip of land, sandwiched between railway lines, stands Battersea Dogs Home. Its frontage is on busy Battersea Park Road, which rises to cross a bridge over the nearby tracks. The segregating effect of road and rail gives the brick building, its additions, and fences a remote air despite the property being in a built-up area near the middle of London.

"How about one by the van, my Lord?" asked the photographer, advancing the film in his camera.

"Certainly," said Stokely who, while cradling a small spaniel in his arms, moved to the side of the vehicle. He put a foot up onto the running board. He looked relaxed and benign in the sunshine of the mild January day.

The photographer repositioned the tripod to capture the Battersea Dogs Home name on the van's side. He framed the photograph, and it appeared as if Lord Stokely had just rescued the dog.

"That's perfect... You are a pleasure to work with, my Lord."

Stokely smiled. "That's all for here, I think." He turned to one of the dogs' home staff. "Yours, I believe."

A woman stepped forward and, with marked deference, took the spaniel from him. Stokely brushed and inspected the front of his overcoat, said goodbye to the rest of the assembled staff, and got into his Rolls-Royce limousine.

"They assured me the dog had been defleaed." He was scrutinizing his coat again.

"Your overcoat has suffered no damage, my Lord," said Vincent Cobden, Stokely's secretary.

"Let us hope not." Stokely nodded, and then Cobden tapped on the glass partition.

The chauffeur put the car in gear and drove away. Next to him was one of Stokely's bodyguards. In the car following the Rolls-Royce sat the photographer, a driver, and another bodyguard.

"Who am I meeting at the orphanage?" asked Stokely.

Cobden gave him several names and the title of their positions. The car was quiet for a minute.

"I think it is time to finalize and publish the book," the earl said at last. "Brooke's reportage and private reports contain some excellent information that I wish to include. His work has allowed me to clarify some of my ideas and I wish now to put them into a definitive form."

"I understood it to be a biographical work, my Lord."

"In part, but the main thrust will be a manifesto detailing the path Britain must take to maintain and strengthen its place in the world. We are weak from the war, and must move quickly to regain our former position."

"I wonder, my Lord, if I might make an observation."

"Please, do."

"The danger in publishing a large-scale work is that it might alienate certain groups whom we may wish to use in the future."

"Like the Communists, you mean? Yes, I've considered that aspect carefully and concluded they are really more trouble than they're worth. Their usefulness is limited because, ultimately, people follow a strong leader and not an ideology. Mark my words, whatever happens in Russia is bound to end in some form of dictatorship. Britain will never accept a surly comrade or a deranged intellectual to be in charge of its affairs."

"But what of the time and money you have spent in courting them?"

"It's not wasted. We know our enemy thoroughly, therefore we can destroy him thoroughly. We don't need the Communists as competitors; and as allies...?" Stokely made a huffing sound. "They would turn on us given the chance. I have made up my mind. We shall use them as scapegoats, characterizing them as alien invaders imposing a foreign system... making the British public loathe and fear them... We shall give the nation a well-defined enemy which then creates the cause to rally behind. Hatred for and then destruction of the Communists and all forms of extreme socialism would ably fulfil that role. But first, I intend to espouse several of their more useful policies and, by rewording them, include them in the manifesto."

"I see."

"You don't approve?"

"My approval is of little consequence, my Lord. The difficulty I anticipate is that, without the appropriate action accompanying the release of such an opus magnum, there will be little real incentive for anything you propose to be adopted by the government."

"That is not my intention. As I often say, the governance of the country must be re-ordered. As for the appropriate action..." Stokely stopped. "At the right time, Britain shall descend into a chaotic state. I believe the Italian fascists have the right idea in fighting the Communists. We shall do the same here and fight them and whoever else opposes us. That is easy to accomplish. But first, we must create a popular movement that appeals to both the traditionalist and the revolutionary. Our newspapers will champion the movement." He stared out of the window for a moment. "I have plenty of backers for the first part. It is the revolutionary wing of the plan that requires building before being set loose. The book will explain matters by setting out what needs to be done." Stokely turned and patted Cobden's arm.

"You see, my friend, we shall sweep away the competition early. All the ugly talk of class struggle and hardship will be replaced by sensible themes of unifying the nation and working towards universal peace and prosperity. The only way to create that unity is through destroying all dissent. Simple prosperity is what everyone wants, and I shall give it to them."

"These are very bold ideas."

"Indeed, and this is the appropriate action that you say must accompany such boldness. Britain's industrial regions are discontented because of unemployment. We need only harness the energy of that resentment to be successful, but we have to move quickly and with certainty to become the dominant voice."

"How can I help facilitate matters, my Lord?"

"You shall help develop a new organization with effective communication for the public's consumption at the local level. Within this organization shall be a strong system of control to ensure everyone's compliance with the overall vision. Through this entity, we shall begin our anti-Communist drive. Next week, we'll meet Brooke and others and, from those meetings, we will draft a comprehensive plan."

"Excellent, my Lord. I welcome this novel challenge."

"Now, for you to meet Brooke, it is necessary for you to telephone the Countess and get yourself included in my birthday celebration dinner."

"Well, I can try... I hardly like to do that, my Lord."

Stokely laughed. "You're a strange bird, Cobden. You don't baulk at revolution and bloodshed, yet appearing too forward in asking for a dinner worries you."

"I have always observed the proprietaries, and for me to trouble Lady Stokely goes against the grain, as it were, my Lord. However, it is an obvious fact Britain needs the new leadership that you will provide. As we can only institute such sweeping changes as you envision through violent overthrow, then we must instigate the process no matter what the cost and no matter where it may lead."

"Well said. I will speak to Mama to spare your sensibilities." Cobden thanked him. Stokely laughed again.

———◦⋈◦———

It was early Thursday evening. At the agency, Ada wore a blank expression and Sophie's patience had worn paper-thin. A fork dropped onto the table in the spare office.

"I'm sure I'll get the hang of this silver service lark," said Douglas Broadbent-Wicks.

"Why don't you 'ave another go," said Ada, any heartfelt encouragement long since absent from her voice.

"Perhaps if it were real food and not just lentils, I might, you know, have a little more success. Can I try it without the gloves, Miss Burgoyne?"

Sophie stepped forward, unavoidably crunching spilled lentils under foot.

"Give me your left glove, please."

"What are you going to do?" he asked, removing it, and then handing it to her. "Hit me with it?" He alone laughed.

Sophie put on the glove. "The spoon and fork, please."

When set, she said, "There are approximately three hundred lentils in a level dessertspoon. Your best score at this point is twenty dropped lentils."

"And that's being kind to you, Mr Broadbent-Wicks," said Ada.

"I have never served with my *left* hand before," said Sophie. "I shall do so now."

Sophie did a quick practise with the spoon and fork. She then picked up the bowl and awkwardly served a spoonful on to the plate.

"How many did I drop?"

"Four or five, miss."

"Oh, I say. That's absolutely marvellous. Well done."

"Good grief! I'm not showing off. I simply cannot understand where you're going wrong. If I can almost manage it with my left hand, why can't you at least do the same with your right?"

"I honestly don't know. It might help if I used *rubber* gloves."

"Rubber gloves in Lady Stokely's dining room?" said Ada. "You must be joking."

"Please, keep practising, Mr Broadbent-Wicks, while Miss McMahon and I attend to other matters."

The two women walked well away from the room and whispered so as not to be overhead.

"He'll get us in trouble, miss, he will an' all," said Ada.

"It's such a pity... He's so open to spying and using different names."

"If he could serve and keep his mouth shut, I'd say he was all right. But he don't *do* those two things, does he?"

"No." Sophie put her hand to her forehead. "Is there anyone you know, or someone in your family, who could work as a footman?"

"Well... One of me brothers could do it, but he might go funny about the spying... I'd rather not ask him, 'cause if he says something to the rest of the family, it would *all* come out."

Sophie was about to reply when a happy Broadbent-Wicks called them.

"I did it! Three times in a row. Come and see."

They returned to watch the demonstration. No lentil escaped the young man.

"I've finally got the hang of the bally thing. It's easy, really."

"That's a partial relief," said Sophie. "You must also remember to be *absolutely* silent at all times while serving... and at all other times."

"Absolutely silent," said Ada.

"You mean like a vow of silence where one chap doesn't speak to the other chaps for years and years on end?"

"Yes. And under no circumstance make a comment such as you just did."

"I completely understand that. Keep a tight lid on the old banter... Ah! But what if I'm asked a question?"

"Answer it as simply as possible, without embellishment, ornamentation or anecdote. Also, remember to whom you are speaking and use the correct form of address."

"Don't worry, Miss Burgoyne, I shall be as quiet as a mouse, until m'lord asks for an extra spud. And, you'll be pleased to know, I still remember all the rules." He smiled. "Be professional at all times — I like that one. Serve from the left, clear from the right, only clear the sherry glass, don't touch the plate, don't lean across, don't turn your back to the table, etcetera."

"Most reassuring," said Sophie. "And the other rules?"

He told them off on his fingers.

"Don't stare when someone is speaking. Don't loiter or stand too close while listening or I'll draw attention to myself. Stay in the background as much as possible. Use hand signals discreetly. If I discover something interesting, I must control myself and make it look as if I have seen nothing — and try to look like a dummy, as Miss McMahon suggested."

"And?" asked Sophie.

"Let me see... Yesss! The butler will be present. Therefore, I must take all my cues from him and not you because, on the night, you will be Miss Phoebe King, the maid... and jolly old secret agent, of course. Exciting, what? I'm so *thoroughly* looking forward to it."

"Excuse me for bothering you," said Yardley, when he had quietly opened the door to Superintendent Penrose's office.

"Why, Mr Yardley. What an unexpected pleasure. Do take a seat." He stopped writing.

"Thank ye, kindly."

"And how are you this evening?" The policeman from Somerset sounded cheerful.

"Personally speaking, never better."

"This is not just a social call, then?"

"I rarely have time for such luxuries. In fact," with a casual move, he hitched his trouser leg slightly before crossing his legs and leaning back, "as recently as last night, I had a very special dinner interrupted in a most importunate fashion. But I suspect my complaint is as taking coals to Newcastle."

Penrose smiled and picked up his pipe. "You might say it is... Mrs Penrose has got used to my working all hours. Now, if I was to go home early unannounced, why, it would upset her arrangements. I'd be vexed, thinking about work, and she'd be shooing me out of the kitchen for being in the way. Conversely, if I receive a telephone call *while* at home... ohh, my, there's nothing more certain to make Mrs P go off like a rocket."

Yardley laughed. "Perhaps you should have Mrs Penrose answer the telephone instead."

"That's a good idea. I might just try it and see what happens... Is it bad news?"

"Hard to say how bad at present. We think Stokely is behind it. Have you met Lord Laneford, the newly installed gentleman at the Home Office?"

"Twice since he's taken over."

"I met him last night at nine thirty. He has a dilemma and

asked me to follow a young chap, a Home Office clerk named Jackson. Our man had been working late, so we followed him when he left a Whitehall office. With Len accompanying me, we trailed him to a run-down tenement house in Pimlico approximately two miles away. Jackson carried a parcel containing copies of HO documents.

"Upon arrival, he knocked on the door. A large gentleman, who had evidently been awaiting Jackson, answered and received the parcel from him. The door then closed, and Jackson left. Within a minute, a light went on in the top-floor flat, presumably the large gentleman's lair. I continued keeping the place under observation, while Len went to fetch Laneford and co.

"The rest of the house was in darkness. At one thirty-five, a motor car arrived containing two men. One of them alighted. He used a key to open the front door of the house. The other remained in the car with the engine running. Somebody switched on the light in the upstairs flat and, within seven or eight minutes, the large gentleman and the other man left the house carrying suitcases. The car departed. At three minutes past two, Laneford's men, accompanied by several police officers, arrived in two vehicles. I left them to it, because as there had been a tipoff, I wanted to keep well out of the way."

"Hmm... So, did his lordship send you here?"

"He did, O perceptive one. Being new to his position, he doesn't know whom to trust at present, except those few individuals he can personally vouch for. Laneford has at least one clerk, Jackson, who he knows is spying for these people, whoever they are, but the more significant point is that between Laneford receiving the address from Len and the police obtaining a search warrant, someone had time to telephone and warn the gang."

"Wouldn't be Len Feather, would it?"

"You know, Len thought the police might suspect him first. He gave vent to *such* howling indignation over the idea that he could not have feigned it. He irritated me so much this morning I had to send him out to do some shopping. No, it is not Len. Furthermore, it is not anyone at the HO. Laneford says he kept a tight rein on things and none of the three HO agents who learned of the Pimlico address after midnight had an opportunity to use a telephone privately."

"Then it was a police officer or the judge who leaked the information."

"It definitely looks that way. I have here the car registration, and some names for you. Laneford is, and I agree with him, reluctant to have anything investigated through the normal channels for obvious reasons." Yardley handed Penrose a slip of paper.

"I'll do this on the strict q.t." Penrose looked at the names. "Judge Morgan." He said the name slowly enough to make Yardley notice.

"Familiar with him?"

"Not personally, but fellow officers sometimes discuss judges who give unusual verdicts or don't direct a jury properly. Let's just say his name being on this list comes as no great surprise... But surely it would be by chance if Morgan were involved?"

"Meaning what, exactly?" asked Yardley.

"Let's assume this outfit to be well organized. We know that at least four people are involved apart from your HO man, Jackson. There are the three men you saw, and whoever warned them. It would be a stroke of luck if, when the search warrant application was made, it happened to be to a judge in their pay."

"Yes, that smacks of it being too coincidental. I take it you are inferring a more systematic arrangement?"

"Unfortunately, I am, and one involving police officers. I hope to get closer to the truth when I've had a gander at the warrant and looked into these names." Penrose examined his pipe. "What were the documents? And why didn't Lord Laneford have Jackson arrested as he left the office?"

"Laneford couldn't or wouldn't say specifically, except that, as a clerk buried among thousands of files associated with factory inspections, Jackson could copy out what he wanted at his leisure. He was careless, though, and a fellow employee reported Jackson, believing him to be up to no good. As for an arrest — Lord Laneford wanted to see who else was involved first, because he could deal with Jackson at any time. However," Yardley consulted his wristwatch, "the gentleman has been under observation all day where he works in case anyone approached him, but the police should have picked him up at his home by now."

"Factory Inspections? Why, that sounds like very dry reading to me." Penrose laughed. "Although there has to be something of value there to whomever it is seeking such information."

The telephone rang. Penrose answered it. At one point he said, "He's here with me now." Then he listened, saying little. He ended the conversation with a curt, 'Thank you'.

"That was the Home Office." Penrose slowly hung up the receiver. "The officers went round to his bedsitter and found Jackson dead. They could smell gas on the landing outside his door, so they broke it down and opened the windows, but were too late. On a table was a quantity of cocaine, a syringe, and an unsigned farewell note. An autopsy will tell us either way, but the detective on the spot thinks it's a murder staged as a suicide. Reckons they were waiting for Jackson when he got home."

"Tut... Poor, silly fellow. Lost his life for a few pounds, no doubt... And he was so alive last night." Yardley got up and looked annoyed. "Whoever did this wanted no loose ends left dangling. What can be so important about factory inspections?"

"We'll see if we can't find out. What I'd like to know is what else are they up to? There are just too many people involved for only the one scheme to be all that they're interested in. Before you go, give me the descriptions of the three men you saw.

"Happy to do so." Yardley sat down again.

"Also, I'd be obliged if your man, Mr Len Feather, would pop round to see me tomorrow."

# Chapter 4

# Repairing to Rotten Row

Fleur de Lis Mews is situated a quarter mile north of White Lyon Yard. Its cobbled street is quite wide and serves well the thirty or so small buildings that line each side. These stables, now mostly converted to garages, once housed the horses and carriages belonging to well-to-do property owners. Only two of the cottage-like buildings now stable horses.

At number eleven, early Friday morning, one of the garage doors was open slightly. Inside, and looking vast and ghostly in the gloom on the left, was Lady Shelling's limousine. To the right, there was another car named Rabbit, an Austin Twenty. This gleaming red vehicle was lit from the side by table lamps with pretty shades. The lamps sat on top of a wooden bench that had a clean oilcloth on it. Spread out on the oilcloth was a large chart. Three people dressed in overalls were studying it.

"Take the grease gun," said Miss Elizabeth Banks, "and give a charge at each of the spring shackle pins — here, and the two at the end here." She pointed out the places on the large diagram.

"Charge?" queried Nick. "Do you mean like a squirt, Miss Elizabeth?"

"I said charge, and I meant charge. But call it a squirt if you must."

He turned away and bent down by the rear wheel. Sophie and Elizabeth leaned in closely to watch him.

"I can't see what I'm doing, Miss and, er, Miss."

"Sorry," said Sophie. She and Elizabeth gave him more room to work.

Nick operated the grease gun and then stood up, smiling. "That was bloomin' *ea-sy*."

"My turn," said Sophie, eagerly taking the gun from him. She used it to grease the springs on the other side of the car while Nick held a lamp for her to see what she was doing.

Elizabeth examined the chart again. "Next on the weekly list is greasing the foot brake cam spindle. You'll find that here." She showed where it was to be found.

Tutor and tutored worked through the list to completion — oiling, greasing, topping up, and generally inspecting the Austin. When they had finished, Sophie said,

"I feel I need some air. I'll just step outside for a moment. We can clean ourselves up properly at Auntie Bessie's."

"Good," said Nick. "This grease gets everywhere." He was wiping his hands with a rag.

"Before you get too clean," said Elizabeth, "there is a very important job still to be done."

"What's that?"

"A good workman always takes care of his tools. So let us clean everything we've used and then return each tool to its proper place in the kit. That way, we will always be able to lay a hand on a thing when it's wanted."

"All right." They set about the task. "Where'd you learn about cars, Miss Elizabeth?"

"Literally, by accident. Sir Damien Boscombe had employed me to catalogue and organize his library when his chauffeur broke a leg. As the house was quite remote and no one else could drive, the chauffeur first taught me how to maintain a car and then, when he could get about, showed me how to drive. It was a 1904 Darracq, a lovely little motor car, but it required a lot of attention to keep it roadworthy."

"So you sort of *had* to learn what to do. Why didn't Sir Damien learn how to drive?"

"He was not a practical type of person. Sir Damien was interested in archeology and only tolerated motor cars as a necessary evil."

"Myself, I'm the other way around," said Nick. "I like motor cars, but don't ask me nothing about archeology. That's them pyramids and old bones, ain't it?"

They finished putting the tools away.

"There is a lot more to it than that, young man."

"I bet there is, Miss Elizabeth, but it won't help me find work, not like knowing how to look after a motor car will."

Sophie re-entered the garage.

"I have just been told that someone stole a car from the garage at number four a week ago. They broke the lock and just drove it away in the middle of the night."

"Oh, dear. How thoroughly dreadful," said Elizabeth.

"It's quite upsetting." Sophie stared at Rabbit with great misgiving, and then she looked at the limousine. "What can we do?" she asked of Elizabeth.

"I'm not sure…" Elizabeth's brow furrowed. "Perhaps there *is* something, though. Nick, please pass me the screwdriver."

The Austin's bonnet went up, and Elizabeth dived in to busy herself. Within a minute, she held up a small item for inspection. "This is the rotor arm," she explained. "The car can now neither start nor the engine turn over. Should a thief try to steal the car… Well, he can't. The plugs won't spark. It's as simple as that."

"You must know everything there is to know about cars," said Nick, obviously impressed by her trick.

"Oh, hardly," said Elizabeth, a rosy sign of slight embarrassment mounting in her cheeks.

"How ingenious," said Sophie. "Well done, Elizabeth. Would the limousine have one as well?"

"Yes, it would." They moved over to the other car to unlatch and fold back the bonnet. "Would you like to try it, Miss Burgoyne.? She offered the screwdriver. "Just undo the distributor cap — that object with the wires — and pull out the rotor arm. Keep it in a very safe place, though."

"I'll give it to Marsden quietly." Sophie began undoing the cap. "He's Lady Shelling's footman and looks after the limousine. Auntie would be furious if she thought I'd been messing about with her car."

"But you're protecting it from theft, Miss Burgoyne." Elizabeth and Nick watched carefully.

"Yes... I'm sure she'll be fine. I would just rather she didn't find out." A few moments later, Sophie had extracted the rotor arm, and smiled triumphantly. "I know little about cars and how to make them run smoothly, but I can now certainly make one *stop* running altogether!"

Sophie and Nick had gone on to the agency. Elizabeth sat waiting in the drawing room at White Lyon Yard. Hawkins, the butler, opened the door and her ladyship entered, dressed in a long, dark grey frock, and wearing a thick, dark blue cardigan. Her hair and face were superbly made up.

"Good morning, Miss Banks, and thank you for coming."

"Good morning, Lady Shelling. It is my pleasure."

"Hawkins, we'll have the coffee in here. Please be seated, Miss Banks."

"Thank you."

They settled themselves.

"I'm sure my niece has explained matters to you."

"She said that you were conducting some research and wished to organize your findings."

"That is correct. It concerns the Stokely family."

"As I have been informed, your ladyship."

"Do you have any qualms about undertaking such work?"

"Well... I wouldn't say qualms, exactly. I do confess to a difficulty in reconciling Lord Stokely's public figure with some of the things I have recently been told. But I trust Miss Burgoyne's judgment in the matter."

"Ah, good." Aunt Bessie got up and went to a small escritoire. She unlocked a drawer and retrieved a pile of sheets of paper. "I've made some notes on what I have learned so far but, if I add anything more, I fear the sense of everything shall irretrievably descend into complete chaos. Here you are. What do you think?"

Elizabeth received the pages filled in on both sides. The first thing that struck her was the old-fashioned beauty of Lady Shelling's penmanship. The second was that what she read made no sense.

"Who is D.C.?"

"Dowager Countess Stokely."

"And what does croup, colic, laryn., influ., lumb., and sci. mean?"

"Her known illnesses, in order, since she was a child. Sci. is short for sciatica."

"Oh."

"My informant, M, that's Mrs Marshall, is a fount of knowledge concerning everyone's illnesses. Gentlemen, I believe, have the equivalent in landmarking a journey by public house. Mrs Marshall does the same in a person's life, only by illness. She's a good-natured woman, but rather morbid sometimes."

"And who is F? The note next to it says Knee, followed by three question marks."

"That's Folger, the Dowager's lady's maid. Apparently, she has a cure for housemaid's knee and it includes turpentine and zinc, but Mrs Marshal was unsure of the quantities or what else went into the preparation. She's going to find out and report back. If it works, it would be a useful remedy."

"I see," said Elizabeth. "So there is a larger story behind each of these brief notes." She held up the sheets that were covered in such brief notes.

Lady Shelling looked her in the eye. "Exactly... It may have crossed your mind that I am in my dotage and about to waste your valuable time. Far from it, Miss Banks. I intend to sieve through the minutiae of the Stokelys' lives in hope of finding useful information. We must expect a good deal of chaff for each kernel that is found. I will record everything I hear, and it is your task to put it into order. Perhaps, in a biographical form for each person."

"Yes, that is a good idea." Elizabeth looked at another page. "Oh, I see you have recorded food preferences... and pursuits... Perhaps if you could give me the key to the initials and explain some of your methods, I could make a start."

They started. They drank coffee and continued. Elizabeth stayed for lunch, and they resumed afterwards. They had tea, but did not stop their work.

"Why would Lord Stokely call his Persian cat Bunsen, I wonder?" asked Elizabeth.

"That is one of those chemistry flame-throwing things... Where is his school-days' page?"

"I saw it a moment ago. Ah, here it is. Page thirteen." She gave the paper to Aunt Bessie.

"Let me see... Yes, here it is. He did well in chemistry at Eton, and the master's name was Byrnewell."

"They must have called him Bunsen Byrnewell, then."

"Undoubtedly. As certainly as night follows day." Aunt Bessie took off her reading glasses. "The naming of the cat demonstrates that Stokely retains a great nostalgia for his schooldays."

"Lady Shelling, may I make a suggestion?"

"Of course."

"Among your circle of acquaintance, is it possible to find a gentleman who was at school at the same time as Lord Stokely?"

"Oh, there's bound to be one. I will investigate and find out... What is your opinion, Miss Banks? Was he a swot, a cad, popular, or a non-entity?"

"I don't like to venture an opinion."

"Not a betting person, eh? Pity. I would put him down as a popular boy, but secretly a cad. Just as he is now."

"That may prove to be the case."

"Now tell me, Miss Banks, what do you intend doing with all this mass of detail?"

"Tabulate and cross-reference it by person, informant, date of the event, and type. Next, I will add information from reference works. From that starting point, and with your permission, I will research public records and combine such useful details as may be found. Hopefully, the results will suggest possible areas of interest requiring further enquiry."

"Excellent. Spare no expense in the matter."

"Ah."

"And what does that ah mean?"

"I am employed by Miss Burgoyne, you see. She allotted two days a week of my time to this project."

"Did she, indeed? I'll have a word with her about that. Two days a week is not enough if we're to get on with the job. Wouldn't you agree?"

"Ah, yes, Lady Shelling, but..."

"But what?"

"I have other office duties."

"Not anymore you don't... Only please don't say I said that to my niece. She often takes things the wrong way and gets furious with me."

Elizabeth thought it prudent to say nothing. She tried to recall an instance when the always pleasant Miss Burgoyne had been infuriated and failed to find one.

Aunt Bessie continued, saying,

"I think we have made a promising start, but that is enough for today. I shall be dining with friends this evening. One gentleman is acquainted with Stokely's Uncle Teddy, so I hope to learn a few things from that angle." Unusual for Bessie, she gave the latter comment an air of great significance by sitting up even straighter, and inclining her head. "Then tomorrow,

I have a fancy to go riding on Rotten Row. The turnout has greatly deteriorated in recent years, but I understand Stokely puts in an appearance there very often. I would like to observe the creature in the wild, as it were... Do you ride, Miss Banks?"

"Yes, but I haven't for many years, Lady Shelling. I used to enjoy it very much when we kept a pony, but that was when I was a girl." A faraway, wistful look came into Elizabeth's eyes.

"According to the newspaper, the weather is supposed to be unseasonably warm and dry tomorrow. A brisk day perhaps — I hope they've got it right, for once. If you have nothing else to do, you could join me. I can lend you a quiet horse with a soft mouth... It is unbelievable, Miss Banks, but I can't get my niece to leave her blasted business alone for five minutes to come with me. Now she's all taken up with that motor car of hers."

"I would love to come," said Elizabeth suddenly, and with a bright expression.

"Would you? Good, that's settled. I'll ask Sophie if she'll *deign* to join us, but I'd bet a pound to a penny she doesn't. I can send the car to your home. What time do you rise?"

---

Contrary to public opinion, weather reporters do not solely rely on the opening or closing of pine cones and the crisp or limp state of their favourite piece of bladderwrack hanging outside on its nail. They use these, certainly, but also resort to barometers, thermometers, rain gauges, hygrometers, windsocks, shipping reports, balloons, mathematics, and current conditions at other weather stations. If all else fails, they look out of the window and give it their best estimate, before couching the forecast in terms often so bland it can cover all eventualities. Saturday morning was a mixed blessing for the weather reporters. They had got it absolutely right in Friday's verbiage, but had failed to be perfect by including the usually safe words 'a chance of showers later.' From Land's End to John o' Groats, there was not a single shower to be found anywhere. In London, specifically around Hyde Park, one would have said that Spring was threatening to irrupt on this unusually warm January day. As a consequence, Londoners were quick to take advantage, and the park was much busier than usual for the time of year.

Aunt Bessie would have lost her bet had she made one. Sophie went riding. Aunt Bessie suspected that she had only done so to chaperone Elizabeth. This half amused and half irritated her.

"I find it astonishing that you could find the time to join us," said Aunt Bessie.

The three women rode side by side at a slow trot, with Aunt Bessie in the middle. The horses were well-mannered and did not mind the spectators on the other side of the railing.

"I have wanted to come before," said Sophie, "but I've been so busy."

"If you had really wanted to go riding, I think you could have found the time."

"I'm here now, so let's enjoy ourselves. It's a lovely day."

"Miss Banks did not hesitate in accepting my offer of some riding. Isn't that correct, Miss Banks?"

"It was very kind of you, Lady Shelling. I couldn't resist such a tempting invitation."

Aunt Bessie smiled. "You are altogether too kind."

Sophie glanced at her aunt, who was still smiling with an air of impervious superiority. An older gentleman riding in the opposite direction reined in his horse to approach them.

"Lady Shelling. How marvellous to see you out and about. Ladies." He touched his low-crowned hat as he greeted them.

"Good afternoon, General Brandt," said Aunt Bessie. "I'd like you to meet Miss Banks, a friend of mine. And this is my niece, Miss Sophie Burgoyne."

"Glad to make your acquaintance. One minute... Burgoyne's. Someone mentioned that name recently. Now what was that in connection with, I wonder?"

"A domestic service agency, was it?" asked Sophie.

"Yes! That's it. A coincidence in the names, I suppose."

"The coincidence is, General Brant, that I am the proprietress."

"Good heavens, is that so?"

"Yes," said Aunt Bessie, "the Burgoyne name has sadly descended into the world of trade."

"Don't say that, Lady Shelling. It's all the rage just now, and needs must, what? But Miss Burgoyne, permit me to say that the ladies who were discussing your agency did so in the most approving terms."

"Oh, thank you so much for telling me. One does one's best, but one never really knows."

The others did not notice as they continued talking, but Elizabeth was smiling quietly to herself, feeling proud to be a part of Burgoyne's.

"But of course, my niece would make a success of anything she cared to put her hand to," said Aunt Bessie.

After a little while, General Brant rode off, and the three women continued. At their leisurely pace, the bits and bridles tinkled and the horses' hooves made a faint thumping noise in the soft sand and the remnants of last year's leaves. The leather harnesses creaked, and the warm, friendly aura of the horses blended with the scents of earth and leaf-mould in the cool air of the winter-bound park. Spectators pointed, leaning on the railing, watching the ambling trio as they passed nearby. A little boy stared, large-eyed, fascinated by the horses and their elegant riders.

Sophie looked along the ride. When viewing the prospect over her horse's dark brown ears, and past the faint steam of the horse's breath, she decided she had been remiss in not falling in with her aunt's wishes before. The truth was, she had feared she may have forgotten how to ride, and Sophie had never been very proficient to start with. She patted the neck of her mount.

"I'm sorry, Auntie, for not accompanying you before. I confess to having had a dread of falling off and making a spectacle of myself — particularly here, of all places."

"Is that the reason...? I wish you had said something at the time. All my horses are very gentle, and you needn't have worried."

"As I now see. I'm glad I came."

"Miss Banks' family used to keep a pony, you know."

"Chester was such a joy," said Elizabeth. "We lived in Wembley... It was all fields roundabout then, and father used to drive a dogcart into town. As often as I could, and when he didn't need Chester, of course, I would be out riding all over the place. It gave me such a sense of freedom... Oh, excuse me for talking so much."

"Please don't disturb yourself, Miss Banks... I, too, had a similar experience in my youth. I'm fortunate enough to be able to keep horses in London, although not for much longer, I think."

"What are you contemplating, Auntie?" Sophie spoke with some alarm.

"It is rather expensive to maintain five horses in town. I had hoped that after the war there would be a return to the way things used to be. My hopes have been disappointed. The day of the horse is over, and many of my friends have given up riding... Age, you understand. I can't justify the horses' upkeep solely for the little riding I do, and I'm not getting any younger."

"Will you sell them?" asked Sophie.

"*Absolutely not!* I shall buy the horses a small farm and have a suitable little man run it and take care of them. I've an idea to collect old donkeys and three-legged dogs and stick 'em all in there, too."

"An animal sanctuary? What a marvellous idea, Lady Shelling," said Elizabeth.

"Do you like it, Miss Banks? And you, Sophie. What is your opinion?"

"I think it is an utterly splendid idea."

"I'm glad you like it, because you have volunteered to take me in your car in search of a suitable property. We'll go in the Spring."

Sophie laughed, and Elizabeth almost did.

They had started at the western end of Rotten Row and, at about the mid-point, a small troop of Household Cavalry cantered into the ride in good order. They belonged to the Blues regiment and were wearing full ceremonial uniforms under dark blue cloaks; the nodding scarlet horsehair plumes atop their brass helmets were the most striking feature against the pale January sky and the muted colours of the parkland landscape.

"It's a relief to see them properly dressed once again," said Lady Shelling. "During the war, what could only be a committee of complete incompetents insisted the Household Cavalry wear khaki while training or exercising their horses. It is such an unbecoming colour."

They trotted on and, nearer to Hyde Park Corner, they descried a growing knot of people clustered around several riders on horseback, and more pedestrians and riders were joining the group all the time.

"I believe we may have our quarry in view," said Aunt Bessie.

"I can see photographers," said Elizabeth.

"The vain imposter," said Sophie. "He probably brushes his teeth with a camera present."

"What a disgusting thought," said Aunt Bessie. "What shall we do now? Join the throng of acolytes? I find the idea distasteful, but I suppose it is necessary."

"I mustn't," said Sophie. "I can't allow him to see me because of the upcoming dinner."

"Of course, you can't, my dear. Miss Banks and I shall ride

on while you... What will you do?"

"I'll dismount and walk, while observing from a distance."

"Very good. We shall report back to you his every insidious and calculated move." Sophie dismounted and heard her aunt saying to Elizabeth, "I do not recall having taken against someone so thoroughly in all me life, Miss Banks. Lord Shelling had to deal with an embezzler once, and I felt some sympathy for the poor fellow. But this one! Why, I would like to..." The rest was lost as the distance increased, but Sophie assumed it included horse whipping, or tarring and feathering, or a long stint underwater on a ducking stool.

Sophie reflected that Lady Shelling had taken an obvious liking to Elizabeth. She supposed Elizabeth was now also a full-fledged secret agent — included through a process of assimilation rather than by consultation and invitation. Watching as they trotted away on their horses, she could see the crowd growing ahead of them, and threatening to spill onto the ride itself. Among the hundred or more people, she observed a policeman's helmet, and presumed he was asking the crowd to move further back. Stokely sat on a tall horse, but this alone marked him out in the distance — there was no special ray of light from the heavens illuminating him. His words did not carry on the breeze. There was no visible reason to single him out as the most important person present but, nevertheless, he was. The crowd was swelling quickly. Buses stopped nearby — she could see their top decks in the distance. A hundred yard walk was all it required to satisfy the curiosity of the passengers who alighted there as to why a crowd was forming.

Hyde Park Corner has always been a busy place, a confluence of a dozen bus routes and the Piccadilly Underground Line. It also surges with traffic heading north-south or east-west, funnelling around the large open spaces of Hyde Park, Buckingham Palace Garden and Green Park. It seemed to Sophie that bus and trainloads of passengers were coming expressly to converge upon one little section in Rotten Row. She had watched for a few minutes while the crowd had swelled to five hundred or more. The streams of people seemed to increase in volume. Sophie had never witnessed the like before, and she found it disturbing — eerily fascinating and inexplicable. Stokely had power. She had known that, but seeing it manifested and hold sway over the many in front of him she found alarming. A bushy-bearded, middle-aged rider in an old tan overcoat on a big horse approached from the west and stopped.

"Good afternoon. An unusually pleasant day for riding, don't you agree, Miss...? I'm sorry, I didn't quite catch your name."

She looked at him and was about to say something about being accosted in such a manner when she became suddenly puzzled.

"Your eyes may be deceived, but not your heart. It is a pity, but I must tear myself away to see what the fuss is about. Excuse me." He touched his bowler hat and geed up his horse.

"Sinjin Yardley, you rogue," she whispered to herself, and laughed.

# Chapter 5

# A network of intrigue

Early on Monday morning, 10th January, 1921, a cold rain battered Central London. Inspector Morton would usually have found a seat on the top deck of the bus instead of standing trapped at the end of the aisle behind the driver's compartment. The top deck was open to the elements, so he could not have smoked or read a newspaper there. He decided it was better to stand, cramped and hemmed in, swaying with every jolt, than to sit helpless in the lashing rain upstairs, sullenly counting the places where he felt moisture creeping in. At least it was warm on the lower deck, but the warmth was of that humid, fragrant variety produced by silent, miserable, close-packed, rain-dampened humanity. The windows had misted up. A seated woman made a spyhole in the condensation with her sleeve, but it filled in quickly and the view outside was depressing, anyway. It was eight o'clock, and a man coughed. It was a long, chesty cough, the type one would back well away from if only one could. The passengers on the lower deck had no escape, so they eyed the unsavoury exhibitionist with venomous disdain before averting their faces. Some calculated whether, by holding their breath for as long as possible, the surely contagious airborne germs would disperse sufficiently that they, too, might not catch a cold or influenza.

Two stops before he got off, Inspector Morton got a seat as the bus emptied of workers who had reached their destinations. Superintendent Penrose had telephoned him at home the night before. He would meet Penrose at nine and then he would find out something. Oh, yes, it would be something interesting right enough. Morton reflected that he always felt a little out of his depth on the cases Penrose gave him. They set up differently to the routine of ordinary investigations. He smoothed his moustache. His stop came and Morton got off to hurry through the Derby Gate shortcut to get to the Yard and out of the rain.

Serving in the Yard's white glazed brick-lined canteen was Mrs Trowbridge — she of the biggest forearms of anyone of Morton's acquaintance. While tea could be obtained from urns, wiser officers knew that the tea from Mrs Trowbridge's massive metal teapot was the better choice.

"Good morning, Mrs T. I'd like a cuppa, hot and strong, please."

"Good morning, Inspector Morton, and I'm sure you need it on a rotten day like today." She dispensed a perfect amount of the liquid into a mug with the accuracy of a sniper and the speed of a machine. "You can have as much sugar as you like, deary." She called everyone 'deary'. "You won't believe this, but we was down to scrapings Friday morning. Then, after lunch, we got a delivery. I've never seen so much sugar in me life. We got sacks and sacks piled up, we have. Where's it all come from, that's what I'd like to know? Hoarders. That's where. They kep' it during the war to keep the price high and now they're dumping it. I just hope the price goes down at the grocers, but it won't."

"It never does, Mrs T."

"Something should be done about it."

"If you swear out the complaint, I'll investigate the matter for you."

"Oh, get along with you, Inspector. I don't have the time and you're pulling my leg. What I have to put up with from you boys, I don't know... Go on, take an extra biscuit. I won't say nothing."

"As long as no one's looking, I will. Thank you."

The daily badinage ended as others in the queue asked for tea. Morton sat and chatted with a fellow detective for a few minutes before going upstairs to his office. At nine, he met Penrose in the latter's room.

"Something serious and underhand is going on, and I don't like it," said Penrose. "You share an office with Bygrave. Has he mentioned anything about the theft of documents from MPs?"

"He remarked about it last week, sir," replied Morton.

"There have been five thefts of documents from Liberal MPs, and all the details of how they were carried out are so similar as makes no difference. Two thefts occurred at the same time. One was in London, and the other in a small village named Llandinam, slap bang in the middle of Wales. Now you can't get from one to the other in a couple of hours, so two different thieves were at work in the two places. Therefore, we're dealing with a larger plot, and an organization behind it. Bygrave will continue working on the cases and pass his findings along to me. I'm now passing them to you, but don't mention this to Bygrave."

"No, sir. Were any compromising documents taken?"

"No one is saying they were compromising. The items and documents all sound very ordinary and quite pointless. That is, they were pointless until yesterday. I have a friend in the newspaper business. We spoke yesterday afternoon, and he gave me an advance warning of something. Take a look at this."

Penrose placed a copy of that morning's London Mercury folded in a way to display an item buried within its pages.

57

Morton read the title 'Dark Rumblings Within the Liberal Party.' Beneath ran the article. 'We find it distressing in the extreme to give credence to unsubstantiated rumours, but when such rumours arise on every side, we are forced to resort to that old adage — there is no smoke without fire. It has come to our attention that the governing party may have slumped into that lamentable state of moral turpitude of those too long accustomed to power. We hope the rumours are unfounded and, although come to us circuitously by various routes, emanate from a single biased source. It may be that in this manner, the hearsay has multiplied and where there was only one event, for example, there are now three very different versions going the rounds.

What are these dyspeptic noises, hinting at a deeper sickness, within the governing body? They signify that public money is being used for private purposes, and certain well-known and hitherto commendable MPs have fallen prey to their baser instincts. As we learn more, we feel it our duty to keep the public informed. We pray that these rumours are unfounded for the sake of the country. Yet if we are presented with hard facts that verify the assertions being made, we shall have no choice but to publish them.'

"That's rather nasty," said Morton.

"Yes, and it's nothing but innuendo that the government can't defend against. My guess is the supposed list of MPs with baser instincts will prove to be no different to the list of those MPs who have experienced a theft recently."

"But a newspaper has to back up its claims with actual facts," said Morton.

"They do. Particularly in court. But a lot of damage can be done between now and then. Also, there's the chance that false documents will be presented to the London Mercury, and those could be used as justification for whatever they publish. Aside from that, all the other newspapers won't want to be left out of this. They'll be looking for Liberal Party scandals and will make much of whatever they find. It's a clever piece of trickery on Stokely's part."

"You believe he's behind this, sir?" asked Morton.

"It's his newspaper."

The statement seemed to settle the matter. Morton wondered what Penrose wanted him to do.

"That's the first part," said Penrose. "There's another. Last Thursday evening, a clerk, a civil servant named Jackson, was murdered. It was made to look like a suicide, but it was definitely murder. He was in the habit of copying out documents in his spare moments and selling them to a third party. Jackson was followed to Pimlico, where he dropped off a tidy bundle of papers. Copies of factory inspections."

"Inspections, sir? What would those be about, exactly?"

"Underage workers, improper hours, unsafe conditions — what you would imagine. Interestingly, responsibility for the Alkali, &c. and Works Regulation Act was passed to the Ministry of Health a year or two back. It has subsequently been discovered that another chap in that ministry is also copying out factory inspection reports on the quiet. These are inspections of factories around London to regulate what gets discharged into the air."

"Why is anyone interested in that? I mean, it would be nice if they *actually* cleaned up the air and didn't just regulate what got discharged into it!"

"Too true. The air's that gritty sometimes you can taste it. Now that *can't* be good for a person. But coming back to what concerns us. There has to be a reason for this sudden interest, only we don't know what it is. The main feature that strikes me, and others, too, is the level of organization behind the schemes. It's not just one or two fellas looking for cheap property, or trade secrets, type of a thing. There is at least a small network involved... We might even be nibbling around the edges of a vast network for all we know. Let's say it's a large network and there does appear to be a lot of money involved — that limits who can be running it. Can't be British Communists — they don't have the cash. The Russians are too busy with their civil war. Germany's out of it for the time being, and most other nations are still licking their wounds. In other words, no one can imagine any foreign power with deep pockets being interested in this type of stuff. So we're looking at a home-grown variety — small or large. That's what you're going to find out for us."

Morton was silent for some seconds. "I'm not sure how to approach it, except by following the man at the Ministry of Health."

"That's already being done. The Home Office has identified several files they believe were copied by Jackson. So you'll take a look at those. The man at the Ministry of Health is a bit more circumspect, but it's hoped he'll leave some traces of his activity, and copies of those files will be forwarded as soon as possible. Hopefully, you'll work up some leads."

"Oh, I see, sir."

"But you can't do any of this work in your own office. I've nothing against Inspector Bygrave, but we don't know the extent of this network's reach or its size. For example, of two possible police officers right here at Canon Row Station, one of them tipped off Jackson's contact after a search warrant was issued, and so the contact got away with time to spare. I count at least four men involved in that operation, and Jackson makes five. If they are controlling the man at the Ministry of Health, that's six. Where else are they active, eh?"

"It's rather alarming, sir."

"Isn't it just? So we have to proceed cautiously. You and Sergeant Gowers will work from another building unconnected with the Yard. Until we can get a handle on this situation, we have no idea who or what we're up against. Neither does the Home Office, for that matter."

Morton blew out a puff of air. "Are you thinking the MPs' stolen documents and the inspection reports are connected?"

"I can't see how directly," said Penrose. "But both sets of circumstances are giving me a similar feeling, as if the same mind had designed both. First, what is being taken is peculiar and superficially useless. Second, there is far more organizing ability devoted to these activities than is warranted for just the crimes themselves. Third... Well, I don't know that there is a third, except that we'd be very unlucky to have two such outfits on the go at the same time."

Penrose got up to retrieve a large pile of files from a table. "Anything I've signed out from Records, I want back. I've included some notes." He placed them in front of Morton. "Go through everything and see what you can find. And a word of warning. Don't leave these files lying about. Keep everything with you and in sight at all times."

"I'll be extremely careful, sir."

---

Sophie was at the entrance to the Foreign Office just before ten. Albright, one of two door-keepers present, was scanning a list on a clipboard looking for the name King, Phoebe. This was her eighth visit where Albright slowly scanned through the lists of permitted visitors. He always started with the wrong list, and he did so again today. She knew he knew she had clearance. He picked up a second clipboard. Sophie could have turned to the exact page for him and pointed out her name, but Albright was not one to be hurried. "King," he said softly while still in the B section and slowly turning pages. He muttered 'King' again while in the Js. "Yes, you're on the list. You may go up. Mr Drysdale's office is just..."

"Thank you. I know the way with my eyes shut. Good morning." Sophie went up the stairs, certain Albright was doing it all deliberately for some obscure reason known only to himself.

Archie welcomed her and apologized for bringing her out

on such a wet, blustery day.

"Now, to come to the point of this meeting," he said. "Over the weekend, an agent was observing Lord Stokely while in Hyde Park. Something of an impromptu public gathering occurred, undoubtedly helped by the nice weather, and a crowd of almost two thousand gathered."

Sophie thought it best not to mention Sinjin Yardley. "Yes, and Stokely gave a little speech. When he made a joke, the crowd laughed even though they could not possibly all have heard what he had said."

"You were there?" He frowned.

"I went riding with Auntie Bessie and he showed up. But I was careful, and stayed right out of Stokely's way, while *she* spied on him. She very much enjoyed herself."

"I'm sure she did... What else did our ace investigator have to report?"

"That the intelligence of the British public has fallen to an all-time low if it is so easily entertained by such a jackanapes. That is a direct quote, by the way. She admits Stokely is handsome, but added that, as he is more inwardly corrupt than Dorian Gray, it would be fitting if his head were a mouldering cabbage. Auntie loathes him."

"The way she expresses herself seems to indicate that. Did she notice anything or anyone else?"

"Another person? In Stokely's entourage, you mean? No, except to refer to them as flunkies."

"Bessie, bless her soul, needs some training if she is to be effective. The thought of what that would entail terrifies me. The agent to whom I refer, a properly trained person, noticed an interesting man among Stokely's retinue. This individual, thirty-five to forty years old, shaven and with a very smooth skin, tall, thin, and exceedingly well-dressed in an expensive beige overcoat and a brown homburg, stood among the cameramen and bodyguards. Stokely now always has at least three bodyguards accompanying him everywhere. This unknown man was careful not to appear in any photographs, and yet he directed the activities of a photographer and a bodyguard on different occasions. They deferred to him. He is someone of importance who hasn't been noticed before. Perhaps he is new, and this was our first sighting. We must find out who he is. So, to that purpose, can you ask Charlotte Terrence if she knows of anyone fitting the description? If she has information, get everything you can concerning the man's background and his position within the Stokely camp."

"I most certainly shall. I'm supposed to see her on Friday, after the birthday dinner."

"See Miss Terrence today and also meet her on Friday."

"Very well... When last I spoke to her, she was irritated at not being herself invited to the dinner. Apparently, she has been in the past, but not for the last two years."

"It is rather sordid," said Archie, who wrinkled his nose, "but we must capitalize on her resentment. I fear she will probably become less helpful in the future."

"I think that a possibility, too. Has she been helpful so far?"

"Up to a point. I suspect she's keeping something back. Her card player's instincts make that almost a certainty."

"Charlotte's a strange woman. You'd think she'd be anxious to make amends after escaping such serious charges. But she doesn't possess the slightest particle of remorse, and it's as if she had done nothing wrong. Some people just think and behave differently, don't they?"

"You mean you find it surprising in her?"

"I suppose I do. She can be quite friendly on occasion, but it's as if she's turning on a tap. When the charm's not needed, she turns it off again. It's the difference between *being* a nice, friendly, and open person, and *pretending* to be one only when it serves a purpose. I hope Charlotte's not in one of her foul moods. It's ridiculous; I'm half her age and have to reprimand her as one would an overwrought and difficult child."

"Some informants go the other way," said Archie, "and will volunteer every little detail of their lives. It's almost as if they wish to purge their souls. Then there are the ones who wish to be friends, and those who lie. There is always some difficulty, no matter who it is. Double agents are the worst. No matter how intelligent a person may be, they all seem to get in a muddle."

"I think I would get in a muddle if I were a double agent. I can barely comprehend the term... Could someone be a triple agent?"

"Oh, yes."

"How absolutely frightful. One could never trust them."

Archie smiled. "One never does."

"I must leave all the double-crossing, triple agents to you. I would find them too, too tiresome for words." Sophie smiled, pleased she had finally used a phrase she liked that she had heard Flora use. "I had better go round to Charlotte's flat. She's probably still in bed."

"Good luck," said Archie.

Sophie had to knock three times on the door to Charlotte's flat before it opened.

"It could only be you at this time of day," said Charlotte. "Come in, and speak quietly. I have a splitting headache."

"Self-inflicted, no doubt. Good morning, Charlotte, not that there's much left of it."

"I hate mornings... So what is this visit about?"

She sat down on a sofa. Sophie sat in an armchair and, once again, admired Charlotte's comfortable and tastefully decorated flat.

"There is a man who is associated with Lord Stokely. Perhaps you know him." Sophie described the tall, thin, well-dressed individual.

"That sounds like Lester Dawkins." Charlotte took a cigarette from a box on the table.

"Do you know anything about him."

"He's important to Roderick. They were always talking." It was one of the rare occasions that Charlotte had used

Stokely's given name. Hearing it always surprised Sophie, and she had to make a conscious effort to recall that Charlotte was talking about the earl. "I don't know what he does," the older woman continued. "Manages business, I should think."

"Were you introduced to him?"

"Naturally, although I found him unpleasant... No, that's not the right word. He made me feel uncomfortable. Dawkins stares at you and it's as though he's calculating something disturbing."

"Isn't that usual in meeting someone? To a certain extent, anyway, doesn't one always try to assess what sort of person one is talking to? Perhaps he just has a funny manner."

"I'm not explaining it very well. The unpleasantness came from my getting the impression he was calculating how he could harm me, but in a strange way... Almost as if he were estimating how much blood I had. Sounds stupid, I'm sure. Anyway, I didn't like him. I remarked that Dawkins seemed odd. Roderick said he has a brilliant mind, but is very unorthodox. I had to be content with that cryptic comment. When he doesn't wish to talk about something or someone, it is best not to irritate Lord Stokely."

Sophie was quiet for a moment. In the little that Charlotte had said, she had heard of two Stokelys. One was Roderick — the man Charlotte was close to when she met Dawkins. The other was Lord Stokely, who must not be irritated by unnecessary questions. "When did you meet Mr Dawkins?"

"Three years ago. Three and a half, actually."

"Where was this?"

"While staying at Chertsey Park. It was in July. Dawkins was there for several days. He and Roderick had many closed-door meetings. I was never permitted into the inner sanctum." She laughed. It was an abrupt laugh, conveying the loss of something.

"Inner sanctum? Was that a room?"

"No. A state of being. He often surrounds himself with men of business and important affairs, and in those meetings, no woman is permitted. I can't imagine what they were discussing... The downfall of a competitor, no doubt."

"Would Ferrers have attended such meetings?"

"Oh, yes... I think Roderick was a little afraid of him. Ferrers threw his weight about like nobody else. He was a brute in every sense of the word."

"Did you speak to Ferrers?"

"Often. He was always pleasant to me. The servants at Chertsey Park used to hide from him, they were so intimidated."

"How did the servants behave towards Mr Dawkins?"

"In no special way that I remember." She put out her cigarette. "I'll tell you this, though. I always imagined that Ferrers could beat someone to death and think nothing of it. Dawkins strikes me as the type who would burn down a town and then get a good night's sleep afterwards."

"Such charming people. What would Stokely do?"

"Conquer a nation and, whatever the casualties, he would think it worth the cost in achieving his goals... The end justifies the means — I heard Roderick use that phrase several times."

"You knew this, yet you loved him?"

"Strange, isn't it? In another era, he would have been a Bonaparte, or a Caesar. Can such types flourish now? I don't know, but if he can, he will strengthen Britain and make the Empire a glorious power once again. That I find tremendously exciting. How he even thinks he can do it, I find beyond my comprehension. You must understand, I did not only love him. I worshipped him... And now he doesn't need me anymore."

"Yes, he has shown that you, too, are expendable. You were nearly one of the unfortunate casualties who must fall if he is to fulfill his vision."

"That's how he sees things. I would give anything to be back where I once was in his affections."

Sophie simply did not understand Charlotte's attitude.

"Is there anything more you can tell me about Mr Dawkins? Do you know where he lives?"

"I know he lives in London. I'm not sure, but he might have a place in the country. He's married, although I've heard nothing about his family. He went to Cambridge and has money. Dawkins doesn't play cards, though. I really don't know much about him."

"Does Lord Stokely play cards?"

"Occasionally, but he's not very good. He prefers horse-racing."

"Out of curiosity, did you ever play cards with Stokely?"

Charlotte smiled. "I did, but I made sure I lost often enough to keep him happy. He's a poor loser."

Sophie easily pictured that he would be. "What is he like when he wins?"

"At cards or in general? You mean generally speaking, don't you? I've never thought about it, but I would say he's like a happy boy no matter what it is that's gone his way. He doesn't boast or become smug, but he does have what I can only describe as a glowing smile."

"I see." Sophie found the idea of a triumphant Stokely quite sickening. "Thank you, Charlotte. I think that's all for today. We'll meet again on Friday as planned."

"Twice in one week?" she said in a mocking tone. "I'm honoured... Why?"

Sophie became suspicious. She could not tell her that she would be at Stokely's birthday dinner. "If and when you meet Lord Stokely, I would like to get your current impression of him while it's fresh in mind."

"I'm not likely to see him until the weekend. I'm told he's going to the Café Royal on Saturday."

"I remember you saying that was a favourite haunt of his. Who is it who keeps you informed of his movements?"

"Miss King," Charlotte smiled, "you've asked me before, and I'll give you the same answer again. That's private."

"As you wish," said Sophie. "We'll meet, anyway. I'm sure I

will have thought of other questions to ask."

"You'll never catch him out. He's too clever."

"Do you want him caught out?"

"Yes... No... There, take your pick. The truth is, I don't really care."

Sophie left shortly afterwards, certain that Charlotte was being a lot less helpful than she could be and possibly untruthful. When she informed Archie of their conversation, he remarked that Charlotte might bear watching more closely.

# Chapter 6

# Dinner at Lyall Place

In Belgravia, there is a tremendous amount of uniformity between dwellings. Firstly, the same architects designed rows of houses or whole streets. Subsequent architects and builders closely followed suit in conforming to the established style. Secondly, the use of the same colour paint for the stucco — white, off-white, or cream — across entire blocks of townhouses furthered the effect. Under a sunny sky, the townhouses dazzled. After sunset, they lifted the gloom of night, and made the thoroughfares lighter, airier. With every front door being black and adorned with burnished brass, it would take a brave soul to paint a door red. Someone did, once, and the outrage of the community was swift and intense. The stern lessor involved acted promptly, and the chastened lessee returned the door to its rightful glossy blackness — almost overnight.

In Lyall Place, near a bend in the road and next to a small park, there was a set of five imposing townhouses with identical façades. The only real distinguishing exception was in the house numbers painted on their impressive columns. Number 109 was in the middle. It was the home of the Dowager Countess, Lady Stokely. Georgiana Musette Cusack, of Anglo-Irish descent, was born in 1859. She had spent her childhood on a small estate close to the Stokely estate, Chertsey Park, in Surrey and, consequently, grew up knowing the family and eventually marrying into it.

Well before the appointed dinner hour of eight, guests began arriving, and a bright and engaging Lady Stokely moved among them, holding a series of brief and convivial conversations. Everyone had assembled in the drawing room where, with drinks in hand, they talked while waiting expectantly for the arrival of the honoured guest. At ten to eight, three cars drew up outside number 109, and Lord Stokely got out followed by half a dozen men and a photographer. After Lord Stokely had entered the house, one of his men stood on guard outside the front door.

When Lord Stokely entered the drawing room, the attention of all turned to him.

"*Mama*," he announced, pausing in the doorway. "You look as beautiful as ever. Simply wonderful." He went to her.

The countess turned upon first hearing her son's voice. The sudden joy on her face was apparent to everyone.

"Roderick, I'm so glad you could come. I know how busy you are."

"No matter how many demands are placed upon me," he kissed her delicately on the cheek, "I always have time for you."

Those nearby felt included in this magical moment, drawn in, as they were, to the tender exchange between a loving mother and her affectionate son — and such a noble mother, while her son, they believed, to be the brightest hope for Britain.

"I've brought an extra guest," said Stokely. "You must forgive me for not telling you beforehand."

"I'm sure we can find a place for him."

"Allow me to introduce the gentleman to you." Stokely motioned to a man with a thin beard and moustache, who had a very innocent-looking air about him. "Mama, this is Mr Nikolai Bukharin, who is briefly visiting England before returning to his most important duties in Moscow."

"Enchanté, Countess Stokely." He spoke with a heavy Russian accent.

"Mr Bukharin, welcome. It is a pleasure to meet you. Will you be staying long in London?"

"Not long. I am here for an important meeting, that is all. Then I must return — my duties demand my presence."

"I'm sure they do. I imagine you must be very busy with both the civil war and the Polish war at present."

"Naturally, countess. Russia is beset by enemies."

"Yes, yes, we'll discuss all that later," said Stokely affably, while putting a hand on Bukharin's back to guide him away.

If Lady Stokely was bemused by a Russian communist leader being unexpectedly invited to her dinner party, she did not show it. She was long used to meeting Stokely's strange acquaintances, and surmised that whatever her son was doing had to be for the good of the country.

Below stairs at 109, Sophie, Flora, and Ada, with four other Burgoyne servants, waited patiently in a row. In front of them stood Mr John Dalgleish, butler to Lady Stokely. He was an older gentleman with the time-tested manner of the ancient retainer who well knows the order and procedure in all the household's affairs. This assembly was partly for a final inspection and partly for a last word before the dinner commenced.

"I will attend to Lord Stokely's requirements in the serving of meat and refreshments," he said, speaking in reasonable, patient, and authoritative tones. "His lordship is very particular in certain matters and how they are to be performed. As I am acquainted with his habits, I shall serve him those things I have just mentioned. Soup, salad, dessert, vegetables, and coffee can be served to him as to any other guest.

"The one rule which must be obeyed at all times is that there shall be no talking among you while in the dining room. If your duties require you to communicate with one another, you must leave the room to do so. This is a standard rule in many houses but, here, and especially with Lord Stokely present, it shall be scrupulously and perfectly observed. Do I make myself clear on that point?"

"Yes, Mr Dalgleish," said Sophie, who bobbed upon answering.

"Then, Miss King, you and your staff may go to your stations. I shall strike the dinner gong in three minutes."

They departed, two maids going to the kitchen, the footmen to the hall on the ground floor above, while Sophie, Flora, and Ada climbed another flight of stairs to the dining room.

The two tall men from Burgoyne's waited in the hall for the gong to sound.

"What's a young chap like you doing as a footman?" The man who breathed the question out of the side of his mouth with his lips barely moving was tall and in his late forties. He had an outdoors complexion and, although perfectly dressed as a footman in black tail coat and starched collar, he looked slightly out of place.

"We're not supposed to be talking," said Broadbent-Wicks, who was similarly attired.

"Keep it down, me old fruit. We're not supposed to get caught, that's all that is."

Broadbent-Wicks observed the way his companion was speaking and, mimicking it, also spoke from the side of his mouth.

"I get it. To answer your question, I can't find steady clerical work, and I'm hard up."

"Ain't we all? Still, pay's good for this racket. Just serve the food and keep yer eyes and ears open."

"I'm Douglas Broadbent-Wicks, by the way."

"God bless us, are you really...? I'm Alfie Tanner."

"Have you always been a footman, Mr Tanner?"

"Nah, son. I was in service years ago, and that's where I learned the trade. Then, I was a platelayer on the railways. Now that was good, steady money and an easy life until I did me back in. Did odd-jobs afterwards up until I was an ambulance driver during the war." He paused for a second. "I got blown up once, you know? Bloomin' artillery shell. Lucky it was just me in the ambulance. You won't believe it, but I come out of that wreckage with nothing but a scratch... Funny how that turned out. Now I clean windows and do the servant game on the side. There ain't a lot of money in window cleaning, but it keeps body and soul together. What's *your* racket?"

"I worked for the civil service until I was made redundant."

"Ain't life like that? You get everything set up perfect and then, boom, out of the clear blue, it all goes wrong. Gobs shut — here come the nobs." He had murmured the quick warning as the door to the drawing room opened.

Sophie found it difficult in the dining room. She brought in dishes and served competently, but she struggled with the urge to set everything down to listen exclusively to Lord Stokely. Most awkward was when she worked her way down the table, away from the earl, who was seated at one end. It irritated her that he had a nice voice. It annoyed her that she could not hear everything he said. Stokely spoke casually on a broad range of topics with those around him. He seemed to show no single person any particular favouritism. This, also, Sophie found objectionable.

Ada met Sophie in the kitchen as they loaded up their trays again. They both looked around before speaking.

"Anything?" asked Sophie in a whisper.

"Nothing much, miss," said Ada.

"Likewise."

They took their trays to the dining room. Within a few

minutes, Flora signalled to Sophie behind the back of Mr Dalgleish. They both stepped unobtrusively outside.

"The foreign gentleman," said Flora, "who's sitting three down from Stokely. He's a Russian communist. Quite an important one, I think."

"Is he? What can he be doing here?"

Suddenly, Flora raised her eyebrows in warning upon hearing the sound of someone approaching.

"I think Mr Dalgleish will advise us regarding the order of serving the desserts," said Sophie, at Flora's prompt.

The butler came out of the dining room and stopped, having heard her.

"You are correct, Miss King. A sorbet shall be served first, then I will inform you what comes next." He paused for a moment in which Flora bobbed and departed.

"Mr Dalgleish, may I ask if you are finding our work satisfactory?"

"I am, Miss King. I have no complaints."

"Thank you."

The butler inclined his head before continuing on his way.

Broadbent-Wicks had so far served with quiet decorum, but his duties had kept him away from Lord Stokely. The young man had marvelled when witnessing Alfie Tanner offering peas to the earl, who refused a second spoonful. Alfie had said, "As you wish, my Lord," in such a deferential upper class accent that if Broadbent-Wicks had stood there with his eyes shut, he would have sworn Alfie's voice could only be the product of Eton or Harrow. He had looked at the older footman in astonishment. Alfie, upon noticing Broadbent-Wick's stare, winked back.

Sophie, under Dalgleish's direction, was more often than not in the vicinity of Lady Stokely. There, she soon learned that two star opera singers, Mr Marion Green and Miss Maggie Teyte, would arrive later to sing a selection of songs from the romantic opera, Monsieur Beaucaire, in which they were appearing. Sophie learned Stokely had attended the Prince's Theatre several times to see the show, and this performance was to be his birthday surprise.

More often than any other servant, Ada served Arthur Brooke, the journalist recently returned from Italy. While serving, she found him nervous and slightly embarrassed. She noticed that his awkwardness increased as soon as he discovered he was seated almost opposite a famous Russian communist leader.

"Brookie." Lord Stokely caught the journalist's attention. "After dinner, I want you to explain your findings in Italy to a few friends of mine."

"I will be pleased to do so, my Lord."

"Excellent." Stokely turned his attention to Nikolai Bukharin. "It is such a pity that you must leave early, because you would have found Mr Brooke's discoveries immensely interesting. It concerns the fascisti's strategies in Italy. What is Chairman Lenin's view of their political aims?"

"He views them as a natural progression in Italy's downfall of decadent capitalism. They will not last long, although they will be problematic while they exist. The issue is the chauvinist fascisti divert attention from the true revolutionary goals of achieving democracy for the masses in Europe."

"Yes, they do… The problem as I see it," said Stokely, "is that they merely wish to create a new ruling elite — themselves, of course." He smiled.

"Occasionally, the simple statement captures the matter perfectly. I believe you have stated the truth." Nikolai Bukharin bowed in acknowledgment of Lord Stokely's perception.

"Comrade Bukharin, I think I shall visit Russia soon," said Stokely.

"What a great honour for the Russian people it would be if you came to our country," replied Bukharin. "You will be made *most* welcome."

"That's kind of you to say," said Stokely.

Flora and Sophie's areas of table service often overlapped. Sitting in the middle of their overlap was Lester Dawkins, the man upon whom Archie Drysdale wanted information. Dawkins, the agents discovered, was a person of few words. The attractive young woman sitting to his left, was not, however. She spoke often to Dawkins and demanded little in the way of a response, apparently content in keeping the man entertained. Sitting across from Dawkins was a young man whom Sophie and Flora decided was probably Lady Georgiana's cousin or nephew. Seated to Dawkins's right was a portly, middle-aged gentleman whom neither agent could adequately pigeonhole. He might be a fifty-year-old industrialist, a diplomat, or a relation heartily enjoying the food set before him. When they had a brief, quiet moment in private around a corner, Flora and Sophie discussed him.

"I can't decide who he is from the list," said Sophie. "I'm sure he's not on it. I wish Mr Dalgleish had used name cards."

"He can't be Stokely's Uncle Teddy whom you mentioned," said Flora, "he's too young."

"Yes, that's true. As far as I know, Edward Fielding was never invited... There have been several substitutions since Mr Dalgleish gave me the guest list. Do you think I should ask him about the gentleman?"

"I don't know. It might look like idle curiosity on your part unless you have a good reason. Anyway, that man eats everything in sight, so you can't use his diet as an excuse. I think it's too late for all that now."

"You're probably right, but I'll try anyway. The other thing is, twenty-nine have sat down to dinner, but I was given a list of only twenty-six, not including Dawkins." Flora shrugged, so Sophie said, "Let's return before we're missed."

The dinner courses were concluded with the entrance and presentation of a birthday cake in which ceremony Lord Stokely took great delight, especially when cutting the first slice. Alfie then removed the cake from the table and proceeded to cut the cake into small portions. Then Ada took a tray of small plates to where Lady Stokely was sitting. Flora also assisted in serving cake. Sophie was not needed at that moment, but her heart leapt into her mouth when she saw Mr Dalgleish signal to Broadbent-Wicks to serve cake to Lord Stokely. She watched, transfixed, her eyes large with apprehension, as the young man carried a single plate on a tray and approached the earl.

Stokely was in conversation when Broadbent-Wicks stopped at his elbow. Stokely looked at the cake and then at the footman. Broadbent-Wicks put the plate down.

"I'm sure you'll be having some of this later," said Stokely.

There was a moment's silence. Sophie's breathing stopped.

"It is to be hoped, my Lord," said Broadbent-Wicks, who bowed and backed away.

Stokely laughed. Sophie breathed again.

Afterwards, the party descended en masse to the drawing-room below. Soon, the opera singers began their recital accompanied by a pianist, and everyone was entertained for twenty minutes. During one song from the opera, and as an amusing conceit, Maggie Teyte serenaded Lord Stokely. Stokely was immensely pleased by this singular attention, and the room shared his joy.

The party continued but, just after eleven, Bukharin left. Stokely said goodbye to him with professions of goodwill towards Russia and Bukharin personally. At eleven-thirty, a curious event took place, and it only became more apparent later to Sophie what must have occurred. She noticed Stokely seemed to be smiling in an artless and unfeigned way. At the time, she could not say what had produced the cherubic expression on his countenance, but the pronounced effect was unmistakable. Charlotte Terrence had referred to it as his glowing smile, and now Sophie had witnessed it.

A little later, Stokely and several guests adjourned to a small room for a private discussion.

"You may smoke, gentlemen. Brookie, come, sit next to me." When Arthur Brooke was seated, Stokely spoke to him. "You're probably wondering why I invited such a very earnest communist to dinner. My reason is simple. I wish to know what the Russians are planning for Britain, and I have found out what it is by simply asking." Stokely laughed. "You may not be aware of this, but three British socialist parties will combine into a single party within the next few days. Lenin has sent Bukharin here to London to ensure Sylvia Pankhurst and those of her faction cause no further trouble. Lenin, you must understand, is a pragmatist. He wants his glorious revolution to thrive in Britain and the only way he believes that possible is by infiltrating and eventually controlling the Labour party and the Trade Unions. Old Lenin's a canny fellow, and I agree with his assessment and methods. Pankhurst, however, pushes for a violent change and the installation of a Soviet-style government in Britain. That will never do. It is suitable for Russia with its large, illiterate peasantry, but not for Britain."

"Thank you for the explanation, Lord Stokely, but I don't understand. You seem to agree with the Communists."

"Do I? Let's hope Bukharin thinks so, too." Stokely laughed, as did others present. Mr Dawkins smiled. Stokely continued, saying,

"They are doing exactly what I want them to do, which makes it easier for us to attack them. However, should Pankhurst spoil the game, she shall be removed. We will let her stay in her track, advocating for women and the poor, but she shall not step a foot outside. Understand, Brookie, I want the communists subversive and muttering in the dark in their foul social club meetings. We shall control the streets and the newspapers, industry and the privileged and, in so doing, we shall save Britain from the communist threat. It's a very simple scheme. Now, tell us all about the Fasci Italiani di Combattimento." Stokely then addressed the room. "Mr Brooke was in frequent consultation with senior members of the Italian Nationalist movement — Michele Bianchi and Dino Grandi, isn't that correct?"

"It is, my Lord. I also met Mr Mussolini on several occasions." Brooke then addressed the whole group. "I was quite impressed with how well-informed and intellectual he was." He cleared his throat. "I know of your wishes to understand the organization. Fundamentally, the strength of the FIC rests on the Black Shirts, the organization's paramilitary arm. It is attractive to ardent nationalists because it provides the means of expression for their discontent. Propaganda alone will not accomplish the changes required in Italy. Enforcement of the vision and the defeat of all opposition is also required. The Black Shirts are organized in a very interesting and effective way..."

Brooke spoke at length, and his audience was quiet, intent upon hearing everything he said. At one point, Brooke explained that he was not a violent man, and expressed with sadness that, if Britain was to be saved from decline, violent means were a necessary evil in defeating the nation's enemies, some of whom held legitimate power, and some, like the extreme socialists, were actively seeking it.

---

It was one in the morning after the dinner, and Sophie, Flora, Ada, and Broadbent-Wicks were in the agency's offices on Sack Lane. As they gave their reports, a distinct chain of events became apparent to them.

"Before going home to his family," said Sophie, referring to her notebook, "Alfie informed me that he heard a car stopping in the road at about twenty past eleven. A moment later, the man on guard outside entered the hall and asked Alfie to fetch the butler. He did so, and then witnessed a sealed envelope being delivered into Mr Dalgleish's hand. In the drawing room, Nancy observed the butler giving the missive to the gentleman whose name we did not know, but of whose name Mr Dalgleish subsequently informed me as being Morris Wilberforce. Mr Wilberforce immediately opened the envelope, read the note, which could only have been several words in length, and then stuffed it into his jacket pocket. He arose. Both Flora and Ada witnessed Wilberforce saying something brief and confidential to Mr Dawkins, who merely nodded in response and remained standing where he was talking to several guests. We momentarily lost track of this message but, and it could be no more than a minute or two later, I saw Stokely beaming like an angel. We presume he had received the message and, whatever it was, it pleased him."

"He has to be a *fallen* angel, I think," added Flora.

"Oh, absolutely," said Sophie. "Is there anything to add to this string of events?"

Ada and Flora shook their heads in answer.

"I didn't see any of it," said Broadbent-Wicks. "Though it's rather *impressive*, following the message all through the house like that."

"It's a pity we don't know what was in the note," said Ada.

"Yes... although it's unlikely to have stated anything *we* would find useful."

"That's right, an' all," said Ada. "We'll never know what was in it or what it meant unless someone tells us."

"It's bound to be something dreadful," said Flora.

"Following on from your thought," said Sophie, "if it is something dreadful and Stokely's involved, then it's entirely possible it's to do with an incident on a large scale... Might it not appear in the newspapers?"

"That's a thought," said Flora.

"What 'appens if there are two bad reports in the papers?" asked Ada.

"Either toss a coin or we could vote," said Flora.

"Vote, of course," said Sophie, "after using as much deductive reasoning as we can muster between us. We know what Stokely's after and the disgusting methods he uses... Does anyone know when the morning editions come out?"

"No," said Flora. "They come out very early, anyway, so please don't ask me to do brain work first thing in the morning. After eleven, and I should be fine."

"It might depend on the paper," said Ada. "I think the earlies come out at about five. But I know there's a later morning edition, 'cause I worked for a family once, and the gentleman, he was a lawyer, used to 'ave two papers delivered at 'ome, and then he used to buy them again at the railway station. Around nine, I reckon that was. He was a great reader, and always 'ad his nose in a book or a newspaper."

"I didn't know that," said Sophie. She looked at Broadbent-Wicks. "I have everyone else's report, but not a full one from you. Did you notice anything of significance?"

"As a matter of fact, I did, and I've been very annoyed about what I overheard."

The three women stared at him. "Yes?" said Sophie, encouragingly.

"Yes, well, just after the opera singers had done their turn, Mr Dalgleish told me to wait outside the drawing room so that, if needed, he could call me in at a moment's notice. I thought he only wanted me out of the way because I was getting underfoot or something. A footman underfoot, what? Anyway, I was standing there looking like a dummy, as you taught me, when Lord Stokely and his mother came out together. They walked right past me as though I wasn't there... After all, I suppose, that's how it should be. They both popped into that small side room and closed the door. I say closed, but it was really only shut to, leaving a gap.

"I said to myself, what would Miss Burgoyne and Miss McMahon want me to do now? Get closer and listen, I answered myself. So I shuffled along sideways to a position nearer the door. Here, I must apologize, because I missed some of their conversation. *But*, I heard that Stokely is having some sort of do at Chertsey Park and needs staff. He said that the locals don't want to go into domestic service anymore. Lady Stokely replied, but I didn't catch what she said. His voice carries, you see, while hers doesn't so much. Well, not at all, at that moment. I felt like asking her to repeat what she'd said."

"I'm glad you didn't," said Sophie.

"Oh, I wouldn't have done that, Miss Burgoyne. Not now." He paused and smiled. "But there was more."

"Ah," she said. "I wonder if we can get into Chertsey Park? Sorry, please continue."

"Not at all. And I honestly have no idea if you can or not. Get in the Park, I mean. What I'm referring to is that they then changed topics, and that's what annoyed me."

Sophie was on the verge of commenting, but decided against it, believing it better to let him continue at his own pace until illumination might finally be granted her.

"Lady Stokely must have moved closer to the door, because I suddenly heard everything she said." He nodded. "You'll never guess what they were talking about."

"I shan't even try," said Sophie. "Please, tell us."

"Lady Stokely said, and I was *most* surprised, she said, 'Roderick, it's time you married. An heir is needed to inherit the title.' I mean to say, I felt very uncomfortable, but I stood my ground." Broadbent-Wicks took in a deep breath and then expelled half of it. "You would *never* guess what he said in reply. You just wouldn't. And this is rather embarrassing for me... I'm sorry, I know this is a debriefing, so I'll be as *debrief* as possible. De*brief*, what?" He laughed. "I rather like that. To continue, he said, 'Mama, find me a suitable bride among this season's crop of debutantes, and I'll marry her. Only, make sure she has a decent settlement, won't you, darling?'"

"He called his mother, darling?" said Flora, a dark look on her face.

"What else did the abominable creature say?" asked Sophie. "What was Lady Stokely's reply?"

"It was surprise upon surprise," said Broadbent-Wicks. "She, her ladyship, replied, 'I know your attitudes towards marriage, but you must do this properly because it is important. At least get acquainted with the girl first. Love may come later if you do.' Then he said, 'Like it did with you and Papa?' Then, she became *quite* angry, and said, 'How dare you? Such insolence.' Then Stokely said, 'I have overstepped the mark, and I apologize. But you have told me often enough that there was no real affection between you two.' At this point, she must have moved away from the door, because I didn't hear what either of them said for about a minute. Then they came back to the door again to leave. Stokely said, 'I shall marry within a twelvemonth. There, are we friends again?' She said in a very sweet voice, 'Of course we are, Roderick. I can never be angry with you for very long.' He laughed, and I shuffled back to my place outside the drawing room, pronto. *There.* What do you make of that!? The bounder should be horse-whipped."

"My aunt would agree with you," said Sophie, absently.

"I find it quite tawdry," said Flora.

"I might, too, if I knew what it meant, Miss Flora," said Ada.

"Cheap, distasteful, and morally bankrupt," she replied.

"Yes, I s'pose it is. Mind you, he'll look after the girl with everything money can buy, 'cause he wants a son. At least, his mother does. But it's funny, her getting on like that. And why doesn't he find a girl for himself? That's what I'd like to know."

"Because he is obscene," said Sophie. "Whoever his victim ends up being will imagine she's entering a lifelong partnership of mutual trust, affection, and respect. Instead, she will have been deceived by him. Undoubtedly, she will become very unhappy and disillusioned."

"I agree, miss, but it won't be the end of the world for her, and some girls might jump at the chance."

"I'm sure they would," said Sophie, "even if they knew the truth. But it's one thing to know this man's attitude beforehand, and another entirely to be wilfully misled by him."

"There is that," said Ada.

"What do you make of Stokely's reference to his father?" asked Flora. "Is there a mystery there?"

"It seems there must be... A loveless marriage between Stokely's parents... The mother complaining to the son about it... Why did she become angry, I wonder...? Any ideas, Mr Broadbent-Wicks?"

"Not really. The entire conversation struck me as unimaginably peculiar and rotten. I didn't know that mothers were even capable of saying such things. I mean, she seemed to hint that the marriage would not disrupt his current circumstances... I don't really like to go any further. Probably, she overindulged him when he was an infant which addled his mind, and she's kept up the same overindulgence ever since."

"I think you might be close to the truth there," said Sophie. "The speed with which Lady Stokely forgave him after the insult is unprecedented. From anger to sweetness in a minute or two? Perhaps the sweetness was only because he fell in with her suggestion."

She glanced at the others and saw they looked tired.

"I think it's time we all went home. Thank you, everyone, for your excellent work. And thank you, Mr Broadbent-Wicks, for discovering such startling information. Hopefully by tomorrow, we can make sense of it. Does anyone have a question?"

Ada and Flora shook their heads.

"I have one," said Broadbent-Wicks. He turned to Flora. "I know you were introduced to me as Flora Dane, but aren't you Lady Laneford?"

"No," said Flora.

"Look at the time! I must get going," said Ada suddenly.

"Yes, it's very late," said Sophie. "Come along, Mr Broadbent-Wicks. You must be going, too. We'll find taxis at the rank."

"Ah, I think I'll walk. My flat's only half an hour away... You look so much like Lady Laneford, you could be related, you know."

"Could be, but we're not," said Flora, hurriedly putting on her coat. "We need two taxis. One for Ada, while you and I share the other, and we'll drop you off first."

"Yes, we'll do that," said Sophie. "Hurry, I'm about to turn off the lights." Flora and Ada were already on the stairs.

"Yes, of course," said Broadbent-Wicks, putting on his hat and coat. "The whole evening's been exceptionally enjoyable. Thank you, and good night."

"Good night," said Sophie. She waited while he descended and then switched off the lights.

# Chapter 7

# Chasing an idea

Sophie left White Lyon Yard at just after nine in the morning. She took a slight detour from her usual walk to go to Liverpool Street Station. There, she purchased four newspapers. The vendor assured her they were the most recent editions. In fact, while she conversed with him, a lad of fifteen came hurrying up to the stand with a fresh stack of newly printed Daily Chronicles tied up with string. This was the newspaper controlled by the prime minister and his friends.

"May I swap?" Sophie asked the seller, holding out the older Chronicle.

"Course," he said, gruffly. He undid the string on the stack and a split second later, Sophie had the latest edition.

"Thank you, and good morning."

She found an empty bench and sat down to scan the headlines and important columns in each paper. While trains arrived and masses of commuters were still disgorging from them, Sophie became absorbed in her task. She found that in reportage there was much similarity between the papers, while in editorial comment there was a huge divergence of opinion and assessment. Despite her close, quick scrutiny, nothing seemed to connect to Stokely, and certainly no calamity, death or financial downfall that would cause him to smile. Folding up the newspapers, she decided on a course of action, and went outside to find a taxi.

"Scotland Yard, please," she said to the first cabbie in the line. "The Norman Shaw building."

"Yes, miss," he replied, and wound up the clock on the meter as she got in.

Sophie settled herself in the back and removed her hat to smooth her hair. Then she sifted through the newspapers to pull out the Express. She wanted to find out what Rupert Bear was getting up to today.

"Why, Miss Burgoyne," said Superintendent Penrose, who stood up when she entered his office. "How nice to see you."

"Good morning, Inspector. I apologize for disturbing you."

"Not at all. Not in the slightest. Anyway, I was expecting your report of last night's doings. Please," he indicated a chair. "What brings you on a visit?"

Sophie seated herself and put the newspapers on another chair.

"I will send a copy of the report over as soon as I've typed it. The reason I'm here is that something interesting occurred, and I wondered if you could help. Allow me, please, to first give you some background information."

"Go right ahead," said Penrose, who settled himself even more comfortably.

Sophie explained the arrival of the note at Lyall Place, followed by Stokely's smiling in a such a marked manner. She ended by saying,

"I've searched the newspapers, but nothing leaps out at me as the cause for Stokely's reaction. So, I thought, perhaps you had heard of a significant event that might give Stokely reason to smile, but was not newsworthy enough to be printed."

"Arh," he said softly, his Somerset heritage seeping into his voice. "Interesting, that." He paused and picked up his pipe. Instead of smoking, he used it to underscore his points as

87

though it were a conductor's baton. "I think I should take you into my confidence. But mind, it must go no further."

"I won't tell a soul. Cross my heart."

Penrose smiled and then explained the string of thefts from the houses of sitting Liberal MPs. Sophie listened and spoke when Penrose paused.

"I see where the burglaries can tie in with Stokely, but not with what happened last night."

"That's because there's another part to it." Penrose became solemn. "An ex-MP, a Liberal named Walter Sturgess, committed suicide last night. They found him hanging from Broom Hill Bridge over the River Frome just outside Bristol. That was early this morning, so the news missed the morning papers, but it will make the evening ones. I've received no proper report yet, although I've put in a request for one. What do you think of that?"

"I'm not sure… Are you suggesting that it *wasn't* a suicide?"

"I'll wait on that one before giving my answer. But here's the thing. Just in the past few days, there was a murder made to look like a suicide. That had to do with the selling of ministerial information. And the only person I can place behind such a performance at the present time is Stokely. Could be that this is how he intends doing business from now on." He put the pipe down. "I'm familiar with those parts around Bristol. Mr Sturgess lived in Keynsham, a town on the road to Bath from Bristol. The Avon runs past and there's a convenient bridge over it if a chap means to hang himself. So why'd he travel the four or five miles from this nearer one to the other? There might be a reason, even a rational one, but it wouldn't surprise me if someone waylaid him on the road, and then drove his car out of the area in case a neighbour recognized Sturgess' vehicle and intervened. Theories are beautiful things, but often enough facts knock 'em for six."

"I daresay they do, but I think your bowling may have taken a wicket."

Penrose laughed. "That's good, that. But we'll see… Did you

discover anything else last night?"

"Stokely brought an uninvited Russian Communist named Nikolai Bukharin to dinner at literally the last minute. We frantically rearranged the table to accommodate him."

"I've heard of that chap, if he's the one I'm thinking of. How do you spell his name?"

Sophie, who had noticed the spelling in the newspapers, told Penrose, who wrote it down. Then Sophie added, "Stokely had a private meeting with four other men. Present were Arthur Brooke, Lester Dawkins, Vincent Cobden, who is Stokely's secretary, and another late arrival named Morris Wilberforce."

Penrose was writing again, so she continued.

"It was impossible for us to find out what they were discussing, because a bodyguard was stationed outside the door."

Penrose looked up and stared at Sophie before speaking. "Had to be important, whatever it was."

"It's very frustrating, this not knowing and having to guess all the time."

"It is that. However, Miss Burgoyne, at least we know they *had* a meeting and, by this list, we now know who Stokely's current confidants are. That's a good step in the right direction... Dawkins and Wilberforce interest me, because I don't know anything about either of them. I'll find out if they have records."

"Could you tell me if you find out anything, please? I'm very interested."

Penrose smiled indulgently. "*If* I can, I might. Depends upon what I discover, doesn't it?"

"They say curiosity killed the cat, and I know it keeps me awake at night. Have a heart, Inspector. I'd be very grateful for *anything* you can pass along."

"I can understand that. I'm in what you might call a perpetual state of curiosity myself. There's never enough information and as for good evidence? Why, it's scarcer than gold, all too often. But there, I'm started on the hardships of the policeman's lot and the day isn't long enough to tell them all. You should escape while you can." Penrose looked pleased with himself.

"Then I shall, and you can get on with your important work." Sophie stood up, as did Superintendent Penrose. They said goodbye.

Arriving at the office, Sophie was greeted by, and returned, a series of 'good mornings'. After she had taken off her coat and hat, she asked Elizabeth to see her privately.

"May I ask," began Sophie, "how the research is progressing?"

"It is keeping me fully occupied, Miss Burgoyne. Although a great deal of information has been assembled by Lady Shelling, there is no part at present that can be truly said to be comprehensive. Everything your aunt discovers, I endeavour to authenticate and verify from public records and reference works. There is rather a backlog at the moment, and I have yet to begin on Lord Stokely's finances."

"If you wish, you could work more hours."

"I'd be delighted to. It's quite fascinating in its way."

"Would you, please?" Sophie smiled. "Are you getting on all right with Lady Shelling?"

"From my perspective, very well indeed. She is a remarkable woman."

"Quite so. Has my aunt discovered anything of use?"

"She has. Although, as far as I can tell, there is nothing particularly damaging to the Stokely family. However, I believe there is a lot more to come and that will undoubtedly provide yet more interesting avenues of enquiry."

"Including scurrilous stories, no doubt."

Elizabeth hesitated. "There have been a few, although so far unconnected with Lord Stokely. I must say, some people's behaviour can be very surprising, and even quite disturbing."

"Yes. The more one learns about certain people, the more

one discovers that ignorance can be bliss... Last night, we got a glimpse into the lives of Stokely's parents. It is definite that theirs was a marriage with very little or no affection."

"Is that so?" Elizabeth thought for a moment. "The eleventh earl, Humphrey, was older than Georgiana by eighteen years."

"Was he? And how old was she when they married?"

"Nineteen."

"That seems likely to have been an arranged marriage. Also, the age difference is not unlike Stokely's current situation in which he intends marrying someone much younger than himself... Humphrey was thirty-seven. When did he die?

"In 1888. He was forty-eight and died of consumption. He had been an invalid for quite some years."

Sophie nodded. "Then how old would Stokely have been when his father passed away?"

"Ten or eleven. I would have to confirm the fact. He is forty-three as of yesterday."

"Oh. So he must have been born soon after his parents married."

"That's correct. Lord Stokely had a younger brother, William, who died during the war. There was a daughter named Florence who died in infancy in the fourth year of the marriage."

"Oh, dear... There was a man about twenty at the dinner last night who wasn't on the list. We think he might be related."

"A young man...? That may have been William's son, Charles."

"Charles Fielding. Then *he* must be the current heir to the earldom, unless I'm mistaken."

"You are correct."

"Tell me, does anything strike you as odd about Humphrey and Georgiana?"

"Only that he was a semi-invalid even before they married. Lady Shelling suggested Humphrey became desperate to produce an heir. She also discovered a subsequent rift

91

between Humphrey and his brother Edward, which arose some years afterwards."

"Where on earth is she getting all this from? It was over forty years ago."

"From Lady Mary Banstead. She's in her seventies now. Her younger sister died three years ago, but she was married to a friend of Edward Fielding."

"Stokely's Uncle Teddy... My goodness, Auntie has such a knack for ferreting out information."

"She most certainly does, Miss Burgoyne. I'm frankly astonished at how frequently she finds the right person to approach, and then gets them to talk."

"Indeed. Thank you, Elizabeth. I look forward to your reports."

After Elizabeth had returned to her desk, Sophie took out a notebook and drew a diagram of the Stokely family tree. Staring at it gave her no inspiration whatsoever. She closed the book and looked out of the window. It had stopped raining, which fact decided her upon a course of action that would answer one of her questions: Where does Stokely go when not in the public eye? She wrote several names on a slip of paper, then went to Elizabeth's desk and spoke quietly, even though the noise from the typewriters further away made it impossible for her to be overhead.

"Please, may I have the addresses for these two companies? I know Stokely's home address."

"Yes, Miss Burgoyne." Elizabeth looked perplexed. "I don't wish to intrude, but Lord Stokely has more companies than these."

"I expected he would have. How many does he have?"

"I'm up to sixteen, and I'm sure there must be others."

"Sixteen!" Sophie puffed out a big breath. "You'd better give me all the addresses you have in Central London. I'm only interested in those."

In the end, Sophie did not get away from the office until eleven as several job applicants came in, interrupting her or

92

Elizabeth.

Even though it was a dull, cold January day after the recent deluge, Sophie experienced that inevitable sense of freedom that comes from riding on a half-empty bus during working hours. She *was*, in fact, working, only it did not *feel* like *proper* work. It had occurred to Sophie that, in order to discover Stokely's personal base of operations, she should survey his financial empire but, surprised by its extent, she now had to adjust her hasty plan. The factories in which he had a controlling interest — home appliances, textiles, furniture, cakes, and canning — were scattered throughout the Midlands. So far, Elizabeth, and Aunt Bessie's research, had also identified Stokely's involvement in coal mines, town gas production, and shipbuilding, but to what extent was as yet unknown.

Working from the list of addresses provided by Elizabeth, Sophie first investigated an insurance company on Lime Street, because it was close to the agency. She climbed the stairs to the third floor to observe unobtrusively the main door to the offices. In glimpsing the interior as two men came out, she espied a blameless and old-fashioned business that certainly would not do for Stokely's headquarters. On Threadneedle Street, Sophie observed a plush, busy stockbroking company, but decided it was too small a place to accommodate the earl and his inevitable followers. Also on Threadneedle, Frobisher Bank, opposite the Royal Exchange, occupied its own building. It, too, yielded nothing but a chance to watch the comings and goings of people about their important business. She could not get inside because a liveried man wearing a top hat was on duty outside, and he would ask what business she had before allowing her entrance. As she *had* no business with Frobisher and could not think of a plausible cover story, she remained loitering on the pavement for several minutes until the uselessness of such activity became inescapably apparent to her.

Next on the list of destinations were the Fleet Street offices of the London Mercury and other papers, hence the reason for Sophie taking the bus. She knew the address was 195, so was at great pains to note the numbers of the buildings as the bus crawled past them. Noting that she was now getting close and that a suitable bus stop loomed ahead, she stood up and rang the bell — unnecessarily, because the bus was stopping, anyway. She alighted. On the pavement, many of the pedestrians walked quickly, as if on Fleet Street one was required to display a sense of urgency in one's affairs. A young lad was fairly running, clutching a bundle of newspapers under his arm, and hopping between kerb and road to avoid obstacles and slow movers.

"Taxi!" An arm-waving man almost shouted in Sophie's ear as he hailed a passing cab. He had just exited a coffee shop and was carrying a Thermos flask and a small packet of sandwiches. Sophie turned and then lined up the coffee shop's window with the entrance to the London Mercury building and found she could get a direct line of vision from inside. She noticed an empty table for two by the window and darted in. First, she put her hat and umbrella on the chair as evidence of her rightful claim of possession. Then she joined the queue and noticed how seedy were her surroundings. The perpetual crush of customers who came in for coffee and then left in a hurry, or sat and drank it hurriedly and then left, had worn out the place. The decoration had a grimy, neglected look and, even when new, the shop had to have looked cheap and awful.

The three people in the queue ahead of her all ordered corned beef sandwiches, while one, carrying a Thermos flask, also ordered coffee. Behind the counter she could see two women making sandwiches as if their lives depended on it, and they were efficient, too. A third woman was grinding beans, while perched on a stool was a small woman, perhaps fifty, who worked the till. Standing and serving at the counter was a man of great girth, with a walrus moustache.

Together they dispatched the customers' orders with alacrity. An altercation broke out between the cashier and the man ahead of Sophie.

"You've short-changed me," he said. "I gave you half-a-crown."

"Oh, no, you didn't," said the woman at the till. "You held out a half-crown, but you were holding two coins and dropped a florin in me hand. You're trying to diddle me out of sixpence! Think I haven't seen that dodge before? You must take me for a mug."

"I'll call the police!" boomed the walrus-mustachioed man, becoming angry and belligerent.

"No. It ain't worth the trouble," said the cashier, soothing him. "It's lunchtime in fifteen minutes."

The customer beat a hasty retreat with the walrus moustache promising to break his neck if he ever saw him again.

"Sorry about that," said the man, instantly pleasant to Sophie, who was a little disturbed at the unexpected turn of events. "What would you like?"

"I would like a coffee and a corned beef sandwich, please."

"Coleman's or house?" he asked.

"I beg your pardon."

"Mustard."

"Oh. What is the house mustard like?"

"It's better than Coleman's, milder you see. A bit like the French Dijon but nicer, 'cause it's a secret recipe." He winked. "It's what most people have who come in 'ere."

"Than I shall try it, thanks."

"We have three coffees and four teas." He pointed at a board where poorly formed chalk letters proclaimed what was available.

"Kenyan," said Sophie, seizing upon the first item on the list with no idea what she was ordering. They settled the matters of cream and sugar between them. Her sandwich on a plate appeared immediately on the counter. The coffee was ready moments later. Sophie paid the cashier and went to her table.

She looked at her early lunch in despair as she removed her gloves. The table was grubby, the plate chipped, and the mug had seen so much use the glaze had dulled. The coffee was still too hot to sip, so Sophie tried her sandwich of corned beef, lettuce, tomato, and mystery mustard. She found it delicious and everything was fresh. Carefully, she blew on her coffee, hoping no one noticed her, and then took a sip. It came as a surprise at how different and rich it was. Sophie had believed her Aunt Bessie's was the best coffee to be found in Britain until this moment, and the new revelation shocked and pleased her. Nearby was a discarded newspaper which she picked up, careful not to get the print on her hands. She settled herself behind it and slowly ate and drank while monitoring the entrance to the London Mercury.

At a few minutes to twelve, customers began arriving in such numbers that the queue soon reached the door, eventually spilling out into the street. She noticed several people carrying Thermos flasks in which to take away their coffee or tea. The tables filled up, which made Sophie feel guilty for dragging out her stay. It became very noisy.

"Do you mind if I sit here?" asked a young man, pointing to the empty chair at her table.

"Not at all," said Sophie, smiling, and wishing he would go away. She slipped her notebook into her handbag.

"Thank you." He sat down with his lunch. He had what appeared to be a chicken sandwich. "If you don't mind my asking, what paper are you with?"

"I'm not with a newspaper." She thought for a moment. "How does one go about getting a job as a journalist?"

"It's not easy," he answered. "It took me a while to get established. You really need an angle, such as being a specialist in a subject that's of interest to the newspaper. Can you type?"

"Yes, I can, and I also know shorthand."

"You want to be a reporter, eh?" He smiled.

"Working for a newspaper has been a long-held ambition of mine," she said.

"I can give you some pointers. What you have to do is go in and talk to editors — as many as possible. When you find one who's sympathetic towards you, tell him you'll do a trial piece and don't take no for an answer. See, if he publishes your work, you'll then have something to discuss." He smiled again at Sophie and then attacked his sandwich.

"Thank you for your kind help," she replied. The man nodded. Sophie looked over towards the London Mercury and froze in disbelief. She stood up suddenly, saying, "Goodbye." Jamming her hat on her head, she rushed outside, clutching her handbag, gloves, and umbrella. Her explosive departure rather surprised the man, who assumed she had taken him at his word and gone to find editors to besiege.

# Chapter 8

# Dear old Fleet Street

Fleet Street was busy with traffic and pedestrians. In front of a shop window on the south side, Sophie watched as Lord Stokely, handsome, cutting a fine figure of affluence in a perfect camelhair overcoat and top hat, spoke to the taller, thinner, but equally well-dressed Lester Dawkins who wore a dark coat. A limousine stopped, blocking the traffic behind it. A bodyguard got out to hold open the door for Stokely, who approached the vehicle and, once inside, he exchanged a few more words with Dawkins, who had not moved from off the step. The car drove away and then another car stopped. Dawkins stared across the street to give a slow, deliberate nod. He got into the second car. Not ten feet from Sophie, a heavyset man, who had been stationary at least as long as she had, began walking eastward on Fleet Street. She was sure he was the recipient of Dawkin's signal, so she followed him. He had a slow, unrelenting gait, yielding the pavement to no one as he walked. His flat cap and thick, rough jacket did not help to distinguish him. Indeed, he looked like twenty other men on Fleet Street just then. Sophie, close behind, studied his back and could see a shiny grease mark on the edge of his collar where his hair rubbed it. He wore a dirty blue neckerchief and was round shouldered. Of his face she had yet to get a glimpse, because he kept his head bowed and did not turn it to the right or to the left.

Although Sophie was certain the man had responded to a signal, by his demeanour and walk she would have said he was despondent. While by following him she hoped to discover something useful, she found among her thoughts that there had sprung up a sense of foreboding. A man of influence and standing had signalled to a scruffy workman by prearrangement. Now, that same workman was unhurriedly doing his master's bidding, which, as far as Sophie could tell, was to amble along Fleet Street. A large clock jutting out overhead told her the time. It was a quarter past twelve. St Dunstan's chiming clock seconded that opinion.

They passed a white-gauntleted policeman on point duty at Chancery Lane, but the workman did not vary his step or look up. They passed by the famous 17 Fleet Street with its wide, low archway, inside which somewhere was hidden Prince Henry's room — the place of his investiture as Prince of Wales in 1610. Although Sophie had noticed the narrow, ancient edifice, the man she followed gave it no heed. A succession of buildings on either side came and went — a blending of history, commerce, arts and community, all veiled beneath a sooty coat deposited by the smoke-laden London air. The Olde Cock Tavern, a bank, newspaper offices, buildings designed by leading architects from a dozen notable eras, followed one after another. Then, unmercifully squeezed by its neighbours, St Dunstan-in-the-West, an architectural gem and a church with a thousand-year heritage, appeared on the north side.

It was lunchtime now, and the public houses and luncheon counters were hard-pressed to keep up with the demands of their customers, many of whom were employees of newspapers. They crammed themselves into the tightest of spaces, hectically talking, smoking, drinking, and eating. The Street was busier than ever with an increase in traffic, and pedestrians crossing where they willed with the indifference of long habit, often perilously close to buses or horses.

Sophie passed alleys, narrow lanes, courts, and roads — Red Lion, Bouverie, Shoe, Whitefriars, Salisbury. Each step now brought into view an additional sliver of the dome of St Paul's Cathedral, which dominating feature stood out ahead, touched now and then by a momentary gleam of sunshine. This masterpiece, made ethereal by distance, seemed to float above a nearer railway bridge while being taunted by the legions of commercial signs that adorned every available space. It was the Vanity Fair of Fleet Street, decked out and mindlessly busy with its own interests and stretched out before an unworldly citadel suspended in air. The incongruity struck Sophie sufficiently that she had to will her attention back to the slow-moving workman ahead of her.

Near the crossroads at Ludgate Hill, the man stopped at a window of a double-fronted shop as though to examine the wares on display. However, Sophie noticed that he stood at an odd angle, and she was sure it was so that he could observe pedestrians while appearing to look in the window. His head was so bowed that his chin touched his chest. Finding herself exposed should he turn her way, she retraced her steps to a nearby lane. There, she took up a position to observe him surreptitiously and not look too ridiculous standing about in the street. Sophie, used to the countryside, had the idea that she was always on display in the city, and that people might notice her and find cause to judge her actions. For a woman to loiter alone in the street was unacceptable behaviour as far as she was concerned, and no one must notice her doing so. Therefore, she frequently consulted her watch as if waiting to meet a friend who was late. It was now 12:27, and it had started to rain. Sophie opened her umbrella.

Within a few minutes, the workman started walking again. The bells of St Dunstan chimed the half hour. Sophie now noticed crossing the street a man who had caught the attention of her quarry. The man, the workman, and Sophie, more or less in synchrony, turned south on narrow Bride Lane. Once there, the workman walked much faster to catch up with the man in front, and Sophie was hard put to it to maintain the pace without actually running. The three of them walked beside an old blank retaining wall while the back of St. Bride's church reared up high above them. Several pedestrians were about, but they all were in a hurry on account of the steady rain. The procession passed the opening to a court on the opposite side of the narrow road, and the workman was now only half a dozen paces behind the man in front, with Sophie fifteen paces further back. Her sense of foreboding increased because she could not understand what was happening.

At the mid-point of its length, Bride Lane swung sharply eastward. In the outside corner lay the entrance to St. Bride's Passage. They all turned into it, although Sophie hesitated for a moment before entering, fearing she might come upon the two men in conversation, which would force her to walk past them. To her surprise, she found a steep flight of stone steps a few yards in, with no one to be seen. The steps rose between brick walls at a right angle and she could not see the top. As she ascended, she heard a muffled cry somewhere ahead, which brought her up sharply. "What's going on!?" she shouted, before climbing to the top. To her right, the passage widened and, for a second, she could see the workman at the far end fleeing into the next street over. But before her, on the wet stones, laid out in the falling, dismal rain, was the man. She went to him, but he was dead; wounded in several places. There was blood everywhere, and it mingled with the puddles that were forming. Stuffed in his mouth was a piece of paper. The scene horrified Sophie. She had not expected it. Unwillingly, the macabre piece of paper seized her attention. She dared not touch it, but she could not miss that there was a design printed on the paper. What she saw seemed to be part of a red hand. Sophie came to her senses and then raised the alarm.

---

At two o'clock, Sophie entered the magnificent entrance of Bow Street Police Station under arrest. A constable and then a sergeant at the station, as well as the arresting officer, had found her difficult to deal with, as she refused to give her name and address. They also vaguely suspected she may have been involved in the murder. She was being held in a dingy interview room.

"I want to speak to Inspector Morton of Scotland Yard," she said again to the sergeant.

"He's not here, is he, miss? While I am. Murder is a serious business, and you *must* give me your name and address. You're under arrest for obstruction. Why make it difficult for yourself and us? Just answer our questions."

"Not until I've spoken to Inspector Morton. I gave my statement to the constable and I would be happy to comply with your wishes under normal circumstances, but there are valid reasons why I can't."

"A murder in broad daylight is not what *anyone* would call a *normal* circumstance. You're not co-operating, and you leave me no choice. A matron will be in shortly to conduct a search of your person before we put you in the cells. While you're there, I'll have a think about the charges to be laid."

"No, she will not!"

The sergeant got up.

"Have you tried to contact him?" she asked.

"We did, but no one knows where he is at present. But that's all beside the point... Make it easy on yourself. Just tell us who you are."

"Oh, dear, dear... I'm sorry, sergeant, but I can't."

He gave her a weary, almost blank stare and then left the room, locking the door behind him.

A quarter of an hour passed while Sophie reflected again that Stokely had spoken to Dawkins, who had signalled to the workman, who assassinated the man, to which fact she was a witness. Stokely would want no witnesses left alive, especially one who might tie the murder back to himself. Sophie had suppressed elements of her account, including her following the workman. If she added her name to her statement, Stokely and his agents could find her. If she used a false name... She pondered whether she should do that and decided she would. Then she thought further on it. The police were not stupid. They would verify her name and address, all the more so now that she had made such a fuss in refusing to identify herself. There was nothing for it. She must stay the course.

The door was unlocked and opened. Instead of the sergeant and a matron, Penrose's assistant, whom Sophie had met before, entered the room. He quickly put a finger up to his lips.

"I'm Detective Sergeant Daniels. You are still under arrest, miss, and will accompany me to Scotland Yard to be interviewed. We'll get your things at the front counter as we go, so there's nothing for you to be concerned about."

In silence, he ushered Sophie out of the room, and then out of the police station, and into a waiting taxi.

"Well, well," said Superintendent Penrose, as he sat in his office with Sophie in front of him. "I can't imagine where you'll turn up next. You'd better give me the complete story, if you please. But first, rustle up some tea, Daniels, our witness looks fair parched."

Daniels left, and Sophie explained what had happened. Penrose nodded occasionally while she spoke, all the while taking notes.

"Hmm," he said, when she finished. "What made you go off

on this jaunt in the first place?"

"I'm not sure, really, except a vague sense of urgency to deal with Stokely sooner rather than later. Also, I thought, observing where he lived and finding out where he worked might be helpful in understanding what he was getting up to. Now I believe he works out of the London Mercury offices."

"That, he does."

"Oh, you knew that... If I had asked, would you have told me?"

Penrose thought for a moment. "Probably not."

Sophie smiled. "Where is Inspector Morton?"

"Can't say. It was lucky that Inspector Bygraves, who shares his office, thought to pass along that Bow Street was looking for him and *why* they were. Otherwise, you'd be in a cell, and up before a magistrate in no time. Then, if you had continued to withhold your name, you'd be facing contempt of court charges, and that's a different kettle of fish entirely."

"Do you mean I'm still in trouble?"

"No. I'll give Bow Street a name, but it won't be your own. They'll think it suspicious, but will drop the charges, and it won't go any further... Lucky for you!" He shook his head. "Miss Burgoyne, you have this mortal bad habit of not telling anyone what it is you're doing. How many times have we had this conversation?"

"But I only went to look at buildings and businesses."

"And creep about following dangerous, violent people."

"I didn't know that was going to be the case."

"Neither did anyone else. Who knew where you were going?"

Reluctantly, Sophie said, "No one."

"Arh," said Penrose.

Sergeant Daniels came in with a tea tray. "They said it was freshly made, sir, and I scrounged some biscuits."

"Any Creolas or Garibaldis?" asked Penrose.

"Only digestives."

"That's a pity, but I'm always hopeful." He addressed Sophie, while Daniels put the cups on the table. "We used to get lovely biscuits before the war, but the Kaiser put a stop to all that. Cost-cutting measures came in and all the good biscuits disappeared. Although, I know for a fact they still get them upstairs." He pointed upwards with his thumb.

"Why don't you bring some in and keep them in a drawer?"

"Because I'd scoff the lot in one sitting." He started stirring his tea. "I'm that bad with biscuits, and Daniels isn't any better. Only he likes Custard Creams, which I'm not partial to."

Sophie sipped her tea. Penrose continued.

"Are you all right?"

"Thank you for asking, but no, I'm not. I feel brittle and empty... Seeing that man lying there in the rain. It came as an utter shock."

"That it would. Things like that are difficult to forget. As a policeman, I soon learned to be matter-of-fact about things. Now, if I were you, I'd talk it over with someone you trust, to get it out of your system or, at least, so that you're not alone dwelling on it all the time. Easier said than done, but you ought to try."

"I will, thank you. But it bothers me that had I not hesitated before going up the stairs, I might have frightened away the killer. You know, just by being another person nearby."

"You may have done, but you didn't know what was coming, did you? Anyway, that fella meant to kill the man right enough. If he didn't do it today, he would have done it tomorrow." Penrose spoke with certainty.

"I suppose you're right. Who was he?"

"We've an idea, but it has to be confirmed, so I don't like to give his name just yet. I'll tell you this, though. He was a union man working for a newspaper, and I really know no more than that at present."

"So why did the killer indecently put that piece of paper in the man's mouth? And what was on it?"

"I don't know why he did. A calling card or a warning,

maybe. It was a small, rectangular sheet with a fist in red and outlined in black, printed on one side."

"Have you seen such a thing before?"

"No. Sometimes there's a handwritten note at a murder scene. It'll say something like 'thief' or whatever. Once, there were words cut out of the newspaper to make up sentences. A printed red hand is a first for me. Smacks of a gang or these anarchist-types trying to intimidate someone."

"Do you think there will be another murder, then?"

"The paper was printed, Miss Burgoyne. You don't print one of anything, now do you?"

"How dreadful. You mean that workman person will strike again? Stokely and Dawkins will decide who dies and send out the butcher?"

"That's about the size of it, but let's hope for the best, shall we? Perhaps they've done as much as they intend... Can't say I've convinced myself of that. The red fist points to the beginning of something rather than its end."

"What an outrageous idea, that they can just take lives on a whim to suit their wicked purposes."

"These types think differently. There's a coldness to them, which isn't normal." Penrose picked up his teacup to drink and, to Sophie's surprise and amusement, he extended his little finger, which was also sausage-like. "We must get evidence to convict. If we can get the killer, we might work up the chain of command... You gave a detailed description, but you didn't see his face, you say?"

"No. I hadn't noticed him before he started walking, and I had no opportunity afterwards. He kept his head down and walked slowly until the end."

"Would you say his walk and the way he carried his head were habitual?"

"They both looked natural to me."

"Detectives will look for witnesses among the shop assistants, office workers, and anyone else they can find, which will include the policeman on point duty." Penrose did not say to Sophie that all the killer needed to do was change his clothes and he would probably never be found. "If he knew what time the man left for lunch, then he must have been in the area several times before to observe his victim's movements. The killer timed it well and chose the most out of the way place in a busy area at the busiest time of day. For a daring attack, I'd have to say, he planned it perfectly. He's no common thug, that's definite."

"Are you suggesting he might not be an actual workman?"

"I don't know. It's only a possibility."

"The clothes looked like they could have belonged to him and worn by him regularly, because he had a greasy collar and his hair was tickling it at the back to make it so through long use."

"Dark brown hair, I remember you saying. Then if you could see the band of grease on his collar, he must have had his hair cut recently."

Penrose watched Sophie's serious face as she recalled what she had seen of the man's back. "I believe you're right, come to think of it. His hair was more neatly trimmed rather than straggly."

"Then he wears his hair longer than most. Oil on it was there?"

"No, I don't think so. It was just dirty-looking."

"So if he has washed his hair since then, it would look a shade or two lighter than what you observed, wouldn't it?"

"Yes, I suppose it would."

Penrose nodded and wrote a few lines. "When it comes to you testifying at the coroner's inquest, just stick to what you observed. Don't go speculating. They don't like that at all. We'll talk to him about your name and such. Depends who it is, but we'll get some kind of accommodation, I'm sure. Hopefully, we'll only need a written statement, rather than you having to appear in person."

"It's very kind of you to go to all this trouble."

"Perhaps. We have to keep your identity secret for your

own safety. What I would like is for you to be present at the inquest. That's just in case the killer decides to take an interest in the proceedings and show up. It has happened before, and it might now. Are you certain he never saw you?"

"Absolutely, I am, and I'll do everything I can to help."

"Thank you, Miss Burgoyne... How's the tea?"

"Well..."

"Stewed, right? We have to go downstairs to the canteen to get a good cup in this place."

---

Aunt Bessie, Elizabeth, Ada, Flora, and Sophie gathered just after five for a meeting in the drawing room at White Lyon Yard.

"The tea at Scotland Yard is absolutely abominable," said Sophie, who was drinking tea from a Royal Crown Derby cup in the blue Mikado pattern.

"Do not mention tea, if you please," said Aunt Bessie, an untouched cup on the table in front of her. "Flora, you would not believe the immense quantities I am forced to drink in pursuit of information. It is such an absurd form of martyrdom."

"Martyrdom, Lady Shelling?" asked Flora. "Yes, I suppose more tea must be quite revolting once you've had enough."

"Exactly... Are you currently appearing in a production?"

"Sadly, I'm footloose and fancy-free once again, because the management and producers show favouritism when casting the parts. The fact is, I don't know any of the right people who could help me... Of course, I might be a ham actress without realizing it."

"Excuse me," said Ada, "but you're the best actress there is. You played that part of a baroness for *days* on end and never slipped up once. You 'ad no script, no nothing. Sorry, Lady

Shelling, for speaking out like that."

"Miss McMahon is correct," said Lady Shelling. "Don't put yourself down, Flora."

"Thank you for your kindness, but that was a little different from a stage performance. I did not have to live up to anyone's expectations, particularly those of fat-headed managers."

"I might have a part for you," said Sophie. "It is the reason for this sudden meeting."

"Ooh, how exciting," said Flora.

"You might find it *too* exciting once you know the details. You are not aware of what happened to me today. So, I shall start there."

To a silent and spellbound audience, Sophie gave a concise account of how she had followed the workman and found the body. Afterwards, she was peppered with questions, and bombarded by comments as everyone had their say about the appalling murder.

"The *idiots*," said Aunt Bessie. "How dare the police even *think* of putting you in a cell? I shall write to... *everyone*! I shall publicize this outrage..."

"No, Auntie. Don't tell anyone anything. We must keep it quiet for safety's sake, which was why I didn't give my name."

Lady Shelling looked at Sophie. "How annoying. Presumably, you expect me to bite my tongue?"

"Don't do it too hard," said Sophie, smiling.

"Do you see, Miss Banks, what I have to put up with?"

Elizabeth, mortified by this appeal, returned an embarrassed smile.

"There is an important matter connected with the murder that I must tell you about." Four expectant faces turned towards Sophie. "When I returned to the office, a letter had arrived by special messenger. It was from Mr Dalgleish, Lady Stokely's butler. In it, he related that Lord Stokely will host some sort of conference or series of meetings at his Chertsey Park estate from the twenty-seventh to the thirtieth of January. That's Thursday to Sunday. Apparently, Chertsey Park is under-staffed at present. To address this shortage, the butler and several other staff from Lady Stokely's house will assist at the event. As Chertsey Park is a large house and the staffing shortage is acute, Burgoyne's has been invited to accompany Mr Dalgleish for the duration of this... whatever it is. He is asking for four maids and two footmen."

"Right into the enemy's camp," said Flora. "How spiffing is that!?"

Aunt Bessie said, "It sounds rather dangerous to me, considering today's killing... Isn't that extraordinary? I never imagined I would ever say such a thing... Oh, well."

"Yes, it is, Auntie." Sophie turned to the others. "It is very dangerous and there's no denying that, should we make a mistake, we must get out as fast as we can or... I think I need not elaborate."

"Do you have a plan for that, miss?" asked Ada.

"Yes. We must travel down by train with Mr Dalgleish and the rest of them. What I thought was that because Elizabeth can drive, she could take Rabbit and stay at a nearby hotel or inn. If trouble arose, we would telephone her and she would come and collect us." Sophie turned to Elizabeth. "I'm sorry for putting you on the spot like this, and I'll quite understand if you don't wish to go. I'm asking you because you already know the situation we're in."

"Oh... ah, I'm not sure that I can." Elizabeth looked worried. "Who would look after my cats?"

The room fell silent.

"A neighbour?" suggested Flora.

"I have very little to do with them, I'm afraid, and it would be such an imposition for me to ask."

"Friends or family?" said Sophie.

"They are all too distant, or too elderly," said Elizabeth. "There aren't many of them, anyway."

"I know," said Ada. "What about Nick? He feeds an 'alf-wild moggy that 'angs about Sack Lane. So he must like them."

"Nicholas is a very nice young man. I find him trustworthy," said Elizabeth.

"Shall I talk to Nick and find out if he's willing?" asked Sophie.

"Would you, please? If he says yes, then I *would* be able to drive Rabbit." She looked delighted with the idea.

"Wonderful," said Sophie.

"Who else is going?" asked Ada.

"The three of us, if you're all agreeable. Then I was thinking of Fern as the fourth. Remember, she has a photographic memory, which could be useful. But it would mean a run down to Hampshire, because I feel I need to speak to Lord and Lady Hazlett in person and also to warn Fern of the dangers. One benefit to this long drive is Rabbit would reach five hundred miles, which means her engine has run in. Then she can have... What is it she has to go in the garage for, Elizabeth?"

"Among other things, to have her big end bearings tightened, and the babbitts inspected."

"*There.*" Sophie smiled. "And when Rabbit's babbitts and big ends have been seen to, she will live up to her name and go as fast as anything."

"What *can* you be talking about?" asked Aunt Bessie.

"Engine things, Auntie."

"I'm glad you understand it, because I certainly don't. It sounds remarkably like gibberish. However, you once asked me to look into the Hazlett family, which I did. I think I, too, would like to go to Hampshire."

"Yes, of course, you can. I was going to ask Elizabeth to accompany me, so that we could spy out Chertsey Park and find suitable accommodation in the area. But if you wish to join us, you will be most welcome."

"Are you going, Elizabeth?" asked Aunt Bessie.

"I think it would be lovely, Lady Shelling, only..."

"The cats!" said Sophie. "I shall talk to Nick first thing in the morning without fail."

"Thank you," said Elizabeth.

"That appears to be settled," said Aunt Bessie. "Let me know when the expedition is leaving, and I shall be ready. I don't want to meet the Hazletts, necessarily, but to escape London for a couple of days would be quite a tonic."

"In the interim, Auntie, I wonder if you and Elizabeth could direct your powers of research upon Lester Dawkins, Stokely's associate."

"Dawkins?" said Aunt Bessie. "Is he on our list?" she asked Elizabeth.

"He is, Lady Shelling, only we haven't got to him yet. We'll move him up to the top, Miss Burgoyne."

"I assume Alfie will be a footman," said Flora. "Who is the other to be?"

"Mr Broadbent-Wicks."

"No," said Ada.

"Yes. You won't believe this, but Stokely made a point of asking for him. Apparently, Mr Broadbent-Wicks made him laugh, and that is the sole basis for insisting he be included."

"Can we give him a code name, then?" asked Ada. "Something short. What's the shortest name in Britain?"

"Um... There's a Bishop of Ely," said Flora. "We could call him Ely."

"That's good. What about a first name?" asked Sophie.

"Eli," said Ada, who had them all smiling.

"Eli Ely? I don't think *any* of us could cope with that."

"How about Leo," said Flora.

"Leo Ely...? Very well, I'll tell him that's his nom de guerre. I hope he doesn't object."

Later, Sophie went to bed. She lay awake with fragments of the day sparking and tumbling in her mind, often returning to the man lying on the wet stones. Without truly knowing why, tears flowed, and she fell asleep only to wake up stiff and unrefreshed, having barely moved during the night.

# Chapter 9

# Important arrangements

"Cats? Over the weekend? Miss, you can't be serious." Nick's face was a pantomime of youthful horror. "I like them an' all that, but it's me time off. The other evenings during the week s'all right."

"I'll pay you," said Sophie.

"That makes it better. I s'ppose, if it's to do with that old geezer, Stokely, I shouldn't complain."

"Shh, don't mention his name. And he's not that old, although he might be a geezer if I knew what that meant exactly."

Nick was laughing and shaking his head. "The way you said *geezer*, oh my goodness, miss. I wish me mates could've heard you."

"Very funny, Nicholas. You've had your laugh. I was going to pay you extra, but now I'm not so sure."

"*Miss*. It just struck me as funny, it did. I'm really sorry, I couldn't help meself."

Sophie stared at him and raised her eyebrows. "One pound for four days. That's two hours daily of feeding, watering, and generally taking care of Falstaff and Desdemona."

"A whole quid! Thank you, thank you. It's very good of you, miss. I promise, them cats will be the best kept in London."

"I trust they shall. Elizabeth will provide you with a key, her address, and all that she requires you to do. So consult with her when she comes in."

"Yes, miss, and thanks again."

With a dark look, she watched him leave her office, knowing for a fact that Nick would treat his 'mates' to an exuberant performance of how she spoke and especially how she enunciated the word geezer.

"Mr Broadbent-Wicks, have you found a position yet?" asked Sophie, an hour later.

"No. I have a sort of half-promise from one place that if I return in a month's time, they might have something for me."

"I may have something suitable, but it is only for four days at the end of January. Lord Stokely is hosting a gathering, and Burgoyne's is required to supply staff for the event. Mr Dalgleish asked for two footmen to be sent. He specifically requested that you be one of them."

"That's awfully rum. Why would he ask for me?"

"Apparently, you made Lord Stokely laugh."

"I did? Come to think of it, that's true. It was over the birthday cake. Although, honestly, Miss Burgoyne, I didn't mean to. I was being silent and professional, just as instructed, yet he left me no choice but to speak."

"It so happened that I witnessed the exchange, and you are not to be faulted. However, it may now mean that his lordship expects some bon mot or other witticism from you should you meet again." Sophie paused, repositioning herself in her chair. "The potential success of the mission demands that you refrain from comment. If cornered, think before speaking, as I believe you did over the cake."

"I admit to wanting to jolly things along, but I will absolutely do my best… Although, just in case I *am* cornered, I might read some of Oscar Wilde's stuff to get a few pointers."

"Ah, no, I'd rather you didn't do that. Just be polite and simply humour the man, but not to excess."

"I believe I see what you mean."

"The motto for this mission is Serve and Observe. That is all we shall do, because there is a substantial amount of risk involved."

"Risk, eh? What sort?"

"We might all be murdered."

"Oh, *come* off it, Miss Burgoyne," said Broadbent-Wicks, his face lighting up. "Now you're pulling my leg."

"No, I'm not. I don't know the reason for this gathering, but it is certainly some type of organizing process to implement a plan. It is important we find out at least some of what they discuss. In the event of discovery, we shall leave and all go into hiding."

"*Hiding.* I say, it really is serious, then?"

"Most decidedly so. Stokely will stop at nothing, and that includes murder and violence. He, or an associate, arranged a murder as recently as yesterday."

"That is totally disgusting. He must be stopped."

"Yes, and we shall play our part in stopping him if we can."

"I agree." He slapped the table. "Um, Miss Burgoyne, I hate to mention this, but I'm rather low on funds at present. What will the pay be?"

"Everyone will receive the same amount, which includes danger pay. Forty pounds for four days."

"Forty! That's a stupendous amount. Forty… Let me see… I really should leave my flat and move into cheaper digs. Yes, I'll do that. And if you pay me at the end of January, and I already have February's rent set aside… I should be able to manage everything if I stop eating for the next two weeks."

"Are you broke?"

"Yes. And I'll be stony broke come the first of Feb, except about then I'll receive forty glorious pounds. It all works out in the end, doesn't it?"

"Why not move now?"

"I've been busy looking for work and haven't really thought about moving. I like my flat, but it really is far too expensive for me under the circs."

"Please wait a moment. I'll be back shortly. When I return, do not mention Stokely or missions... or anything else. Understood?"

"Absolutely."

Sophie returned, accompanied by Miss Jones, who was a severe-looking woman and the manager of the typing pool. After the introduction, they settled themselves.

"As I mentioned to you, Miss Jones, Mr Broadbent-Wicks is looking for a room."

Miss Jones turned her attention to the young man. "I live in a ladies-only house, Mr Broadbent-Wicks. However, on our road, the landlord has converted many buildings and there are often rooms to let and the rents are quite reasonable for what you get. The buildings are large, there are public gardens and shops nearby, and the turnover of tenants is quite high in some houses only because commercial travellers rent them by the week or month. Some houses include a breakfast and dinner, but that's extra, of course."

"Oh, Miss Jones, where is this Utopia? I must fly there at once."

Miss Jones, unsure of his manner, hesitated while staring back at Broadbent-Wicks. Then one of her rare smiles broke out. "It's in Dalston."

"Dalston? Does it have a tube station?"

"No, but the railway station is only a short walk, and the service is reliable. I use it myself."

"Then it can have no better recommendation," said Broadbent-Wicks. "I'm *very* interested."

"Perhaps you and Miss Jones can discuss the matter once we have finished," said Sophie.

"Yes, that would be marvellous," responded the eager young man.

Miss Jones left.

"I must emphasize that Miss Jones and the other typists are not aware of *any* espionage activities."

"They won't hear it from me, Miss Burgoyne. On that subject, my lips are most firmly sealed."

"Good. Now, to continue..."

Sophie explained matters. It took some time for them to settle on a false name, because Broadbent-Wicks had balked at the choice of Leo, yet he did not mind Ely. He explained that when he was a small boy, his Uncle Leo when visiting often tickled him into hysterics — once to the extent of making him expel his dinner on the carpet. These experiences resulted in Broadbent-Wicks not caring for the name of Leo, so they settled on Dan Ely.

By the time Broadbent-Wicks left, he was best of friends with Miss Jones — who had taken a liking to him even before he fixed a sticky key on her typewriter, had two pounds in his pocket, loaned by Sophie to tide him over, and was off searching for a new place to live. Happy that his prospects had so suddenly and radically improved, he decided he was a very lucky chap.

---

"My dear Soap," said Archie with tender concern. "Please, sit down. How are you?"

She had visited him at the Foreign Office with newspapers under her arm.

"As long as my time's occupied, I'm fine. Thank you for asking."

"It's a rotten business. Penrose told me about it... You almost spent a night in the cells, old thing. What did Bessie make of that?"

"Ha! She blew up, naturally. She's a dear. Calming her down made me feel better, as well as in knowing she was so outraged."

"Yes, it's easily imagined. I'm glad you came, because I wanted to talk to you but, at a guess, I think you have an idea in mind."

"Two or three related things. Look at these newspapers."

A column in one had the heading *Brutal murder in London*. The report stated that a secret group of anarchists, known as the Red Fist, had carried out the assassination. A second paper carrying the same story said the Red Fist was a subversive communist faction. The third echoed the others, but called upon the authorities to act speedily to expunge the Red Fist — a group of murderers who wished to start a revolution.

"The remarkable feature of these newspapers," said Sophie, "is that none of them belong to Stokely. And what does Stokely's London Mercury and National Chronicle say? 'Murder near Fleet Street', and then report the bare facts, omitting any mention of the Red Fist. Why, I have to wonder, should this be the case?"

"Stokely's distancing himself, that's obvious." Archie swivelled his chair from side to side. "As for the other papers, it is possible that reporters may, on occasion, display the mentality of a pack. Someone fed each of them the same or a similar story, and it was sufficiently lurid and sensational for them not to bother checking the source. Or the source might usually be unimpeachable in their eyes. Something along those lines, I would guess. The result is what you see here. I doubt very much that there is any collusion between them or that a Stokely agent orchestrated the various papers. Is that what you were thinking?"

"It crossed my mind. I couldn't see how else they all leapt to roughly the same conclusion so soon."

"Well, it could just be a case of Fleet Street mania. Anyway, we now have a good idea what Stokely's doing, thanks to you, but it comes at an awful price. If you had not witnessed the events preceding the murder, we would be in the dark... Stokely is going after the revolutionary groups, which is likely to include the communist parties, or party, I should say. They've united into a single party, guided by Moscow's intervention. Nikolai Bukharin mediated between opposing factions and they have all joined under a single banner. I should think they'll make a public announcement today or tomorrow."

"Then why was Mr Bukharin at Stokely's party?"

"Stokely wished to create an optical illusion... Buying time or diverting suspicion away from himself to keep Moscow on side. We shall see in due course."

"That due course might be short. The agency is going to Chertsey Park at the end of January. Six of us will be working there."

"What's this?" He sat still. "How did you manage that?"

"Only by agreeing to a proposal. Our work at Lyall Place suitably impressed Mr Dalgleish, Lady Georgiana's butler. Stokely is having a big get-together at the end of January and, as I'm informed, it's more to do with his business than anything else. We got in, because Chertsey Park is understaffed. There, Sweet Boy, what do you think of that?"

"Phenomenal."

"Yes, it is," said Sophie, who clapped her hands together and laughed. "There is the possibility of danger in this mission, wouldn't you say?"

"Potentially fraught with it."

"I have five of the six places filled, and I'm hopeful of the person I'd like for the last place."

"Hold on. I can send someone with you."

"No, you can't."

"I think I must. It's for security reasons and for your safety."

"Balderdash, as they used to say. Our security and safety lies within our doing our jobs properly. You can't foist an amateur on us. They'll make a muck of it, and I'd be ill with worry. It's out of the question. Our motto, which I made up

119

today, is To Serve and Observe. I refuse to add Blunder to it."

"Have you finished?"

"I can continue if you wish, but I think I've made myself clear."

"Perfectly, thank you. I shall not insist, because I can see I would only be wasting my time. You will, however, submit to me all the details of your operation. You must inform me of the names and addresses of everyone who's going so that you do not inadvertently take a Stokely agent along with you."

"That's ridiculous."

"Sophie, it is not ridiculous. Lord Stokely's agents and operatives have infiltrated the Home Office, Scotland Yard, and the Foreign Office. Reviews are presently ongoing in many departments, including the more secretive ones." He paused. "You met a Stokely agent when you came here, although I doubt very much he understands he is one."

"Who was that?"

Archie looked blankly at her before saying, "If you guess correctly, you must promise your attitude towards him doesn't change in the slightest."

"Who on earth do you mean?" She reflected upon who she had met since entering the Foreign Office. "Not Albright, the door-keeper?"

"Close. The fellow who sits next to him."

"Why don't you arrest him?"

"Stokely would merely recruit someone else, and it would take time for us to find out who it was."

"What can he do, though?"

"He keeps a record of who meets whom, and when. It has a slight value in some quarters. The value of such information increases when the individuals who meet have senior positions or important business to conduct. You should understand that he already passed your name on before today."

Sophie went quiet as she considered what she had just heard. She looked at Archie, and then away. When she looked at him again, she said, "I can't change my name for Chertsey

Park."

"That's true."

"Is it possible they would cross-reference the name Phoebe King at the FO with Phoebe King from Burgoyne's?"

"Yes. How likely that is or what they make of it if they discover the match, I cannot say."

"Oh, dear... I must go. I have no choice but to go, and I can't change my name." She shrugged. "So that's that."

Archie could not recall her looking so unhappy ever before.

"You need not go. We are getting closer to Stokely... Whatever is brought back from Chertsey Park would be undeniably useful. Perhaps a suitable person could change places with you, subject to your stringent vetting."

"It's not like that. We function as a team and are used to each other's ways." She thought of young Fern at Lady Holme, and Broadbent-Wicks, who needed very close attention. "No, the die is cast, so we need not discuss it further."

"I understand. You know that once inside the house, you will be on your own. We'll provide some help, but I must consult with others first before I can say what that help will be."

"We have an escape plan," she said brightly.

"You had better tell me what it is."

Sophie explained about Elizabeth and the car stationed nearby to be summoned by telephone if need be.

"Are you sure all seven of you can fit in the car?"

"Not without getting rather squished. But if we have to make a run for it, I don't think we'll be worrying about that."

Archie nodded. The matter dropped.

"Wasn't there something you wished to tell me?" asked Sophie.

"It isn't urgent. Only that the London Mercury is continuing its assault on the government's morality and the other papers have picked up the theme. The interesting parts are in the letters to the editor sections. Some hot exchanges are developing, and I wondered if you might have a look to see if you can provide insight into any of the correspondents. Your agency may have provided staff or services to them. Just a thought."

"I'll do that. Although, isn't this a Home Office matter?"

"Yes."

"I can always tell when you know something interesting but are keeping it back."

"That sometimes works both ways. Usually, I have to chase you down after the fact to wrench the information from your stubborn grasp. I must insist that you be entirely forthcoming about what you intend to do at Chertsey Park, and keep me, or a designated person, informed while the operation is ongoing. We'll work out the details on how it's to be done. For the moment, I need your solemn promise that you will pass along information at regular intervals."

"I promise to do so. But..." Archie closed his eyes and shook his head as Sophie continued, "I can't promise to send messages at an exact time, because of the type of work we do."

"I can appreciate the difficulty. It is your commitment to send such communications that I need."

"I gave my word and will keep it." She started collecting her things together. "How does one get around the Stokely spy on the door?"

"Simple really. We unlock another entrance when needed."

"Fancy having to creep into your offices? Some elements of this spying business are utterly farcical. I wish everything about it were farcical."

"Don't we all. And it's espionage, if you please."

"Sorry.... What do they call it in the HO?"

Archie stared at her. "You're fishing."

"Trying to. As you're not biting, I shall leave. Have a lovely day, Sweet Boy."

"Good day." He stood up. "Telephone before dropping in next time, so I can give you a guided tour of the Post Room and backstairs."

"I'll definitely call to take you up on such an irresistible offer... Oh, have you found out anything about Lester Dawkins?"

"He is being investigated." Archie smiled and folded his arms.

"Ho-hum... Cheerio, Archie."

# Chapter 10

# Wildlife

On Monday morning, 17th of January, Rabbit finally cleared the built-up areas of London. Strictly observing the speed limit, Sophie drove along the open Guildford Road. Her chauffeur's uniform was hanging up in her bedroom wardrobe, but she was wearing the matching cap, because she adored it, and her leather coat. Her jack boots were barely noticeable beneath her long dress.

"We have left civilization," said Aunt Bessie from the back seat. "The last acceptable hotel was overlooking the Thames."

"Elizabeth has to be stationed as near as possible to Chertsey Park for the plan to be effective," said Sophie.

"We want to see if we can find a place in Ottershaw," said Elizabeth in the front, who was in charge of the map.

"I've never heard of the place," said Aunt Bessie. "No one has."

"There's bound to be an inn with rooms available on a road like this," said Sophie.

"How quaint," said Aunt Bessie. "At least I won't be staying there. I'm sorry, Elizabeth, that you are being put to such an inconvenience."

"I don't mind, Lady Shelling, I really don't. Except... I've never been in a public house before."

"Which is the proper behaviour for a genteel woman," said Aunt Bessie.

"I take it you've never been in one?" asked Sophie.

"Good heavens! Of course, not."

"Neither have I," said Sophie.

"Oh," said Elizabeth. "How does one go about booking a room?"

"I really don't know," said Sophie.

After a momentary and expectant silence in the front, Aunt Bessie said,

"I'm not having anything to do with it. I've never booked a thing in me life, and I'm not about to start now."

"I suppose Hawkins booked the hotel in Southampton on your behalf." Sophie referred to the butler at White Lyon Yard.

"How else would we be staying there if he hadn't?"

"Have you ever stayed in a hotel?" asked Sophie of Elizabeth.

"Twice as a child... Later, we didn't have the means."

"It was the same with my family... When we find somewhere, we'll go in together to negotiate the terms."

"Oh, thank you," said Elizabeth with evident relief.

They arrived at a roundabout on the north side of Ottershaw. Five roads radiated from it.

"There's a garage ahead," said Sophie, while changing gears and braking. "We'll stop for petrol and ask for assistance."

She brought Rabbit to a stop in front of the pump that stood against a square, utilitarian, white-washed building consisting of two garage bays with green doors and an office. A large, ruddy-faced man in overalls came out of his office lair and strolled over to the driver's window.

"Good morning, miss. What can I do for you?" Although only in Surrey and a few miles outside of the metropolis, he had no hint of a London accent.

"Can you fill it up, please?" said Sophie.

"Yes, miss."

After removing the cap, the man pumped the lever until the petrol flowed.

"Do you have a can as wants fillin'?" he called.

"It's already full, thank you."

"Arrh."

The proximity of the attendant invoked complete silence in the car. When finished, he came to the window.

"Four and a half gallon, at three shillin', which will be, let me see now, ah… thirteen shillin' and sixpence. That's cheaper now the tax has come off. They do say it will go down further. Shall I look at the oil?"

"Yes, please, and top it up as necessary."

"Arrh."

He opened the bonnet. Sophie was close enough to talk to him as he worked.

"Are there any hotels in Ottershaw?"

"Lord love you, no, miss. There be rooms in public houses, though."

"Could you recommend one?"

He came to the window with the dipstick in his hand. He put his foot on the running board and bent down to look in the window.

"Three ladies. That's unusual. You're all a-wanting rooms?"

"It's just for one of us for four days at the end of the month."

"Arrh… Just the one… Well, you could try The Otter, but they only have lodgers, so there's no point. The beer's good there. Now the Plough does a rare ploughman's lunch, as one moight expect with a name loike that, but they have no rooms. The Queen's Head has rooms, but they be the size of kennels, and from what I hear, no dog would touch the food there, eh? You might want to give that one a miss. No, your best bet is the Gardeners Arms. Very nice there, it is. Clean rooms and good food, and you can't ask for more than that."

"Where is it?"

"Down that road." He turned and pointed. "No more than a hundred yards, by Coach Road."

"Thank you, we shall inquire there."

"Tell 'em, Bert sent you. My brother-in-law is the landlord, and my sister Agnes does the cookin' and lets the rooms. She's a foine cook, an' when she sets down such a great heaping plateful as she does, no one ever asks for seconds."

"Is that so?" said Sophie, who now had a doubt about the food. "Does the Gardeners Arms have a telephone?"

"Yes, and it has electrics, hot and cold water, indoor lavs, and radiators, as well as a fireplace. I put the radiators in, so I know it's snug."

The three women had winced simultaneously at the word lav.

"Thank you... May I ask why Ottershaw has four public houses? How many people live in the village?"

"Oh, nigh on seven hundred. But there be five pubs. The Fox and Hounds is run by a chap named Smith from North London. It ain't so much that we've taken against him because he's foreign; it's just he throws his weight about, and him a newcomer. T'ain't right."

"Ah... Five public houses for seven hundred people. Are you all very thirsty?"

The garage owner knitted his eyebrows together for a moment, then threw back his head to laugh loudly.

"*Thirsty*... Made my day, that has. No, it's the passing trade, you understand. Come here in the summer and you'll see it proper busy."

"That makes sense now... I wonder if you would also be so kind as to give us directions to Chertsey Park."

"I can do that. Take that road over there, go to the end, an' turn left to go up Gracious Hill. Before you get to Chobham, you'll see the Park on your right. It can't be missed... Are you visiting?"

"No, passing through. Out of curiosity, we wanted to look at the house while we were in the area."

"Right." He spoke in a different tone. "Best not to stop in there."

"Is there something wrong at the Park?"

"Well now, miss. I don't say nothing against the earl with him being such a gentleman and the squire hereabouts, but the Park is that poorly run."

"Do people from Ottershaw work there?"

"Arrh, an' most of 'em want to leave. It's best I say no more."

"I understand."

Sophie looked at the dipstick he was still holding. The garage owner looked at it, too.

"Oil's foine, miss."

"That's good, and thank you very much." She gave him some coins. "Keep the change."

"Well, that's koind of you, miss. You have a safe drive. Good day to you, ladies."

Sophie drove to the Gardeners Arms and parked in front of the gate in a white wicket fence. They stared at the building, which was really two smaller, different height houses knocked into one. Its white-washed exterior looked clean, and the place appeared to be well kept. The only jarring feature on the exterior were the painted signs — particularly one of them. The massive lettering shouted the words Milk Stout.

"Why have they done that?" asked Lady Shelling. "Do people passing by become seized with the desire for milk stout simply upon reading the sign?"

"It is odd."

"I've drunk milk stout," said Elizabeth. "It's quite strengthening."

"So the advertisements inform us," said Aunt Bessie.

"It's the carbohydrates in it," said Elizabeth. "I think the sign is meant to encourage nursing mothers to enter the premises."

"What word did you just use?" asked Aunt Bessie.

"Carbohydrates. It's a technical term for sugars. For milk stout, they add sugars derived from lactose, hence the term milk can be used."

"It sounds filthy. Are we going in, or shall we sit here all day?"

"You're coming, too?" asked Sophie.

"I want to see what happens. But don't go throwing my title about."

Sophie turned towards her aunt.

"Don't look at me like that. I've changed my mind, that's all."

They got out and entered through the porch — three women who had not booked a room between them and had never been in a pub before. The interior was warm and cheerful, dimly lit, decorated with horse brasses, knick-knacks, and photographs on the wall, all of which made it feel welcoming.

"It's nice and clean," whispered Sophie. "What do we do now?"

"Go up to the counter," whispered Aunt Bessie. "There isn't anywhere else to go."

A young barmaid was pulling a pint for a customer, and their eyes fixed upon her as she operated the beer pump handle. She looked up, saw them, and said cheerily,

"Be with you in just a moment."

She finished with the customer and came over.

"What'll you 'ave? You can sit in the Ladies' Room if you loike."

She pointed to a door with the appropriate sign on it.

"Am I to understand that you are referring to the conveniences?" said Aunt Bessie, horrified.

The barmaid barely suppressed a fit of laughter. "Oh, no, ma'am. It's the room where the ladies sit to have their drink."

"Do they drink milk stout?" asked Sophie.

"Some do. Is that what you'd loike? A bottle o' milk stout?"

"No, no," said Sophie hurriedly. "Bert directed us here about a room. Is Agnes available?"

"I'll fetch her for you." She went to a doorway behind the bar to shout "*Mum!*"

From somewhere far away, a loud voice, diminished by distance, shouted back.

"Wh-*at*!?"

"*Rooms!*"

No shout came back. The barmaid said reassuringly, "She'll be down in a minute."

The allotted time elapsed and a very round woman with a bright face barrelled through the doorway, speaking as she walked.

"I'm ever so sorry to have kept you waiting, loike. Ooh, three ladies. How long are you staying?"

"Good Morning, Agnes. Um, Bert sent us."

"Did he? You've come to the roight place, you have."

"We wish to book a room for one person."

"Ahh," said Agnes, visibly disappointed.

"It's for four days."

"*Ahh,*" said Agnes, her spirits restored.

"Yes. It's for the twenty-seventh to the thirtieth of January."

"The twenty-seventh, you say," said Agnes. She took down a small calendar from a hook and began counting out loud. "So you'll be leaving Monday morning?"

"That's correct."

"Roight. It's just you, miss, is it?"

"No, it's not for me. It's this lady who will be staying."

"Excuse me. Are you visiting someone, madam?" she asked Elizabeth.

"No," said Elizabeth. "I'm here to study the winter habits of the wildlife in the area."

"*Wildloife?*" The landlady's surprise was shared by Sophie and Aunt Bessie. They all stared at the reddening Elizabeth. "You mean loike foxes...? And adders? Thems about as wild as they come in these parts. Not like in Africa."

"Yes," said Elizabeth, floundering. "Foxes."

"Oh." Agnes looked doubtful, but tried entering the spirit of the moment. "We have plenty of rabbits and squirrels. There's deer, royal ones, from the king's lands... I know what you moight loike," she added cheerfully. "We have a spider what skitters across the water... But it's not the time o' year for them, though."

"Perhaps I'll find one hibernating," suggested Elizabeth.

"You moight at that, madam. It's foive shillin' a day for room and dinner, with foive shillin' in advance to hold it, please. I'll give a receipt."

"Before we settle, do you have a room with a view?" asked Aunt Bessie.

"View? Well, there's really only the front, back, and the soide to choose from. We live on t'other soide. Garden looks nice Spring onwards, but it's a mournful ruin this time o' year."

"May we see the rooms?" asked Sophie.

"Yes'm, there all empty, except for one."

She bustled from behind the bar and took them through a door which led to the means of going upstairs. There they examined the rooms, ending up in the one overlooking the garden.

"I'll take this one," said Elizabeth.

"Very good, madam. You can adjust the radiator if it gets too hot for you. Dinner's at six-thirty. You can have it downstairs or in your room on a tray."

"I understand Lord Stokely lives nearby," said Sophie. "We thought to drive past his house."

"It's a big house and very grand." Her attitude had changed, as if she begrudgingly admitted such facts.

"Is there any ill-will held against his lordship?" asked Sophie.

Agnes hesitated at the abrupt question. "Not against him, no... He's a lovely gentleman by all accounts, though I've not seen him these past six years. Trouble is, he don't spend much time on his estate loike he should. Always up in London on business, and then he's off to foreign parts at the drop of an 'at. No, it's not him, because he don't have enough hours in the day for what he does. It's that man he has there running things." Agnes nodded emphatically.

"What does this man do?"

"More'n he should *and* what he shouldn't. But I dursn't

say anything against him, because some in the village... There, now. You're not interested in our little affairs, and I'm a-clacking away when you just want a room."

"Here's the five shillings," said Sophie, smiling. "I'm sorry for taking up so much of your time."

"Don't you worry about *that*, miss, and thank you very much. What name do I put down?" She had a receipt book and pencil at the ready.

"Ophelia Woodhouse," announced Elizabeth, heroically.

Sophie and Aunt Bessie sought to govern themselves at this further surprise from their companion.

They all returned downstairs and said goodbye to Agnes, who disappeared back through the doorway whence she had first appeared. After a brief consultation amongst the remaining negotiators, Sophie approached the bar.

"Excuse me. May we have a bottle of milk stout served in three glasses, please?"

"Three glasses?" The barmaid looked puzzled.

"Did I ask for it incorrectly?" Sophie's colour heightened, and she added hurriedly, "Should I pay extra for the additional glasses?"

"No, just the beer. I'll get it for you." As the barmaid busied herself. "You've taken a room, have you?"

"My friend has."

"If she's from London, she'll find it quiet here. T'other roads are much busier at night, but not this'n."

She put the glasses on a tray. Sophie paid and took charge of it. She returned to the others and suggested,

"Let's adjourn to the Ladies' Room."

They went in and it was empty.

"It's not as nice in here," said Elizabeth.

"It has a forlorn air," said Sophie, setting the tray on a table.

"You look like a barmaid," said Aunt Bessie.

"No, I don't." She sat down. "I've served beer and cider at harvest-time, but it's funny my never having been in a public house before when there are so many of them. Cheers. I think that's what they say."

They tried their milk stout.

"I still don't like beer," said Sophie.

"I'm quite enjoying mine," said Elizabeth.

"When we get home, remind me to tell Hawkins to order in a crate." Aunt Bessie dabbed her lips with a fine cambric handkerchief. "I rather like it. I thought it would be vile but, surprisingly, it isn't. Strengthening, you say, Elizabeth?"

"Supposedly, it is, Lady Shelling."

"That is an eminently useful excuse... Sophie?"

"It's Phoebe, remember."

"Yes, yes, *Phoebe*. Why didn't you ask the barmaid about Stokely?"

"Because they are all one family in this house and they're bound to talk about us. If we mention Stokely all over the place, they'll become suspicious. However, Auntie, you've raised a good point. Elizabeth, or should I say Ophelia — that came as a shocker — do you think you could get them talking about Stokely? I'd like to know what it is the villagers have against the man in charge."

"Of course, Miss King. That person must be quite awful by the sounds of him."

"There's no butler at Chertsey Park," said Aunt Bessie. "Otherwise, the Dalgleish fellow wouldn't be going. Therefore, it must be only the estate manager they've taken against."

"I think so, too," said Sophie. She looked at her watch. "We must be on our way soon."

"Don't hurry me. I'm savouring my drink."

"But we have to reach Winchester by teatime. Father is expecting us."

"Henry won't mind if we're ten minutes late. As a vicar, it is required of him to have a forgiving nature. If he says anything, I shall remind him of that fact."

"You won't do any such thing."

They got away and, as they passed through the roundabout, Bert waved to them while filling up another car. The road took them past some cottages, and then a few scattered farms situated on cleared land among woodlands until they came to the end.

"Homewood Road," said Elizabeth, reading a sign, and looking at the map. "It's not far now. Gracious Hill is next, then we should see the estate."

"Why is he the Earl of Stokely?" asked Sophie. "There's no place in the area with that name."

"Ah-ha," said Aunt Bessie. "I'm glad you asked. Elizabeth and I have discovered a great deal. The earldom is ancient. Originally, a branch of the de Bohun family had the title and held extensive lands in Cheshire, south of Manchester. The name Stokely is common to several places in that area. For want of a male heir, the line died out with the third earl. The title was put into abeyance and then extinguished. It was recreated in 1661 and given as a reward to Humphrey Fielding, second Baron of Longcross, which place is in this area. He was gifted the 612 acres we are about to see from the remainder of the Chertsey Abbey estate that hadn't been already given to others. There was a substantial house on the grounds at the time, much bigger than Fielding's own, so he moved into it, and started collecting the rents."

"Then Stokely has two titles?"

"Yes," said Elizabeth. "He's the twelfth Earl of Stokely, and the thirteenth Baron of Longcross."

"Double-cross, you mean," said Sophie.

Aunt Bessie laughed. "That's far more suitable for the creature. Elizabeth, tell Phoebe what else we discovered." She became excited. "This is a corker!"

"Well, Miss King, it's rather speculative, but there are strong signs that something odd occurred about the time of Lord Stokely's birth."

"Excuse me for interrupting," said Sophie, "but we're approaching the estate and I must be careful about stopping in case Rabbit draws attention. I'll drive slower, though."

They followed a long, dilapidated fence next to the road

that marked the border of the estate. Three farms then appeared side by side and, although they looked tidy, there was no marked evidence of prosperity to them. The fence continued again before changing to a high brick wall — weather stained and inexpertly patched in places. At last, Sophie slowly drove past the wide entrance with its stone columns supporting heraldic devices. Through the gates, they could see the house at the far end of the open drive.

"Is anyone coming?" asked Sophie.

"No, dear," said Aunt Bessie, peering through the small rear window.

Sophie stopped the car.

"How many bedrooms would you say?"

"There has to be at least forty," said Aunt Bessie. "Do we not know for certain, then?"

"Unfortunately, we don't," said Elizabeth. "The architect was George Dance the Younger. The house cost £14,200 and was built between 1771 and 1774 after Mr Dance had finished Newgate Prison."

"The earl could have saved the two hundred by dispensing with the faux castellation," said Aunt Bessie. "There's far too much of it for my tastes."

"There's supposed to be a fine parterre garden," said Elizabeth.

"Is there? I'm still grappling with the Newgate Prison connection," said Sophie.

"Drive on, there's a lorry coming," said Aunt Bessie.

They set off again.

"He's let it run down," said Sophie.

"It's *dreadful*. With his millions, he can easily afford its upkeep."

"He might be a miser, although not in the traditional sense." Sophie changed gear. "Elizabeth, what were you about to say before we stopped?"

"It concerns his birth date. He was born Jan 12th, 1878. Georgiana and Lord Stokely, Humphrey William Fielding, were married on April 10th 1877. According to the records, Roderick Fielding was born almost exactly nine months later."

"Ah. I'm not sure I'm following you."

"His full name is Roderick John Humphrey Edward Fielding. The first time I can find the use of Edward as a family name was for his Uncle Teddy. Edward Fielding was an army lieutenant, later raised to a captaincy. He was posted to South Africa, and departed for an extended tour of duty in February 1877."

"I'm rather baffled. Where is this leading?"

"Be patient," said Aunt Bessie.

"Yes, so, the brother of the earl, Edward Fielding, remained in South Africa, but briefly returned to England at the time of Lord Humphrey Stokely's wedding. He returned to South Africa immediately afterwards. He returned twice..."

"Cut it a little shorter," said Aunt Bessie.

"Well," said Elizabeth, "the upshot is that every time Georgiana gave birth, Edward had begun his leave in England ten or eleven months earlier."

"But they weren't married," said Sophie. "And Roderick was born within the, um, time limit, so to speak, while Edward left in February."

"May I, Elizabeth?" Aunt Bessie took up the narrative. "Four months before she was supposedly due to give birth, Georgiana stayed with relatives in Ireland, and then returned nearly two months after the birth. She was away five months, nearly six, while Lord Humphrey stayed in England because he was an invalid. Then, the last part is that Roderick Stokely's birth was falsely registered in England over two months *after* the event, and well outside the forty-two-day limit."

"Are you saying... No, you're further ahead than I am. What's your conclusion?"

"Roderick Fielding is illegitimate as far as the titles are concerned. He was born in Ireland about two months earlier than stated on his birth certificate. That's certain. However, Georgiana and the Fielding brothers covered up the indiscretion between them, but we're not sure exactly what they did. We believe the younger brother, Edward, is Roderick Fielding's father. In fact, the father of all Georgiana's three children. There's an outside *chance* that Lord Humphrey is the father, but I suspect he was incapable of producing an heir. So, you see, Roderick has no legitimate right to the title until *Edward* Fielding dies."

"What on earth were they thinking of?"

"Protecting Georgiana's reputation, I imagine. Consider Georgiana's viewpoint for a moment. Will she fall for the charms of a dashing officer of twenty-eight and foolishly get into trouble? Or was she dazzled by the idea of a title, and so married a sick man, eighteen years her senior?"

"I have to think this over," said Sophie.

They drove through Chobham in silence

"If this is the chink in Stokely's armour, how do we make use of it? We can't prove anything."

"No, but consider this. I'm firmly rooted in the ways of the last century and thus familiar with them. I'd give odds of twenty to one that Stokely knows nothing about his parentage or that there is even a secret to be discovered. The absolute last thing a family would do was to tell the child anything. Hush it all up, that's the way they always did it. In the seventeen hundreds, it was entirely different. The nobility had illegitimate children all over the place and didn't care who knew it."

"But wouldn't Edward inherit the title when Humphrey died?"

"Yes, which makes me think there must be another reason for this decidedly odd arrangement... Haven't found it yet, though."

"Then to confirm the theory, we need only find out if Georgiana and Edward loved each other before and after the marriage."

"Yes. I'm sure Georgiana has kept some fascinating letters from Edward, but you won't find them at Chertsey Park. Men burn compromising documents while women always keep 'em."

Elizabeth quietly cleared her throat. "I'm sorry, Lady Shelling, but that is not always the case with men, although I'm sure it is for many of them. I've organized the private libraries of several gentlemen and, in each instance, I sorted out correspondence thrown higgledy-piggledy into boxes. As these papers and diaries spanned decades or centuries, it was quite an eye-opener to find what was available for anyone to read if they cared to open a box."

"There you are, Phoebe. Send the gel with the photographic memory up to the attics at Chertsey Park. When she comes down blushing, you'll know she's found something interestin'."

"Auntie, please."

# Chapter 11

# Red Fist and blackmail

Late the next day, with Elizabeth and Sophie sharing the driving, the expedition returned to London in triumph. Aunt Bessie had changed her mind once more and, at Lady Holme, had met Lord and Lady Hazlett, who were at first bewildered and then positively delighted that she was in their house. The Hazletts honoured their side of the strange arrangement Sophie had made with them, whereby Fern, the young maid with the photographic memory — which skill was unknown to the Hazletts — was loaned out to Burgoyne's Agency. For its part, the agency supplied a replacement for the duration of Fern's absence. After the Hazletts and Sophie had agreed on the matter, Sophie privately informed Fern of the risks involved in any future 'missions' with the Agency. Fern said she had thoroughly enjoyed pretending to be Dora Datchet before and looked forward to doing so again, despite the dangers. Sophie impressed upon her it was indeed dangerous work, while Fern remained adamant, becoming shocked upon learning how much the job paid.

When parking Rabbit in Fleur de Lis Mews at the end of the

return journey, the odometer read five hundred and fourteen miles, which small accomplishment pleased Sophie. At White Lyon Yard, a note from Superintendent Penrose awaited her. He informed her that the inquest for the Fleet Street murder was on Friday, the 28th of January, so Sophie could not go because she would be at Chertsey Park that day. She was a little disappointed because she had never been to an inquest before.

On Thursday, the 20th of January, a few newspapers continued a modest, questioning attack on the Liberal coalition government over personal expenditures, some with foundation, while the London Mercury refrained from commenting on the morality of sitting MPs. Neither did the paper seem interested in the Red Fist Gang, which organization inflamed the other periodicals. This inflammation became acute after the report of a Monday night steamfitters' union meeting in Leeds being broken up. Unknown assailants had hurled bricks through the windows. One of the attackers had wrapped a paper emblazoned with a red fist around a missile. Fleet Street speculation ran wild about who was behind the nearby killing and the violence visited upon the Leeds' meeting. The press, save for the mute London Mercury, agreed it must be subversive revolutionaries and extremists, while a minority stated outrightly that it had to be communists.

Penrose had assigned Inspector Morton and Sergeant Gowers a blackmail case. In a single-roomed office on a floor of seedy offices, in a disreputable building in a rundown area, the two men had been working through files from the Home Office and the Ministry of Health, searching for something that could be of use to a criminal organization. On the first day of their labours, the project had looked manageable, with only a dozen files to go through. Since then, messengers had brought over two hundred additional files, delivered in daily batches. The detectives reviewed each morning's delivery and returned the files by the end of the business day.

"This is driving me barmy," said Gowers, as he sat with a

typewriter in front of him. "The factory inspection reports aren't so bad, but otherwise the Ministry of Health files are a joke. I can't read the writing on half the stuff... What do you think this report says, sir?" He held out a handwritten paper. Morton took and scanned the page of quirky, illegible scrawl.

"No idea. I can only make out the words in the title. Government something Establishment."

"You make establishment out of that?" Gowers was looking over his shoulder.

"Yes."

"I didn't. I make the middle word out to be lymph."

"Lymph? Can't be... That's something in the body, I think. Are you sure?"

"I know the p looks like a t, but that's definitely an m in the middle."

"All right, but what you take for an l looks like an s to me."

"Symph isn't a word, sir. Lymph is... Government Lymph Establishment. But that can't be right."

"Hmm... That's definitely smallpox in the first paragraph." Morton pointed at the word.

"Oh, yes. What should I do about it?"

"Sounds like you should burn it." He handed the page back. "But if we can't read it, no one else can."

"Very good, sir. Just a reminder, we have to leave soon to meet Mr Johnston."

"I haven't forgotten."

Later, Morton and Gowers arrived by car at a large, comfortable house on a quiet road called Prospect Hill — the home of Mr Johnston, M.P. for Walthamstow North. Morton opened the iron gate in the high wall which surrounded the property. They entered and Gowers knocked on the door.

"Nice place," said Gowers, who carried a square leather case. Morton nodded.

A middle-aged maid answered the knock. She surveyed them apprehensively.

"We're from Scotland Yard," said Morton.

"Please, come in. Mr Johnston's expecting you."

They both said thank you and wiped their feet on the mat before entering.

"He's in the study. If I may?" The maid took their hats and hung them up on the stand. "It's this way, please." She opened a nearby door and announced, "The gentlemen from Scotland Yard are here to see you, sir."

"Send them in please," said Johnston, seated at a roll-top desk. He stood up. The detectives entered when the maid stood to one side.

"Good morning, gentlemen," said Mr Johnston, a short, wiry man of about fifty.

Morton and Gowers in unison replied, "Good morning, sir."

The maid left, closing the door quietly.

"You must forgive Mrs Wilson for appearing anxious. As with many honest souls, dealings with the police fluster her."

"We come across that quite often, sir. I'm Inspector Morton and this is Detective Sergeant Gowers."

"Thank you for coming. Let us sit at the table, shall we?"

They sat down at a round table of highly polished, dark stained wood. Johnston was opposite, with his back to the window. Placed squarely in front of him was a large manilla envelope. The room was a welcoming and tastefully decorated one. Although there were filing cabinets and other office impedimenta, the room also contained many books on shelves, the subjects of philosophy, religion, economics and political thought being well represented.

"In here is the objectionable communication." He placed a hand on the envelope. "It was dropped through the letter box sometime Tuesday night, or so Mrs Wilson informs me. It was subsequently handed to me with the morning post at about nine-thirty. Being an M.P., I receive a considerable volume of mail and I did not open the letter until approximately ten o'clock. As soon as I opened it, I could see what was afoot. I considered telephoning the local police but, being aware that our small, local station might not have the best facilities for dealing with such an important and delicate matter, I had my secretary contact Scotland Yard.

"I can tell you no more because that is the extent of my knowledge. Indeed, it is the accumulated knowledge of the occupants of this house. Concerning the contents..." Mr Johnston pushed his chair back and stood up. He gripped the lower part of his jacket lapel with his left hand and used his right hand expressively, as though in the House of Commons. "They are distasteful in the extreme. But what they hint at.... Ah! Who can say? Certainly, I have *no* concept of what it is they are suggesting. I am being blackmailed, gentlemen, but I give you my word it is without substance. It is without foundation. I would laugh it off as a jest... *If...*" He raised a finger, "my reputation were not at stake. My life is an *open* book. I possess *no* dark secrets. There is no taint in my life... *But...* To simply *say* it is nothing does not adequately deal with this outrage.

"Political opponents and unfriendly elements of the press will be uncharitable towards me. They may say, 'Oh, it's *something* all right.' The likelihood of this unavoidably damaging attitude means the matter *cannot* be bruited abroad. I have no weapons to fight against the invisible. I am inadequately equipped to grapple with hidden enemies and slanderers. In short, gentlemen, I desperately need your professional help. All must be done in a discreet, private, and professional manner. I'm sure, I am certain, you conduct *all* your investigations with tact and dignity, which is a great credit to you personally, and to the fine institution in which you serve, the Metropolitan Police. Thank you."

"Ah... May we see the letter, Mr Johnston?" asked Morton.

"Without question." Johnston slid the large envelope across the table to Morton.

"Who has handled the letter?" asked Morton, who peered inside the envelope and then slid the contents onto the table.

"Only myself. Naturally, Mrs Wilson touched the envelope when she picked it up. Yet as soon as I saw the contents, I thought, this is one for the proper authorities, and remembered to be cautious about leaving fingerprints. At present, I have yet to tell Mrs Johnston about the thing. I wish to keep my home and my family undisturbed by such unmitigated and undeserved trash."

The envelope lay on the table addressed to Mr Nigel Johnston, M.P. in block letters. Beside it was a half sheet of cheap writing paper folded in half. Gowers held it up using a long pair of tweezers. Then he opened it out flat on the table, weighting the corners.

"That's Stephen's ink," said Gowers.

The detectives read the note, which was written in the same block letters as the envelope. It said,

Mr Johnston, I know about Miss R and the public money you took. £300 buys my silence. If you don't pay, the press will, and I got evidence. Don't go to the coppers or else. I'll write again soon so get the money ready.

"I have to ask, sir," said Inspector Morton. "Is there a Miss R?"

"No. It's absurd. Of course, there isn't. However, I have a wide circle of acquaintance, and consequently I know several Miss Rs, but whether the man means a first name, nickname, or surname I can't say."

"Would you be more friendly with one rather than the others?"

"Well... yes. I suppose I should tell you. I call in at The Councillor once a week, sometimes twice, and meet a few friends there. Only for an hour. Usually, a barmaid named Ruby serves us. She's a delightful person, full of good humour. I have only ever spoken to her as a customer. I assure you, nothing has *ever* transpired between us."

"I see. Where will we find this pub? You should understand, Mr Johnston, that we must check to make sure that the blackmailer is only taking a chance, and using his knowledge of your acquaintance with Ruby. And do you have her last name?"

"I don't. The Councillor is on Erskine Avenue on the other side of the high street. Surely, if this fellow is watching Ruby, he might learn you are policemen."

"We'll make sure he doesn't, sir. Now the mention of public money. What might that be about?"

"I can't say. I'm on two committees. The important one concerns determining the best methods of production, how to ramp up production when there's an outbreak, and the stockpiling of vaccines."

"Vaccines?" said Gowers. "Would that include smallpox, sir?"

"Certainly. Smallpox and tuberculosis vaccines are our major considerations, but we also have the responsibility for cholera, typhoid, and malaria vaccines. Those are important in the colonies, you see. But storing the doses in tropical climates far from production centres is nothing short of a nightmare."

"I'm sure it is," said Morton.

"The other day, I heard someone mention the Government Lymph Establishment," said Gowers. "I thought they'd made a mistake."

"They were correct, sergeant. The GLE is vital to Britain's vaccination scheme."

"Thank you, sir. I'd never heard of it before, so it came as a surprise."

"Have you had a burglary in the past month?" asked Morton.

"No. Why do you ask?"

"You're a Liberal M.P..."

"No, no. Conservative. But I'm an ardent supporter of the coalition government, and wish Lloyd George to continue on as Prime Minister. He has my firm support."

"Sorry for the mistake, sir," said Morton. "I live in Earl's Court, you see, so I'm not really up on what happens in Walthamstow."

"London will always be parochial, so no offence taken,

145

Inspector."

"Yes... As I was saying, there has been a rash of break-ins where the thief took nothing of a marketable value. Have you noticed any strangers loitering in the street? Or are you missing anything?"

"No, to the strangers. It's odd that you should mention it, but I can't find my 1920 diary. We've looked everywhere, and I'm sure I had left it in a desk drawer."

"Are you missing anything else?"

"Not that I'm aware of."

Gowers looked around the room and then got up to approach some long curtains. He drew them back, revealing a French door leading to the back garden. He unlocked and opened it, examining the lock and woodwork with a magnifier.

"What are you doing?" asked Johnston.

"Someone forced the door... Recently, I'd say."

Johnston and Morton came over.

"Do you see that small notch on the latch bolt?" asked Gowers. "It's got a shine to it. Someone used a chisel to force it back. And see here on the frame. The back of the chisel, or whatever tool they used, has left an indentation in the wood. See there... A bit of the paint layer has flaked off."

"How is this possible? I had the lock fitted only two years ago."

"It's a Yale night latch, and the door doesn't fit the frame properly. It's likely the house has settled and created a gap between the door and frame. Here, I'll show you how it's done."

Gowers went out and closed the door, which locked behind him. From an inside pocket, he took out a wallet and selected a thin, but stiff, strip of metal. He used the strip on the bolt and, in less than ten seconds, had the door open. The ease with which Gowers unlocked the door horrified Johnston.

"Perhaps you should look through your desk, sir," said Morton.

Johnston went to his roll-top desk and hurriedly searched. The detectives noted which drawer he opened first, and that he returned to it to look through a second time.

"I'm not sure," he said while still looking. "A few documents have gone... Nothing *that* important, you understand? Receipts and a bundle of unimportant letters from constituents."

"If you could write out a list, please, that would be helpful," said Morton.

"A list? Yes, I will. I'm not sure I can remember everything."

"When did you first miss the diary?"

"End of last week. Friday, I believe... This is atrocious. You must find the devil who broke in..." Johnston worked himself into a temper and delivered an angry monologue.

Gowers fingerprinted Mr Johnston and Mrs Wilson to exclude theirs from the prints taken from the blackmail letter. It was then they learned Mrs Johnston was in Wales visiting her mother, and could not have touched the letter. When they had finished, the detectives drove off and parked out of sight of the house.

"Now we know," said Morton, who lit a cigarette.

"Could you open your window, please, sir?"

"I'll stand outside..." He got out and spoke through the open window. "So the information leaks and the burglaries have the same goal in mind. To cause trouble for the government."

"Yes. Ordinary blackmail's a dodgy game unless they get hold of compromising letters. But this, I don't get it. What do you think of Johnston?"

"We'll take him at face value for the present. He gave out Ruby's name quick enough, so we'll find nothing there. If there's an actual Miss R, I don't think we'll find her unless we tail him. He's not the criminal, though."

"Yet he's lost something important that he's not telling us about," said Gowers. "The way he went for that drawer... Do you think he's benefitting from his position on the committee?"

"I don't know… Vaccines. Is there money in them? I suppose there is when you multiply by millions."

"That makes one think the financial angle might have some legs to it. Maybe the thief stole company documents from Johnston."

"Maybe. We need to know if this blackmail is based on fact. Talk about treading carefully. If Johnston thinks we're investigating him, he'll cause no end of trouble. Anyway, we'll let Penrose worry about all that."

"Pubs are open. Shall we try The Councillor and see if Miss Ruby's working?"

"Might as well."

Ruby Murray, twenty-nine, was as Mr Johnston had represented her to be. When Gowers took her aside for a quiet talk and asked her what Mr Johnston was like, she said he was a 'thorough gentleman', 'liked a bit of a joke and a laugh', and had 'nice manners.' When asked if she was married, she replied she had been engaged for three years and would marry in June, because she and her fiancé, a carpenter, had saved enough to buy a house. Gowers mentioned that there had been a burglary and asked Ruby if she had seen anyone observing Mr Johnston's movements, to which she replied she had not. Morton and Gowers determined that Ruby was not Miss R, if there was one, but believed the blackmailer might have chosen her as a foundation in launching a baseless allegation against Johnston.

---

On Thursday, the twentieth, the Speaker of the House called upon a Labour MP to state his question. The MP rose. His question was this: Would the Home Secretary explain why members of the coalition government control companies which routinely employ underage workers and which frequently contravene the regulations governing factory discharges into the air?

The Home Secretary adroitly minimized and deflected the question, claiming he had no knowledge of such regulations being broken. In the follow up, where the Labour M.P. insisted that these facts could be found in public records, the minister replied the matter would be investigated, but it would take some time before he was in a position to report back. The House then moved onto the next question. What alarmed those of the government benches was that, throughout the exchange, the Labour M.P. held a small sheet of paper which they could only assume to be a list of names. No one could guess whose name might be on the list.

The next morning, the London Mercury printed the complete list of six names and the companies, accompanied by caustic editorial comments. As a result of this damaging revelation, the government floundered — convening hasty meetings to search for a solution.

Superintendent Penrose did not like the events that were unfolding, but he was pleased he had a clear picture now. Like a spider in the middle of a hidden web, he felt every breeze of attitude and opinion flowing through his network of strands, and every inadvertent brush which might mean something or might mean nothing. Now he sensed something large caught in his web, something sending tremors, and he believed he knew what it was. How to approach it, though? The catch had strength. How to subdue it? That was dangerous. Too early and the thing would cause harm. Too late and it would escape. He knew he needed many strong silken bonds to effect a successful capture.

"It's all one scheme of Stokely's," he said to Inspector Morton, who sat opposite him in Penrose's office. "Burglaries and thefts from Members of Parliament and then blackmailing them. Stealing information from the civil service and then using it against the government." He paused to unclasp his

149

hands, which had been resting on his stomach. "Then there's the Red Fist business and a murder of a moderate union man... They're parts of a whole, and there must be more coming... He's making a big play and it'll get much worse before we end his game."

"Can't we arrest him on suspicion?" asked Morton.

"Nothing will tie back to him. He'll get off, we'd show our hand, and he'll come after us. It's not the danger to ourselves so much; it's that, if he beats us, Britain will go down the drain, and he'll be in charge. We have to stop him now, or it'll be too late and we'll be finished. We're not in a position to move. Not yet. Which brings me to the reason why I wanted to see you.

"Stokely's having a do... Well, not a do as such, more like a confabulation among all those who work or are associated with him. He's plotting something big and means to put his best effort into it. He's organizing for a big and sustained push... That's what I reckon."

"Like a revolution?" asked Morton.

"This'll end up thereabouts, right enough, if it's not stopped. At the moment, he wants to cover everyone in muck, to make himself shine all the more, but he'll not stop there... The Red Fist business is a sham. It's only him wanting to destroy his competitors by getting *them* blamed for the violence and killings that *he's* doing. There's more of that to come, I'm sure of it."

"If I might say, sir. Having me and Gowers review files — well, it's us just playing catch up. We'll never get ahead of what he's doing."

"Raring to go, are you? That's handy, because I'm taking you off that job. Continue with the Johnston blackmail case, though. Ever been to Chertsey?"

"I've driven through it."

"Arrh. Stokely's estate is about five miles outside, near to Chobham. You'll be on hand in the area with a detachment of picked men come the end of the month. You see, Burgoyne's Agency will be inside the house when Stokely has his party.

We have hopes of them getting something on the quiet. If there's any trouble, you're to go in at once. You'll have a search warrant, just in case, but you won't execute it unless advised to do so. You'll go in armed and take no nonsense. Arrest anyone immediately for obstruction or anything else you can think of, Stokely included.

"Should you get inside, gather any documents that might look useful... If we get a few of them behind bars, then we'll have a chat. It all has to be done lawfully, though, so we need to be called in by someone in Chertsey Park. A call for help, and you can batter down the doors. No call, and you stay put. Are you ready for something like that?"

Morton breathed out heavily. "Yes, sir."

"You'll be sticking your neck out where Stokely's concerned?"

"I understand that, sir."

"Good man, Morton. If we're called in, make the most of the situation."

"I'll do my best, sir. Let's hope it's a quiet affair, then."

Penrose laughed gently. "We can hope. Make sure you're prepared, though."

# Chapter 12

# Planning stage

On Monday evening, the 24th of January, Sophie, Flora, and Ada alighted from a taxi, and walked through the archway at the Foreign Office, to be met by Archie at a back entrance. He held the door open while they filed in silently. Inside, the only persons they passed as they made their way to his office were two bored clerks in the telegraph room, and a cleaner slowly polishing the parquet flooring in a corridor. Once in Archie's room, they all sat down to discuss the upcoming operation and some of the expected difficulties that might be encountered.

"Circumstances require that I inform you about Lester Dawkins. He was a Royal Artillery Captain until June 1915, when a medical examination revealed his hearing was impaired. Soon afterwards, he joined the Intelligence Corps. In 1918, they promoted him to the rank of brevet Major for his achievements, which promotion the army subsequently confirmed. He left the army in early nineteen and found a job in one of Stokely's companies. They met, and an association, or friendship, developed between them in which Dawkins became an executive in several of Stokely's companies, more recently including Frobisher Bank.

"Although we've ascertained that much, we don't actually

know what it is he does within Stokely's organization. Up until now, we thought he was only a business manager and nothing more than that. He's a reserved man, cautious of speech, thirty-eight, and married with two children, but has been separated from them for three years.

"His war record is respectable, except there is talk of an incident in France in 1917. Dawkins shot an escaping prisoner of war whom he had been interrogating. Although the official record exonerates him completely, the private opinion of two people who were near the scene at the time is that he deliberately executed the prisoner to make a second one give up information. Dawkins got the information he sought. This possible action of his demonstrates he may be a ruthless individual who will do whatever he thinks necessary to achieve his ends. Dawkins is also a capable interrogator. "

"That's ghastly, if true," said Sophie. "How reliable are these privately held opinions?"

"The informants appear to be ordinary, honest men. Neither man has a grudge against Dawkins, and there's no reason for either to have spoken unless he believed he spoke the truth. Also, their stories still agree on all major points and our interviews with them were conducted just within the last few days. So they have both remembered the same three-year-old story independently of each other. *That* is significant."

"Gosh," said Flora. "It's all quite disturbing. You're warning us to be careful around Dawkins, aren't you?"

"Indeed, I am. You cannot count on any person present at Chertsey Park as being an ordinary person. You must assume that anyone you serve or speak to is a Stokely agent. Any of them may be trained to look for suspicious behaviour or extract information useful to Stokely. It is certainly true of Dawkins, and it is more than likely true of the others with whom you will come in contact."

"We shall be extremely careful, Archie," said Sophie. "All of us are very much aware of the necessity of conducting ourselves as professional servants first and not to take chances. I have impressed the dangers upon everyone that, if we do not behave ourselves perfectly, we will draw unwelcome attention. We will only listen to conversations."

"That's most satisfactory... Should a mishap occur, there is a plan in place. You have your arrangement for Miss Banks to come and get you if you need to leave. If you need to leave immediately because of an imminent threat or emergency, telephone this number... What are you doing?"

"Writing it down so that I can memorize it."

"Hmm. Just make sure the notebook doesn't enter Chertsey Park with that number in it." He gave the telephone number, adding that she could also use it to submit her daily reports.

"They write everything down at the Home Office," observed Flora. "How is Lord Laneford these days?"

"I presume he's well," replied Archie. "I've heard nothing to the contrary."

"Is he involved with this escapade?"

Archie adopted his blank look, which meant the three women opposite him knew he was about to become non-committal or even fib.

"Oh, I don't think so."

The secret agents now believed Lord Laneford was involved in some capacity.

"Should you meet him, give him our regards," said Flora.

"I second that," said Sophie.

"He's such a nice gentleman, Mr Drysdale," said Ada. "He was no trouble at all."

"I take it, gentlemen can be troublesome sometimes, Miss McMahon?"

"Ooh, that they can, sir. But it's the nervy ones who are the worst. Always fussing and causing no end of work. I did for one who 'ad me buttering 'is toast, as if he couldn't butter it 'isself like everyone else does. I never did get it right, 'cause he kep' changing his mind. I think he did it deliberate just to be awkward, 'though don't ask me why."

"I wonder if Stokely is fussy," said Flora.

"Probably," said Sophie. "He insisted on serving himself at Lady Georgiana's house. And he always takes the best of what's offered."

"Why don't we just poison him, then?" asked Flora. "It would save a lot of bother and we could do so by putting it in the best piece of meat or whatever is suitable. What's a good poison for that?"

"Arsenic," said Sophie. "But you must dissolve it properly... We could put it in his meat with a hypodermic needle."

"Would that be before or after it's cooked?" asked Ada.

"I don't know... Then it's probably easier just to put it in his coffee," said Flora. "Imagine if one accidentally stabbed oneself with the needle."

"I wouldn't like to risk that," said Ada. "I'd vote for in 'is coffee."

"Yes, I think that would be easier. Then there's also strychnine," said Sophie. "Rat poison for a rat."

"That couldn't be more suitable," said Flora. "How does one administer strychnine? Do you know, Archie?"

"It's a powder, I think. Strychnine is bitter, so it could also go in his coffee. For form's sake, I must ask you this; you're not serious, are you?"

"Don't worry, we're only speculating," said Sophie. "I always thought spies had secret poisons. Dastardly foreign ones do in books."

"Your choice of literature seems to confuse two very distinct professions. Espionage agents are only interested in acquiring information from or disseminating false information to their opponents. It is the assassin who is knowledgeable about poisons."

"Oh... Then the FO has never assassinated *anyone*?"

"Not to my knowledge. We prefer drinking tea with our enemies while discussing sane courses of action. The government of the day does not always permit pleasantries when making its demands. We must then couch those sometimes outrageous demands in the least offensive diplomatic language possible." Archie smiled. "As for espionage agents: every country has them. Indeed, it is a requirement to have them if one wants to be considered an advanced nation."

"What about the HO? Do they have assassins?" asked Flora.

"You'll have to ask them. There may have been past British government involvement in scandalous things, but I can only speak of what I know, which is the Foreign Office. However, the government is, and always has been, strongly opposed to illegal dealings overseas, but that stance does not prevent individuals acting badly in secret or on their own account."

"We shall keep up the FO tradition by not acting badly," said Sophie, smiling.

"The other man of interest at Stokely's party, Morris Wilberforce, is a factory manager and wealthy. Aged forty-four, he's married with three children. He has the knack of turning ailing businesses around, and getting the most from his workforce without unduly disturbing the union, if one is present. He oversees one of Stokely's businesses, but has several prosperous ones of his own. Wilberforce is an alderman for the municipal borough of Birmingham and is hot on education and reform. Although unassuming, he is quite an industrious organizer. That's all we have on him at present."

"He's seems to be hardworking and respectable," said Sophie. "What's he doing associating with Stokely?"

"Hopefully, you'll be able to tell me," said Archie. "I'll add that he also represents a type or class of follower. There's many a wealthy or influential person who's enamoured with Stokely, simply because he whispers free-trade and lower taxes into their ears to win them over." He looked at each of them. "Please be careful, for your own sakes."

"Thank you, Archie, we shall endeavour to be so," said Sophie.

He smiled, then asked her, "Have there been any changes

to the travel plans?"

"No. We still travel by train there and back with Mr Dalgleish. Cars from the house will ferry us to and from the station."

"I'm rather glad Dalgleish is going," said Archie. "Scotland Yard has nothing against him, and he doesn't have much to do with Stokely these days, although Stokely has a suite in his mother's house, which he uses occasionally. Dalgleish was the former butler at Chertsey Park, but went to Lyall Place with Lady Georgiana in 1911. I don't think you can trust him in any extraordinary sense, but at least he's not your enemy."

"Do you think the rest of the other staff will be a problem, Mr Drysdale?" asked Ada.

"Yes, I do. Stokely always uses others to carry out his reprehensible operations, and some servants at Chertsey Park may well be of that number. I believe that if you treat everyone the same, Miss McMahon, you shan't go wrong."

"Thank you very much, Mr Drysdale." Ada smiled.

"My pleasure, Miss McMahon."

Ada's smile increased. She could listen to the way he said her name all day long.

"Do you have any further questions?" he asked.

"Only to enquire after Victoria," said Sophie. "How is she these days?"

The three agents leaned in slightly to catch every nuance.

"She's very well. Thank you for asking."

"Please pass along our regards," said Flora.

"I shall do so... Our? But you haven't met Victoria, have you, Flora?"

"No. I hope to soon."

"Hmm."

"Why don't you get us invited to Mr Redfern's estate?" asked Sophie.

Archie leaned back in his chair. "First, what's all this 'us' and 'we' business?"

"We're staunchly on your side, every one of us," said Sophie.

"And if you get us invited to Redfern Manor, or whatever it's called," said Flora, "we can go to work on old man Redfern."

"Ah, no. No, no, and no. Are you in this, too, Miss McMahon?"

"Pardon, Mr Drysdale?"

"I asked, are you in on this scheme, too, Miss McMahon?"

"Oh, yes, Mr Drysdale. We all 'ave your best interests at 'eart, and if we can work it, we'd like to try 'aving a go at Mr Redfern."

He stared at each of them in disbelief. Somehow, every time these three ladies came to his office, at some point a state of confusion descended upon him.

"Simply out of curiosity, what do you propose doing?"

"We're not yet entirely sure," said Sophie.

"It all depends what type of man he is," said Flora.

"If he's a pompous old... person, we'd 'ave to threaten him somehow."

"Threaten him...? Please, say on."

"Well," began Sophie, "we thought that if he's as difficult and unreasonable as he appears to be about a marriage settlement, we'd suggest he put you on the board of directors of one of his companies. Or something like that. Whatever it is that wealthy people do for friends when they want to slip some money their way. Then he'd include you in the family business and your polite charm would win him over. Anyway, if he refused, we'd point out that he would never see his grandchildren, and, by his own actions, he would destroy Victoria's promising career, which, by the way, we decided is the only reason he doesn't want her to marry *anyone*. He's only finding fault with *you*, because he's extraordinarily proud of his daughter. He would do the same with any other suitor."

"Unless they are as rich as he is," said Flora.

"Or, they 'ad a title he couldn't ignore," said Ada. "So don't take nothin' personal, Mr Drysdale."

"That's right," said Sophie. "Don't let him get you down. We believe his bark is worse than his bite, and he doesn't want Victoria to leave her position. She's far, far too valuable to him, so he's only saying nasty things to put you off. If he wins and you go, he'd claim he was right all along about your motives. He's testing you. We mean to test *him!*"

After a long pause, Archie said,

"Your inordinate interest in my personal life does, on the one hand, amount to pure meddling, but I find it extraordinarily touching, nonetheless. I hope that you never get within ten miles of Redfern, but I confess to being interested in seeing what would happen if you did. However, your deliberations have brought out one or two points that I've failed to observe. For those insights, I wholeheartedly thank you, as I do for your moral support. Can we please leave it at that?"

"We knew you'd say no," said Flora. "You should discuss it with Miss Redfern."

"Can we drop the subject, please?"

"Should you change your mind," said Sophie, "we're willing to have a go."

"I do not doubt your zeal for a moment, thank you. And that is the end of the subject."

They went on to discuss other matters. When the agents were leaving, Archie took Sophie to one side.

"While you're at Chertsey Park, I'll be anxious to hear from you, so report as arranged, and be careful of telephone extensions."

"I will. Is there anything else?"

"Only to wish you the best of luck." He looked at her and then grinned. "There is something else, quite inconsequential, only you mustn't tell her. I find it delightful the way Miss McMahon pronounces *Mr Drysdale*."

At Scotland Yard, Morton and Gowers sat in a private room so as not to be overheard.

"They've finalized a plan," said Morton, "and I can tell you about it now. We have to go to Chertsey Park."

"Where is it?" asked Gowers.

"Well, near Chertsey, but a few miles outside. Close to Chobham."

"The King's Head in Chobham's a nice pub."

"Glad to hear it, but we're not going there. This is an important job, so we'll be on our best behaviour. We might have to enter the estate on short notice, so there's no propping up the bar for any of us."

"There's more than two of us, sir?"

"Yes. There'll be sixteen plus two drivers and we'll be carrying revolvers with rifles on hand."

"Blimey, sounds like I should make out a will."

Morton stared at him. "Come on, pay attention. This is serious."

"Sorry about that, sir. Please continue."

"We're after Stokely's organization and we're to arrest everyone on sight for whatever charges are appropriate under the circumstances. The idea is to get as many of them in jail as possible, whether or not we lay charges.

"Now then, we only go in when ordered to do so. That decision is not up to us, but we'll be ready day and night. We'll have two Black Maria's and three cars. We'll put the small fry in the local nick, and take the others to the Brixton nick first."

"Brixton? Why not bring them here?"

"We're going to shuffle them around so it takes the lawyers longer to find them."

"Oh, in transit."

"That's right. If there are no charges, we must keep them out of circulation for as long as possible. That's all I know about that."

"When's all this taking place?" asked Gowers.

"Starts Thursday and ends Monday."

"That's all right, then. I don't mind going."

"What do you mean, you don't mind going?"

"Fulham's playing away at Lincoln."

"You and your Fulham... That's an FA Cup match. What do you reckon?"

"They *should* win, but whether they do remains to be seen... Why are we hanging about for four days?"

"Because Burgoyne's Agency will be inside Chertsey Park."

"Will it now? That's very interesting. So, we'll be like back-up for them, sir?"

"That's right. There'll be six of them present. Everyone else is a suspect until we can determine otherwise. I'll hand out their names should we have to enter the premises. We'll have a warrant, so there's no problem on that score."

Morton consulted a file in front of him.

"You might not be aware of this, but Mr Johnston M.P., who is currently being blackmailed as we know, left the government benches today and crossed the floor of the house to sit as an independent."

"What's going on? He supported the government last week."

"Oh, yes. So I reckon the *blackmailer* got him to do that. Perhaps that demand for money was for *our* benefit. The real motive — the Stokely motive — is to keep chipping away at the government, never mind the money.

"Inspector Bygrave says here that there is no Miss R that he can find, and he's good at this stuff. What he *did* find out is that Johnston's a shareholder in a company which often employs underage labour. Only the way the company works it, is that, if they admit their guilt before it goes to court and promise never to do it again, they only pay one pound in costs. It means no judgment ever gets brought home against them and they're not threatened with closure. It's a real racket, apparently, but it's new to me. Anyway, Johnston may not even have known that the regulations are being circumvented in this way, until the blackmailer told him.

"That information is damaging enough to him personally that, rather than wait for the government to kick him out in shame when the blackmailer releases the information, Johnston walks with his head high as if he's against the government on principle. That's an easy choice for him to make. The blackmailer lets him alone afterwards, because he, or rather Stokely, has got what he wants — a shaky government."

"Yes... There was that list published the other day of M.P.s connected to misbehaving companies."

"Johnston's company is not on the list." Morton closed the file. "Stokely's behind all of this. Perhaps we can do something about him this coming weekend."

"Stokely, ooh... a pint says he wriggles off the hook."

Morton paused to consider the proposition. "You'll have to give two to one on that."

"Two! I suppose we both want the same side of the bet... Look, I'll be very sporting about this, as you're the senior officer. I'll take the other side. A pint says we get him, sir."

"All right, you're on."

# Chapter 13

# The dormitory

The house at Chertsey Park from the front was impressive, not only in its size but also in its symmetry, and was mostly Palladian in style. The central block with its columned entrance dominated and drew the eye, while its two wings at their lesser height extended just a shade too far, as if someone, not necessarily the architect, had insisted as an afterthought that he needed some extra bedrooms. What principally detracted from the whole at a distance were the tightly jointed sandstone blocks. Their warm, aged colouration was perfect, but from the far end of the drive, the blocks presented as a smooth, featureless wall that begged for more ornamentation. The simple lintels over the windows were inadequate for the job. Instead of ledges, carvings, or insets, the viewer's eye had to be satisfied by the decorative parapet at the very top of the wall. The castellation singularly failed to make the house look anything like a castle and seemed an odd choice. All in all, though, it was an imposing edifice. Heading towards the house, three cars proceeded along the drive.

In the leading vehicle, a limousine, Sophie sat in the back next to Mr Dalgleish. Opposite, sitting on folding seats, were two maids from Lyall Place. In the front passenger seat sat Mr Broadbent-Wicks. Nobody spoke. As they drove towards the house, Sophie surveyed the grounds, which were covered in a thin blanket of snow. The land was open for a distance of several hundred yards around the house until it reached the grey-brown line of bare trees. Rather than the grassland or fields she had expected to find surrounding a country estate, she saw open heathland which, to the north, rose and extended as far as she could see.

"The estate adjoins Chobham Common," said Dalgleish. "Long ago, it was all open fields to the trees, but the heath has reclaimed them."

Through the car window, Sophie studied the heathland and saw clumps of pale bracken piercing the snow cover, patches of eight-foot high, dark green tangled gorse, a stand of birches, several lone pine trees and, in the flat areas everywhere in between, a thick, snow-mottled and uneven carpet of winter-green heather. Further to the north, under a grey sky, distance had compressed the appearance of the undulating land into a simple black-and-white pattern of a snowfield intersected by lines of gorse.

"It's a sight to see when the heather blooms," said the butler.

"It must be lovely. That's in July and August, isn't it?" asked Sophie.

"Depends on the type, Miss King. Bog Heath comes first in June, then Ling, and Bell. The flowers last into September and October."

"Did you grow up in the area, Mr Dalgleish?"

"I'm from Sunningdale, on the other side of the common, so I'm familiar with its ways."

Sophie looked at him and smiled. "You're almost home, then."

"In a certain sense, I am. I have relatives in Sunningdale, and I was footman, and then butler here for many years. This is the first occasion I have been back in some time."

As the car drew closer to the house, Sophie sensed a change in Mr Dalgleish. He became tense, and she wondered what had produced the effect.

The car came to a stop at the servants' entrance at the rear of the west wing. Sophie got out. Upon closer inspection, the house looked much better now that the details of the old stone became evident. Standing outside, with views along gravel paths next to the long side of the wing, the structure now manifested itself to Sophie as mightily impressive by its size, and a triumph of ingenuity raised up in the raw land. Its attractive sandstone was a reassuring warmth in a chill landscape and a well-built stronghold against the elements. But of danger without there was none, yet — she knew all the danger lay within. The surrounding snowy lawns, although narrow, restrained the advance of the wild heath. Sophie understood what had produced the change in Mr Dalgleish as she watched him now taking inventory of the several signs of dilapidation on the building and the general decline of the estate since his last visit.

The servants' entrance was, in its own right, a tastefully executed feature with a porch, double doors, and windows on either side. Sophie now saw, as the butler was seeing, the discoloured and peeling paint of the window frames, the remnants of a bird's nest in a corner above the door, and the dull brass fixtures and chipped paint on the door. She knew that Mr Dalgleish would not tolerate such things at Lyall Place, but whoever was in charge at Chertsey Park did, and it obviously pained the butler to see the disrepair. Sophie busied herself so that he did not catch her studying him as he studied the obvious lapse in standards since his day.

The party of servants from London were soon inside with their suitcases, and they lined up in a wide corridor which led to the kitchen and pantries. There were ten in all – seven maids and three footmen. Where they were standing looked clean, but Sophie noticed more signs of wear and tear through use. Mrs Newnham, the Chertsey Park housekeeper who was about fifty, spoke in whispers to Mr Dalgleish, so that the rest of them could not hear what was being discussed. A maid and footman from the house had accompanied Mrs Newnham, and she now signalled to them, while also making it apparent she had no interest in meeting the new arrivals.

"Can you follow me, please?" At the signal from the housekeeper, a young country girl stepped forward and spoke to include only the maids. She sounded and seemed hesitant, as if she were doing something wrong.

"Are you showing us to our rooms?" asked Sophie.

"Yes, that's roight."

"Attics?" asked Ada, gloomily.

"Yes. How d'you know that?"

"A wild guess," said Ada. "What's your name?"

"Bertha."

"We're all pleased to meet you, Bertha," said Sophie. "I'm Miss King. This is Miss Carmichael, Miss Walton, and Miss Datchet. We're from Burgoyne's agency. We weren't formerly introduced to the others from Lyall Place, so they'll have to answer for themselves." Sophie laughed. "Shall we go?"

"Yes, miss," said Bertha, a little bewildered, recognizing Sophie was of a different class and rank.

They left the corridor to ascend a servants' staircase of ample width. The first floor was of a similar generous height to the ground floor, yet the size of the rooms and the appointments denoted they were for the less exalted guests. Someone had recently painted the walls, the high wainscot, and the moulded ceiling, while on a pedestal in an alcove a plaster bust of Dante gave at least a pretension to intellectual dignity. In climbing to the second floor, it was as if they had crossed a boundary on the other side of which money had suddenly become scarcer. The party stopped on the landing to look along the corridors and saw a dark wooden waist-high wainscot that thirsted for polish, chalky and distempered walls which were cracked, and a ceiling with a large, old and bulging stain where water had come in from whatever lay above. The dingy corridors felt cool and smelt musty.

"Is this floor used for anything, Bertha?"

"Nothing, miss, not now. It used to be for the higher-up servants, but there ain't been any o' them for a long time. They wor' gone before I come here and that wor' two year ago."

"I see," said Sophie, intrigued by this piece of information. "Please, lead on."

The snake of maids trouped up the final flight, fearful of what they might find after the floor below. When they arrived, they felt some relief. Although the ceiling was low and slanted, the corridor was wide and Bertha led them past closed rooms until they arrived at a large, square dormitory which occupied the corner created by the front and the side of the house and where all seven visiting maids could sleep. It was clean and tidy although sparsely furnished except for the beds of which there were four doubles and four singles.

Ada shivered, and said to Sophie, "Coo! It's brass..." — then she remembered a former conversation they had had about making indelicate remarks. "It's like the North Pole up here, miss."

"We'll get a fire going," said Sophie. "Oh. Who put the heather on the pillows?" Sophie smiled when she saw a tiny dried sprig on a clean pillowcase.

"I did, miss," said Bertha, now self-conscious. "It's for good luck."

"What a nice thought. We could all do with some luck, couldn't we?"

"Right enough, miss," said Bertha, who smiled.

"The doubles will be warmer," said Ada. "Wait a mo!" She addressed an older maid from Lyall Place who was putting her suitcase on one of the beds nearest the fireplace. "Don't go grabbin' nothing until we sort out who gets what."

"I saw it first," replied the maid, whom they had not met before. "Anyway, who put you in charge? You're just temporary, and I'm a parlourmaid."

"Yes, well, I'm a parlourmaid, *and* I've been a lady's maid, so I outrank you. You're not grabbing a bed until we sort it out."

"We'll draw lots for the beds," said Sophie.

"You're not over me, and I've claimed this bed," said the parlourmaid.

"I hope you'll be reasonable about this. There are seven maids present who must share this room. I am in charge of three maids, while you are in charge of two."

"What are you making a fuss about? There's the bed opposite. You take that."

"No, that's not how we're going to do it. We shall toss a coin. Whoever wins gets the beds closest to the fire first, but after that we'll take turns."

Everyone's attention was riveted upon the exchange.

"What if I don't want to?"

"Let me see... I could put you out of the room, or report you to Mr Dalgleish or, if this a sample of your behaviour, make life extraordinarily difficult for you while we're here. Which would you prefer?"

Only the sound of the wind in the chimney made a noise.

"Have it *your* way, then," said the parlourmaid.

"Thank you," said Sophie. She took out a penny. "Now, everyone choose a bed-fellow."

"Nancy, do you snore?" asked Fern.

"No, I do not."

"I shared a bed wiv a maid once," said Fern, "and in the middle of the night, she woke me up with this 'orrible snort like a trumpet. I thought the house was coming down. Then, she took to grunting and mutterin' to herself. So you don't do anythin' like that?"

"No, Dora, I don't snore. What about you, though?"

"Oh no, I'd never do that. Shall we share a bed, then?"

"All right. We'll call tails."

"Shall we share?" asked Flora of Sophie. "I swear that I have *never* snored in my life, but I'm rather concerned about your habits."

"I blare the whole night long like a foghorn," said Sophie, smiling.

"I'll keep a peg handy, then. How about heads?"

Sophie nodded. Everyone was ready. She tossed the coin, and it landed on the floorboards — tails.

"Ha!" said Ada, who immediately put her suitcase on a bed near the fireplace.

The two younger maids from Lyall Place had also called tails.

"We never do that, as we got our own rooms," said Bertha to Sophie.

"Where are they?"

"Maids are all at back o' this wing, miss. Some's in attics, and some's on the floor below. Men are in the east wing."

"There's no coal!" called Ada, pointing at an empty scuttle.

"An oversight probably," said Sophie. "Where shall we find it?"

"You can't touch the coal." Bertha was panicked. "I'd have brought some if it wor' given me, but no one said, an' I don't like to ax for it."

Her reaction puzzled Sophie. "I'm sorry. I'm failing to understand you. Do you mean there's no coal?"

"Oh, there's coal."

"Then why can't we have some?"

"I'd give you some of moine, but it wouldn't heat this big room."

"You get an allowance of coal?"

"Yes, miss."

"Then who's in charge of it?"

"Mr Kemp, but you mustn't go talking to him."

"Why ever not?"

"He's not noice." She was still worried. "You'll have to ax Mrs Newnham and she'll ax Mr Kemp, only…"

"Only what?"

"She's scared of him." Bertha hurriedly added, "But please don't go a-sayin' I said that."

"I won't, I promise." Sophie straightened her coat. "Right. I shall be back shortly. Bertha, where shall I find Mr Dalgleish?"

"But you're to go to the kitchen once you've settled."

In the staccato phrasing of barely repressed annoyance, Sophie said, "I am *not yet* settled." Then, in her usual tone, she repeated, "Where shall I find him, please?"

"Second floor, t'other wing. It's the big room by the servants' stairs. Go by the first floor, miss, because nobody's here, yet, and it's noicer."

"Thank you." Sophie then sallied forth.

"We're off to a good start," said Flora, who was standing with Ada and Fern after Sophie had left.

"Won't she get into trouble?" asked Fern.

"Oh, yes," said Ada. "But I bet we get coal soon enough... Bertha, come over here, please."

"Yes?"

"What's up with Mr Kemp, eh...? Come on, tell us, we'll keep our traps shut."

"He's loike the master of the house, he is." As she began whispering, she glanced over her shoulder. "They do say as he gets money off everything, and gets more for hisself by being a moiser towards the house. Kemp don't give nothing away for free. No." She shook her head. "There's plenty o' coin for beer and spirits for him and his men, and that comes out of *our* food and coal and such-loike. Just betwixt us, he's a *pig*, that he is, though I never said it if anyone wants to know. And he has nasty ways *and* a bad temper."

"Why is he here, then?" asked Flora

"He's nothing but a gamekeeper who 'appened to please his lordship, so much so that he give him the estate and the house to run. And ever since then, they say, the house has gone downhill."

"I can't fathom why Lord Stokely would do such a thing," said Flora.

"Give the devil his due. Kemp provides good shooting for his lordship whenever he has a moind to bring his friends. The partridge and grouse are plentiful on the estate. Even see pheasant sometimes, 'though they be a rarity on the heath as a rule."

"Oh, I *see*," said Flora. "Then Lord Stokely treats this place like his hunting lodge."

"Yes... I s'pose that be about the soize of it. At least until now, with this here weekend."

"Hadn't we better go down to the kitchens?" whispered Fern. "We don't want to cause more trouble if we can help it."

"We ought to, an' all," said Ada. "The guests will arrive soon, and I reckon we've got plenty to do."

---

Elizabeth arrived at the Gardeners Arms at midday, immensely satisfied with Rabbit's performance on the road since its return from the garage. She had noticed the car was quite noisy when accelerating, but quietened down upon reaching its cruising speed. Once, after accelerating hard, she spotted a constable on a bicycle, which made her careful and mindful about the speed limit thereafter.

To support the idea that she was a naturalist, she had brought with her some very sensible winter clothes and wellington boots, a loaned pair of binoculars, a notebook, a Thermos flask, a supply of sandwiches and biscuits, and a hastily acquired knowledge of the flora, fauna, and geography of the area. She had a list of animals ready in the event she had to explain herself. Elizabeth secretly hoped no one would speak to her but, if cornered, she was ready. Her research had sparked a genuine interest, and she hoped to see an otter, a badger, and a red kite. If she had to venture out at night, she would pretend she was a devotee of the tawny owl.

She occupied her room in the inn without incident, which process came as an unexpected surprise, for she was sure something would go wrong up until the moment she actually stepped into the back bedroom. The novice naturalist was soon rewarded with the sighting of a hare in the back garden. Elizabeth instantly took out the binoculars to observe the feeding hare, smiling as she watched. A red squirrel, tiring of hibernation, came into the garden searching for food it had buried in the autumn. A few birds flew in. For a minute, the peaceful scene played out, then a door banged somewhere outside, and the garden emptied. Elizabeth wrote her first entry in her notebook, which she had entitled Observations of an Ottershaw Naturalist.

In the village hall on Church Road in Sunningdale, seventeen policemen were lounging about on chairs and camp beds. Ostensibly, four of them were in uniform and on duty, while the rest were in their shirtsleeves, including Inspector Morton and Sergeant Gowers. An eighteenth man had his feet up while sitting in front of a radio set reading a newspaper. Outside, exciting the curiosity of small children and causing much speculation among adults, were three cars and two black marias. The more precocious passersby had tried to ask a variety of questions whenever an officer came outside, ranging from the childish 'What are you doing in there, Mr Policeman?', to the mature inquiry that began along the lines of, 'Forgive me for being inquisitive, officer, but...' The police response, with minor variations, was always, 'I'm not at liberty to say, but I'll tell you this much. We're testing a theory.' Sunningdale was not satisfied with this, and said as much in the butcher's, greengrocer's, and newsagent's, although the proprietors of those establishments welcomed the increase in trade the new arrivals had brought. Along that line, Mrs Worthington, a local policeman's wife, and her sister, Freda, were joyful even while they slaved constantly, being tasked with providing three meals a day for eighteen men who relished their food. This sudden influx of profitable income, flowing from the coffers of Scotland Yard, had given the sisters a cause for celebration in the middle of an otherwise dull winter.

The village expressed its dissatisfaction again over dinner and in the pub. Certain members of the debating society, who met once a fortnight, exchanged intelligent views of a more indignant nature after the unceremonious postponement to the following week of their meeting. As it was only Thursday, the village had yet to gather within the church precincts to say anything about the police, although the verger of nearby Holy Trinity stopped to stare hard at the line of vehicles parked outside the village hall. The vehicles told him nothing, neither did the constable he approached.

All in all, Sunningdale was proudly energized and very put out at the same time, because it *knew* something important was going on. This certainty arose when the GPO rigged a temporary telephone line to the hall first thing in the morning.

"If we had a football," said Gowers, inside the hall, "we could get up a game."

"No." Morton continued reading his newspaper. "See those windows? They're made of glass."

After a minute, Gowers said, "I should have brought a book."

"Don't keep on, or it'll be another round of exercises for everyone."

"Yes, sir."

"If you're bored, go outside for a walk, but don't be too long about it."

"I almost too bored to get up."

"We've only been here for a few hours." Morton looked up.

"Well, it has been several days since I arrested anyone... I suppose I *could* go for a walk."

"The locals will pester you with questions."

"Not if I tell them we're working under the Official Secrets Act. I wonder what they'll make of *that*."

"Go on, buzz off, for goodness' sake."

"I'll assume that's an order, sir, so I'll be on my way."

Sophie walked along the wing's first floor, passing numerous bedrooms, in a rather featureless yet refined corridor in pale blue and white. Upon climbing a short flight of stairs, she entered the main building to be met by an astonishing sight that made her slow down to better take in what she was seeing. Along this shorter corridor were doors that had to be twelve feet high and ceilings that had to be nearer twenty. Surprising as these were, they were the least of the changes, for it was the rich and thick dark blue carpets, the quantities of gilt-framed old paintings hanging on plum-coloured walls, and the mouldings on the ceiling picked out in gold-leaf, which produced the overwhelming effect that she had entered a vast space of great opulence.

She walked very slowly, glancing at paintings worth a fortune, but what drew her attention all the more was the golden glowing space ahead. As she stepped from the corridor, her jaw dropped at the extent of what lay before her. The exterior of the house had not prepared her for this interior.

It was a Roman temple or a forum that functioned as a hall, and from floor to ceiling must have been all of fifty feet. She stood on the white marble floor of the piano nobile in a portico and looked up at the gold domed and coffered ceiling inspired by the Pathenon. She stepped across to a wrought-iron railing between two immense fluted and carved alabaster columns, each in the variegated colours of puce, tan, and strawberry. Below her lay a sunken level, which was the ground floor. The walls there were lined with alabaster panels of the same colours as the columns. She counted the columns. There were sixteen in all surrounding the entrance, and they supported a banded frieze, which in turn seemed to support the domed roof. In the white painted walls behind the columns surrounding the entrance were a series of alcoves, each containing an old Roman statue — some were complete and some damaged. Sophie noticed doors to two other principle rooms, remarkable in themselves, but it was the third, central entrance at the back of the hall, if that's what it could be called, that demanded her attention.

Stretching away from the tall double front doors, a long red carpet crossed a brilliant white marble floor and continued up thirty marble steps, which began full width of the entrance at the bottom, tapering to become half width at the top. The carpet continued on and arrived at an entrance that possessed its own semi-dome, which repeated the ceiling's gold coffered design. The carpet passed under a pair of closed doors. Sophie could not resist the temptation. She opened one to discover the plain red carpet joined a patterned sea of red, with another magnificent ceiling overhead. It was only a glimpse she had before quickly shutting the door on the scene of splendour that she had not the time to investigate just then. Later, she learned, that room was called the Grand Salon. She realized that the building may have cost fourteen thousand, but the interiors had cost several times that amount.

"Mr Dalgleish. May I speak to you for a moment?" asked Sophie.

Sophie had found the butler on the first floor of the east wing in conversation with Mrs Newnham. She had to wait until they had finished and Dalgleish beckoned her. Mrs Newnham gave Sophie a cold, unreadable stare.

"This is Miss King, Mrs Newnham. She is in charge of the staff from the agency."

"Good morning, Mrs Newnham," said Sophie, who then bobbed a perfunctory curtsy.

The housekeeper hesitated before replying, "Good morning, Miss King." Hers was a cheerless greeting.

"You wish to communicate something?" asked Dalgleish.

"I do. All the maids are to sleep in a dormitory in the attic. It is very cold there, and although there is a substantial fireplace, we have no coal."

"No coal, Miss King?" He turned to the housekeeper. "Mrs Newnham, would you be so kind as to direct Miss King in this matter?"

The housekeeper remained silent. Forewarned by Bertha's explanation, Sophie thought the woman might be shaking. She was certainly mute and struggling to answer. Dalgleish, impassive, waited for her reply.

"Is there a difficulty with the coal supply?" he asked.

"No." She managed that much, but was unwilling to speak further.

"Then how shall we solve the problem of the unheated dormitory?"

A barrier broke. "You may as well know that Mr Kemp is in sole charge of the estate. He... He guards the coal."

"Guards the coal?" repeated Dalgleish.

"He, uh, he has funny ways of doing things, and I, um, have to submit to them." This admission brought her no relief. If anything, her distress increased.

"I shall speak to him at once, Mrs Newnham. Where shall I find this person?"

"Please, don't."

"This is not right. The situation must be rectified immediately. Where shall I find him?"

"In the Gun Room... I expected Kemp to do something like this."

Dalgleish gave her an enquiring look, hoping for elucidation, but when it became obvious none would be forthcoming, he said,

"Excuse me, Mrs Newnham."

"May I accompany you?" asked Sophie, as Dalgleish turned to go. "It will save time so that we can start on our proper duties all the sooner."

"A good point, Miss King. Yes, you may."

In silence, they walked to the Gun Room on the ground floor of the west wing.

# Chapter 14

# A bear in its den, and a lion in the hall

The door to the Gun Room was ajar, and Sophie heard a fragment of conversation uttered by a London man.
"... So I said to him. 'You do it again...'"
Dalgleish pushed the door open and stepped inside. Sophie followed him. A hefty man in his late twenties stopped speaking, his hand still up and pointing towards another man sitting across from him at a large oak table. This man, in his fifties and seated in an oak swivel chair, was cleaning a shotgun by pulling a cord and cleaning patch through the barrel with his sinewy hands. He turned to Dalgleish and noticed Sophie standing just behind him.
"You're interrupting a private conversation," said the older man, in a voice full of accusation and challenge. One could tell he was tall, even though seated. There was no doubt his weather-roughened complexion would turn dark copper in the summer months. His grizzled beard of several days'

growth contrasted with his black hair. He spoke again. "You're Dalgleish. And who's this?" He looked again at Sophie.

The room lined with firearms made his insolent tone all the more menacing. It was a large, low, square room with barred windows. The guns were scrupulously clean, and some of them very expensive. Kemp aligned the barrels of the shotgun he held with a window to inspect them.

"You are Mr Kemp, I take it. As butler to the Fielding family, it is not my custom to knock on the doors of rooms for general use."

"You're wrong there, ain't you?" He put the shotgun down on the table. "See, I run things here and I've no need for a butler. They're useless to me. What you do up in London is your business, and I've no interest in it. What you do down here is my business. Like the others, you'll knock on doors in future."

The young man started grinning while Kemp was speaking, and continued to do so in the silence that followed. Kemp's behaviour appalled Sophie, and she doubted if Mr Dalgleish had ever been so rudely treated before.

"No," said Mr Dalgleish.

"No?" Kemp now smiled. "You reckon you'll have a word with Lord Stokely about me? Try it, and see what 'appens."

Sophie would have counted to ten to bring herself under control, but she became impatient.

"Where do you keep the coal?" She snapped.

"None of your business. If you want some, it's five shillings the scuttle's worth." He paused. "Chilly in those attics, ain't it? We're short on coal and the upkeep of the Park is something terrible. I'm just trying to save his lordship's money, so you maids, or Dalgleish here, will have to pay."

"*Ridiculous.* I'll find it myself," she said, and turned to go.

"No, you won't!" Kemp stood up.

"Yes, I will. You're an extortioner, and you're not getting a penny. What criminal nonsense it is. Do you think you can *actually* get away with this stupidity?"

"Miss King," said Dalgleish. "Please, permit me." He raised a cautionary hand. "Mr Kemp, we shall take what supplies we need while we are here without reference to yourself. Good day."

With that, Dalgleish and Sophie left the room.

"Shut the door, will you, John?" Kemp said to the young man. He smiled to himself and sat down.

John got up to do as bidden. "Are you letting them off?"

"No choice," said Kemp. "They're not the right type. Far too mouthy for me to squeeze anything out of them."

"What will Stokely do when he hears about it?"

"Ah, don't worry. We're like brothers, and I do a lot for his lordship, as you well know." He picked up the shotgun. "Now, what was it you were saying?"

"Oh, yeah... So I said, 'If you do it again,' then I tapped his bonce with a beer mug and down he goes, 'you'll get a lot more of that.'"

Kemp gave a short laugh.

---

The Grand Dining Room possessed a mahogany table which rested upon seven pedestals and was thirty-six feet long, once all the leaves were added. To stand at one end and look down its polished length was a feast for the eye. If one studied long enough, it would be seen that only a single leaf stood slightly proud to the rest. On close inspection, the wood's even pattern appeared to be submerged under a clear, glossy red-brown lake.

"It's magnificent," said Sophie, carrying two large and heavy, folded tablecloths.

"Looks like a lot of work to me, miss," said Ada, who carried two more.

"We'd better be quick, or the others will be here with the crockery. Mr Dalgleish said there should be a two-foot overhang at the ends, and for the overlaps not to be visible from Lord Stokely's end."

"Which end is that?"

"The far end." They put the linen on the table. "So we'll start at the other end first and make sure the tablecloth is in good order."

They began laying out the cloth and were looking for something to weight it so that it didn't move, when three footmen in livery arrived each carrying silver epergnes or baskets. Dalgleish followed and supervised their actions, sending Broadbent-Wicks to the end where Sophie and Ada were working.

"Hello, Miss King and Miss Carmichael. What do I do with these?" Broadbent-Wicks held two silver baskets.

"Don't speak," said Sophie, as she and Ada pulled the cloth taut. "Put them on the table."

He put them down together.

"I should have explained," said Sophie. "One in each corner, please."

"Oh, to weight the bally thing down, what?"

"No talking," whispered Ada, "and go away immediately."

"I'll get the hang of it, Miss Carmichael, don't you worry." He left as they began laying out the second tablecloth.

Dalgleish and the footmen left the room.

"Fern said that two vans arrived from London full of food. The first that come was from Fortnum & Mason's, and the other was from 'arrod's."

"Do you think they had a race on the way down?" asked Sophie. They smoothed the second cloth into place.

"That'd be a laugh if they did, miss. And, she said, the French chef has arrived with his staff and some of them are wearing those hats... Funny objects, ain't they? Fern says, the chef 'isself has the biggest and floppiest one of them all. She can't pronounce his name though, because it's French. It's something like For-her-knee-a?"

"Um... That must be Fournier."

"Say it again, miss."

"Fournier."

"Fern was close, then, when she said it."

"I wish he were doing our cooking," said Sophie.

"That's right, an' all. Talk about thin soup. I had to hunt for a potato, I did. That Kemp's a wrong-un'. No one likes him... Stealing from the servants' food, I ask you?"

"It's reprehensible. He needs to be removed."

"That would be difficult... Butler's coming back."

As they adjusted the last tablecloth, the footmen returned, now carrying baskets of silver cutlery. Alfie Tanner and three maids followed with piles of dishes.

"Arter'noon, Miss King, and you Nancy," said Alfie. "On the table, yes?"

"Yes, please," replied Sophie.

"With *pleasure*," he whispered in his posh accent this time, and then retired to bring more dishes with all the stately decorum that a severe major-domo could ask for.

After a few moments, Mr Dalgleish approached to speak to Sophie and Ada. "I shall lay a sample place, and you are to use it as the pattern for the rest of the table." He laid out the dishes and cutlery with unerring, white-gloved efficiency. "When the glasses and side plates arrive, place them in their usual order. The table shall be set for twenty-eight, so allow thirty inches for each guest. You will find this useful." He handed Ada a length of red cord. "It is exactly thirty inches in length."

"Thank you, Mr Dalgleish," said Ada. "We used to call it the Idiot String. Do you call it that 'ere, sir?"

"I am aware of the term, Miss Carmichael." He turned away and left the room.

"He *nearly* smiled," whispered Ada to Sophie, as they began laying out the dishes without using the cord.

"That's what you always do, get people to smile or cheer

them up."

"I find life goes much better when it can be done."

"Yes, but don't waste your time on Kemp, though."

"No, I won't. Stealing left and right. It's not just him diddling the servants' food and coal, miss. They say he lets people 'unt on the lands and keeps the money he charges them. And it's reckoned he shoots deer sometimes."

"He's a *dreadful* creature... Deer hunting isn't illegal, though, as long as it's authorized."

"It is illegal round here, 'cause this estate used to be the king's forest or something, and you still can't 'unt the deer even now excep' by special licence. They said it's three months' 'ard labour if Kemp's caught. Bertha thinks ten years would be about right for him."

"She's probably correct... You should have seen Mr Dalgleish talk to Kemp. How he kept his temper, I don't know, but he did... Poor soul. It was awful seeing him treated so abominably at his age."

"What a shame... As far as butlers go, I like him," said Ada. "Aren't these plates beautiful?"

"Yes, and they're old, too." Sophie turned over a plate with the hand-painted, open design of flower sprays and exotic birds, to examine a crude yellow anchor mark. "I think this might be Chelsea."

They continued setting places. The parlourmaid from Lyall Place, whose name was Beech, entered the room with a pile of napkins. Sophie and Ada briefly looked at each other, then carried on. Miss Beech began folding napkins at the other end of the table.

Dalgleish was no longer present, so Sophie said to Ada, "I'll be back in a minute." She approached Miss Beech. "Isn't that Bishop's Mitre?"

"That's right."

"May I try?"

"Suit yourself."

Sophie took a napkin from the pile and began copying Miss

Beech's actions. "It was Pyramid at Lyall Place."

"Lady Stokely prefers it."

"I hope we can put the past behind us," said Sophie.

"I don't know."

"There." Sophie had finished. "It's not as good as yours. I'll try again." She undid her work.

"It takes practise... If you don't get the two points identical, it won't come right."

"That's where I went wrong... Have you worked here before?"

"Never. And never again, I hope."

"It's not at all well run. I think Mr Dalgleish is upset by the changes since his time."

"I'd say. In the olden days, it used to be a proper showplace, right up until Mr Dalgleish left. Not now, though."

"It could be again."

"Yes... How they dare to serve us that muck they call food, I don't know."

"It's not the cook's fault, though."

"No, but Mrs Potter's no good... Trying her best, I suppose, but she's not up to it."

"Where are you from originally?"

"Sidcup in Kent."

"I'm from Winchester. What do you think?" Sophie had refolded her napkin.

"Yes, it's good enough."

"I'll do one more, then I must get back to laying the table... It's a big party. Twenty-eight here and as many again in the Second Dining Room."

"There'll be forty-four in there."

"Really? Seventy-two all told. It has to be something important."

"No one's said anything, so I don't know. What I've heard, but don't tell anyone this, that it's going to be all men."

"All men...? It must be about business."

"Oh, definitely. Or politics, because I heard there's an M.P.

coming."

"Ah, and a French chef."

"Yes. He works permanent for his lordship. He's taken over the big kitchen and there'll be food deliveries from London every day except Sunday, of course."

"Perhaps there'll be some leftovers... Unless Kemp gets to them first."

"I do hope not... No one has a good word for him, that's all I know... I'm glad we've got coal now... What happened there?"

"He was trying to make us pay for coal, *and* at an exorbitant price."

"*Pay* for it? I never heard of such a thing... For him to keep the money, I suppose. Oh, how wicked!"

"Upsetting, isn't it?"

"It is that."

"What do you think?" Sophie showed Miss Beech her attempt.

"That's coming along, that is. Leave it on a plate."

"I must be off." She smiled at Miss Beech and returned to where Ada was working.

"How'd it go, miss?" whispered Ada.

"Quite well. We're on speaking terms now, anyway. I'm certain *she's* not a Stokely spy."

"That's good... What was that palaver over the napkins?"

"I pretended I didn't know Bishop's Mitre."

"I was goin' to say, 'cause you taught me it. I remember you saying that, when you was a little girl, you did it for your father, sayin' 'ow he should be a bishop."

Sophie smiled. "That always brings back fond memories."

They continued working along the table. Maids and footmen returned frequently with yet more items. While all the members of staff were thus occupied, guests began arriving, and Dalgleish and two footmen attended to them. The first four guests proved to be well-dressed, well-spoken men on Stokely's staff, and they brought with them many boxes of papers which they did not allow the footmen to handle.

Broadbent-Wicks helped carry in their luggage. He noticed one of the arrivals in Saville Row tailoring with the overcoat and jacket unbuttoned. As the man had got out of the car, Broadbent-Wicks caught a glimpse of a pistol in a shoulder holster.

---

"Psst!"

Sophie had been walking along the first floor corridor at about two. She turned to find Flora beckoning her into a side passageway. She joined her friend.

"I've been looking for you," whispered Flora. "I've collected reports and information."

"Good, because I haven't seen anyone in ages other than Ada."

"That's because the house is enormous and we're being sent all over the place. First of all, have you seen the back of the building?"

"No."

"Ah. You know how the front of the house is rather boring? Well, the back isn't. In fact, it's lovely. There's this garden that must be absolutely beautiful..."

"Excuse me. Are these rooms empty? We don't want to be overheard."

"No, I checked that first."

"Is your narrative leading somewhere?"

"Of course, it is, Phoebe. I found two informants outside. Just go and see the back for yourself. That will save me from explaining it."

"Yes?"

"Right. So there are three telephone lines. Two private lines upstairs, and one downstairs with three extensions."

"*Three!*"

"Shh. I know. It makes it awkward for us. On the ground floor, the general line runs into the office, with extensions to the adjacent Muniment Room, Gun Room, and Butler's pantry, only there's no butler here. Upstairs, Stokely's office has two lines, one with an extension in the State Bedroom, but it's thought to be broken."

"Muniment... That's for the estate documents, isn't it?"

"That's right, because I looked in. Have you seen the State Bedroom?"

"No."

"It is *definitely* fit for royalty. You must see it."

"Have you seen the Entrance Hall?"

"No. I was told to keep to the second floor. I don't know how it's done, but that corridor misses all the principal rooms and hall in this great big loop."

"Go along the first floor, then you'll see a sight. In fact, you'll see it now, because I need you to come with me."

"I can't. I have something to do."

"You must. We need to go to the Grand Dining Room. You must watch the door, while I get the names from the place cards that Mr Dalgleish put out. It's very important. Then we have to go to the Second Dining Room."

"Don't bother, because they're not putting any place cards out there. Phoebe, I might get in trouble if I'm too long. I'm supposed to be starting the preparations for tea."

"Just make up an excuse or say I asked you to help me with..."

"What?"

"I can't think of anything."

"But we're wasting time. I only have four more things to tell you.

"I don't believe it. Four?!"

"Mr Broadbent-Wicks, alias Dan, said he saw a man wearing one of those gun holster thingies with a gun in it. The type that goes up the armpit. One of Stokely's agents, obviously, but dressed like a gentleman. He arrived with three similar gentlemen and two drivers. They brought in some suspicious boxes. Alfie believes a few of the boxes contain money. Very interesting, don't you think? How many items is that?"

"Three."

"No... It's two. Number three is that there are kennels for the gun dogs but, supposedly, there are also two big nasty brutes among them who are Kemp's favourites. Sort of a Hound of the Baskerville type of breed. Do you know about Kemp?"

"Yes, I met him."

"He sounds dreadful... Ah, so that's why we have coal in the dormitory, I suppose. What a brick you are. Well, anyway, he sounds dreadful. Tell me all about that later. Four... The estate has three working horses, and that's all there are here. Stokely stables his riding horses near Windsor. I got the impression from a gardener informant that he has a property there."

"Although fascinating, how does that help?"

"Ha, I nearly forgot. The garage is by the stables. There were eight cars parked in it before anyone arrived. Two cars were decrepit, but the rest looked new or newish, anyway."

"Why are there so many?"

"Exactly what I asked myself, but I can't think of a good reason. Why don't you ask Stokely when you see him? Phoebe, we must go at once."

They set off. Flora gasped while crossing the Entrance Hall. In the Grand Dining Room, Sophie hurried around the table, writing shorthand notes. Flora watched the corridor from the door.

"Quick, Mrs Newnham and a maid are coming."

"Just three more names."

"Under the table? It looks fabulous, by the way."

"Not the table. That door at the back." Sophie pointed with her pencil.

"I'll see if it's locked." Flora hurried off. She tried the single door in the corner. "It's open. Come on."

Sophie scribbled the last name, then ran the length of the room and through the doorway. Flora shut the door, plunging them into the darkness of a short, windowless passage with a lower ceiling, ten feet high. A moment later, they heard a main door open. Both women listened intently.

They heard indistinct noises followed by silence. Then the main door closed. Sophie tapped Flora's arm. She cautiously opened the door.

"All clear. I simply *must* leave," said Flora.

"Do so. I'll investigate these rooms."

Flora nodded and slipped quietly away. Sophie examined three rooms. The nearest was a spacious lavatory. Opposite that was a small sitting room furnished in the French Empire style. The last door opened onto a very large smoking room in late Victorian dark wood panelling, with brown leather chairs and sofas, and dull red oriental carpets. It could easily accommodate twenty men, and forty at a pinch. Sophie noticed a spiral staircase which appeared to lead to another room above, of probably similar proportions. From the smoking room, two doors led elsewhere, but she had not the time to continue further and, in any event, feared being discovered. At least she now knew that, should Stokely disappear after dinner, this was where he was likely to go. While cautiously leaving, she gave a brief thought to the name of the guest of honour. She knew it, because it was a famous name, and she wondered what his presence might mean.

At half-past two, a convoy entered the drive. The cars containing guests halted at the front entrance. The vehicles conveying Stokely's personnel either turned away to the west wing side entrance or continued on to the garages and other essential outbuildings at the far end of the east wing.

The long-standing custom for the staff at Chertsey Park, when the earl had been away for an extended period, was to stand ready for inspection at the top of the interior marble staircase. All the presentable staff did so now, waiting in a line against the wall between the doors of the Grand Salon and those of the Anteroom. Dalgleish stood alone, to one side of the bottom stair. Opposite him were three of the well-dressed and, so far, taciturn aides.

Several footmen unloaded the vehicles. Alfie, at attention, held the front door open. Stokely entered. His entourage followed at a respectful distance.

"*Dalgleish!*" said Stokely, as though he had not seen the butler for years instead of just two weeks ago. The earl strode across the wide marble entrance to the staircase. Stokely paused in front of him.

"My Lord," replied the butler, bowing.

"I know you're busy now." Stokely spoke clearly, and the marble hall gave a ring to his voice. Every person could hear him. "But later, you and I shall have a talk about the estate. I have a few ideas."

"I look forward to hearing them, my Lord."

"Where am I heading?"

"Refreshments await in the Anteroom."

Stokely did not answer. He turned and looked towards one of the unknown gentlemen, who then fell in behind the earl. Dalgleish, at the perfectly timed moment, moved to precede the earl, and they ascended the stairs.

The servants' line had stood to attention with Sophie near the middle, her eyes straight ahead, and nerve-wracked. She had feared that Stokely would know the real reason she was present as soon as he saw her. As Stokely had slowly passed, looking at each servant, footmen bowed and maids bobbed, each quietly saying their name, followed by "my Lord." She had overheard Alfie utter the phrase in his refined voice and suddenly wanted to scream with laughter. She had managed her turn, though. Stokely entered her field of vision; she bobbed and swore fealty, as they all had; then he passed on. What had surprised her was that he seemed older close up — older than in photographs, anyway. The set of his features in profile betrayed as much emotion as that of a monarch on the obverse of a coin. Sophie had reminded herself that although she had said 'my Lord' it counted as nothing, because it was to a traitor who, if he achieved all his aims, *would* have coins struck bearing his image. All titles and honours flow out from the king or queen, but here was a man, a murderer and destroyer of lives, who would change that arrangement. No matter. She had given her word, and had given it falsely, and she felt ashamed.

"They're well-turned out," Stokely had said to Dalgleish.

Once the master had left, the butler silently snapped his gloved fingers and the line of staff scattered to its various stations and duties, with Flora, Ada, and Miss Beech assigned to the Anteroom.

# Chapter 15

# Head counts and speeches

Travelling among the guests in the convoy were two newspapermen. Having shared a car on the way down, they entered the house together and stopped just inside the doors because a queue had formed while Stokely spoke to Dalgleish.

"What do you think?" asked Jack Long, editor of the London Mercury, referring to the classical elegance of the immense hall.

"Frankly, I'm astonished," answered Jeremy Rushton, editor of the Albion News, which would soon publish its first issue. "Oh, to be a plutocrat... Is the rest of the house as Romanesque?"

"No, not at all, although some rooms will still knock you silly. However, our bedrooms won't be so grand."

"I imagine not... Did you see Auckland of the Times? He's behind us somewhere."

"I didn't," said Long. "What's *he* doing here?"

"Stokely must be frying a bigger fish than we thought."

"Yes... You and I should keep our wits about us."

"Sound advice, I'd say... Ah, we move, at last."

The footmen were kept busy as guests frequently arrived by car, either private ones or those of the house sent to collect people from the station. Sophie learned that the scheduling for Stokely's vehicles was in the hands of the mysterious, well-dressed aides. Neither Dalgleish nor Kemp had anything to do with the matter, except that several of Kemp's men had been seconded as drivers.

A storm swirled, its locus being the largest kitchen of the Kitchen Court. There, Monsieur Fournier, the genius of the storm, barked an unceasing stream of French commands at his staff. He also, in French, liberally cursed the stove at which he was working. It was not a place to enter unless one had business there. Across the small, paved, rectangular courtyard, in another kitchen, was Mrs Potter — sulking in her own domain — who had been demoted to sous-chef and put in charge of some vegetables, some baking, and a few other minor chores.

"Who does 'ee think 'ee is?" said Mrs Potter, standing next to a sink and glaring across the courtyard, although Monsieur Fournier was invisible to her. "What right do 'ee have to come here and take over? Answer me that."

"I don't know, Mrs Potter," said a kitchen maid who always thought it best to agree.

"There's nothing wrong with my cooking that he should take over."

Here, the maid privately and completely disagreed, but appeasingly said, "I know, Mrs Potter. He should have stayed in London. Or, better yet, he could go back to France."

"Yes, 'ee should. I'd loike the chance to do for his lordship just the once. It's *never* given me... It's all Kemp's fault."

The maid failed to trace Kemp's connection to the matter. "It's so unfair."

"You said it. Him always a-keeping me short on supplies... You tell me, how's a body to cope under these conditions?"

"I don't know how you do it."

"Ahh... There, done. Run these carrots over. That a Frenchman, an *undercook* moind you, should show *me* how to cut a carrot — well, it beggars belief. 'Course I know Julian Carrots! I cut 'em that way before 'ee were born."

"I know... But he spoke ever so noicely."

"Take them carrots and watch your step. I'm a-*warning* you..." She waved a knife at the maid. "...Don't go making eyes at no Frenchman, or 'ee'll carry you off to France before you can say Jack Spratt."

The maid picked up the large bowl. As she walked across the yard, she dreamed of France, picturing herself being carried there. Upon entering the maelstrom, she saw Monsieur Fournier and Sophie in conversation. The chef was smiling, and once he twirled his moustache. They were speaking mostly in French.

"Non, Mademoiselle King, do not apologize. Your ability to speak French, eh bien, c'est magnifique. A rarity among maids, but then I can see you are the professional."

They had been discussing specific points about the timing and order of various courses, which attention both pleased and calmed the man. Sophie's ostensible purpose for bearding Monsieur Fournier in his den was to ask him if he had any special presentation requirements for particular dishes, although no one had ordered her to do so. Sophie's actual, but hidden, objective required Ada's coaching in the delicate art of 'how to become friendly with a chef while he's busy'.

"And you are an artist, Monsieur Fournier. His lordship is very lucky to have you prepare his dinners.'

"Oh," he said, smiling, and with a slight and very French shrug.

"Unfortunately, my staff and I must endure what the household cook provides." Sophie sounded depressed.

"Quel *dommage*."

"English cooking, Monsieur Fournier, and mostly boiled turnips and potatoes at that." She sighed.

"Mon Dieu! That is abominable."

"We must put up with what we're given, I suppose." She looked sad and spoke without hope. "Forgive me for troubling you with my little problem."

"Not at all... Un moment! I will set aside un petit quelque chose pour vous.. How many staff do you have?"

"There are seven of us." Sophie had the maid's dormitory in mind.

"Seven... There will be plenty remaining after the dinner. Come here at eleven and I will have une belle surprise set aside for you. Ask for it, if I am not present, hein?"

"Monsieur Fournier! I don't know what to say. How lovely and so immensely kind of you."

"Oh, it is nothing."

"I must leave you, but thank you for *such* a marvellous treat. You are a godsend."

Monsieur Fournier was gratified. So was Sophie.

The dinner began with a toast. Lord Stokely rose from his chair at the head of the table, but placed a hand on the sleeve of the gentleman sitting to his right. Everyone then rose, except for the guest of honour.

"Ladies and gentlemen," there were, after all, two women among the guests. "You will be relieved to hear that I shall *not* unduly delay your dinner." Polite laughter followed. "I want to take a moment of this august company's time, to honour one worthy person in particular. For more than a decade, his newsreels have informed us, and his cinematic documentaries from around the world have educated, entertained, and delighted us. Indeed, upon entering *any* cinema, he is unavoidable." There followed a great deal of laughter. "French by birth, we have taken him to heart as one of our own. His name represents a most *beloved* British institution, while other countries hold dear his work, too. To you, Monsieur Charles Pathé, good health, sir, and long may you continue in your endeavours."

The company gave good health and sipped from its glasses before sitting down. Pathé rose. In his fifties, he was spry and dapper, possessing a friendly face adorned by a small moustache.

"Thank you, Lord Stokely, you are too kind... Ladies and gentleman, I have been remiss. Had I understood how splendid this evening would be, I would have brought my camera with me." Laughter. "What would the title card of this scene say...? I believe I have it. — You'd be hard put to find a more excellent host than — Lord Stokely!"

"Hear, hear!" They clapped enthusiastically.

Pathé raised his glass. "I give you, Lord Stokely." The table followed his lead and responded, "Lord Stokely!" They all sipped and sat down again.

Immediately, and with silent efficiency, the first course of the dinner arrived.

Later, outside of the Grand Dining Room, Flora met Sophie out of sight around a corner.

"They're all bankers and industrialists down Dawkins' end," whispered Flora. "Ready?"

"Yes." Sophie held her pencil and notebook.

"On the left. Fourteen is a representative from Rothschild's. Thirteen is shipping, I think. Twelve is Frobisher's. Eleven is one of the aides."

"Ah, good. He's the last of them."

"On the right. Fourteen is Baring's. I haven't got thirteen. Twelve is mining, but don't ask me what. Eleven is aviation."

Sophie took down the information, having numbered each place at the table to match with the names collected earlier.

"I've got information from the others," said Sophie. "It's mostly newspapermen at Stokely's end. One's from South Africa, and another from Australia. In the middle, one woman is a doctor, and we don't yet know what the other woman does. Of the men identified there, they all seem to represent businesses of every type. Dotted about are more of the mysterious aides."

"Eavesdropping on the surrounding guests, no doubt. What's going on in the other dining room?"

"Nancy and Dora said it's all men and, as far as they could tell, they work for Stokely, but hale from different parts of Britain. Besides that, there's nothing much of interest there at present."

"I wonder what it's all about. As soon as I have more, I'll signal you... Don't lose that notebook," said Flora.

"Ooh, I shan't do that," said Sophie.

"My feet are killing me," said Broadbent-Wicks, who was now Alfie's equal at whispering from the side of his mouth. The two footmen stood side by side by the dining room's main doors.

"You're not used to all the bloomin' stairs. Come out window cleaning with me, and the ladder work will soon get your legs in proper condition."

"I suppose it would... Are you offering me a job? Because I need the work."

"I might. It gets busy sometimes, and I'm on me own. Window cleaning's a very competitive trade. If I'm not there, the shopkeeper'll bring in another bloke soon enough, and that'd be good night for me."

"I can see that. How would I know when you wanted me?"

"Where d'you live?"

"Dalston, I think."

"You don't know where you live?"

"Yes, I do. It's that I've only recently moved there, and I believe I've made a good choice, and won't have to push off again any time soon, but I'm not sure yet."

"Well, Dalston's a bit far out, really. My routes are all in Stepney... It might work."

"I'll see what I can do. If it doesn't work out, I'll have to condition my legs some other way."

No one at the table appeared to want the footmen's services just then. Dalgleish came in. Both men watched him for the few moments he remained until he went out again.

"Can I ask you something?" asked Broadbent-Wicks.

"What?"

"Why don't you have a false name? I'm now Dan Ely, while you're still Alfie Tanner."

"It's very simple, mate. I don't like it. Miss King and Miss Carmichael lumbered me with a few monikers, but I didn't take to the notion. They had a second go with Miss Walton present. Cor, blimey, talk about having a laugh at my expense. They went through a list of names that turned me stomach. It ended up with them wanting to call me Phineas ffiske-ffroggart. Double fs and double-barrels, 'sides it being a mouthful. I told 'em I'm having *none* of that. I said, call me Alfie Tanner, but don't call me nothing else, thank you very much. However, I said, I'll put on a posh voice when working to confuse people as to my *real* identity. So here we are. I speak la-di-da when needed and keep me own name."

"Are you still annoyed with them?"

"*Oh, no*. They're all lovely girls — as good as they come. But they're a bit on the cheeky side when they're all together. You have to watch 'em close, or they'll take liberties."

"I hold Miss King in the highest esteem," said Broadbent-Wicks. "I also think Miss Carmichael and Miss Walton are admirable."

"So do I... What you on about?"

"Please do not make derogatory remarks about them."

"Come again?"

"You referred to them as cheeky."

"I did, me old cock-sparrer, 'cause they are. How would you describe 'em, then?"

"Genteel. And Miss Carmichael conducts her work to such a high standard that she, too, is ladylike."

Alfie slipped into his refined voice. "Well, pardon me, my lord."

"Apology accepted."

Alfie laughed quietly to himself before saying, "I wish I was your age again."

While hearing brief snippets of conversation, the agents were hard put to make much of them. A danger was to infer significance when there was none. A frustration was witnessing comments without hearing responses, or vice versa. Sophie polled the others infrequently, because her own duties kept her too busy for much else. What she knew was that in two full rooms, there were up to twenty conversations in progress, and she had difficulty making sense of either the parts or the whole. From her own narrow observational slice, she found that the diners, journalists mostly, talked about a wide range of unsurprising topics, but she also heard the words reorganize, plan, and revitalize used by different people, which led her to believe that Stokely had invited those who were influential in their fields for a special purpose, and the choice of the field or business sector somehow fitted with his plans of eventually governing Britain.

With the penultimate course served, Sophie accompanied Flora to the kitchen.

"What are the bankers talking about?" asked Sophie.

"Money."

"Can you be more specific?"

"I can't. It's all capital this, that, and the other, and I don't understand what they mean. I get the impression they're running short of money and would like some more."

"They can't be, surely? Give an example."

"Um… The man from Frobisher said the capital requirements were enormous, but the money to be raised was not all needed at once. The Rothschild's man said he was concerned about the adequacy of the gold reserves, to which Frobisher said something about proper ratios. Then, the Baring's man asked when the first series was to be issued, and would it be fixed or something something? I also missed everything before and afterwards."

"Series of what? And what could he possibly mean by fixed?"

"No idea. Bankers don't talk like normal people, so who can say?"

Arriving at the kitchen brought the conversation to an end.

As Sophie returned to the Grand Dining Room, Ada passed some information to her.

"Dalgleish is busy for the moment. Can't stop, but you ought to know this. Alfie says they'll all be out hunting early tomorrow morning on the 'eath. He says not to go near Kemp and his men, 'cause they're a bad lot."

"In what way?"

"He said they all look like crooks to him, and nasty ones at that."

"Goodness, I suppose I knew they would be. How nasty does he think?"

"Cut-your-throat types. And Bertha says there's always two or three knocking about the place, but sometimes there are as many as eight of them *plus* Kemp. She thinks they're all 'ere tonight."

"Oh, dear. Also, there are the four men in evening dress who are aides, spies or whatever."

"*And* the bodyguards and the drivers, and those are the ones we know about. There could be more sittin' around the tables. We're right in it, miss, and no mistake."

"So it seems. We'll just do our work and keep our heads down."

"*Yes*, and here's 'oping we get to *keep* our 'eads, an' all."

"Everything will be fine, but I must get the guest list out of the house tonight, so I need to make two telephone calls. One of them is to Elizabeth, so she doesn't worry about us."

"I'd an 'orrible feeling you were going to say that about the telephone. Do we 'ave a meeting first?"

"I doubt it shall be possible, under the circumstances. Get information from the others, then only we two need to meet."

Ada nodded, and they quickly walked off in different directions

---

The Grand Salon was long, wide, and tall. The walls above the wainscot had been covered in panels of Ciselé velvet of a slumbering red that was nearly maroon. The linked pattern of flowers and urns was offset by a deep, muted pink satin ground. There would have been too much of it had not so many large paintings been hung in the room — good or great paintings, too, with pride of place going to an interior scene of a family in a Spanish palace by Diego Velázquez. Along the walls were sofas and tables standing on a marble floor, although the centre of the room was covered by a massive red hand-woven carpet with a lozenge design. The carpet had no furniture resting on it, perhaps with the intention that guests should just stand and talk or listen to others, or stare up at the ceiling which, importantly, constituted the other half of the room. Overhead was a coved and coffered ceiling in various golds and complimentary colours. Its sides were deeply patterned and, although the indentations were regular in shape and tapering in size the higher they went, they suggested the 'eyes' of a peacock's feathers. The actual central portion of flat ceiling was an oblong, formed and painted in such a cunning way that it looked like a skylight with a summer's sky above. The guests from the Grand Dining Room began to enter.

"This room makes one feel rather small," said Jeremy Rushton, looking up as they all did.

"That's the desired effect for when meeting a potentate," replied Jack Long.

"Yes... It's extraordinarily well done, though."

"I've been to Chertsey Park before, and it never fails to impress... Have you spoken to Auckland?"

"Briefly," replied Rushton. "We said hello."

"I'm finding him stand-offish, actually."

"Could that be the Stokely taint?"

"It comes with the position, old man. You know that by now, but Auckland's pretty decent as a rule, even if the Times *is* a competitor."

"Perhaps it's dyspepsia, then. The dinner was superb *and* very rich."

"Could be. I'm going for a wander to meet people. Care to join me?"

"Yes, I will. Let's get a drink first."

Rushton signalled to a nearby maid carrying a tray. Ada approached and served them.

Stokely was treated with deference. To speak to him, individual guests were summoned by one of the mysterious men who were adaptable, educated, well-spoken, and vigilant. Standing near the fireplace, Stokely held these brief interviews while a bodyguard stood nearby, searching the room continually. Similarly, Lester Dawkins seemed more liable to scrutinize an individual than to talk to him or her. Sophie thought him enigmatic, and was careful not to be caught looking in his direction, or anyone else's, for that matter. To her, knowing that she was in the same room as two men complicit in a recent murder, the room's atmosphere seemed sinister and out of touch with reality. Could these decent-looking men in this fabulous room really be the devils she thought them to be, knew them to be? She felt the strain of her pretense, and she saw glimpses of the same strain in her friends' faces.

Sophie, Flora, Fern, and Miss Beech were tasked with taking the trays around, while Dalgleish oversaw both them and the dispensing of drinks at a table in an adjacent room. In the Grand Salon, the agents found it well-nigh impossible to do anything useful in regards to their mission, except to serve drinks. Between wary Dawkins, the bodyguard, aides-de-camp, as Sophie thought of them, and Dalgleish, there was allowed no opportunity to loiter near anyone, and certainly not near Stokely.

The guests from the second dining room entered. Being more numerous, and with some having met before, they naturally formed larger cliques. Among these, and it came as no surprise, the agents saw that Morris Wilberforce was a man of great standing among his associates. Slowly, the hierarchy of Stokely's organization became apparent.

The Salon, having filled up with guests, kept the servants busy for a time. Quite noticeable now was a widespread excitement in the room; an anticipation that something would happen. The atmosphere even affected those from outside of Stokely's business empire.

Several of Stokely's staff began giving directions to the guests, and they moved back to create a space. For once, Stokely stood alone — an elegant and handsome host, at ease in front of his fireplace. They all fixed their eyes on him and the room became quiet, with only a few whispers being exchanged. Stokely waited.

"My *friends*... Thank you for coming..." His manner was intimate, as though he were having an exclusive fireside chat with each person present. "This is a tremendous moment..." His fine, clear voice became the only sound. "All of you are here with one goal in mind. The transformation of Britain. The nation shall be great again. Perhaps greater than it has ever been before." He paused, as though considering his words. "Our current government tries, but it is weak and its policies ineffectual. It taxes heavily only to waste money. Why? Because the government, any democratic government for that matter, lacks the efficiency and singleness of mind of the business enterprise. Here, in this room, is such a wealth of business acumen as could form an effective decision-making body fully capable of running the country. We need only to organize, which is why you are here.

"You *know* I'm not talking about revolution. I am referring instead to the desperate state of our failing institutions. Our aim is to assist the government. To strengthen it. To overhaul it before it is too late. You have seen the recent news. Corruption, scandal, self-aggrandizement. Ah, the list goes on, as we all know. Well, it is time for men, and ladies, like ourselves, who are blessed with skill and capacity, to come to the nation's aid. Not one of us standing here wishes to see our country sicken and die while we stand by doing nothing. Ask yourself. Search the *depths* of your hearts. Do you want Britain to fail...? If not, then we *must* act."

The mesmerized guests forgot to drink what was in their glasses. The staff had nothing to do while Stokely spoke. Sophie slipped out of the room.

# Chapter 16

# Hunting grounds

Various offices occupied the ground floor of the west wing. It was a plain, functional area meant for the management of the house and the estate. Currently, it was Kemp's domain, although his bedroom lay in a remote part of the east wing, as were the rooms set aside for his men. In some respects, Kemp performed the duties of a butler, but one orientated to satisfying a specific set of his employer's whims. Hunting and shooting, the formal garden, wines and spirits — these were the estate manager's preoccupation, because those things were all that interested Stokely at Chertsey Park. Professionals from the town of Chertsey regularly came in to maintain the gardens, and they came more frequently in the spring and summer. Similarly, wines and spirits were delivered from London. To manage everything else — the staff, supplies, the routine upkeep of the house, and managing the shooting — Kemp received a fixed payment every month from Lord Stokely. By various methods, Kemp siphoned into his own keeping a goodly amount of money additional to his wages. With inflation, Kemp's extra income from this source had fallen dramatically since the war. This meant he would have to have a word with his lordship and, to do so, the account books had to be in order.

In the poorly lit and deserted corridor, Sophie walked slowly on the balls of her feet, trying to prevent her heels from clicking on the polished wooden floor. She was looking for the telephone and various extensions that Flora had discovered in the west wing. The only room whose use and position she knew for certain was the Gun Room, which had a light in a wall sconce outside. With all doors shut and no names upon them, she could not determine which room was the office. The Gun Room was locked, but that was really the last place she wanted to use. Sophie noticed an overhead wire coming out of the plaster by the door and then, secured by staples, going up and across the corridor to enter the room opposite. A second wire came out of that room and went into the one next door. Another wire emerged and went to the room next to that, with a final wire stretching back overhead. Telephone wires — Sophie felt pleased with herself for discovering this, and approached the room she had identified as the office, where also the telephone line entered the house.

As she reached for the handle, a faint glow under the door became apparent to her. Then someone spoke inside the room.

"That's everything I could do." The voice seemed to belong to an older man.

"Do you think the accounts are in good enough order?" This voice sounded like Kemp's to Sophie.

"Um... Not if anyone looks too close. Otherwise... Well, I've done my best, Mr Kemp, that's all I can say."

"It'll be fine. I'll show him this list of expenses and he'll see the place needs more money... Here you go."

"Thank you very much, Mr Kemp. I'll be going now, but send for me if there's anything else I can do."

They continued speaking, but Sophie had to prevent them from finding her. She moved away and quietly entered a nearby room, closing the door behind her. It was dark, and a brief flash of her torch revealed that this was probably once the butler's room and was now disused, judging by the litter accumulated on the table. Just to be sure, she hid behind a large cupboard on the side furthest from the door. Sophie pressed herself into the corner and controlled her breathing.

While she waited, she considered that, if she had walked along the corridor, they would have seen her had they come out immediately but, now she was hidden, they were taking an age in leaving. Eventually, the door across the corridor opened, and she heard them depart. When certain they had gone, she switched on the light to use the telephone.

---

While Sunningdale settled down for the night, the police in the village hall were vigilant, although they looked bored to tears. The telephone had not rung for several hours and it came as a minor explosion to the inmates when it rang now. They all scrambled to their feet. Many moved nearer to the telephone.

"Yes," said Morton to the operator, who had put the call through. "Hello...? Yes.... How is it going?"

He listened to Sophie's report, which she delivered in a London accent. She had modified it for the operator's benefit, in case she was listening in, making it sound as though Sophie was talking to a gentleman friend about the trials of her work.

"And I've got something nice for you, Morty." Sophie called him 'Morty', because she had no idea what his first name was.

"That's sweet of you, lovey," said Morton, the colour rising in his cheeks, and a strange, ardent glitter in his eyes.

"I'll get a friend to bring it over, 'cause I can't get away, as you well know."

"It'll be a shame not to see you."

"We'll meet soon, don't you worry."

The knot of policeman, gathered around the telephone,

wondered why the inspector in charge of them suddenly looked so uncomfortably warm.

"See you soon, then. Good night, ducky."

A strange noise preceded Sophie's response of, "Good night, dear."

Morton hung up the receiver. "All right, as you were," he said to the nearby men, who drifted away.

"Ducky?" queried Sergeant Gowers after the others had gone.

"Don't... It was because the operator might be listening and we can't go out there except in an emergency."

"I know all that, sir. It's just your choice of words took me aback a bit."

"What should I have said?"

"*Anything* else would have been better."

"Too late now, isn't it?"

Agnes of the Gardeners Arms knocked on Elizabeth's back bedroom door. She answered.

"There's a telephone call for you downstairs, Miss Woodhouse." Agnes was so visibly excited by the unusual occurrence of a guest receiving a call, it was as if the communication was from Buckingham Palace.

"I'll come right away," said Elizabeth, who was ready to go out apart from putting her hat on, which she now did.

"Were you expecting a call?" asked an inquisitive Agnes as they descended the stairs.

"I rather think I was," said Elizabeth.

"Oh?" said Agnes, wanting to pry further.

They arrived at a tiny office behind the bar. Reluctantly, Agnes gave Elizabeth some privacy.

"Hello?" said Elizabeth, and then listened, until she ended the call by saying, "In half an hour... Yes, goodbye."

Although Agnes had not listened in, she wore an expectant look and was nearby when Elizabeth emerged from the office.

"I'm going out," announced Elizabeth, buttoning her coat.

"What, now?" asked Agnes, aghast at the idea.

"Yes." Elizabeth swallowed hard. "A friend of mine has seen a tawny owl, so I'm going to have a look at it."

This declaration nearly rendered Agnes speechless. "You're going to see an owl? At noight? But they bring bad luck."

"Um... Not if you deliberately go to observe one. I shall have to be quick or I might miss it."

"Oh. We lock the doors at half-past eleven."

"I shouldn't be that long... Perhaps you have a key I could borrow?"

"A key? No, it's never come up before, so we don't give out keys. And my husband's loike clockwork, he is. He always has the door bolted by half-past."

"I don't wish to cause a disturbance, so I'll be back in time. Goodbye."

"Goodbye," said the mystified Agnes, addressing Elizabeth's retreating figure.

Sophie crept out of the house. It was a chill night under a half moon, and she pulled her coat close about her. There was no snow on the driveway, but it lay as a thin blanket everywhere else. This made it easier for her to see where she was going. As far as Sophie knew, Lord Stokely was still delivering his speech and, therefore, she hoped she was immune to discovery from departing guests. Her eyes adjusted to the low light as she crunched along on gravel where the snow had melted and the water had frozen again. She looked across a white wilderness of strange, lumpy forms. The trees several hundred yards away were invisible.

As she approached the still hidden road, Sophie noticed a soft yellow glow moving westward — Elizabeth, she hoped; but she would make sure first. Sophie hurried and risked turning on her torch to guide her steps. The pillars of the gateway set in the wall loomed ahead of her out of the dark. She could now hear an as yet unseen car and dashed for cover behind a gorse bush. The car slowed and its lights illuminated the gateway. As it turned into the drive, Sophie crouched lower. A big limousine drove in, its black shape blocking the snowy landscape beyond it. When it was a safe distance away, Sophie returned to the driveway, brushing snow off her coat. She heard a second car stop on the road, to her surprise, one with its lights off. A tiny voice floated to her, saying, "Miss King! It's me!" Sophie hurried towards Elizabeth.

"I followed that car," began Elizabeth, sitting in complete darkness, with the engine running, "but I took the precaution of switching off the lights so as not to give myself away. I know it's illegal, but I really had no choice, Miss King. I hope you're not cross with me."

"Absolutely not. I think you have done splendidly."

"Oh. Thank you."

Sophie could hear the blush and breathlessness in Elizabeth's voice. "Take this list of names to Inspector Morton as soon as you can." They groped in the dark to effect the transfer.

"I'll go at once," said Elizabeth. "I have the surrounding roads memorized, and I believe I can get back in time before I'm locked out."

"That is *such* a nuisance."

"Yes, but it's made everything all the more thrilling. I apologize, Miss King. I really have to go. May I purchase a torch for the office tomorrow?"

"Of course, you may. I should have thought of your need for one."

"I'm so sorry. I didn't mean to infer anything."

"Don't worry. You made a simple request for a necessity."

"Thank you. And I'll go to the library in Chertsey to study the habits of tawny owls. Goodbye."

"Goodbye and good luck."

Sophie stood back from the car to watch the dark shape until its lights came on as it drove away to Sunningdale. She returned to the house, wondering why Elizabeth had taken such an extraordinary interest in owls.

Stokely had finished speaking. The crowd knew it had heard something momentous and, in the hush that followed, hesitated before applauding, because what they had heard, and what had sunk into their hearts, seemed worthy of something beyond applause. Applause came nevertheless, and it was thunderous, accompanied by cheering. The Grand Salon had never before witnessed such a scene.

There was business to be done, however, and the occupants of the room broke into smaller groups, still energized by the speech.

"Lord Stokely," said Charles Pathé, "let me congratulate you on delivering such a stirring and patriotic address. Intelligent thinking, directness, and passion are an overwhelming combination."

"Thank you, monsieur. It is what I feel burning within me."

"You mentioned you will deliver a series of speeches soon. Send your itinerary to my office, and my cameras shall be there."

"You are too kind. I shall forever be in your debt." Stokely smiled, and he looked charmingly innocent.

Some guests, including Pathé and several bankers, began leaving shortly after eleven. Those who remained were Stokely loyalists, and the aides efficiently organized them into two groups by discreet whispers. The larger group entertained themselves in a drawing room. The smaller group, with Stokely among them, gathered into the smoking room that Sophie had investigated earlier.

"It seems we are not to be numbered amongst those of the inner sanctum," said Jeremy Rushton of the Albion News, after the division had taken place.

"That's a good thing, to my mind," said Jack Long of the London Mercury. "When he's decided what he wants done, we'll hear soon enough."

"I have heard a good few speeches in my time, but that was one of the best, if not *the* best." Rushton sipped his drink. "You know, I completely lost my objectivity and got caught up in the moment. If Stokely had said, 'Into the breech,' I wouldn't have hesitated; I would have vied to be first."

"And upon sober reflection?"

"He made some very good points. How about you?"

"Oh, I agree. Talking's one thing, and doing's another, though... I wonder how all this will play out?"

Of all the people present, only Auckland of the Times had not fully appreciated Stokely's speech. At least, it looked and sounded as though that were the case — the journalist had made certain comments to a few of his fellow-newspapermen. Afterwards, Auckland made a couple of attempts to speak to the earl privately, but always one of the young men deferentially and immovably prevented him from doing so. Without saying goodbye, the journalist left after eleven, having brought his own small car.

He set off and, driving at a reasonable speed, headed for London along the empty country road. After a mile or more, the lights of a vehicle appeared in the darkness behind him. After another mile, the car, a large one, was close behind, but not unduly so. The two vehicles continued on, passing some cottages and farms along the Holloway Hill road. A very short distance ahead lay the Guildford Road. As Auckland slowed his car to make a turn, the vehicle behind increased its speed. Auckland saw it come closer and closer until it inevitably collided. Instead of stopping, the second, heavier car pushed on, powering Auckland's car forwards. He struggled to brake, saw trees in front of him and, as a last resort, tried to turn. His car rolled over and smashed heavily into a tree, before ending up on its side. Two men got out of the second car — one carrying an iron bar and a lantern, and the other a can of petrol. They looked up and down the then empty Guildford road. The man with the iron bar peered through the smashed windshield. "Do it," he said. The other emptied the can of petrol inside the car. A third man, the driver, turned the big car, in readiness, northwards on the Guildford road. With the petrol ignited, the two men outside clambered back in, and the car sped away. Soon, Auckland's vehicle was engulfed in flames.

Inside the smoking room, Stokely's secretary, Vincent Cobden, handed out fifteen copies of a document to the people seated in comfortable chairs. Stokely addressed the room.

"Cobden here has done a splendid job of organization, as you will soon see from his report. You will work from a London office with a hand-picked staff to accommodate your requirements. Any questions?"

"Where will the offices be, my Lord?" A man at the back asked the question.

"A small hotel is being converted for your use. Where is it exactly, Cobden?"

"Suffolk Place, opposite St. Mary's Hospital, and near to Paddington Station, my Lord. The work is almost complete."

"That's fairly central. Our purpose is to form a government-in-waiting. To this end, we must recruit suitable allies both within the political sphere and, more importantly, influential people outside, so that when the time comes, we are ready. Dawkins will be in charge of security and Wilberforce of finance... Dr Rudd, you will be responsible for health and identification."

"That is most welcome news, my Lord," said the only woman present in the room.

"Good. You will all find your duties align with your talents. In the not too distant future, you will assume control of the civil service, to rebuild it into an efficient system. We aim for an orderly and swift transition, to allow new government policies to be implemented without delay. Clear communications are vital in this area. Shall we say a month for your initial reports on what needs to be done?" Stokely looked about, and everyone nodded in agreement. "Is that everything for now, Cobden?"

"There is the matter of remuneration, my Lord."

"Naturally, you will all be paid," said Stokely, smiling. "Read through the report and we'll meet again tomorrow to make any adjustments to the plan deemed necessary. That will be after the early morning shoot, of course. Who's turning out for it?"

There was a show of hands and some comments back and forth until Stokely said,

"Dr Rudd, do you not shoot?"

"No, my Lord."

"If you are not averse, accompany me tomorrow. I recently read a paper on the current state of thinking in eugenics, and would value your opinion upon its usefulness for Britain."

"It would be an honour, my Lord."

---

At the end of an exhausting day, a maidservant's day, seven women forgot their tiredness while partaking of a glorious midnight feast in front of a roaring fire in their dormitory.

"I don't know how you managed it," said Miss Beech, pushing her last piece of chicken around her plate so as not to miss the tiniest soupçon of Monsieur Fournier's sauce suprême. "I heard him shouting, and I wouldn't have gone near him for all the tea in China."

"I wonder how much tea there is in China?" asked Flora.

"I think there are over four hundred million people," said Sophie, "so that must represent a huge consumption of tea. Thousand upon thousands of tons."

"There you are, Miss Beech," said Flora, "It might be worth facing an irate French chef for all that amount of tea."

"You know what I meant, Miss Walton. It was a figure of speech." Miss Beech smiled. The appearance of unexpected food had completed the thaw of her icy reserve. "What I asked was, how did you manage it, Miss King?"

"Well, it helped that, underneath his rather flamboyant exterior, he's a decent man who appreciates a little recognition and a chance to be kind to others. Besides that, I learned from a great teacher, didn't I, Nancy?"

"I can't speak with me mouth full," said Ada, trying not to laugh, her hand covering her mouth because it *was* full.

"Sorry for catching you unawares," said Sophie.

"It's a shame about the others," said Fern. "Fancy working here and not getting enough to eat."

"I found out how they work around it," said Flora. "Someone, who shall remain nameless, bakes pasties and pies after Mrs Potter has finished for the day. These are then secretly distributed among the servants." With significance, Flora added. "Some of the meat and vegetables destined for Kemp and his men do *not* always arrive."

"Ooh," said Miss Beech. "Well, good for them, that's what I say."

"I agree," said Sophie.

"But wouldn't Mrs Potter notice if her stock was going down?" asked Ada. "I know I would."

"I didn't ask," said Flora.

"Perhaps she thinks Kemp's men help themselves and is too afraid to say anything," said Sophie.

"That must be it," said Ada.

"And as for Mrs Newnham, the housekeeper, she hasn't a clue."

"She's good-natured, really," said Fern. "Only she hates it here and doesn't know what to do. I thought about it, and I could see how I'd be the same."

"Does she want to leave?" asked Sophie.

"She doesn't talk much, miss, so I dunno. But I think she's in such a state of fright, she can't do *anything*."

"Yes, I saw that," said Sophie. "It must be hard when you come to think of it. Mrs Newnham took on a job for which she was qualified, yet found herself saddled with Kemp. I'm certain that when he interviewed her, he gave no hint of his real nature."

"I'm sure he didn't," said Miss Beech. "I'm equally sure Lady Stokely knows nothing of what goes on here. I think she would be horrified if she found out."

"She'd *definitely* be horrified," said Flora, thinking of Stokely's enormities, which comment earned a swift, warning glance from Sophie.

They ate pastries and talked. Miss Beech told the two maids in her charge to go to bed, as she did herself. The agents lowered their voices to barely above a whisper so as not to disturb the others.

"Anything else?" asked Sophie. Fern and Ada shook their heads.

"Lord Stokely is a tremendous speaker," said Flora. "He'd get my vote if I had one."

"What do you mean?" asked Sophie.

"Just that *if* I were voting, I'd vote for him no matter what the other candidates had to say. It's because he's so impassioned and dedicated." She lowered her voice further. "Of course, I wouldn't *actually* support him, knowing what we do. I can see how he's so popular, though. He says what everyone wants to hear and does it beautifully."

"I found him a bit like that, miss," said Ada.

"I didn't take to him," said Fern. "It was all about 'im, even though he never mentioned hisself once. Like one of them blokes at the fairground, who'll shout anything they can think of to get you to spend money on something you don't want."

"You're right, come to think of it," said Ada. "As soon as Stokely started talking, I said to myself, 'ere we go, it's goin' to be nothing but 'ot air. Then, the longer he spoke, the more

I listened, and I forgot who I was listening to, so I ended up thinking what he said was all right, even though at the back of my mind, I know he's a stinker."

"I haven't heard him speak," said Sophie. "The way you describe him brings a scripture to mind... The words of his mouth were smoother than butter, but war was in his heart."

"That suits him perfectly," said Flora.

"We'd better turn in," said Ada. "They're all shooting dicky birds early in the morning."

"That's horrible," said Fern.

"I don't like it, either," said Sophie.

"Ah! Why don't you tell us about the time *you* went hunting?" said Flora, smiling.

"No, it's too late for that," said Sophie.

"You've been 'unting, 'ave you, miss?" asked Ada.

"I see I have no choice. Very well. Come closer..., all of you." They moved in, and Sophie spoke in a whisper. "My Uncle Raymond lives in Scotland, and there's a very long story attached to *why* he's there. Anyway, he lives in a small castle with a lot of land, and is, in a sense, the laird, although he's English. Tormodden Castle is actually his *wife's* family seat, and Uncle Raymond is a justice of the peace. We've stayed at the castle numerous times. One thing you should understand is that Uncle Raymond no longer *sounds* English. He's immersed himself in the life there and sounds as Scottish as they come, and you can't tell him apart from a true Scot. He insists he's lost the ability to speak like an Englishman. I think that's all nonsense, but he's adamant about it. The local population has a great respect for him, because he has their interests at heart.

"Tormodden is set in a wild country of lowering crags and windswept hills, and icy streams tumbling down through dark forests to join rivers in the glens. Highland cattle wander about and game abounds. There are salmon and trout in the streams and deer in the woods. One summer, when I was fifteen and at a loose end, I considered hunting. I couldn't bear to kill anything, but I could see that tracking quarry over hills and through forests must be exciting in its way. I decided I would *pretend* to hunt a deer. I dressed warmly, because it can be cool in the summer when the wind blows. Then, secretly, I took a shotgun down from the wall in Uncle Raymond's study. I made sure both barrels were unloaded and crept out of the house with it.

"I walked for miles without finding a thing to hunt. Not even a rabbit to creep up on. It was most irritating. There I was, the intrepid huntress, empty shotgun at the ready, and all the animals had scurried away, no doubt to watch from their hiding places, laughing. I gave up my hunt and returned.

"On the way back, and now quite close to the castle, I followed a path which entered a small forest on the estate. The air was sweet, and it was pretty inside, with the sunlight streaming through the trees. The path, quite overgrown in places, ran beside a stream. At a certain spot, I suddenly came upon two very rough-looking men who were fishing. They were using hand-lines, so I knew they weren't guests. I stared at them, and they stared back. One of them said something and stood up. I couldn't understand him, but he sounded gruff and dangerous to me. Stupidly, I said, 'What are you doing?' I was only fifteen, remember? The other one got up. He spoke, while pulling in his handline. Poachers! The thought scared me. Then, without thinking, I pointed the shotgun at them. The first one said something more. I thought he was threatening me, so I pulled a hammer back as if I meant to shoot. Guess what they did?"

"What did they do?" asked Fern.

"They put their hands in the air and surrendered. I *couldn't* have been more astonished. The only course of action to take that I could think of was to march them back to the castle and have Uncle Raymond deal with them. So that's what we did, walking in single file. The two poachers were in front while I nervously hoped they didn't discover the shotgun was empty.

"When close to Tormodden, I felt relieved it was all over

and started feeling a shade pleased with myself. A surprised servant ran to fetch Uncle Raymond when we appeared at the door. My uncle came outside and, to my extreme horror, he began laughing. He inspected the shotgun and laughed even louder and showed it to the two men. Uncle Raymond then started speaking in the local dialect, and the two men answered him. I didn't understand a single word they said as they went back and forth. He then gave them half-a-crown each. They tugged at their caps, smiled awkwardly, glared at me, and walked off. It turns out he knew the men well and employed them often. He had allowed them to fish on his property as long as they only took what they needed for their families and sold nothing, which, he said later, they never had. My uncle also promised the men that neither he nor I would tell a soul I had captured them. This was to preserve their reputations. It was all *most* embarrassing, and I hid in my room, *absolutely* mortified."

# Chapter 17

# Shoot

More snow had fallen overnight and, although Friday had dawned grey and cloudy, the sky began clearing around eight, producing a drop in temperature.

Ten local men, beaters carrying sticks, were outside at the end of the east wing. They stamped heavy boots on flagstones to keep warm and their breath was visible in the air. Kemp and another man met them, accompanied by a small pack of six eager dogs from the kennels. There were two springer spaniels, a cocker spaniel, two labradors and a retriever. As soon as Kemp stopped, the small cocker spaniel wanted to wander and had to be recalled twice by Kemp's sharp whistle. A minute later, three other men emerged from the house to join the group. All were dressed in layers of old, heavy clothing, with woollen hats or caps with earflaps, gloves, scarves, and gaiters or puttees.

Of those present, Kemp was the tallest — a rangy man, with a loose-limbed, slouching walk. Kemp carried a shotgun broken over his arm. "Put that red scarf inside your coat," he said to one man. "Right. This is the last shoot for partridge and pheasant this season. When his lordship and his party come out, you'll go up the hill a quarter mile to that ridge and form the line there. Drive towards the road. Keep the line dead straight and dead slow at all times and let the dogs flush out the birds. You'll have five with you, and I'll have some on the gun line with me and the pickers-up. There won't be any outside dogs. Do this right, boys, and I'll be happy. So will his lordship, and that'll be good for all of us."

He gave more directions. When he had finished, he left the group with only the cocker spaniel following him.

Sophie loathed the idea of the organized destruction to come. However, she had no choice but to fulfill her duties. Working with several other servants, she carried trays of sandwiches and bottles of drink to the Steward's Room on the ground floor of the east wing. The long, low-ceilinged, comfortable room was decked out with hunting paraphernalia and there were framed hunting prints lining the wood-panelled walls. The door to the grounds had three windows on each side. In the centre of the room was a heavy oak table, covered with an old, marked green baize cloth. Laid out in two rows on top were a variety of scrupulously cleaned and polished shotguns and a pile of ammunition boxes. Lying in the centre of a row on a strip of purple cloth lay a pair of matched shotguns with rose and scroll-style engravings on the plates. Sleek, because the hammers were hidden, the well-balanced guns with their flamed walnut stocks looked expensive. Undoubtedly, these were Stokely's guns.

From her tray, she took covered plates of sandwiches to put onto a side table against the wall. Upon returning to the kitchen, Sophie passed the open door of a nearby room. In it were folding chairs and various boxes that were obviously about to be moved outside. The room was half full of odds and ends. On one wall, old coats and jackets were hanging on a long row of hooks. She passed by the room but then began to frown, and finally stopped abruptly to retrace her steps, because something had caught her attention. She looked in again. A couple of hooks in, along the row, she saw a rough, old jacket hung outermost on top of several other garments.

What had drawn her back was the inch-wide, shiny grease mark on its collar. Sophie's mouth opened in disbelief. She was sure it was the jacket she had seen worn by the Fleet Street murderer, although it was perhaps foolhardy for her to feel certain unless the same man put it on. The noise of someone coming made her move away. It was only another maidservant about her own age, but Sophie did not want to be found being overly curious about old clothing. The two young women talked while returning to the kitchen together to bring out more food to the Steward's Room.

"Who lives in the east wing?" asked Sophie.

"Apart from guests, that'd be the footmen and Kemp's men. Sometimes in the summer gardeners and labourers stay temporary."

"And on which floors are the servants?"

"Ground, second, and attics. Why? Do you have a beau among 'em?" The maid giggled.

"No, I do not!"

"You'd be mad if you did. They're a slovenly lot for the most part... But there's a few of them what go up to London often, and a couple o' them look tolerable, but I'm not sure any of 'em are decent. None of them go to church, but they'll go to the pub fast enough."

"It sounds as though *you* have your eye on one."

"No. I have a fiancé, I do. I'm only doing this work until Lady Day and them I'm finished here. This place is not run properly. They axed me to work another quarter, but I said, no, I wouldn't."

"When are you getting married?" asked Sophie.

"July. And my husband-to-be will inherit a farm one day. So then I'll be a farmer's wife. How about that?"

"I hope you'll be very happy."

"That's kind of you. It's true I'm looking forward to the day, and not just to get out of here."

Sophie smiled and could not help but think of her own situation. Sinjin Yardley came to mind with some fondness, quickly followed by Inspector Morton's use of the word 'ducky', which nearly made her laugh outright.

She returned to the Steward's Room, carrying more food, passing the now closed door of the room in which she was interested. Careful not to be seen, and waiting for an opportune moment, on the way back she opened the door, intent upon searching the jacket. She was too late. The jacket had gone, which could only mean that the man who owned it was present. The danger she had formerly perceived as a remote possibility was now acute and imminent. Sophie hurried away, uncertain what to do about this discovery. However, she had no time even for thought just then, because of the mountain of tasks to be accomplished before the guests ate, and ate again, at lunch, and at tea, and at dinner.

---

Inspector Morton had relayed the names of the guests, with accompanying notes, to Scotland Yard. With nothing to do in the village hall, he was looking over the report again, only this time he studied Sophie's handwriting, trying to deduce if her penmanship revealed anything about her character. The words were, as he had found with most ladies' handwriting, neatly and regularly formed, but that told him nothing as to what she was thinking. Sergeant Gowers broke into his reverie.

"Are we going to do the exercises now, sir? Or shall we save them for later so we can get *really* enthusiastic?"

"You're a right comedian."

"But you're not laughing, sir."

"Don't you know any proper jokes?"

"Only a few, and they're not very good. Do you?"

"No... Come to think of it, I'm also horrible at telling a story."

"I'm not too bad at that. What about poetry?"

"Come off it." Morton wrinkled his nose.

"Singing?"

"Now, I'm all right there, and when I'm in a group, but not a solo," said Morton.

"I think I sing a little off key," said Gowers. "At least that's what somebody told me once, but I've never let it stop me... Actually, I really enjoy singing."

"There's a piano in the corner. I bet one of these chaps can play it."

"Bartlett plays piano. He can sight read, too, and there's sheet music in the office."

"Bartlett!" shouted Morton.

In Ottershaw, the word had gone about that Miss Elizabeth Banks was an eccentric, but probably harmless as long as she found birds and animals to study. Elizabeth was unaware that she and the car she drove were now famous and the very latest thing in the village. Bert at the garage smiled and waved to her as she went off to town. Elizabeth was extraordinarily happy with life at present. Her only concern was whether Nick was looking after her cats properly. She reassured herself that he was and also hoped he remembered to lock the door when he left each evening.

As often as she could, Sophie watched from windows in different rooms, searching for the man in the old, greasy jacket. When she finally saw the jacket, it came as a surprise to find that Alfie Tanner was wearing it somewhat peculiarly over a raincoat. He was working behind the gun line, so she hurried to find her own coat to go out and talk to him.

It was cold, and Sophie shivered. Shotguns thumped nearby as they spoke.

"It's like this, miss," said Alfie. "They told me first thing I was to work out here and I'd only brought a raincoat with me, 'cause me only overcoat is a bit too shabby for this place. It's freezing, so I asked if they had an overcoat I could borrow. They didn't, but had some old jackets. This one looked the warmest, but it smells. I didn't want to mess up me raincoat, so I wore it over the top. Better to be warm even if I do look stupid. Know what I mean, miss?"

"I understand, perfectly. Who gave it to you?"

"Big chap named John. Youngish, and always hangs about with Kemp... That's him over there."

Sophie turned to look

"I've met him... Was there anything in the pockets?"

"Just rubbish, which I chucked away. An old bus ticket..."

"How old was the ticket?"

"Years old, I'd say. There was a cigarette that had fallen to pieces, a bit of string... That's about it."

"Thank you, Alfie. I'd better get back."

"So had I, miss."

Within a few minutes of her going inside, a police car arrived. The local constabulary, to whom the car belonged, was rather in awe of the nobility at Chertsey Park and so parked off the drive and well away so as not to disturb the earl's shoot near the house. A sergeant and a constable got out to walk the hundred yards to the entrance. Soon they were interviewing Mr Dalgleish. They informed him that Mr Auckland of the Times had been in a nasty accident and had died of his injuries at the scene. Auckland's family had informed the police that he had been a dinner guest at Chertsey Park. It was a routine enquiry into an accident. The motorist had missed a turn in the dark and overturned his car, which then burst into flames. They considered that was all there was to it. The police simply asked what time Mr Auckland had left, which Dalgleish answered. They then asked for confirmation that Auckland was alone in the car and whether any other vehicles had departed at the same time. Dalgleish said he would enquire and let them know by telephone. Although shocked by the news, Dalgleish maintained his dignity, mentioning that Lord Stokely would be greatly saddened by the dreadful occurrence, while adding his own condolences.

The news of Auckland's death spread through the house. Dalgleish informed a member of Stokely's staff, and so those outside soon learned of what had happened the previous night. After hearing of the tragedy, Sophie became suspicious. She met Flora and then Ada at different times and told them of the accident and about the jacket. Ada and Sophie were again setting the Grand Dining Room, only this time it was for luncheon. New guests were due to arrive mid-afternoon and onwards.

"Are you certain it's the same jacket?" asked Ada, as she arranged a place setting.

"Almost a hundred per cent. If it is, then one of Kemp's men wore it when he killed the man near Fleet Street. It also means the whole Red Fist business is Stokely's doing... Watch out. Others are coming."

They continued working as more items were brought for the table by several maids, because all the footmen were still outside. When alone again, they resumed their conversation.

"Did you see the papers? Them Red Fists struck again last night."

"Oh, no."

"Yes. It was on the front page. They firebombed an 'ouse with the people inside. The fire spread and six 'ouses went up in flames. No one died, but there were two injured. One was a fireman. Them bloody Red Fists want stopping, they do an' all. Anarchists and Communists, the paper said. I never knew they could get something so wrong. It makes my blood boil. The real anarchist is outside shooting little birds. Somebody should shoot 'im!"

"Nancy, shh. You must keep it down."

"Sorry, miss. But all them people lost their 'omes. And for what, I ask you? Because he's bloomin' wicked."

"Where was this outrage perpetrated?"

"Coventry."

"Oh... The distance makes it unlikely it was anyone we've

seen so far. However, they might arrive this afternoon."

"I'll tell the others to keep a lookout," said Ada, who had regained her temper.

"What do you think about Mr Auckland's death?"

"It missed the papers... I dunno. Could be an accident."

"He was at our table yesterday evening, but not in one of our sections, and to think he's gone... Did you notice him at all?"

"Not really. I know who you mean, though. He was on the opposite side to mine... I didn't see him talking much."

"I would imagine journalists are quite glib and loquacious as a rule. Perhaps he was the exception."

"So are you thinking, Stokely 'ad 'im done in?"

"Yes, I am. They might have sabotaged his car to make it crash."

"Like the brakes, you mean? I read that in a story, once. The 'ero was driving to rescue the woman he loved. The villains had 'er tied up in an old farmhouse and were threatening to kill 'er unless she told them where the jewels were kept. While they're doing that, he's driving along this road on the cliffs at top speed, but has to brake and swerve to miss a body lying in the road. Nothing 'appens when he brakes, because another villain had sawed through 'em, which the 'ero didn't know nothing about. So there he is, 'eading full speed for a fence on the cliff's edge, and that's all there is between 'im and certain death. That's what the story was called, Certain Death."

"What happened?"

"I dunno, miss. It was in an old magazine, and I never found the next installment. Very annoying, 'though I s'pose he got out of it somehow."

"I would be annoyed, too."

"If a car's all burnt, could the police tell if someone fiddled with the brakes?"

"Elizabeth might know... Wait a moment. I have an idea. I've oiled and greased all sorts of things on Rabbit's two brake systems and the rods used are quite thick... Silly me. It's even *much* simpler than that. Mr Auckland had to brake and steer to turn onto the road when he left Chertsey Park. If his brakes *or* steering didn't work, he would have crashed on the road outside."

"Oh... Does that mean all that stuff about brakes in Certain Death was rubbish?"

"It might."

"Somehow, that makes me feel better. But let's say they didn't fix Mr Auckland's car. 'Ow'd they work it?"

"I really don't know. But think of this. If they meant to kill him, they wouldn't have left anything to chance. Even if the brakes or steering were sabotaged to fail *eventually*, they could have gone at anytime, and while at low speed. The saboteurs must have done something completely different, of which we're unaware. I'll consult with Elizabeth on the matter."

"Mr Auckland was with the Times," mused Ada. "Why would they invite him to dinner and then kill him afterwards?"

Sophie stopped setting the table. "I hadn't thought of that aspect." She started working again. "Yes, why? They could have killed him anywhere, come to think of it."

"Then I reckon Stokely took against him right 'ere, at this very table.... Godfathers."

"I believe you've hit upon it... Ooh! How about Mr Auckland discovered a secret detrimental to Stokely's plans or of a threatening nature? Stokely tried to get him on side, or bribe him, or whatever. Mr Auckland refused, and that... was the end of him."

"It must be something like that, miss. It's all getting a bit too much, if you ask me... It's ridiculous. Stokely's right here. We know all this about him, and the police can't touch him; don't even know to touch him, except a few of them do. If a nipper in the East End stole a loaf of bread, the Old Bill would be on him in a flash. The world's mad, that it is."

"It is unfair... The real difference is that Stokely works

carefully and in secret. If he also stole a loaf of bread, the police *would* go after him then."

"Only he'd give a couple of quid to make them go away."

"Probably."

It did not take them much longer to finish laying the table.

"This looks so lovely," said Ada. "I would never think to 'ave yellow on a plate, but seeing it laid out like this, I've changed my mind completely."

"Would that be for your future cottage?" Since carrying in the first stack of luncheon plates, Sophie had been admiring the pale yellow and white Worcester porcelain with its simple rustic scenery.

Ada laughed. "I 'ope so."

The calm derived from the routine in the elegant dining room dissipated as soon as they left to find Mr Dalgleish. He was one of the few male servants remaining inside the house, therefore all enemies and threats were outside and the noble house seemed the better for their absence. The shooting had stopped and, when they failed to find Dalgleish, Sophie and Ada went their separate ways — Ada to do work and cover when possible for Sophie, while Sophie herself hoped to observe the men coming in from outside.

From an empty bedroom on the second floor in the east wing, Sophie had a foreshortened view of the returning men below. Most of the guests clustered around Stokely, who was in high spirits. It was difficult to tell who was who, as everyone was bundled up and wearing headgear, but she knew the one woman present, she who was a doctor. The people stood out starkly upon the trampled snow of that part of the gun line nearest to the house. Among them, she picked out Dawkins, tall and aloof, as though he did not belong, yet he carried a shotgun. A few men and dogs were still working the snow-laden heath. Broadbent-Wicks was one of them. Muffled with a scarf, his bowler hat and overcoat suitable for the streets of London seemed incongruous in the rough open ground.

The beaters were coming off the heath in a ragtag way. Sophie identified him at once, even though she was viewing him from the front for the first time. He was one of the better-dressed beaters. The quality of his warm, green hunting jacket was evident even at a distance. From high-up, his full-fleshed, thirty-year-old face was unremarkable, except he unexpectedly had a heavy moustache. It was his unvarying and unyielding walk across gaps in the heath that set him apart; that is, set him apart for Sophie. There was nothing outlandish in his gait, but she had studied it exclusively on Fleet Street until his little idiosyncrasies of walk were all that she could remember him by. Worried, and with her heart pounding, it took a minute to control herself sufficiently to go and investigate.

# Chapter 18

# A strange dance

Kemp and several of his men were busy taking care of shotguns and ammunition, returning them to the Gun Room. The Steward's Room was noisy, packed with animated, ruddy-faced, bright-eyed, laughing men, who excitedly recounted their morning's exploits. They warmed themselves by the fire or with drinks. The flagstones were wet wherever the soft melting snow slipped from their caked boots. The corridor outside was busy with those on errands or employed in packing away items. Sophie stood by a staircase at the end of the corridor and could get no closer without discovery. She glimpsed her man only once, but he entered a room, and did not re-emerge.

Then, carrying his bowler hat, yet still in his overcoat, Broadbent-Wicks slowly came towards her, but he was walking oddly. She stepped back, puzzled. He came around the corner.

"Ah," he said. "Good morning, Miss King."

"Good morning. Are you all right?" She asked, because he looked so stiff and uncomfortable.

"No. My ears hurt. From the cold."

"Dear me, they're bright red... Take your gloves off and put your hands over them."

"But my hands are freezing."

"Oh... Um..." She looked into the corridor to see if anyone was coming. "Stand still." She reached up and put her hands over his ears.

"Ahh!" He looked horrified at the pressure of her palms gently cupping his ears.

"There's no frostbite that I can see." She then realized the enormity of how close she was to him.

In this awkward and rather intimate arrangement, Broadbent-Wicks began appreciating the setting, especially as his ears were coming back to life. He smiled. Sophie saw this and, increasingly embarrassed that she was holding a man's ears and almost embracing him while doing so, let go the same moment.

"I think that's enough," she said abruptly. "Warm them slowly, and don't rub or they'll come off."

"How tremendous of you. My ears feel much better, thanks. You're a lifesaver. Well, ear-saver, what...? By the way," He lowered his voice, "what are you doing here in this area of the house?"

"I'm tracking a man. Please go. I'm sure you're wanted elsewhere."

"Which man?" He frowned as he spoke and turned his head slightly towards the Steward's Room.

"Mr Ely, please go away." As he didn't move, she added, "It's one of the beaters, if you *must* know."

"Oh... I rather thought as much. I forbid it."

"I beg your pardon?"

"I forbid that you watch the beaters. They're uncouth and an altogether disgusting lot of foul-mouthed brutes."

"Nevertheless, I shall watch them, and you must go."

"If it is necessary to observe them, I shall watch on your behalf."

"For goodness' sake. What *is* the matter with you?"

"I have no wish to cause offence, Miss King. Absolutely none. But it is far beneath your dignity as a lady, and you're an awfully fine one, to even observe such men as these."

"Tosh! We will discuss it later, when I shall set the matter straight. For now, and incredibly, there is a modicum of sense in what you say. I can't get close enough to those men to ascertain very much, whereas you *can* with relative ease. The beater wearing the smart green hunting jacket is the one in whom I'm interested. He has a moustache, and…"

"That sounds like Miller."

"You've met him?"

"We've spoken several times, and he's one of the better behaved ones, as it happens. A quiet chap, who has a room near mine. I say mine, but I share it with another fellow, and, of course, I don't actually *own* the room. What has he done to attract your interest?"

"Ah. I'm not sure. Um, just find out all you can… But whatever you do, *don't* go overboard. Keep it normal and stick to ordinary topics. Don't talk about important or secret matters, or *anything* about Stokely."

"Miss King, I assure you, I shan't be blithering like a complete idiot where Miller is concerned. Do you believe he's a spy?"

"Not necessarily. I think he might be of a violent nature, though. So *do* be careful."

"Don't worry, I will not upset him and will just talk normally, as instructed. But I'll keep my beady eye on him."

"I hear someone coming."

A sound came from the corridor, and Sophie ran up the stairs to get out of sight. Broadbent-Wicks walked slowly after her while removing a glove. He gingerly touched an ear with an icy finger.

The unceasing round of servants' work continued, pausing only for meals prepared by Mrs Potter and her staff. To those of Lyall Place and Burgoyne's, these meals, besides having a minimally nutritious value, produced a blank bewilderment among the eaters as to how Mrs Potter could be relied upon to alter ordinary food to such an extent as to make it unrecognizable or tasteless. It was noon, and the second sitting in the servants' dining room. Burgoyne's Agency, except for Mr Broadbent-Wicks, sat at one end of the table.

"I believe I've found a piece of beef," said Flora, poking about in a bowl of watery stew. "Why is it so pale?"

"No, that's fish, isn't it?" said Ada, who, while staring into a similar bowl, sniffed at it. "Smells fishy."

"I'm not having none of it," said Fern.

"We shall have to live on bread and butter," said Sophie. "After this is over, we'll go to a lovely restaurant and stuff ourselves silly."

"That sounds more like it," said Alfie. "I've had worse than this, though. During the war, I reckon some army cooks were working for the Germans. They were sent to demoralize us, which they did."

"Poor Alfie," said Flora. "How about this idea? We'll ask Elizabeth to bring us a food parcel."

"Although risky, it's a good thought." Sophie looked at her watch. "Probably too late for today. Everyone put in a request, but please, don't ask for anything that spoils."

"Digestives and a bar of chocolate." "Wensleydale cheese and pickled onions." "Blackcurrant jam tarts and clotted cream."

"No! Not like that," said Sophie. "One at a time and keep it simple. The parcel has to be brought in surreptitiously. Gladys, jam tarts with cream are completely out of the question."

After some lively discussion, they produced a sensible list.

"I noticed Mr Dalgleish gets better food than what we do," said Fern.

"I'm glad he does," said Sophie.

She was about to say more, but the noise of several men entering the servants' dining room brought a halt to all conversation. They sat down at the other end of the table, and their loud, raucous talking dispelled the congenial, homey atmosphere of the room.

"They're putting me off my stew," whispered Flora, making the others smile.

Kemp, Miller, and two more also sat down. Sophie felt very uncomfortable from the moment she saw Miller. It was tense and difficult enough at Chertsey Park, so she had not told the others of his being the Fleet Street murderer. The last thing she wanted, and what she was certainly struggling with now, was for all her friends to stare at the man, wondering what a murderer did and said in an ordinary setting and, thereby, to give themselves away.

"I think we should be goin', miss," said Ada, quickly, even though their break was not over.

"We may as well," said Sophie.

They stood up and began collecting their plates. Someone called from the other end.

"Don't go, girls! You brighten the place up."

The room became silent. The men stared, smirking and whispering, while the Burgoyne staff, on edge, cleared their part of the table with downcast eyes. Two maids entered with food for the men. As Sophie and her staff left, a burst of vulgar laughter followed them out.

"I'm sorry about that, miss," said Alfie, as they walked to the kitchen. "There's a couple of 'em who want a good clout, and no mistake."

"They most certainly do. They make it all so unseemly."

The agency staff left their plates with the dishwashers. Once away from the kitchen, and after Alfie had gone, Sophie asked,

"Have any of you been bothered by those?"

"One of 'em said something nasty to me," said Fern.

"I've escaped so far," said Flora.

"I haven't said nothing, 'cause of the situation. But oh, *yes*," said Ada. "About an hour ago it was. If one of them geezers don't watch himself, I'll cosh him, I will an' all."

"Try not to," said Sophie. "I know it's awful, but find me

immediately if anything happens again, and we'll see what steps can be taken. Otherwise, avoid them completely. It's only another two and a half days. Hopefully, they won't be about the house except at mealtimes."

"I won't cause no trouble, miss."

"Which one was it? Not that I know any of them."

"A little weasely git who thinks too much of 'isself... Sorry, miss."

"I don't know that one. I'll tell Mr Dalgleish, but I fear he cannot do anything."

"Then there's no point in telling him," said Flora.

"Best drop it, miss," said Ada. "I'd really rather have some food."

"Ooh. If they're all in there eating, I can use the telephone. I'll give Elizabeth the list and arrange a meeting for tonight. Hopefully, she can bring something."

They went their various ways, with Sophie heading to the ground floor of the west wing. She walked by the now deserted Steward's room in the east wing, then passed through a tunnel that lay below the steps of the entrance hall to come out in the west wing. It was empty, as she had hoped. Quickening her steps, she arrived at the butler's room, as she thought of it. She opened the door and received a shock. Broadbent-Wicks was sitting on a table eating a sandwich. He stood up, sandwich in hand, and then picked up a plate piled high with them.

"I say, Miss King, would you like one? They're jolly good. Beef this side, chicken the other." He offered her the plate.

"Ah, yes, I would, thank you." She took one. "Why are you in here?"

"It's nice and quiet. I was watching friend Miller, who is very boring, don't you know, and I overheard one of Kemp's men say there should be a lot of food left over after this morning's shindig. Miss King, I put two and two together. I considered the beaters would descend upon the food as a plague of locusts and, if I were going to supplement the rather meagre rations, I'd have to get in ahead of them. Therefore, I took the initiative. While the guests were present, I entered the Steward's Room. It's remarkable when you think of it. That a chap can just stand there saying absolutely nothing and it's considered normal behaviour. So I stood there, doing nothing."

"Did anyone remark upon your presence?" asked Sophie.

"Yes, and no. I only spoke to Lord Stokely. Ah! Before you say anything, let me rephrase that. He spoke to me, and then I answered, and we had a jolly old chinwag."

"What on *earth* did you say?"

"He had been talking to all the chaps and then came to get something more to eat. He said, 'I remember you. Guarding the food?' He had a sort of glint in his eye, probably because he was thinking of his birthday cake. To which I replied, 'My lord, I am observing the depletion of your sandwiches with trepidation.'"

"You *didn't* say that?" Sophie was stunned.

"Yes, I did."

"What did he say?"

"He laughed like anything, while I kept a straight face. Then he said, 'We'll be gone soon, so I think you're safe. Tell me, do you have an opinion on the current government?'"

"Oh, *no*," said Sophie.

"To which I replied, 'It is always to be hoped that the government does well by the nation, my Lord. However, I fear the current coalition government needs a better vision.' I said all that guff, because it's the sort of guff he's always saying. Then he said, 'Yes, it does. What's your name?' I told him, and then he said, 'What's a fellow like you doing as a servant?' So I said, 'I must work, my Lord. Jobs are scarce, and I find I'm quite suited to this occupation.' Of course, I didn't mention I was *spying* on him as well. He wouldn't like to hear *that* sort of thing."

"Did it cross your mind to say it?"

"No, I don't believe it did."

"If it had, would you have said so?"

"I doubt it. You told me not to, for one thing. Besides, what would be the point of spying on a chap, only to go and blurt out that's what you're doing? That doesn't make sense, Miss King."

"What else?"

"He said, 'Yes,' while putting a sandwich on his plate. 'You'll allow me this one, Ely?' I said, 'My Lord is always free to take what pleases him.' For some reason, which I cannot understand, he laughed like anything, wagged a finger at me, and toddled off. Anyway, they all bundled out of the room a few minutes later, and I rescued a plate of sandwiches from Kemp's minions. I'm saving a few for Alfie... Oh. What are you ladies doing about food? Please, I insist you take the plate."

"Thank you, but please keep your spoils of war. We're getting by... Mr Ely, you must continue to be careful. Avoid interactions as much as you possibly can."

"Most certainly. I shouldn't have gone for the sandwiches... Something of interest. They're all going to roll up their shirtsleeves this afternoon and get down to business in the ballroom. They're going to organize all sorts of things."

"Give an example."

"I mostly heard snippets, but one gentleman was bleating to another something about identity papers and the importance of controlling serial numbers. The other said the papers should contain fingerprints and photographs. Then the first fellow said costs had to be kept down. It sounded very boring, but then some chaps like that sort of thing."

"How puzzling."

"And Stokely bagged the most birds."

"That doesn't surprise me. Did you find out anything about Miller?"

"Not directly, because he disappeared for a long time. What I observed is that he and two others form Kemp's inner circle, so to speak."

Sophie gasped as a thought came to her. "Show me where

to find his bedroom."

"You mean right now? Shall I bring the sandwiches?"

Broadbent-Wicks, plate in hand, stood guard on the landing, while Sophie searched Miller's small bedroom. It contained a single bed, a wardrobe, a chest of drawers, and a chair that served as a nightstand. The bedclothes were pulled up, rather than the bed being properly made. Underneath were two pairs of shoes and a suitcase, which she pulled out. The case was dusty and unlocked. Careful not to disturb even the dust, she found summer clothes inside and, rather than waste time rummaging through, she put the case back.

Hanging in the wardrobe were a good suit, two well-made shirts, two raincoats — one reversible and expensive, an ordinary overcoat, a jacket, and three pairs of trousers over the same piece of bent wire. Hats and gloves were on the top shelf, ties and scarves hung from a bar on the door. An expensive pair of shoes, a pair of wellingtons, and another suitcase, which proved to be empty, lay on the floor of the wardrobe.

She had left the chest of drawers to last, because she found the idea of rooting through drawers full of men's smalls quite distasteful. The top drawer contained a miscellany, including handkerchiefs, a shaving kit, a cigar cutter, and a corkscrew. A short note from someone named Betty Leach of Crescent Road, Woolwich, asked Albert — Miller, presumably — to visit soon, when he had a chance, but to give her a couple of days' warning, because Fred had been poorly recently. There was no accompanying envelope, but the letter looked recent. The next drawer down was full of shirts. The third drawer was what she dreaded the most. In the fourth drawer was a large knife, a short leaded stick, a Webley revolver, boxes of cartridges, and lying carelessly on top of these were papers which she did not even need to unfold — approximately ten Red Fist handbills. She took one.

Sophie was leaving, on the point of shutting the door quietly, when she heard Broadbent-Wicks pipe up.

"I say, Miller. Fancy a sandwich?"

She heard footfalls ascending the stairs as she began tip-toeing away.

"Nah, mate. I'm full up."

"Are you sure? These are jolly good. They're left over from..."

Sophie heard no more, because she was around a corner and hurrying down a corridor towards another staircase, determined to make her telephone call to Elizabeth. Several things crossed her mind. Miller was a Londoner, but not a cockney. His wardrobe showed signs of older impoverishment and more recent access to funds. Another thing was that only Broadbent-Wicks could make standing about by a staircase with a plate of sandwiches seem normal.

---

The Ballroom that could accommodate fifty revolving and sweeping couples, with space for a hundred to watch them, had been converted into a working area. In this room of mirrors, tables, spaced at wide intervals, now covered two-thirds of the floor. Sixty men and a woman, separated into small working groups, hammered out the frameworks of policy and procedure that a government-in-waiting would need if it were suddenly called upon to govern. They did not create out of thin air, but worked according to mandates, guidelines, and timetables designed for their specific areas of interest. Standing and watching this hive of industry, Vincent Cobden, Lord Stokely's secretary, smiled with satisfaction. The inspiration and overall design of how New Britain would look when the changes were accomplished came from the mind of Lord Stokely. But the nuts, bolts, girders, and mechanics for such a feat of engineering were fabricated by Cobden. He watched with pleasure as the assembly of his juggernaut began. There was much work to do, but it had truly started. At the end of Britain's current age, this revitalizing machine would roll forth, destroying all in its path, to become the one true idol of the nation. Stokely would pilot the machine, but Cobden would oversee that it functioned correctly and according to plan.

At one table, the guidelines for government communication were being studied by six newspapermen, only two of whom were from Fleet Street. The others were British nationals from Australia, South Africa, India, and Canada. Jack Long was the chairman. For over an hour, they discussed how the government could best keep the nation informed. The principal question was, would the announcements and reports come through a government-run newspaper, or be fed to carefully selected newspapers? They early on decided that a free publication was necessary, if they went with a government-run paper.

"Looks like we've touched bottom on the matter. I suggest we take a ten-minute break," said Long. "We'll come back to vote, and see where we land." He pointed at a prominent sign. "As there's no smoking in here, I suggest that those of you who do follow my example."

Long got up and headed for an exit. Jeremy Rushton followed and caught up with him.

"I didn't know you smoked," said Long.

"I don't, usually. Can I beg one from you?"

Long offered him his case containing small cigars. "They're quite mild." They lit their cigars.

"What do you make of all this?" asked Rushton.

"I'm as surprised as anyone."

"But it smacks of treason," said Rushton.

"No, I wouldn't say that. It's all in the materials — about how what's being done here is to prepare a contingency plan to be implemented only in case of an emergency." Long blew out a stream of smoke. "Such as a communist revolution, when the government's down and out for some reason. Under those circumstances, this makes sense."

"I read it, too... If it were just a few of us in a room, thrashing out the matter, that's one thing. But look at everyone here. They're all doing the same as we are. It's far too organized to be dismissed as anything but a serious undertaking."

"Look, the way I see it is that it's *his* money, and he spends it how he likes. His doing this is the same as building that type of entrance hall with all the statues. It's a grandiose gesture, nothing more."

"I think it's darker than that. For example, what we're discussing amounts to little more than facilitating government propaganda. If it's to be a government paper, then the independent press will not have access to it until everyone else does, and circulation will drop. We'll be forced to report days later when interest has waned. Conversely, if a few newspapers are selected, then they will become puppets, or they'll lose the franchise."

"Oh, I agree with you. We're all Stokely men here, so guess who'll get the franchise? Anyway, what's the best we can do? Resign? He'll find someone else. You've got a conscience...? They can be rather expensive sometimes. But I honestly believe all this is just show. Some of it's for us, some of it's for future use when he's attacking the government. He wants to be a statesman, and this is his way of going about it. I'll show myself loyal, but he can't bring off a coup. It's impossible. Come on, Rushton. Surely you can see that?"

"It is extreme, I agree. But these are turbulent times. Suppose Stokely's posturing is actually real? Just suppose for a moment that he really intends the overthrow of the government. Surely he would do the very things we see happening here today."

"I don't disagree with you. For example, how is it possible

for him to control all the people in this room? Any of us can walk out when we like and sell a lurid story to a paper. No one is forcing us to do this work. We'll do it, whatever Stokely's motives might be, because it's only an academic exercise. Nothing more than that. He's given us room and board, and we're asked to turn in a few reports. What's the harm?"

"I wish I could believe that whole-heartedly. It's the scale of the thing that concerns me."

"It's an eye-opener all right." Long finished his cigar. "How are you going to vote?"

"A government newspaper is an awful idea. I can see it as a weekly or monthly for legal notices and announcements, after the press has received proper press-releases. I wouldn't have a problem with *that*."

"I'm the same. Also, otherwise we might do ourselves out of our jobs." He laughed. Rushton smiled.

"There is that to consider."

# Chapter 19

# Plans large and small

From about three onwards, new guests arrived while Sophie and Ada again set the table in the Grand Dining Room for dinner. Before they had finished, Mr Dalgleish came in to put out the name cards.

"Are there many more new guests, Mr Dalgleish?" asked Sophie, as he placed cards close by.

"Fourteen, Miss King. Mrs Newnham informs me that only two are staying, the rest are dinner guests."

"That approximates to the number of yesterday's dinner guests."

"Indeed, it does." He finished putting out the cards. "I trust you are finding everything satisfactory, Miss King?"

Sophie stopped laying the table. "Yes, Mr Dalgleish. Except for the food."

"Miss Beech has also informed me of such. I spoke to his lordship on several matters, and the quality of food for the servants was among them. He referred the matter to one of his aides."

"That's excellent, Mr Dalgleish. I wonder, who are those

aides that I see around the place? I find them rather mysterious."

"Quite understandable. They are his lordship's administrative staff and fulfill a multitude of duties. They are gentlemen, well-educated, and facilitate in both his business interests and public engagements. There used to be two, but I believe his lordship's staff has now increased to eight or more."

"Thank you. May I also ask if Burgoyne's staff is meeting your expectations?"

"More than meets, exceeds, Miss King."

"Thank you, Mr Dalgleish. Miss Burgoyne will be gratified to hear such a report."

"I shall communicate with Miss Burgoyne upon returning to Lyall Place and inform her of my satisfaction." He gave her a slight bow before leaving the room.

As soon as he had gone, Ada went to the door to watch the corridor. Sophie then raced around the table, recording names and their positions. 'Good grief,' Ada heard her say, as Sophie stood by the place-setting of the guest of honour.

Every person from Burgoyne's was busy, right up until they sat down for their dinner at six. The room was crowded now, and so the agents had to be careful what they said.

"At least this time it's identifiable," said Flora, examining the filling of her slice of pie.

"It even tastes of chicken," said Ada, who had just sampled some.

"I like it," said Fern.

"Mr Dalgleish's request appears to have worked, so we might survive after all," said Sophie. She lowered her voice. "I'm meeting you know who at eleven."

"Who's that?" asked a puzzled Broadbent-Wicks, who did not lower his voice.

"Shh," said Ada. "Elizabeth."

"Ah, got it," he whispered. "I know who you mean. Shall I come with you?"

"No, thank you," said Sophie.

"This is the best thing we've had out of them kitchens," said Alfie Tanner. "But supposin' it don't last, eh? Like this is a one off. I reckon we ought to get seconds before it all goes, and keep it in reserve, in case such beneficence dries up of a sudden," his accent rising several classes as he enunciated the last phrase of his speech.

"Go and talk to Mrs Potter, then," said Ada.

"Come off it, Nancy. You're the expert at that sort of stuff."

"No, it don't always work the same with a woman cook. Mrs Potter already gives Kemp's men extra, so she'll be all right with you asking for more."

"I don't know about that. We'll need at least two pies."

"There were six left when we got our dinners," said Fern.

"I can't see her giving me two pies, but I'll give it a go, and we'll see what happens."

"Can I come?" asked Broadbent-Wicks eagerly.

Alfie considered the request. "Can't 'urt and might be better if you did."

As soon as they had finished, the two men departed for the kitchen. Other servants began leaving the table.

"Dora." Sophie spoke softly. "Can you find a moment to leave the second dining room later?"

"That's tricky, 'cause there's a lot of 'em in there, and we're kept busy."

"Hmm... We have to get into the Muniment Room. That's where they keep important documents. The door was open, but it's been locked for all of today, so you will go with Ada."

"Miss," said Ada. "we'll never bring it off, us nipping out from two dining rooms. We'd never get the time straight between us."

"Yes, you're right. Then it means a night raid."

"We'll need a lookout," said Ada.

"I'll do that," said Sophie.

"I'm not being left out of this," said Flora. "Surely we need two lookouts?"

"Getting out of the dormitory quietly is going to be hard enough," said Sophie. "If we all leave, and Miss Beech or another wakes up, there'll be no one to give an excuse for our absence. You must be the dormitory lookout."

"What can I tell them...? How about you had a surfeit of chicken pie? It disagreed with all three of you, woke you up, so you went for a walk to ease your stomach pains."

"That might tempt fate, but it will have to do."

"What are we going to look for, miss?" asked Fern.

"Old documents or letters, dated about 1877. We'll be searching for references to Lady Georgiana, Roderick Fielding, and Edward Fielding."

"Fielding? Would they be brothers, miss?" Fern was perplexed.

"Roderick is Lord Stokely, and Edward is his Uncle Teddy."

"Do you mean to tell me Stokely ain't his surname?" Fern could not believe her ears.

"No, that's his title. Fielding is his family name."

"I didn't know that. So having a title is one name, and the one you're born with is another. Is that the same for all the lords and ladies?"

"For the vast majority, I believe," said Sophie.

"I made the same mistake when I started," said Ada. "You learn something new every day."

"Don't you just," agreed Fern.

Alfie and Broadbent-Wicks waited patiently in the kitchen for an opportune moment to speak to Mrs Potter. She was so busy, and in such a bad mood.

"I don't reckon our chances," said Alfie. "She won't give us as much as a slice."

"You never know. All we have to do is ask."

They waited for several minutes more. Mrs Potter knew they were waiting. She even guessed *why* they were waiting. At the same moment as she decided to give them a piece of her mind instead of a piece of pie, an incident occurred.

One of Stokely's staff, a particularly smartly dressed and efficient young fellow, also entered the kitchen. He approached Broadbent-Wicks.

"I believe I'm addressing Mr Dan Ely."

"I believe you are, too," answered the smiling Broadbent-Wicks.

"Lord Stokely sends his compliments and wishes you to have this." The young man produced an envelope from an inside pocket and handed it over. "There's no reply." He smiled.

"What a surprise. Well, tell his lordship, thank you, anyway."

The young man smiled again and left immediately.

This transaction caused Mrs Potter, and several other witnesses, to be seized by a monstrous curiosity.

"It's probably just a thank you note, or something," said Broadbent-Wicks to Alfie. He tore open the envelope and looked inside. "Ten pounds!? That's *mighty* generous of him. I shall thank his lordship profusely when I see him next."

This shocked the now silent kitchen, dumbfounded it, as much as if all light had suddenly turned green.

"Sorry for keeping you waiting, Mr Ely," said Mrs Potter, coming forward. "Is there anything I can help you with?"

"Yes, there is, thank you," said Broadbent-Wicks. "We'd like four chicken pies, please."

"Four...? Oh, I'll have to make some more, then."

"And never stop making them, that's what I say. Let me tell you, Mrs Potter, your chicken pies are superb. Why do you think we're here?"

She thought about it, and slowly came to a remarkable conclusion. If two of the earl's footmen were in her kitchen, and one of them was in high-standing with his lordship, then it must follow that his lordship had ordered the pies. He would partake of them.

"I never thought I'd live to see the day. Oh, I do hope they're good enough."

"Do not concern yourself, Mrs Potter, because they absolutely are."

She was no end pleased. In short order, the footmen whisked four pies on two trays from the kitchen.

"You are *so* jammy," said Alfie, as they walked away. "How do you do it?"

"Do what?" asked Broadbent-Wicks.

"Ten quid *and* four pies? I should be so lucky."

---

Cars arrived and brought guests to the house. Footmen bearing luggage escorted them to their assigned rooms. Teatime came and went but, for those in the ballroom, the tea came from urns and the occupants served themselves, because the household staff was not permitted to enter.

Those working in the room became enthused about what they were doing. Give a specialist a technical problem in the abstract to consider and he or she will work at it until a solution is reached. The room full of specialists did just that. They debated and voted. They wrangled and compromised. Steadily, the pile of unresolved issues dwindled, while the piles of notes of solid worth for draft reports grew. Around this work, a sense of camaraderie sprang up. Naturally, there were the usual problems of conflicting characters and stubbornly held opinions but, under a gloriously painted ceiling in a scintillating room of mirrors and chandeliers, such disturbances as can afflict a meeting were neutralized. Besides, no one dared disappoint Lord Stokely; rather, they wanted to please him.

At six o'clock, while the servants ate, those of the ballroom were dismissed from their labours, allowing them to prepare for their own dinner. They were under instruction to reassemble early the next morning. Although the spigot of discussion had been turned off, it dripped, and continued to do so until they met again.

In the Gun Room, Kemp and another man laboured over the shotguns, scrupulously cleaning and bringing them into perfect working order for tomorrow morning's clay pigeon shooting.

Isolated from all this activity, Stokely remained in his private smoking room to consult with Dawkins, Wilberforce, and Cobden. From time to time, one of the efficient young men would bring a telephone message first to Dawkins, who relayed it to the earl. These encoded messages superficially sounded innocuous, but the underlying content appeared to be of significance to Stokely and to those with him.

It was dinnertime. Although the menu had changed and the guest list was different, the slow, rhythmic dance of traditional service was identical to the previous evening. Footmen and maids dressed in black glided silently about the long table with perfect timing, effortlessly dispensing food and drink as and when needed. Most guests barely noticed the servants, unless they appeared quietly at their elbow and a decision had to be made. The process was painless for the diner, because the servant, preferring not to speak, politely uttered only that which sufficed to get the food on the plate. Those guests habituated to such service gave scant attention to a servant, while those less acclimatized showed awkward concern over not making a fool of themselves.

Stokely addressed the assembly. He introduced the guest of honour, lauding him greatly, and the table responded with applause. Being world famous, the guest needed no introduction. Guglielmo Marconi, sometimes called the father of radio, rose from his seat. A short man, one could not help but notice the shape of his head and his ears — the ears of the man who listened to faint signals in the ether. Fastidious in dress, one might have taken him for a lawyer or a banker, or a Roman patrician of ancient times. In his late forties, he had lost his lean, taut look of earlier years. He spoke English fluently, with only a trace of an Italian accent.

"Lord Stokely, lady and gentlemen — a thousand thanks for such a kind welcome. I was grateful to receive an invitation and have been greatly anticipating this evening at Chertsey Park. Imagine my surprise when I stepped out of my car, into the dark of the English countryside, and then into *such* an entrance hall. I thought at once, my driver had taken a wrong turn somewhere and we had arrived in Rome!" He waited for the polite laughter to subside. "Thank you."

The dinner began. It became apparent that Lord Stokely wished to monopolize Marconi's attention from the outset.

"I know you must soon be aboard the Elettra again, so I will come straight to the matter, which I only hinted at in my letter to you."

"I am intrigued," said Marconi.

"My aim is to put a radio receiver in every British home. At the start, the cost of a receiver will be high, with only wealthy households able to afford them. However, as developments continue to be made, such costs will surely decline while the quality of the broadcast and reception improves."

"I can agree with your last statement, but I do not follow what it is you want to do. A business venture, perhaps?"

"By necessity, it must be so. Radio is still in its infancy, but it is only a matter of a few years until radio broadcasts shall become a part of everyday life. Before that happens, the government shall regulate the industry. I wish to get a start in radio before that involvement so that I may contribute what I can to the regulations. I wish to be in on the ground floor, as they say, in entertaining and informing the British public."

"May I ask why?"

"I need to speak to all the people of Britain, and radio will be the most efficient way of doing so."

"Ahh... I comprehend."

"Yes, I thought you would. The Dutchman, Idzerda, is already broadcasting a weekly entertainment program. We can pick it up here, in England. Others will follow his lead. I intend going much further in founding a British broadcasting network, but I need your help with the initial design, the ongoing development of the radio, and the establishment of the network."

"This is fascinating, Lord Stokely," said Marconi. "You are opening up a vista of possibility that I have ignored. At present, the field of broadcasting is a wilderness where amateur enthusiasts roam. Business is not there, because profits are not there. Marconi is not there. But if there were an adequate network of transmitters broadcasting the same signal... I shall think about this."

"I appreciate your willingness to indulge me."

"I warn you, the costs will be enormous."

"I'm aware of that. I shall build proper manufacturing facilities."

Parts of conversations were overhead by Alfie and Ada. Soon, Sophie knew that Lord Stokely was determined to do something on a large scale in radio.

Course followed dinner course, and the conversation between Stokely and Marconi turned into a different avenue.

"Have you met Mr Mussolini?" asked Stokely.

"No. I have not had the opportunity. I travel so frequently that I am rarely in Italy these days for any length of time."

"What is your opinion of him?"

"When he was a socialist, I knew nothing about him, and cared not to know more. After he changed direction and as soon as I heard of his vital space doctrine, I understood that, at heart, he was a man who wished to strengthen and expand Italy into those areas taken from us in the past. I changed my opinion of him. He fascinates me now."

"He means to make Italy a great power, and I believe he should."

Marconi became quiet. "That is a surprising statement, Lord Stokely."

"Then I'll go one further. Britain and Italy should be allies in not only reviving themselves to their former glories, but also in shifting the balance of power away from many of the old institutions. Europe has changed because of the war. Something new shall emerge, while tired politicians and aging diplomats cling to the past and their old ways of thinking. Socialism must be stopped. Pure democracy will make a nation weak. The new power and antidote is a ruling elite drawn from all classes of society, governing in the best interests of the people."

"Are you suggesting that you would see all of Britain's traditions swept away?"

"No, not at all. They only need be reinvigorated with the proper meaning and direction. Britain will slowly lose everything she currently possesses unless changes are made. The communists are a present threat to the nation. Take this Red Fist business, for instance. Outrages are being perpetrated, and the government has so far done nothing. In Italy, Mussolini is taking on the communists and beating them — literally and figuratively. That same dynamic action is needed in this country."

Marconi nodded. "I can sympathize with your viewpoint... Italy and Britain... Our countries are in quite different positions, but we both face the same obstacles on our paths forward... I am most interested in hearing more of your ideas about broadcast radio."

The next course was served.

"Lord Stokely," said Marconi, "in early spring, weather permitting, my yacht will sail in British waters. Perhaps you will do me the honour of coming aboard for a day or two's cruising. I can arrange for a demonstration of our current work."

"I would be delighted, my dear Marconi," said Lord Stokely.

"Excellent. I feel we have several matters to discuss further. Only two assistants may accompany you, as passenger space is limited on the Elettra. It is a working vessel, after all."

Stokely smiled. "I fully understand. When we sail, I shall bring business plans for your consideration."

"Yes, that is a good idea. My staff will prepare specifications for a radio and a network of transmitters. A word of caution, Lord Stokely. You may find the manufacturing costs prohibitive for a radio designed to be used at home."

"There are ways of making an expensive item affordable. Leave all that part to me. I employ some brilliant people who are astute at building demand, where demand does not presently exist."

Marconi nodded. "I must compliment your chef on an exquisite dinner."

Stokely beckoned Alfie, who approached. "Bring Monsieur Fournier here."

Alfie bowed to the earl before going to the kitchen.

---

Stokely spoke to the guests in The Grand Salon. This time, he presented a bright future in which funding for research and technological advancement would be forthcoming. This was attractive to his audience, many of whom were academics, engineers, and scientists. He spoke of peace through military strength, health maintained by proper diet, and nurturing of the young of all classes through education and fitness. He said that the future was theirs to construct, and mentioned large-scale building projects, rejuvenating struggling industries, and developing a strong export economy to solve the ever-worsening unemployment problem. "As of last month, almost a million workers are idle!" he cried. "At the current rate of increase, that number has already been surpassed, but the count is not yet in. Consider it, my friends, not as the current government does — a millstone around its political neck, but as an opportunity for the nation to rebuild and strengthen itself, drawing on this great pool of available labour. In the interim, there will be suffering, continuing discontent, and a general air of hopelessness. Now is the time for us to step into that gap and put the nation back to work. The war is behind us. We, and our allies, won that war at a terrible cost. Let us not lose the peace we so richly deserve."

He continued on, imbuing the future with certainty of fulfilled hopes and wishes — fully realizable if only the appropriate action were taken at once. In this, he reassured his audience, who felt secure while listening to him. Everything would be all right. During the speech, Dawkins slipped out of the room.

Upon entering Stokely's office at the far end of the first floor in the west wing, Dawkins saw an aide on the telephone, scribbling out a message. The call ended, and the aide brought the message to Dawkins. He read it and looked at his watch. 10:15 p.m.

"Right on time."

"Yes, sir. Is there anything else I might do?"

"Not at the moment."

The younger man returned to the desk. Dawkins, still holding the note, approached the window to look out. Clouds obscured the moon, and it was dark below, except for where the outside house lights penetrated. As he watched, he saw a brief gleam somewhere about the drive and near to the road. He observed the point near the house where the drive emerged from obscurity. Patiently, he waited. His reward came at last — the sighting of a figure on the edge of the darkness and carrying something heavy. This figure seemed to avoid the light, but he saw enough to be sure that it was a woman in a hat and overcoat and that she was carrying a box.

"Have you noticed anything odd about the servants?" Dawkins said this as he turned away from the window. He put the note in his pocket.

"No, sir, I haven't... Oh, except Drummond says one of the agency maids is an actress. He said she's dark complexioned, rather pretty, and therefore quite memorable."

"I know who he means. So she's an actress, is she? What about any of the others?"

"They all seem to be normal servants, as far as I can see. The ones from Lyall Place and the agency know their jobs.... There's Ely. Lord Stokely finds him amusing. He's upper middle class, but apparently he can only find work as a footman. I haven't spoken to the others, so I really couldn't say more. Is anything the matter, sir?"

"No," said Dawkins slowly. "Stay here for another hour in case there are developments."

Dawkins left the room but, instead of returning to the Grand Salon, he went to the servants' staircase in the west wing and stopped to listen. He took out an automatic pistol, checked it was operational, switched the safety catch off, and returned it to his shoulder holster. Then he went slowly and softly downstairs.

# Chapter 20

# A stop on the stairs

"Ophelia, where are you?" whispered Sophie. It was pitch black by the gates to Chertsey Park.

"Silly thing. That's me, isn't it?" Elizabeth spoke from an unexpected place away from the road.

Sophie flashed her torch momentarily and found Elizabeth standing by a bush.

"I'm ever so sorry, Miss King, but a tawny owl was hooting up in this tree."

"Why are you fascinated by owls?"

"It's only tawnies. I'm using them as my nighttime cover story for Agnes at the Gardeners Arms. She must think I'm mad, but that can't be helped."

"Well done. I have an envelope containing important notes and evidence."

"Evidence! Oh, how *marvellous*, Miss King. Do you wish me to take it to Inspector Morton?"

"At once, please. It's vital he gets it tonight."

"I will hasten to Sunningdale immediately. The road permitting, of course. There are some icy patches."

"Yes, do be careful. Are you all right? How are you coping with leading a double life?"

"Splendidly, Miss King. I've never before been so exhilarated."

"Good, but let us hope it gets no more exhilarating than it already has. Did you bring the supplies?"

"I did. The box is rather heavy, though. Will you be able to manage it?"

"I don't know. Where is it?"

"On the backseat." Elizabeth switched on her torch and opened the door. "There."

"Best switch off the torch."

"Yes, indeed."

"Here's the envelope."

"Thank you."

"We'll meet again at the same time tomorrow."

"Understood."

"Best of luck, Ophelia."

"And the same to you, Miss King."

"Good grief, this *is* heavy," said Sophie as she hauled the wooden box out of the car.

"Could I be of assistance?"

"I think I can carry it. You had better go, because of the time."

"You are correct, of course. I'd be at a complete loss if they locked me out of the public house. Goodbye." Elizabeth soon drove away.

Sophie carried the box but, after a minute, it felt as though her arms were being pulled from their sockets. Mentally, she reviewed the list of contents, and although each item was of no consequential weight, she now realized the combined total was a little too much for her. It was the sort of weight that pulls one forward and makes carrying a race between pain versus distance — on legs unable to move fast enough. Pain won, and she had to put down the box to shake her arms for relief. When she picked it up again, she knew snow had got onto her smart overcoat, but she sincerely hoped no dirt was mixed with it. To avoid soiling her coat, Sophie now kept to the unspoilt snow at the sides of the drive and stopped every twenty paces — she counted them. Each time she picked up the box again, it felt a little heavier. When reaching the lighted area, she stopped to rest before making the final dash — if such a name can be given to the ungainly quick-march she was compelled to employ. Then she hurried towards the servants' entrance, which slow sprint ended with her face distorted due to the agonizing pain in her arms. "Ugh," she said, as she plonked her burden on a step. She decided that next time, if there were to be a next time, Broadbent-Wicks could lug the box up the driveway.

Getting from the entrance to the staircase was difficult, as servants were about. Sophie seized an opportune moment when the hall was clear and marched across to the staircase. Somehow, she ascended the first flight without being seen or heard. When she turned the corner, a man standing on the next landing barred her way.

"Ahh! Sorry, but you frightened me, sir."

"What do you have in the box?" asked Dawkins. He spoke slowly in a low, even voice.

She had recognized him at once, but it now sank in how dangerous this man might be. He was a former intelligence officer, one with a reputation for efficiency and ruthlessness.

"Food supplies, sir." She put on a London accent.

He did not answer, but only stared, betraying no emotion or hint of what he was thinking.

"What time is it?" he said at last.

"I'm not sure, sir. After ten, though. May I pass? The box is very heavy."

He neither answered nor moved a muscle. Sophie balanced the box on the bannister. It was unnerving being under Dawkins' silent scrutiny and, although her arms hurt, that pain was now the least of her problems.

"Sir, why are you detaining me?" Her breathing was rapid, partly from her exertions, and partly due to the palpable tension. She considered how to reach her cosh without dropping the box, if he meant violence, and saw she was severely disadvantaged. It occurred to her to retreat downstairs.

"What is your name?"

"Phoebe King, sir."

"I'm not detaining you."

Dawkins then moved to one side, allowing her barely sufficient space to pass, although he could have yielded a lot more room. Sophie would have to brush past him. She saw that for her to do so was his challenge, his test. Without consciously thinking it through, she understood that, if she passed him now, he would have exerted control, and prevailed. Dawkins would have won, but Sophie was unsure what it all meant, and there was still the implicit threat that he might become violent. Under this invisible pressure, she sought a way out.

"No, sir. I'm not allowed to pass family or guests on the stairs or in the corridors. The box is quite safe, sir, and there's plenty of room for you to get by, if you please."

He continued staring for a moment longer, then turned and went upstairs. Sophie felt immense relief at his departure, followed by a spasm of anger. She ascended slowly, pausing at each turn to rest, and hoping he had truly gone.

A little later, after Sophie had put the box in the dormitory, she met Flora in a side corridor.

"A few of them are going to be sloshing it back into the small hours... What's the matter? You look sick."

"I've just had an awful experience with Dawkins."

"The rotter! Tell auntie Glad everything."

"No, it wasn't like that. He was doing some sort of intelligence officer thing. It was quite unnerving."

"Oh. In what way?"

"Well, I was bringing in the food supplies..."

"He didn't confiscate them, did he?"

"No, *listen*. He must have seen me from a window and then ambushed me on the servants' stairs in the west wing. He just blocked the staircase and wouldn't let me pass. Not at first, anyway. He saw I had a heavy box and just stood there, staring at me."

"How unspeakably rude. What did he do next?"

"He just stared, as though his eyes were boring holes into me. I felt guilty and uncomfortable and quite fearful."

"Naturally, one would."

"Then he asked questions about the box and my name, but slowly, as if watching for my reaction."

"Ah, so that must be one of the sneaky ways intelligence officers behave."

"It wasn't very nice."

"Are you sure he wasn't smitten with you?"

"It would be horrific if he were. No. It was as though he were trying to control my mind."

"That's disgusting. Then it wasn't about the box?"

"It couldn't have been. I hope he hasn't discovered us... I gave him my name. Do you remember my telling you about the Stokely man at the FO who was collecting names? He recorded my name, too."

"Do you think we should leave? I mean, if Dawkins is on to us, and you in particular, we're in danger. They've got guns, this is a very remote house, and we already know there's a murderer in our midst."

Sophie sighed. "I've been thinking of nothing else. We can't leave now with the job half done... Help is only a telephone call away."

"Then ring up Elizabeth."

"I can't. Inspector Morton might arrest Miller on suspicion of murder, and Elizabeth can take us away, but it will ruin everything. Stokely will not only escape charges, but he'll also then be on the alert. We'll actually be putting ourselves in greater danger if we leave. Stokely will come after us."

"I wish you hadn't said that."

"We must stick it out as best we can. Did you discover anything?"

"Nothing useful. Two men were discussing atomic energy. Do you know what that is?"

"I've never heard of it."

"Then it can't be important. I've learned something, though. I believe I could now spot a scientist in a crowd of people. After seeing half a dozen of them together, I noticed they all come across as a bit vacant. As soon as you serve food to one, he looks bewildered, as if he just woke up in a strange place and wasn't the least bit hungry. Also, their staid clothes give them away. And type of spectacles. Then, when they speak, no one except another scientist could *possibly* understand what they're saying."

---

Inspector Morton received the notes from Elizabeth. She had been uncomfortable and almost mute on her visit the day before, but on this, her second visit, their politeness reassured her she was under no threat of arrest. After she left, Morton read the notes, saw the Red Fist handbill, and telephoned the electrifying information to Scotland Yard. He got a call back almost immediately from Superintendent Penrose, who gave him instructions.

"Lads! I've got some important news, so try to look like police officers."

The men got up from beds and chairs to gather around him.

"Seen one of these before?" Morton held up the Red Fist for them to see.

"Where did you get that from, sir?" asked Gowers.

"Bit of a turn up, eh?" said Morton. He addressed the men. "So the agents inside Chertsey Park have identified the Fleet Street murderer. His name's Albert Miller, and he has a sister or an aunt in Woolwich. He lives at the estate, but we don't know how long he's been there, so he might have digs elsewhere. He's about five-eight, thickset, round face, big moustache, short brown hair, walk is slow and deliberate — I don't know what's meant by that. Anyway, if and when we're sent in, nab him. Watch him, though. Assume he's carrying a firearm."

A constable put a hand up.

"Go on," said Morton.

"If he's one of the Red Fist gang, what's he doing at Chertsey Park?"

"Smart lad. It looks like the Red Fist being anarchists or communists is all claptrap. It's just a front. Stokely and his underlings are running the Red Fist. Miller had a few of these sheets among his possessions."

The officers murmured, expressing disgust.

"Can't we go in now, sir?"

"No. Strict orders. It's Stokely we're after. We could arrest a dozen Millers and never catch Stokely. Even if one of them grassed on him, he'd never make it to the courtroom. No witness, no case, nothing. Yes?"

"What happens to Miller if we aren't called in, sir?"

"That's not our worry. However, if we *are* called in and one of you arrests him, the arresting officer gets taken down the pub afterwards and stays until he has to be carried home."

They cheered.

"All right, all right... As things are warming up, we need to reorganize. Day or night, six of you must be ready to go at a moment's notice. There's enough of us to split the duty into three shifts..."

---

At one-thirty, Sophie, Ada, and Fern crept from the dormitory wearing dressing gowns over their nightclothes because the house was noticeably cooler away from the fireplaces.

Flora lay awake in the dormitory, ready to enact a sudden and acute bout of dyspepsia if any of the other maids woke up.

The three women crept downstairs to the unwholesome second floor of the dark, silent west wing. The only illumination they had was over the staircase landings. No one was about, so they continued down. The first floor was better lit, with dim lights in the corridor, but was just as empty. They reached the ground floor and turned away from the kitchens towards the Gun Room and other offices. These lay around a corner lit by a single lamp. Once into the long, straight corridor, the only light they had ahead of them was at the far end in the distant east wing, as viewed through the intervening tunnel.

"I'm getting nervous," whispered Fern.

"Shh," said Ada and Sophie in unison.

"I only spoke, 'cause I don't know if me photographic memory works when I'm worried."

"It has to work, Dora," said Sophie. "Breathe deeply... Think of something beautiful... Imagine this is only a game."

"I'll try, miss."

"And if that don't work," said Ada, "think what you'll buy with the forty quid that's coming to you."

"I know exactly what I'd buy," said Fern. "Miss King, where did you get your dressing gown from? It's lovely, and it looks warm. "

"We'll discuss that later. Just think about dressing gowns until you're inside."

"And slippers. I could do with a new pair. Oh, and I also need..."

"Shh," said Ada.

The three agents moved cautiously forward, leaving the light behind them. The corridor was lined with rooms on either side, and became very dark. At one point, they passed a shadowy alcove with an entrance in it. Through the windows on either side of the door, the faintly glowing snow on the heath made this corner seem all the more chill.

"Feel that bloomin' draught," whispered Ada.

"Shh," said Dora.

At the Muniment Room door, Ada began her lock-picking operation. Sophie held the torch, while she and Fern positioned themselves to watch either end of the corridor and shield the glow. After they heard a soft click in the lock, Ada opened the door. The three of them entered the room. The torch revealed rows of account books occupying ancient shelves against the walls. On the floor in the middle, former managers and housekeepers of different eras had stacked wooden boxes in rows beyond a very plain, early Victorian table that had a hideous crack in its warped top.

"Don't switch on the light," said Sophie. "If anyone's outside, they'll see it, and might come to investigate." She watched the corridor from the doorway. "Here, take the torch." She gave it to Ada.

"It smells musty in 'ere," said Ada.

Ada played the torch beam along various shelves. "1834... 35... Here we go. "1875... 76... 1877."

"There's a lot of dust," said Fern as she retrieved the account book for 1877, placed it on the table, and opened it.

"Then no one's touched it for years," said Sophie from the doorway.

"Blimey, they spent a lot of money back then," said Fern.

"Must have been a big staff," said Ada. "Miss? What we after? Perhaps you'd better come and look. I can't make 'ead or tail of it."

"Let's change places."

Sophie took the torch and began scanning the pages.

"How does it work, miss?" asked Fern, staring at a page written in a tall, forward sloping script.

"I'm just getting to grips with how they did it here... There are several cash books and a general ledger bound together in this volume. Basically, there was a general bank account for the estate. Nearly all payments and receipts would have been in cash. The estate manager and the housekeeper would each keep an account of their own cash float in their separate cash boxes. When tenants paid their rents, the manager would deposit surplus funds in the bank. When money was needed, someone would cash a cheque at the bank. Each float had to be balanced to the penny. To summarize and make sense of it all, a clerk would post each type of expense and income to the general ledger. From there, the clerk transferred the totals onto a separate sheet and totted them up to arrive at the profit or loss for the year."

"All that's in there?"

"Yes. This section is for the house... See the pages for cutlery, and linens... This one's interesting. On the 29th of March, there was a large purchase of linens from Harvey Nichols department store. Let's look up furniture... Yes, here. See that. A large bed from Druce & Co. of Baker Street on the 28th of March. Those items must have been for the wedding on the 10th of April."

"That's a lot of money for a bed, miss," said Fern. "Do you think it's still here?"

"I'm sure it is... I doubt this book will tell us much more than it already has. I had hoped that there would be records of a special bank account, or the earl's personal accounts. Correspondence would be an even better find."

"What about that, miss?" Fern pointed the torch at a large metal cabinet, six feet tall.

"It looks promising," said Sophie. She tried the closed door. Although unlocked, the door opened with a loud scraping sound, producing pained expressions on their faces. Inside were five shelves of deed boxes — three to a shelf, with two empty spaces on the top shelf. "I wonder how they're organized."

The boxes were of different sizes and patterns — several older oak boxes on the bottom shelf, while the rest were metal with numbers. She took one out at random that had a nine painted on it, and brought it to the table, saying,

"Ooh, my poor arms haven't recovered yet... It's locked."

"Do you need me, miss?" asked Ada.

Before receiving an answer, Fern said,

"Hold on, there were a lot of keys on hooks inside the door."

They sorted it out quickly because the keys were marked with numbers corresponding to the boxes.

"That's stupid, that is," said Ada. "Why 'ave the key right by the box?"

"I think their only concern is fire, said Sophie. "There'll be nothing of value in here, like bonds, cash, or jewellery."

The box contained various legal papers, architectural drawings, and business correspondence from an early date.

"I've got it," said Sophie. "The numbers correspond to the different earls. We want number eleven for the 11th earl, Humphrey Fielding."

Fern set box eleven on the table and it was soon open. Sophie took out some documents and began searching through them. Further down, she found bundles of letters tied with ribbon. One small bundle of several letters in their envelopes was from Edward Fielding. All were from overseas, with the last postmarked 14th March, 1877, Johannesburg, South Africa. Sophie carefully took out the note to read it.

*Dear Humphrey,*

*I hope this letter finds you in better health than in recent weeks.*

*I cannot express sufficient gratitude for what you propose, and I acquiesce to all your wishes. As you say, Georgie must be shielded at all costs, but that you are the one to bear the burden demonstrates immeasurable kindness on your part, and I am proud to be your brother. Doubtless, you do not feel the same towards me. It galls me to have left England, leaving the woman I love in such distress. I cannot bear to see myself in the mirror. There is no excuse for my behaviour, so I will offer none.*

*My CO is a good fellow. He couldn't allow me the extra leave. Instead, he's sending me to England to attend a meeting as his representative and there to deliver a report. I booked my passage, and I shall arrive at Southampton, 9th of April and return to Jo'burg on the 16th. It will be difficult for me to leave Georgie so soon after our marriage, but there is no other way that I can see. Under no circumstance could Georgie come out here, and she wouldn't want to, not with the way things stand.*

*I won't write again before we meet, as my return will probably precede my letter.*

*Your eternally grateful brother,*
*Edward.*

"It's unbelievable," said Sophie, who put the letter and envelope into her pocket. "Edward married Georgiana, but all the documents make it appear as though Humphrey married her. Oh, la, they must have arranged a special licence and a private wedding ceremony with a minister who didn't know either of the brothers."

"So, Edward is Uncle Teddy, right, miss? He married her, but did it in the earl's name?"

"That's what it looks like to me. The marriage was not legal because of the falsifying of signatures apart from anything else but, between the brothers and Georgiana, they decided it counted as a proper arrangement. The earl must have thought highly of Georgiana... Perhaps he loved her, too... The upshot is that, on the surface, the arrangement shall make Roderick Fielding the twelfth earl, when really he has no legal claim."

More searching in the deed-box produced things of interest, but nothing relating to the marriage between Humphrey and Georgiana, or the births of any of the three children the couple was believed to have produced.

"We should go soon, miss," said Ada.

"Yes. I'm finished."

"You're taking the letter, are you?" asked Ada.

Sophie paused and looked very serious. "Someone said to me once that Stokely needs to be fought with his own weapons if he's to be defeated. I think that's true. I'm not stealing, although my conscience says I am. I'm collecting ammunition."

"I'd take it, an' all," said Ada. "So don't you worry, miss."

Fern yawned. "Can we go to bed now, please? There's nothing for me to do."

"Perhaps there's something for you in Stokely's box. Let's look, shall we?"

They did, but only found a few unimportant documents. While Ada put the box back, Fern looked along an adjacent shelf and found some frames. She took one down.

"Here, look at this, miss," she said.

Sophie came over. In all, there were eight expensively framed pencil drawings signed RF — Roderick Fielding. They were youthful and fanciful — the work of a semi-talented young artist who needed tutoring, but conveyed what he intended. Among them was a series of three London landmarks, only embellished and altered. RF had renamed Buckingham Palace 'The Palace of the President.' The Houses of Parliament were no longer Westminster Palace, but had become 'The Hall of Deputies and the People's Congress.' In a setting that was probably meant to be Hyde Park, he had depicted a great Roman colonnade. In its centre was a raised podium; before it was a large, paved, open space. The drawing was entitled 'Fielding Square.'

"Can you remember drawings?" asked Sophie. "These three?" She separated them from the rest.

"They're difficult. I can remember 'em, but I'm not very good at drawing 'em out again."

"Gladys is, so perhaps she can help you."

"That'd be nice, miss," said Fern. "If you don't mind, can you turn round please? And don't talk to me afterwards or I'll forget."

Ten minutes later, the three agents crept back along the passage. Ada guided Fern who, with bulging cheeks as she sought to hang onto the memory of the drawings, had lost the capacity to walk in any specific direction without her hand being held. Sophie had taken some paper and several pencil stubs for the drawings to be reproduced.

They returned to the dormitory, where Ada sneaked in to bring Flora out.

"They're all dead to the world, at present," said Flora. "I'd have dropped off myself if you'd been any longer."

"I'm relieved you didn't," said Sophie. "You're needed to do three drawings with two copies of each. Stokely drew them, and they reveal his treasonous thirst for power as being of very long-standing."

"I think I must be tired to the point of delirium. Are you really asking me to do six drawings in the middle of the night?"

"Yes. Dora has them stored in her brain. You'll have to work out how to transfer them to paper without Dora being unduly disturbed. Otherwise she forgets, you see."

"Couldn't you have just taken them?"

"Yes, but they are not evidence of criminal behaviour. However, our having copies allows us to play a game with Stokely's mind if we get stuck in a difficult position. I learned that trick from Dawkins. So think of the drawings as insurance. A set will go to Elizabeth for safekeeping and for possible future publication. If we possessed the originals, we could be charged with theft. If we have facsimiles, Stokely won't know how many sets we have, or who we've given them to. Do you follow?"

"No, not at this time of the morning. Six drawings?"

"You could make it nine, if you like."

"You talk such piffle sometimes, Sophie. Six, and that's all you're getting."

# Chapter 21

# Pull

On Saturday, Kemp was out early, shotgun in hand, with two huge dogs — mastiffs crossed with bulldogs plus a touch of something else. They stayed close by as he walked northwards in the now melting snow, uphill towards Chobham Common.

"Heel, you brute," he shouted angrily, if one strayed too far. Yet when he halted, and the dogs came close, he patted heads, speaking in a soft friendly way, as if to children he loved.

Kemp studied the sky and tested the wind. The breeze out of the west had brought a rising temperature. Now he knew how the morning would go, and in which direction to set the traps that launched the clay pigeons. Although Lord Stokely was a reasonable shot, Kemp did not want him shooting into the wind, where variations in the breeze would make the flight of the clays more unpredictable. This would cause a lower score and a displeased earl, especially as the nature of shooting in winter also often dropped the score averages. Stokely employed Kemp to ensure excellent shooting, and the gamekeeper was determined never to fail in meeting the earl's expectations.

Lord Stokely had eaten his breakfast in bed. His valet had

laid out a tweed suit. He dressed the earl, finishing by holding up the jacket with its leather shoulder patch. Stokely turned and put it on. The valet, moving around his master to face him, adjusted the breast pocket handkerchief to perfection, and then applied a soft brush to ensure there was not a speck of dust to be found on the entire ensemble. With the ritual ended, the earl left his private apartment for his office. Stokely was exuberant because the weekend was going well. He had won the confidence of Pathé and Marconi, as well as a dozen other influential men, including several bankers, whose financing capacity would be necessary in the future for certain large projects. The earl entered the office.

"Well?" he asked.

Two aides leapt to their feet. "Good morning, Lord Stokely," they said in unison. One of them then became the spokesman.

"Everything went as planned, my Lord. We received confirmation during the night."

"Good."

"I've laid out the newspapers on the table for you, my Lord."

Stokely walked to the table where the aide had folded seven different publications to display the headline or lead story.

'Red Fist Inferno', 'Factory destroyed in suspicious blast', 'Two killed in deadly explosion', 'Munitions factory in ruins – Two dead', 'Manchester's tragic night of fire'.

Stokely read the headlines and then turned to his aides.

"They really should have sold the controlling interest to me. Now they have nothing."

"I didn't know that was the case, my Lord."

"Yes. They turned my offer down a year ago. When selecting targets, I remembered them." Stokely smiled. "Anything else?"

"Not at present, my Lord. Although tonight will be busy."

"Gentlemen, keep up your good work. Come Monday, the nation shall be presented with the solution to the Red Fist's reign of terror. Relating to that, I'd welcome your opinions on the suggested name for the organization to accomplish the task — The National Peace Movement."

Both young men murmured approval, because they already knew Stokely had chosen the name, and they accepted whatever he said. They believed in him and the cause.

He left the office. Servants made themselves scarce at his approach. He strode through his house considering what should be the colour of the NPM armbands, and the design for the uniform, in readiness for the time when the organization would be established on a proper footing. Lithe in his movements, he quickly descended a staircase.

"Where's Kemp?" he asked a man he encountered outside of the Gun Room.

"I'll find him at once, my Lord." The man hastened away.

Stokely entered the Gun Room and began examining shotguns while he waited. He had been there slightly more than a minute when Kemp entered.

"Good morning, my Lord," said the gamekeeper.

"Shut the door," said Stokely.

Kemp closed it.

"What's this I hear about you stealing from the servants' food and coal?"

"I have the accounts ready for your inspection, my Lord."

"Don't even try. I put you in charge, and I can see for myself the place is falling to pieces."

"It's the inflation, my Lord."

"It's your stealing, Kemp. I'll bring in a butler to take over the house, and someone to oversee the estate. They'll run things properly and you'll leave both of them alone so that they may. Do I make myself clear?"

"Yes, Lord Stokely."

"Very good. With your hand removed from my pocket, you'll suffer an abrupt drop in income, no doubt."

"That's a bit hard on me, my Lord, seeing as how I look after your special work."

"It's because of such work that I haven't discharged you."

"Fair's fair, though. You've asked a lot more of me in the last twelvemonth than when I first started."

"Then you should have said something. Your behaviour *here* reflects on *me*. Do you realize that?"

"I didn't think of it, my Lord."

"*Yes*, well, it does. You're fortunate I'm in a good mood this morning. I intend remodelling the house, so your stewardship was ending, regardless. You'll stay on as gamekeeper at the same rate of pay. I'll also pay you regularly for the other work, instead of by the job as we have done in the past."

"As this is a new arrangement, my Lord, how much would that be?"

"Five hundred a year, and your men get paid independently for each job. Any complaints?"

"None, my Lord."

"Good, because I need something done right away. I hired a fellow to start a newspaper. His name's Jeremy Rushton and he's in the house at the moment. From what I've been told, I may have made a mistake where he's concerned. Have a man follow him for a week. Let me know at once if he acts suspiciously."

"And if he does?"

"You'll send someone to deal with him. Now, about today's shooting. My uncle will arrive soon, so please ensure he has an enjoyable morning."

"I'll take good care of him, my Lord."

Stokely left, and Kemp smiled. He reckoned he had lost financially, but life had just got easier for him. Also, he could still do private shoots on the side — if he squared away the new butler and the estate manager.

The term 'Rise and shine' is familiar to all. The female contingent of Burgoyne's Agency fulfilled the first part, but failed to shine. There was not so much as a dull gleam between them, even after they had eaten their breakfasts. During the night, Flora had produced six drawings, guided closely by Fern. When looking at them, Fern said they were close enough, Sophie had a hazy recollection of the originals and said they would do, and Ada was unsure why they had bothered, although she was complimentary to Fern and Flora. Still, the result was that there were two sets of three detailed drawings — reasonable facsimiles in the manner of Roderick Fielding — which included the titles and artist's initials. Sophie hid them, her notebook, and Uncle Teddy's revealing letter on top of a rafter in an unused part of the attic.

A little later, Ada met Sophie in a corridor, where they spoke briefly while remaining vigilant.

"You won't believe it, miss," said Ada. "More guests are coming today, 'cause I got a butcher's at the guest list when Mr Dalgleish weren't looking. 'Alf of them are women, and one of them is none other than her great self, Charlotte Terrence."

Sophie's eyes looked like saucers. "Oh, *no*. No!"

"Oh, *yes*. What are we gonna do?"

"Hide?"

"We should, an' all. It's not just you an' me, is it? She thinks Glad is Lady Laneford. What will she say when she finds Lady Laneford's working as a maid?"

"I can't imagine."

"Can she be trusted?"

"Not really. I don't know how she will react. I could have a word with her first, before she discovers us for herself."

"I s'pose, miss."

"Warn Gladys, should you see her. I can't stop now, and I need to think this over."

"I 'ope you come up with something. It'll take a miracle to stop it all going wrong."

With those ominous words, they parted. As Sophie walked

away, her tired mind raced without finding for her a way forward. She did her work, all the while picking at the Gordian knot of a problem, but no strand came loose. By herself in the library, she straightened chairs, plumped up cushions, and did a quick dusting. The fire had been laid, but was yet to be lit, so the room felt quite cold. This coolness came as a relief to Sophie, because her head felt hot. She hoped she had not caught a chill and put it down to not enough sleep. Her arms were stiff and sore from carrying the box. Thoughts of Dawkins kept popping up. She needed to think clearly, but her mind would not co-operate.

Charlotte Terrence was coming to Chertsey Park. She could not move past the bare fact, although she foresaw the ensuing danger as a scene. It played out in The Grand Dining Room where she was serving peas. Miss Terrence, seated next to Lord Stokely, would turn to him and say, '*You see that maid? I know for a fact that she's a secret agent... Look, there's another one.*' The scene ended. Even if things did not transpire in *that* way, the consequences of an unintentional slip-up by Charlotte would be dire. It threatened the wreck of everything — all the plans of those who opposed Stokely. Sophie worried over what might happen to her friends at Chertsey Park. Regarding herself, she struggled to remain calm, while fear hammered on the door, demanding admittance.

---

"*Uncle* Teddy!" The few people listening could tell Lord Stokely loved his uncle. They could hear the affectionate warmth Stokely was feeling when he lingered over enunciating the nickname. They could see the radiance of his smile. At that moment, Stokely's uncle was being helped out of his coat by Alfie, while Broadbent-Wicks took charge of his bags. Stokely came down the marble steps of the entrance towards his tall, slightly stooped visitor, saying.

"I'm so glad you could come."

They shook hands. Edward's grip was still firm. Seeing him, thin now, one could divine he was athletic once. His full head of white hair was not unlike Stokely's for length and waviness. He had a kind face, but really it was the droop at the corners of his eyes that gave him his soft, sad look, which may have suggested romantic melancholy in the distant past.

"How are you, my dear boy?" At seventy-one, Edward Fielding had a quiet, faded voice, as though his throat were sore and he had to be careful when speaking. "I saw your mama yesterday, and she sends you her love."

"That's sweet of her... And what were you two talking about, hmm?"

"Oh, this and that. The old days, of course."

Stokely looked about, making sure no one was nearby. He lowered his voice.

"Do you know, I'm surprised you two never married. You have always got along so well together."

"Is that what you think?" The impertinence momentarily pleased Edward Fielding, before he became circumspect. "You should not talk of your mother so. Or myself, come to that."

"Forgive me, uncle... Did you bring your old Jeffreys with you? I hope they're safe to shoot."

"There's nothing wrong with my old guns. They'll outlast me and *you*, by a broad margin."

"I'm sure... What do you think? Shall you and I visit the Purdey showroom to see what you fancy?"

"That's very kind, but far too extravagant. Much too much. Save your money."

"You always say no to things. However, I have some stamps that will interest you, but we'll keep those for later."

"That's my real weakness, as you well know."

Stokely smiled. "Shall we have a drink before we go outside?"

"A good idea," said Edward. They walked together. "I can't understand this weather. It's so up and down."

"Did you get any snow in London?" asked Stokely.

"Hardly anything. Then it soon melted. The roads are clear, and that's the main thing."

---

Fern noticed it first, followed by Ada, Alfie, Sophie, and finally Flora. Although in different parts of the house and busy working at various tasks, all five of them came to understand they were being watched. They kept their heads down, knowing that trouble was brewing. Several of the well-dressed aides had taken it upon themselves to observe the agents' activities. This surveillance did not amount to so very much, and all it really did was reveal the fact that the aides harboured suspicions, and that they had no idea of having given anything away. For there is one thing the well-trained servant shall never do, and that is to look a person of the household in the eye. Additionally, when work had to be done, no servant would stop to return a stare from another employee, albeit a well-tailored one. However, Broadbent-Wicks did things differently when he noticed a glance in his direction. He walked over to the aide standing by a column in the entrance hall. They were about the same age.

"Hello, do you want me for something?"

"Ah, no," said the surprised aide.

"That's funny. I was sure you did." Broadbent Wicks frowned as a thought came to him. "Um, do you have a title?"

"No, I don't." The aide was now puzzled.

"Thank *goodness* for that, otherwise I would have just made the most *colossal* blunder, what?" Broadbent-Wicks looked at his uncomfortable companion. "I say, are you going outside for the shooting? I must, but I really don't see the point. Unless they want me to pick up the broken clay pigeons. Or do they just leave them out there?"

"Leave them, I think."

"That seems rather untidy, but then, what do I know...? Tell me something. What's your opinion of Lord Stokely? Personally, I find he has quite a wonderful sense of humour and is surprisingly generous."

"Excuse me, I have work to attend to."

"Yes, of course you must work, seeing as you don't have a title. Thanks for the pleasant chat." Broadbent-Wicks lowered his voice and leaned forward. "I have to talk on the *sly* or the world will stop turning." He laughed. "Servants aren't supposed to talk, as you probably know. Like children, they may be seen, but not heard. Perhaps we'll bump into each other again later. Cheerio."

---

"Pull!" A spinning clay launched into the air. The man swung his shotgun quickly and fired. The second clay flew lower. He fired again. The referee behind the guns recorded a hit and a miss. In foxholes, in front of the gun line, two trappers reloaded the traps. They made changes in both direction and elevation before throwing the next pair of birds. "Pull!" called the second shooter in the line of seven.

At the same time, work was continuing in the ballroom. Among the participants, ideas had grown like mushrooms overnight. They were enthusiastically proposed and often soberly accepted by others around the table. Cobden continued to observe with relish the dedication to this great work, and, today, he was more frequently consulted on procedure and overall design of the government-in-waiting. In an odd spare moment, he wondered what title denoting his position he should use in the future. As he was at present styled as a humble servant — V Cobden, secretary to Lord Stokely — he thought a simplification of this would add a certain grandeur and recognition that had so far been lacking in his life. He decided he would sign future documents and reports above the new appellation, Secretary Cobden. Pleased almost to giddiness by the contemplation of this daring change, Secretary Cobden went for a walk around the room in a mildly swaggering manner completely foreign to him before today.

The agents communicated with one another cautiously, since they understood they were all being watched. In Sophie, this produced a change. Instead of worrying in a state of not knowing and being ignorant of the enemy's intentions, she now saw the dangers clearly. She wished they did not exist, yet now they had been isolated and were identifiable, she could address them. Dawkins suspected the Burgoyne's staff to be agents. There was nothing she could do to erase his suspicion. Yes, they might just do their duties and play everything straight, thereby avoiding any further attention, but there was no point to that. Stokely would still exist as a threat, and a growing, murderous, red-fisted threat at that. As dangerous as Chertsey Park had become, Sophie saw that, under the current circumstances, there was no safer place for herself and her friends. To leave was to confirm all of Dawkins' suspicions. He would tell Stokely. They would send Miller and others after them. To carry on without doing their secret work would allow Stokely to win. However, she knew there was no guarantee of success even if they did continue their spying. Good evidence, Stokely-destroying evidence, was unlikely to be left lying about. Instead, she decided, they must do things differently. She went to find Flora.

"It's getting rather rotten," said Flora.

"Yes, and we must do something about it."

"What exactly do you have in mind?"

"Not a great deal, at present. However, I'll make sure Miss Terrence doesn't cause any trouble. As soon as she arrives, let me know."

"What will you say to her?"

"I have several ideas, dependent upon her state of mind. If she's for us, then good. If she's against us or lying, I'll know what to do."

"Ooh, can I watch?"

"No."

"What about Dawkins?"

"He's more difficult. At some point, he'll decide if we're a threat or not to Stokely and his precious plans. But think of this. He doesn't know who we work for, does he? Dawkins has to tread carefully. He can stare all he likes and it won't get the silly man anywhere, because he doesn't know *anything*."

"Are you sure?"

"Reasonably sure. But even if he found out about us, he'd realize the police know we're here. Therefore, we are safe."

"I'm not convinced, Phoebe. I feel there must be a hole in your logic, but I can't see it at the moment."

"Even if there is, we must go on the attack."

"You didn't get enough sleep last night. Obviously, you're deranged. What do you mean, *attack*?"

"Simply this. We have one enemy in the house, and that's Dawkins. The others don't matter, not even Stokely Stink-pot. They could imprison us or murder us, but they won't, because others know we're here and they would understand that. They won't do anything, so we're safe for the present. Stokely would not want adverse publicity. Do you think all those bankers, and Marconi, and the rest of them would do business with a man who's in the newspapers because there are murder investigations on his estate?"

"Stop mentioning murder, for goodness' sake... I follow what you're saying, but what is it you intend to do?"

"Outwit the intelligence officer by not being fearful of him."

"That's easier said than done, but please be more precise."
"We shall trick Dawkins."
"*That* I understand."
"Good. We'll have a meeting and put our heads together."

Sophie met Broadbent-Wicks.
'We're having a meeting at midday, so make certain you have lunch with the rest of us."
"Right-o."
"Now, tell me. Has anyone been watching you?"
"No, I don't think so."
"I am surprised. I'll tell you about it at the meeting. Just be careful who you talk to and do only your footman's duties until further notice."
"Absolutely. May I ask a question?"
"Yes."
"Suppose we've made a mistake about Stokely? What I mean is, he seems like an awfully nice chap for an earl. He gave me ten pounds yesterday."
"So, I understand. He's behind the Red Fist business. A factory was blown-up last night. The blast killed two people. He is *not* a nice chap."
"But he was here. You saw him yourself."
"Mr Ely. He pays people to commit the atrocities. All his efforts are towards his becoming the leader, and probable dictator, of this country."
"He hasn't actually said that. I read some materials in the ballroom with no one seeing me. He has some good ideas, although some of it's complete rubbish. You see, if he means that British society should be organized more fairly, then I'm all for that."

Sophie put a hand to her forehead in exasperation. "I don't know what to say. Everything points to his being a murderer, a blackmailer, a liar, and one who wishes to become a tyrant."

"I believe everything you say... It's just that *I* haven't seen it. I've always had the habit of wanting to see things for myself and I can't help it. My father and mother often get annoyed with me."

"Ah. I imagine they do. How about this? Stokely intends moving into Buckingham Palace and renaming it, The Presidential Palace."

"He can't do that! It's not allowed. It belongs to the Royal family."

"Well, he drew a picture of it when he was a young man, and gave it *that* title. So he's had the idea of taking control for years and years. We have a copy of the drawing."

"That settles it. Say no more, Miss King. He really has to be stopped. The man's mad."

"I don't understand how you failed to see the connection between Stokely and all the terrible things that have been going on."

"Because it was all hearsay. I've seen no proof he's done anything wrong. It's possible he has, but it's not proven. Please understand, I trust your judgment implicitly, and willingly fell in with your wishes. You said he was evil, so evil he was. That some of his ideas were reasonable made me see him in a different light. When one thinks of a criminal, it comes as a surprise to find they have good qualities, too. Also, Stokely's been pleasant to me personally. Now that you possess evidence of his dreams of being king, president, or a high and mighty grand poobah, that's all I need to be convinced of your original estimation. He is a traitor, and has had treacherous thoughts for years, as you say."

"Thank you for your explanation. I can picture you on a jury, in a very, *very* long trial."

"That's how I sort things out in my mind, as though all the arguments are in front of a judge, where the matter is pleaded back and forth. Your having such a drawing clinches it for me. Perhaps it's not good enough for courtroom evidence, but it shows the way the man's mind works, and what he's truly after. In other words, it fits with what's going on here. I can no longer give him the benefit of the doubt."

"This knowledge won't make you act differently towards Stokely?"

"Good heavens, *no*, Miss King. At all times, while acting as a footman, I'm most careful to conceal I'm a spy. Lord Stokely shan't be alarmed by me. And if his head is full of all that sort of muck, and he's dissembling to conceal it, I'll make sure I'll dissemble him one better. Or something like that. You understand what I mean."

## Chapter 22

# Watching and whispering

Charlotte Terrence left her service flat to go out to the street and step into the back of Lord Stokely's Rolls-Royce. She had always been a naturally attractive woman but, as the years had gone by, a little more art was necessary to maintain standards. Recently, she had changed the way she did her make-up, going from the dramatic eyes and lips that a young woman could carry off, to a simpler, more blended look. She had benefitted from the change. The car drew away from the kerb and, through the window, she watched winter-wet London go by. She nestled in a corner in her expensive fur coat and hat, and felt more light-hearted than she had for some considerable time. It was so long ago that she had been this happy that she could not quite recall when it was. Blankly looking out, she slowly remembered. It was the last time he had shown interest in her. Now he had sent a car; not just any car, but his own limousine.

On the telephone, Lord Stokely — her Roderick — had sounded pleased to speak with her, interested in what she was doing, and happy to invite her to Chertsey Park once more. She had quickly forgotten all her accumulated resentment over his neglect of her. It was forgotten instantaneously, really. Charlotte did not stupidly believe that his passion for her had suddenly rekindled, but she hoped it might and, given half a chance, she would see that it did. She knew him well, though; well enough to expect him to ask a favour of her. He often had, and usually they were not onerous requests, unlike the last occasion when he had insisted she do something she really had not wanted to do. Although that scheme of Stokely's had ultimately failed, she had played *her* part well. It was then that she had met Miss Phoebe King.

Miss Terrence was not a success with other women. She rarely developed with them anything more than a superficial friendship, mainly because, as a professional gambler, there were few other women in her field. Those that were gamblers were also competitors, and those outside of gambling did not understand the gambler's life, or how a woman could be involved in such a 'low pursuit.' Those same hypocritical women in society who could talk to a *man* who gambled took pains to cut her dead. At first, she thought it was grossly unfair. Then, when she had learned that she could have some fun at her critics' expense, she had scored off them. Now, she no longer cared what others thought. But Miss King was different.

She considered Phoebe King, who was of the type that usually would have nothing to do with her. Nominally, she was of her class, almost twenty years her junior, and also very annoying because she withstood being manipulated. She had seen Miss King dressed in a chauffeur's uniform and as a woman of business, yet also knew her to be an agent — some type of spy for an agency of which she did not know the name, but to whom reports had to be given on the activities of Lord Stokely. If she did not report something regularly, the small, yet steady, supply of money would dry up, with the decision to pay or not to pay resting with Miss King. Well, she would have something to report subsequent to this Saturday and

Sunday, and so the money would stream in for longer. But what if... what if Roderick returned to her? *Then* handling the annoying Miss King might become a problem.

When Charlotte arrived at Chertsey Park, she was in good time for lunch. She did not know it, but her arrival heralded a change in the house. Stokely considered the guests arriving in the late morning and early afternoon to be his friends, rather than useful business or political acquaintances. The morning's shoot had been a relaxed affair, too, where Stokely scored the highest. Saturday was a holiday for Stokely, although he did not view it as such. For those in the ballroom, there was work, although rewarding, and no holiday until the sun went down. Yet they were aware that Saturday night would bring a more relaxed, convivial atmosphere where drink flowed freely. Most were returning to their homes Sunday morning, and the word was that Lord Stokely was exceptionally pleased with their progress.

After an early lunch, the agents were prepared for Charlotte when she arrived. She did not know Alfie, and so he took Charlotte's luggage to the assigned bedroom, while Broadbent-Wicks went to find Flora, who in turn told Fern, who delivered the message to Sophie. Ada then covered Sophie's work while she set off to deal with matters.

While hanging up her clothes in a wardrobe, Charlotte heard a soft knock on her door.

"Enter," she said.

"Good morning, Miss Terrence. Luncheon will be served at one o'clock."

Charlotte stared while her look of surprise turned to one of irritation. Finally, she said, "What are *you* doing here?"

"I'm a parlourmaid. May I add, miss, that although luncheon here is a relaxed gathering, the food is served promptly."

"So you're here spying." Charlotte smiled.

"I prefer you didn't mention my presence. You are also likely to recognize other faces. Please don't acknowledge us. That would be bad for business."

"Oh, how *rich*..." Charlotte was enjoying the idea of the situation, but then her manner changed. "He's not being arrested?"

"Not as far as I'm aware, but then I'm not a police officer."

"Whatever you are, he's too clever for you... I've been meaning to say this for some time. I'm not being paid enough. As you can see for yourself, I'm here, and it took a tremendous amount of persuasion on my part to be invited. It has cost me a packet to come. If you doubled what I'm paid, I suppose I could live with that."

"You know very well that I do not decide your remuneration. I can only refer the matter."

"Then why don't you telephone someone who *does* decide? And do it now."

"Because, Miss Terrence, you will not extort money based on this situation."

"I said nothing like that. You're leaping to conclusions."

"I have leapt to only one conclusion — that if Stokely, or anyone else, discovers we are more than servants, he shall most assuredly hear of what *you've* been up to recently."

Charlotte took out a cigarette and lit it. "You wouldn't dare. If you can't give me more money, you don't have the power to fire me, or let Lord Stokely know what I've been doing. You're bluffing."

"There's a chance I'm bluffing, but I thought you'd know me better by now. How will Stokely react when he finds out you've betrayed him...? As I mentioned, Miss Terrence, luncheon is served promptly at one. Is there anything else?"

Charlotte ground out her cigarette in an ashtray. Sophie waited a moment. After receiving no response, she inclined her head, then silently left the room.

"Was it all right, miss?" asked Ada, when Sophie returned to resume work.

"I believe so. Miss Terrence is a difficult person, and I find her very wearing. She wants to twist everything around all the time. I can't understand people like that."

"Neither do I, but there's a lot of 'em about. I 'ave a brother like it. No matter *what* you say to him, he 'as to say the opposite. If you said, 'It looks like rain,' he'd say, 'No, it don't.' If you come back with, 'I won't need my umbrella, then,' he'd say, 'Are you silly? You just said it looks like rain.' 'Cause he's like that, I never talk to him much."

"What would happen if your brother and Miss Terrence met one another, I wonder?"

"Ha! I don't think they'd last two minutes. But the big thing about my brother is, he has 'ands."

"Hands? What can you possibly mean?"

"Well, he's a good-looking boy, and he's free with 'em, if you get my meaning. He'd take a shine to Miss Terrence pretty quick, even though he's only nineteen."

"Oh."

"He's the only one in the family like it, and we all wish he wasn't. Mum and Dad say they've had trouble with him and girls ever since he was twelve."

"Good grief."

"I know. So what I'm saying is that Miss Terrence might get a surprise. But from what you've said about her, my brother might get put in his place,"

"Let's hope we never find out. For the present, we have to assume Charlotte will keep quiet. Next, we'll deal with Mr Dawkins."

"Those fellas aren't watching like they were first thing this morning. Do you think we're off the 'ook?"

"No, I don't. That would be too good to be true."

"I can see that. What worries me, miss, is if we 'ave to scarper sudden-like. We'd 'ave to telephone Miss Elizabeth first, then wait for her to come and get us. A lot could 'appen while all that's going on."

"Very true, and it bothers me, too."

"Glad says there are a lot of cars in the garage. Couldn't you drive one of them?"

"Yes, *if* I had the key. Elizabeth says she doesn't need one to get a car started, but she never showed me how to do it."

"That's a pity. Who keeps the keys, then?"

"A-ha! I believe you've hit on something. The keys should be kept in the garage."

"I'm 'appy to 'elp, that I am, but we should sort it out, and quick."

"You're right. And thank you for covering so much of my work. I'd be lost without you."

"Oh, don't say nothin', miss. We're all in it together, ain't we?"

"Most certainly, we are."

"Even if it does all go to pot."

"*Please*, let's hope that doesn't happen."

---

Lord Stokely had taken Charlotte Terrence to one side after lunch. In a private room, she sat in a chair while he remained standing.

"I'm so pleased you came, Charlotte. You're looking lovely, my dear."

"Am I?"

Stokely smiled. "You are always lovely." He spoke with tenderness.

He casually moved about the room, carelessly examining objects.

"I have been remiss in not seeing you more often... There's been much to do of late..." He turned to her. "Business, you understand. It's quite remarkable how much time it takes up."

"I can imagine," said Charlotte. She enjoyed watching Roderick, as she always did, but she was nervous, too. All her feelings for him were returning. He had invited her once more. This great man of Britain had singled her out again. Dare she hope? "You've always been busy, and you're so often in the news these days... Often escorting a lady, I notice."

"True. Many events demand I bring a companion... They mean nothing to me. Passing fancies only... Not like you." He came to her and took one of her hands in his. "We have always understood one another. I can speak to you in ways that I cannot with other women."

His eyes fixed on hers. For Charlotte, in that moment, a surge of emotional well-being, if not euphoria, flooded back, erasing the wilderness of time since last she knew he loved her.

"Is there anything I can get for you? Would you care for a drink?"

"Not at the moment, thank you."

He let go of her hand.

"What have you been doing with yourself?"

"Not a great deal... There's no one else at present."

"Isn't there...? Then shall we have a private supper together later?"

"Yes."

"I would send everyone packing early but, as I mentioned, business intrudes. This is rather a big weekend for me, and there are a few necessary things to be done before we meet later. To that purpose, I wonder if you would do me a small favour? It will be thoroughly enjoyable for you... Right up your street, in fact."

"Roderick," she said in a soft, patient way. "What is it?" Charlotte was unsurprised by his asking something of her. It was the way he was.

"I have many guests staying, as you can see. I don't know most of them, but I must be able to trust them. I had an idea that if they got up a card game, those who like to gamble, especially after a few drinks, could not resist the temptation. Before they even arrived, I mentioned there would be card games, so those who have the habit will have come prepared.

You would sit in on the games and tell me of anyone who had a weakness for cards, or anything else, for that matter. You see, if they have a vice, it could become awkward my employing them, which would be detrimental to my plans. Your doing this small service for me will make me so grateful."

Charlotte studied him. Yes, she would do what he asked, and be happy doing so, but her wave of well-being had received a check, and she saw plainly the reasons for her invitation. It then occurred to her that she might make mention of having recognized a few of the servants, and suspected them of working against him. Charlotte could have done this — given away Burgoyne's Agency to gain favour with Roderick. Now she understood that whatever attention he was paying her at this moment would be short-lived. There was no point in telling him anything. She was a gambler and reacted according to her way.

"That's a good idea. It'll put an edge on the game, too... I brought my cheque book with me."

"You don't intend losing, do you?"

"No. Winning is never guaranteed, though. I can only play what cards I'm dealt."

"Naturally. However, you will not need your cheque book." He went to a desk to open a drawer. "I think it would be more interesting for your opponents if you put cash on the table." He brought an envelope to her. "Three hundred pounds. I don't need it back."

Charlotte, the gambler, took the envelope and said, "Thank you... This should impress some of them. Are any of these men rich? It's important I know. Because, if they are, three hundred won't make a difference."

"This is why you are perfect. Let's see who sits down at the table. Then I will have someone provide that information, and anything else you may require."

"That will help. I'm quite looking forward to the challenge."

"That was my hope. I'm terribly sorry, Charlotte — a house full of guests, and so many demands upon my time, means I must leave now, but later on..." Stokely bent down to kiss her, then left the room.

Charlotte, the woman, sadly wondered why he could not just love her.

During lunch, Lester Dawkins had surreptitiously observed Sophie's movements. It seemed to him she was on edge, but not unduly so. A maid bringing in a box late at night — he had believed her when she said it contained food. A maid startled by him on the stairs — her reaction was reasonable. Miss King's voice had changed. Her exclamation placed her as county, of the upper middle class. Her subsequent speech had a London, lower middle class accent. He had met women, and some men, who attempted to sound a class or two higher. This made Miss King unusual in trying to sound a couple of classes lower. Dawkins had since learned she was the manager of the agency's staff, so it was no great surprise that she had answered well beyond that which a nervous maid would answer. Then she had met his challenge and refused to walk past him. He found Miss King interesting — not much less so were the other two maids in the dining room — one an actress and the other terribly efficient. Neither looked like spies to him, and an impoverished actress earning money as a maid was, again, a valid and reasonable explanation. But, taken as a group, although the three maids were performing their duties at luncheon excellently, he thought they seemed too knowing, too aware, now that he studied them carefully in a series of sly glimpses.

Flora and Ada had a hurried conversation outside the kitchen.

"I thought I was gonna' die," said Ada. "He never took his eyes off us."

"Yes, but we did it," said Flora. "Although, I had the urge to shove food in his face."

"We don't want to waste good food on *his* smarmy mug."

"Dawkins also strikes me as an oily character, so, yes, *bad* food would be more appropriate for him."

Ada laughed. "A bucket of slops, eh?"

"Perfect!" said Flora.

In a nearby corridor, Sophie spoke to Alfie and Fern about Dawkins.

"Remember, if he speaks to either of you, just say you were hired to do the work and know nothing more."

"And look stupid, you mean," said Alfie. "It always works with the upper crust, and did wonders for me in the army."

"I can do that an' all, miss," said Fern.

"Yes, I'll do the same," said Sophie. "Perhaps we'll have a competition later to see who looks the most stupid."

They all smiled.

"Do you know where Mr Ely is at present?" she asked.

"Haven't seen him since we ate," said Alfie.

Sophie could not find Mr Ely — Broadbent-Wicks — because at that moment he was trailing Mr Kemp. Broadbent-Wicks had just exited the Grand Dining Room when he noticed Kemp hurrying towards Stokely's office, so he followed him. The gamekeeper had left his usual ground floor haunt and, to Broadbent-Wicks, he seemed particularly suspicious.

Kemp knocked on the door. Someone inside said, 'Come.' He entered. From where Broadbent-Wicks was standing, and while the door was open, he was sure he heard Dawkins say, "There you are, Kemp. I have a joke for you." This puzzled the footman, who tried listening at the door, but heard nothing. Not wanting to be found in such an odd place for a footman, he departed to take up his position in the entrance hall. That was where Sophie found him — standing at the bottom of the stairs.

"Psst," said Sophie, leaning over the railing when no one was about.

Broadbent-Wicks looked up.

"I want a word with you in private."

"At once, Miss King."

He ascended the stairs.

"Let's find a quiet place where no one can see us," said Sophie.

"Um, no need, Miss King. If you hide behind that pillar and whisper, and I stand outside the main door, we can hear each other perfectly. Sort of like the Whispering Gallery at St. Paul's."

"How interesting. Let's try it."

They discovered it worked well. Sophie, behind a nearby pillar, unseen from below or by anyone in the corridors, could hear and be heard by Broadbent-Wicks, who stood outside the entrance to The Grand Salon, twenty-five feet away.

"Have you heard anything useful?" whispered Sophie.

From the side of his mouth, he whispered back, "Only the usual rubbish. 'Hello, how are you? Such a magnificent house, blah, blah.' Although one chap said, 'What a waste of money.'"

"It's a pity Stokely doesn't have his conversations out here."

"He wouldn't do that, because he knows how the sound carries."

"Yes. May I ask where you've been for the last two hours?"

"I was told to stand here by Mr Dalgleish. Guests pop in occasionally, but I was standing about doing nothing for so long, I thought I may as well follow people."

"Who?"

"Kemp, for one. Apparently, Dawkins wanted to tell him a joke, although that didn't sound quite right to me, but I could hear nothing else, because the door was too thick. "

"I don't know what to make of that."

"A bit of a damp squib. Anyway, I also trotted after Miller."

"You did? Where was this?"

"By the Gun Room. I say, Miss King. I'm getting rather good at following people without their noticing. And if they spot me, I stand still like a footman should, and they think I'm part of the scenery."

Sophie groaned. "Did Miller spot you?"

"Only once but, because we're quite chummy, I spoke to him, otherwise it would have been ridiculous."

She shut her eyes. "Tell me what you said."

"Because you forbade me to talk about Stokely, the Red Fist, and all that, I said to him, 'It's a pity about Mr Auckland dying in that car accident. Do you think he was drunk?'"

Sophie's mouth opened in disbelief. "What did he say?"

"He went rather red, then said, 'Yes, it was a pity,' and he didn't know anything about it. So I said, 'I understand newspapermen drink like fish.' To which he replied, 'More than likely.' I noticed he was hesitant and, knowing he's a murderer and that I shouldn't upset him, and the place is full of criminals, I had a luminous thought, quite the inspiration, really, and said..."

Sophie gasped louder than a whisper.

"'... I don't want the coppers to come nosing about asking *me* awkward questions.' Miller seemed to like that. He smiled, then said, 'That's right, mate. You know, I had you pegged as light-fingered from the start. That's a good racket, with your high-class accent and monkey suit. A word of warning, though. Don't go nicking stuff from this place. Give it a miss, 'cause you don't want trouble from Dawkins.' So I said, 'I thought *Kemp* ran the show here?' He replied, 'Nah, you got it wrong. Kemp gives us the jobs and a place to stay, but it's all on Dawkins' say so. You must know that?' So I said, 'Of course, I know Dawkins is in charge of operations, but I didn't know he was in charge of Kemp, too.'"

"Oh, well done!"

"There's more. Miller added not to go asking questions about Mr Auckland. Miss King, he said it in such a way that it made me think *he* had a hand in it. I thought it best to drop the topic, so I said, right-o, and buttoned up completely — not wanting to give the game away, don't you know."

Sophie always felt she was on shifting ground when talking to Broadbent-Wicks. "Weren't you afraid?"

"Afraid of what...? Oh, I see what you mean. Um, not exactly. I found it jolly interesting, though. He must be some sort of assassin, who goes round bumping people off when there's a call for that sort of thing."

"How do you view him, morally speaking?"

"He should have the book thrown at him, of course. Which is a pity, because otherwise he seems like a decent chap. Still, he shouldn't be killing people for money. That's very wrong... Someone's coming. You might want to toddle off."

Toddle quickly she did and in bafflement, arising from Broadbent-Wicks' easy going attitude to anything and everything. At least he had now confirmed that Auckland's death was no accident. Kemp's men had murdered him. Not understanding *how* they had committed the dreadful crime bothered her greatly.

# Chapter 23

# Probing attacks

During the lull in work, between having prepared for Saturday's dinner and serving at teatime, Sophie took a few minutes to consider her position at Chertsey Park. Concerning Miller, she could see that, as the only eyewitness to the Fleet Street murder, it was she alone who could identify the assailant. She asked herself if her testimony, based solely on the way the man walked, would be sufficient. She doubted it was, and further doubted that she could give that testimony in isolation from all the other circumstances of her work. How could she stand up in court and say she routinely spied under contract for the FO and Scotland Yard? That was impossible. At least she had identified the murderer; the rest of it was out of her control.

Evidence. It always came down to that. For the death of Mr Auckland, she had none, yet his killer or killers were in the house, of this she was certain. Perhaps Miller was also involved in Auckland's killing. While she was thinking this over, she concluded she had no evidence, and no testimony — nothing to convince anyone that charges should be laid, let alone that the case should be tried in court.

Her growing sense of futility increased further when considering Stokely. He unwittingly may not be an earl, and he had possessed grandiose ideas from an early age, but neither of these facts made him a criminal. She could prove he housed Red Fist men and murderers, but not in any way that would prove him culpable. If there were no evidence to present for either of the two murders, and the Red Fist handbills proved nothing by themselves, Stokely remained in the clear, without taint attached to him. She asked herself what she had expected to find at Chertsey Park and had no answer. Here she was, in amongst the inner workings of a treasonous machine, unable to stop it. There had to be a lever somewhere, or a delicate flywheel which, if tapped, she could dislocate and bring everything to a halt. Rendering her inability to find evidence even more painful, the newspapers brought daily reports of violence perpetrated by the Red Fist. With her time at Chertsey Park running out, Sophie felt the pressure to succeed, knowing her failure meant harm and suffering for innocent people.

After meeting Dawkins, Kemp returned to The Gun Room where his associate, John, was working on a disassembled shotgun.

"Leave that. I've got a job for you."

"Oh, yes?"

"Dawkins's got an itch he wants scratching. You know them servants down from London? He thinks they're wrong-uns. Some of them, anyway. Not the ones from Lyall Place."

"Wrong in what way?" asked John.

"Thieves or police, I suppose. He wants you to get chummy with a girl named Dora Datchet. She's about eighteen or twenty."

"I think I know who you mean. What have I got to do?"

"Make her talk. Get her drunk, promise her marriage, threaten her, whatever it takes. Only, he wants it done today."

"He don't want much, does he? These things take time."

Kemp shrugged.

"What's the pay?" asked John.

"A few quid, I suppose. He didn't say. Dawkins is anxious, though, and you don't want to disappoint him, do you?"

"No need to tell me that. Is he after anything in particular?"

"Yes. He wants to know about the people she works with and if they're up to no good."

"Getting her drunk's the easiest, but she's got to like me first."

"You've always done all right with the girls, so run along and come back with something useful. Make up a story if you have to."

"But what if she knows nothing?"

"Like I said, make it up. Dawkins won't know the difference and you want to get paid, right? Anyway, John, you'd better get on with it."

The young man found Fern having a cup of tea by herself in the servants' hall. He walked in nonchalantly and stopped. Fern noticed him and he came over to her.

"Hello," said John, brightly. "A penny for your thoughts."

Fern smiled at the unexpected question given by the man with a friendly face. "What do you mean?"

"You look sort of sad, sitting there by yourself. Like you need cheering up." He sat down opposite her.

"No, I'm not sad."

"Thinking about something important, I reckon."

"I s'pose."

"I'm John and I believe you're... Dora Datchet." He spoke playfully. "That's a nice name... I tell you what, Dora, why don't you come to the party later?"

"What party's this?"

"We have one nearly every week. A few of us get together and have a fine old time. It's just us smarter lads and pretty girls." He winked at her. "We have a gramophone, and there's a bit of dancing, food, drink, and a good time's had by all. You should come along. You'll really enjoy yourself."

"I can't, I'm working. And I have to be up early."

"Ah, don't worry about that. We don't go too late, because

we *all* have an early start."

She hesitated.

He leaned forward. "Just come for half an hour. That won't kill you... I'll tell you something, though. You'll *laugh* like anything. There'll be a couple of fellas there who tell the best jokes, and the way those two banter back and forth, you won't believe it. Talk about funny."

"It sounds nice."

"And it is. I'll take you there, but don't tell anyone you're going, otherwise *everyone* will want to come. Just go as you are, and I'll get you in. So, I'll meet you here... What time do you get off?"

"It's supposed to be ten, but the work always goes later than that."

"What, like ten-thirty?"

"Yes, about then."

"Right, Dora, my girl, I'll be waiting for you here at ten-thirty, right on the dot. I'm pleased you're coming. You'll have a lovely time. I know you will."

"That's ever so nice of you. Thank you."

John smiled at her as he got up. "Bye, for now."

Fern watched him go, delighted that this friendly man had invited her. It would be her first time going to such a party.

---

Although Sophie had arranged a time to meet Elizabeth, she wanted to confirm it. Also, she was in two minds about telephoning Inspector Morton, having realized that her notes might be insufficient to explain the increasingly risky situation. She had to tell him what was going on, and get his advice on the dangers of Dawkins' suspicion, Miss Terrence's presence, and her own theory about Mr Auckland's murder.

All that would take time to explain, and would be difficult under the constant threat of someone picking up an extension or the operator listening in. Sophie would try, but she really needed to meet Inspector Morton in person to relate everything properly.

As she paused at a corner on the ground floor of the west wing, Sophie became vigilant and cautious. The corridor was clear, but before she could take a step, the door to the Gun Room opened. Kemp and another man came out. She drew back. They were too far away for her to hear what was being discussed. She heard another door opening and risked taking a peek. It was the Butler's Pantry door, but the men did not enter. Kemp pointed up to the telephone wires, spoke, then shut the door. Sophie slipped quietly away, certain that, from now on, they would monitor the telephone line.

It took her several minutes to get over the shock, having seen in her mind's eye the total collapse of their emergency plan. If she could not get to a telephone, how was she to summon help? She and her agents might have accomplished much, as long as they had remained hidden and unnoticed. That carefully crafted covering was now being pushed and tested. They may have already pierced it. The game was up, and the agents had to leave. What galled her the most in this ignominious retreat was that Stokely remained secure yet again. Failure! — it irritated her no end.

Ada was putting china away. Sophie entered the room just after Mrs Newnham had left.

"What's the matter, miss?" asked Ada, as soon as she saw her.

"We're leaving tonight. There's no point in us continuing here, because they're on to us. I've just discovered they're going to be watching the telephone. That means I can't ring up to report *or* summon help."

"Oh, no! I'm ever so sorry," said Ada. "I know you expected to get stuff on Stokely, and we got some, but not what you'd 'oped for. At least we tried, eh, miss?"

"We did. However, this was our one chance, and we'll never get another. I'm sorry, I'm rather upset over this disappointment."

"Don't be, miss. Something always turns up in the end. If *we* don't get him, someone will."

Sophie smiled at her. "You're right, of course. I think I was expecting too much. I'll tell the others to get their things packed."

"What time are we leaving?"

"Eleven. Before then, I really should talk to Mr Dalgleish and Mrs Newnham. I can't bear to let them down, so what on earth can I say?"

"They won't be 'appy whatever you tell 'em. Put it down to Kemp and his men. They'll understand that all right."

"Yes, I suppose that sounds reasonable. It's also a near truth rather than a total fabrication. I really hate lying, but I'm doing so much of it these days."

"Aren't we all? Still, you can 'ardly tell 'em the truth, can you? But I know exactly what you mean, miss. It's one thing to cheat the crooks, but quite another to trick decent people."

"Yes, although ultimately it's for their own good. The less they know, the safer they are... Oh, look at the time: I've done nothing useful today, and I've been meaning to go to the garage to find the keys."

"Do that now, miss. I'll look after things in the 'ouse."

Sophie went up to the dormitory to get her coat. From there, she followed a path, to the east wing ground floor, which was least likely to bring her into contact with anyone who might think to either follow or stop her. Several times she waited to avoid staff or Kemp's men on the stairs and in the passages, but eventually she got outside and without incident.

Exiting through a side entrance, she saw that the garage lay towards the rear of the house. Several cars were parked outside the brick block with its row of five closed double doors and a side door. The building was only ten years old and occupied the site where large stables had once stood. A small and similarly aged stable block, kennels, and an old barn were situated even further away. She could hear the occasional bark of a dog, the sound being carried on the soft breeze. The air was noticeably milder now, and the snow was completely gone from the shovelled areas. No one seemed to be about just at that moment so, walking briskly, she headed towards the garage as if she had business there.

Inside the garage was one big open space laid out for the parking of ten cars. They had parked older cars along the back wall, which left enough room for a second car to be parked in front of each of them — corresponding to each pair of doors. The only exception was Stokely's limousine, which exclusively occupied the nearest space. She found a rack of hooks with keys hanging on them right inside the door. Twelve of the hooks identified the car to which the key belonged, and there were seven keys remaining. Quickly, she surveyed the keys and then the cars. She discovered that there were only two she knew how to drive, both being Rolls-Royces — a car she had driven before. The controls and instruments of the other vehicles looked so vastly different to anything she was used to. This meant that if she had to steal a car in an emergency, it would either have to be Stokely's, or the car that was under a dust sheet at the far end. She suddenly felt guilty in considering the theft of an earl's personal car, so she crossed the garage to see if what was under the sheet was drivable.

She lifted the front of the heavy sheet of sailcloth and doubted it was a running car. The old Rolls-Royce had a headlamp broken off and a crumpled front mudguard. Its radiator was dented, while one of the pair of spring assemblies protruding between the front wheels was deeply scored down to shiny metal. Sophie dropped the sheet. If any of the vehicles at Chertsey Park were in perfect running order, it would be Stokely's car. That settled her choice, and she dismissed her scruples.

A vehicle came to a stop outside the garage. Sophie hid behind a car at the back, not wanting to be found poking around inside. She heard the side door open and then footsteps within. She counted the seconds while holding her breath, expecting to hear the jingle of a key being placed on a hook. If it occurred, she did not hear it, because the door opened and closed again, and silence reigned once more. She crept from her hiding place and left the garage. With no one about, she began walking and passed the cars parked outside. At that moment, a man came out of the house opposite. He stopped and lit a cigarette.

Jeremy Rushton was tired of talking about newspapers, Stokely's renewed Britain, and supposed emergency plans to aid the government. He had smoked earlier in his life, but the strain of being at Chertsey Park had made him indulge the habit again. It was a good excuse for him to get away from the others, the oh, so ardent others, who were still working in the ballroom. He had chosen this moment to decide the timing of his resignation from Stokely's newspaper. It would mean a lot less money, but he would get a job in Fleet Street soon enough, and especially as he had a story to tell about Lord Stokely's scheme. Those were the things he had intended to contemplate. Instead, the young woman, obviously a maid, approaching from the garage, caught his attention. He smiled at her as she drew near, and she returned a cordial but shy nod of her head.

"Excuse me a moment. I don't wish to hold you up. Do you work here in the house?"

Sophie halted to reply. "Yes, sir."

"My name's Rushton. I work for a newspaper, one that belongs to Lord Stokely."

"Do you, sir?"

"Yes. I simply wanted to ask if Lord Stokely has had many meetings like this one."

"I wouldn't know, sir. We work for an agency and this is our first time here."

"Ah, I see. Extra staff for the additional guests. Do you know anything about Lord Stokely's aides? The busy young men who seem to be everywhere?"

"I'm afraid I don't. They keep themselves very much to themselves. Why do you ask?"

"Just curious. They seem to be over-vigilant to me. As though they're watching the guests. I wondered why they're doing that."

By his manner, Sophie believed him to be troubled and definitely not one of Stokely's inner circle.

"They have been observing us, too."

"*Really.* Now that is interesting. I'm sorry to have kept you."

"Not at all. May I ask you a question, sir?"

"Please, go right ahead."

"Is Lord Stokely planning some new form of government?"

Rushton was suddenly cautious. "I don't know about that. The work in the ballroom is more in the nature of creating an in-depth prospectus; making others aware of how the government could be run more efficiently in specific ways."

It became apparent he was not talking to a maid, but a social equal.

"I'm glad to hear it. Good day, sir."

"Before you go. Why did you ask that?"

"Because I think it would be a risky business if he were."

As Sophie entered the house, Rushton thought over what she had said, which essentially confirmed his own views. These were the ones he had diligently been suppressing for the sake of his career. He rushed in and caught up with her.

"Sorry to be a nuisance. It's my reporter's habit of pestering people. Do you know something?"

"If you have doubts about Lord Stokely, be guided by them."

"Sage words... But they come too late."

"How so?"

"I mentioned his aides and their vigilance. I believe it is unfavourable towards me."

"Oh, dear... Then put on an act, and get out as soon as you can. That's all I will say."

This time, he let her walk away.

After quickly cleaning her shoes, soiled slightly from being outside, then generally tidying herself, Sophie joined Flora in the corridor outside the kitchen just before teatime.

"Mr Dalgleish was looking for you," said Flora. "He wants to discuss tomorrow's meals. Apparently, and I got some of this from Mrs Newnham, dozens of trade unionists are arriving, and Stokely wants to tone down the landed gentry act, so he won't be using the Grand Dining Room. They'll all be mucking in together at a single trough in The Second Dining Room."

"That's one way of putting it," said Sophie. "What do you think he's up to now?"

"Organizing that general strike business, I should think."

"What an absolute wretch he is. And if it's not that, it will be something equally bad or worse."

An aide entered the corridor, and Flora whispered,

"Here comes an errand boy."

He turned his steps towards them.

"Miss King, Mr Dawkins wishes to see you. If you would follow me, please."

"Do you work for Mr Dawkins?" asked Sophie.

The young man — a year or two younger than Sophie and Flora — hesitated, and his reply came uncertainly.

"Yes..."

"Then you don't work for Lord Stokely?"

"Yes, I do."

"How is it you work for both of them?"

"That's beside the point. You are to come at once."

"I work for an agency, which was employed by Lady Stokely. Sir, I do *not* work for Mr Dawkins. I am *not* subject to his orders. He is a guest and should behave himself as one. That is all I have to say to your Mr Dawkins. Please inform him of this."

A flush of anger suffused the man's face. He turned on his heel and left them.

"How absolutely spiffing," said Flora. "I must say, you reminded me very much of Auntie Bessie."

"I'm out of all patience with these creatures. Who do they think they are? They may have holed us below the waterline, but we'll go down fighting."

"Not literally, I hope."

"No, of course not. We're leaving with Elizabeth at eleven. If we can't, we're going to steal Stokely's car to make our getaway. And if he dares call the police, he'll not press charges, because I shall publish the fact that he is not even an earl. I hadn't wanted to before, because it's not nice to pick on someone in that way. But he and his demented minions leave us no choice. Before we leave, he'll know that we mean business. And as for Dawkins? Pah!"

"Would you keep his Rolls-Royce?"

"No, that really *would* be stealing. I'll park it outside a police station."

"What's prompted this change? You've become quite militant."

"Only a quarter of an hour ago, I spoke to a man named Rushton. It was obvious he's realized he's made a blunder in working for Stokely. Mr Rushton must have guessed that all the work they're doing could be the blueprint for a coup d'état. He also mentioned those wretched aides. They're keeping him under surveillance, and he's worried. They can't go around acting like a secret police force for Stokely. I've had enough of it, him, them, everything."

"So I see. Do be careful, though. What I don't understand is why antagonize Dawkins?"

"He suspects us. He will always suspect us, because he's already convinced we're up to something. If we don't stand up to him, he'll gain control and I won't let him. We're all feigning ignorance at the moment, but Dawkins won't believe that. Therefore, we may as well come out in the open."

"What a blooming pickle," said Flora. "It reminds me of a play I was in... Oh, yes. That's it! Sophie, I mean Phoebe, how about this for a plan?"

Sophie looked at her watch. "It's teatime. Tell me on the way."

# Chapter 24

# Everything stops for tea

The guests entered the drawing room at four o'clock. At first, the footmen assisted them. When Mr Dalgleish saw the maids were more than enough to serve the number of guests, he sent Alfie and Broadbent-Wicks to stand outside the door.

They stood, almost statue-like, and began their odd whispering from the sides of their mouths.

"We're hoppin' it, then," said Alfie. "Can't say I mind. Having them blokes keep staring at me is getting on my nerves. I swear, I'd biff one of them if it went on for much longer."

"I don't think you should," said Broadbent-Wicks. "Miss King wouldn't approve of it."

"Then it's a good job we're going."

An aide approached Alfie to say brusquely,

"Come with me. Mr Dawkins wants to see you."

"I've been posted here to serve the guests in the drawing room," answered Alfie. "Your not a guest, mate. If Mr Dawkins wants to speak to me, he can come here himself. Now run along, sonny; you're spoiling my view."

"You'll regret this." He then addressed Broadbent-Wicks. "You. Come along with me."

"Yes, of course, I will. I'll be another five minutes here."

"What?"

"It's only five minutes. Time flies, as everyone knows. It's because I'm busy."

"You're just standing there doing nothing."

"Correct. It's my job, you see. Well, a big part of it. I also serve at meals, carry luggage, clean the glass and silver-plate, and do many other things. Have you any concept of how scrupulous Mr Dalgleish is over the spotlessness of the silver? Where I'd give it the once over, he wants it shining as it did the day it was made... I suppose it was at its shiniest then. Anyway, the old boy is very particular about his lordship's silver."

"Who put you up to this?" The aide stared from one to the other.

"Don't know what you mean," said Alfie.

"Could you explain the question, please?"

"You think yourselves very funny, don't you?" said the furious aide, who then stalked away.

"I don't think he liked that," said Alfie.

"No, it was rather rude of us. Still, Miss King said not to do what they say and to be tricky."

"But you said you'd go with him in five minutes," said Alfie.

"No, technically speaking, I didn't say that. At the end of five minutes, I was going to enter the drawing room for a while, or I might have gone in and then out through another door. It would all depend on where I could stand to the best effect for the dignity of the household."

Alfie chuckled. "We're all going to end up on the carpet, though."

"Yes, you're probably right. How will you conduct yourself when we do?"

"Pick a point on a wall and stare at it. When questioned, I'll say I know nothing. If Dawkins is *really* angry, I'll do to him what I did to my commanding officer when he blew his top at me. I stared at his epaulette while he stood in front of me and crossed my eyes. He took it I was dim-witted, so he stopped shouting."

"Why was he shouting at you?"

"It was early in eighteen at Amiens and the front line was moving forward. It had gone quiet, so a mate and me took an ambulance out to go scavenging. We struck it lucky. There was an abandoned German dugout with a lot of food in it, so we filled the ambulance and went back. Wouldn't you know it? My mate starts crowing about what we've found, and handing out German sausage to the others. That got the two of us caught and up before the CO. Although he let us off, he took all the food, including a bottle of schnapps. I'd already hidden my share, so he didn't get that. You have to be prudent with these things."

"Indeed, you do. I'll do something different, though, so Dawkins doesn't catch on. Besides, he won't be wearing epaulettes."

"Speak of the devil," whispered Alfie.

The two footmen stood to attention and stared ahead. Dawkins passed by to enter the drawing room without comment or acknowledgement.

Within the drawing room, Lord Stokely was in high spirits and, as usual, the centre of attention. To those who had not previously met his Uncle Teddy, he was prompt to introduce him.

"Now, this is Miss Charlotte Terrence, whom I'm sure you've met before."

"Oh, yes. I know Charlotte," said Uncle Teddy. "How are you, my dear?"

"I'm very well, thank you. It's a pleasure to meet you again."

"The pleasure is all mine. I recall we last met three years ago…"

Stokely left them talking and drinking tea together.

Dawkins came up to the earl shortly afterwards to speak to him privately. He had noticed Sophie, but ignored her.

"Any news?" asked Stokely.

"Nothing to report," said Dawkins. "I came to inform you that everyone is ready and in position."

They stood apart from the rest. The guests had formed into a series of small groups, earnestly engaged in teatime conversation. The room buzzed with discussion, but not of cabbages and kings. Instead, it was of Innsbruck, Cannes, and Venice, cars and horses, theatre shows and nightclubs, who had been seen out with whom, and whose marriage was finally falling to pieces.

"The key thing is that there be no delay," urged Stokely. "The story has to make the Sunday papers and the deadline to include a new story is much earlier than for the dailies. They won't break down the front page after eleven, and The London Mercury cannot be the only paper reporting the riots. They *must* start the action on time."

"They will, my Lord. There shall be no mistake."

"Glad to hear it. Now, for tomorrow, ensure everyone becomes a trade unionist for the day. We may pay these union men but, without their influence, a general strike will be delayed for months. It needs to come on quickly, so we must placate them. They're a bloody-minded lot. Push them too hard, and they'll dig their heels in over some absurdity or other."

"I've spoken with everyone who will come in contact with them. They fully understand they must espouse socialist principles, and that what we're doing must be seen as helping to further the aims of the labour movement. Fair wages and benefits, good working conditions, and all that. Make no mistake, my Lord, these unionists are coming here only for the money, so it needs to be impressed upon them they'll get no more without first delivering results. They'll play the game, and there'll be a strike. Once they've infected the unions with the idea, the process will become irreversible."

"The conditions are certainly ripe for a strike." Stokely drank some tea. "Miners, dockers, railway workers — when they act in concert, they'll paralyze the country. Then the other unions should join them. But we absolutely *cannot* have the print unions going out." Stokely laughed. "Beforehand, I'll raise the pay rates on my papers to see if I can't buy myself a little goodwill... Staying for tea, Dawkins?"

"Thank you, but I can't. I have a small matter requiring attention."

"Anything I should know about?"

"It can keep, my Lord."

"Very good."

Stokely rejoined his guests while Dawkins left the room. He had meant to speak to the footmen on the way out, but they had gone.

After tea, Mr Dalgleish approached Sophie as she was clearing tea things away.

"Miss King, Mr Dawkins has requested your presence in the first floor office. You may leave what you're doing."

"Thank you, Mr Dalgleish. Did he mention what it was about?"

"He did not confide in me."

"Thank you."

Dalgleish nodded and left the drawing room. Before setting off, Sophie tidied herself. As she smoothed her hair, she noticed her hand was trembling slightly.

She knocked at the door of the office. Dawkins bid her enter.

"Miss King," he said. "Close the door." He was alone, and sitting behind a desk.

"I prefer to keep it open, thank you."

There was no change in his impassive face. He held out a hand towards a chair.

"I'll remain standing," she said.

"Then at least do me the courtesy of coming forward a step

so that we need not raise our voices."

Sophie advanced half a pace. "What do you wish to see me about, Mr Dawkins?"

"Who do you work for?"

"Lady Stokely."

"Don't try to be clever."

"Is that everything, Mr Dawkins? I have a great deal of work to do."

"You'll answer my question."

"I have given my answer."

"There are consequences to your actions. You realize this?"

"There are consequences to yours, too. If that's everything, I'll bid you good day."

"One moment. Did Scotland Yard send you?"

He studied her face for a reaction, while Sophie sought to control herself in the increasingly tense atmosphere.

"No."

"Your name was already familiar to me."

He watched her again. So far, he had not surprised her, as she had been prepared for something of this nature. Sophie now knew for certain that Dawkins had connected her name to the Foreign Office, via the spy who recorded the names of all visitors. It meant he had Archie Drysdale in mind. She was unsure of this, but she thought Dawkins was not quite sure, either.

"Was it? If that's all, just inform Mr Dalgleish if you wish to speak to me again."

In a weary gesture, Dawkins raised a hand for her to stop speaking in the way she had been so far.

"You see, if I knew who you worked for, you might also be of some use to *me*. Such work could be quite rewarding."

Sophie hesitated, spotting the obvious trap. He knew she was an agent of some sort, and there was no avoiding it anymore. "How much?"

Dawkins laughed. "It doesn't work that way."

"It does for me. You think about it. Good day."

"We'll speak again," Dawkins called after her.

Sophie gladly left the room and shut the door. Halfway along the corridor, she put her hand to her forehead, believing she might have seriously blundered in copying Charlotte Terrence. She wished she could speak to Archie or Superintendent Penrose.

"Cobden," said Stokely, as he lounged in a chair in his private apartment. He looked over the top of a report at his secretary.

"Yes, my Lord?"

"There's a maid here who was at Mama's house, so she has to be from the agency. She's very attractive."

"Which particular one do you mean, my Lord?"

"She has dark hair, quite tall... I thought she might be Italian or Spanish, but when I met the servants, she proved to be entirely English. Well bred, too, by the sounds of her."

"I believe I may have seen the lady in question, my Lord. She is a beauty, and naturally so."

"Yes... Make sure she serves me at dinner."

"I will attend to it, my Lord."

"As you know, Mama wishes me to marry, and I gave my word to find someone this year. This maid has taken my fancy, so find out if there's any impediment to her marrying."

"Shall I ask Mr Dawkins to make enquiries?"

Stokely put down the report. "No. He has enough to do. You look into it. As long as she isn't already married or doesn't have children, there should be no obstacle."

"Very good, my Lord."

"It amuses me, Cobden — the idea of a servant girl being raised to the highest rank in the land."

"It would look well in the newspapers, my Lord."

"Wouldn't it?" said Stokely, smiling. "Or in a Pathé newsreel. Quite a romantic fairy tale."

"I will enquire at once, my Lord."

Kemp met with six men by the kennels.

"Right, this is how we'll work it. Two of you'll be outside. I want one down by the gates at all times, while the other patrols the house with a dog. If anyone comes out as shouldn't, stop them immediately. Get their name and the reason for being out. Now, if they look dodgy, hold 'em and give a shout. The rest of us will be awake and alert in the Gun Room. This is straight from Dawkins, so get it right. No one's to go off the estate, I mean *no one*. Got that?"

"Even if they're one of the guests?"

"Don't matter who it is. Point your gun, and, what with the dog, they won't be going anywhere."

"Which dogs are we using?"

"Only big ones. They'll take turns like we all will. But don't no one dare let a dog off the lead, or it'll be after a fox. I'm not spending hours looking for it."

"What a way to spend Saturday night."

"Grumble to Dawkins about it, not to me."

"What if someone wants to come in?" asked another man.

"How about that? We've got a thinker. Carry their luggage, of course."

"Do you mean that?"

"You really are dim. If they're guests, which they won't be, let 'em in. If they're not, shoot 'em, because they'll be poachers or spies."

The others laughed.

Ada was busy putting crockery on shelves after tea. She was in a large, windowless room dedicated to storing the household china. The walls were lined with cabinets and, in those with glass fronts, many stacks of plates with gleaming gold edges hinted at the beauty that lay within. Ada enjoyed putting the china away. She was quick, but so careful with the expensive items — a skill perfected through long practise. The reason for her satisfaction was that a meal, today's tea, had been successfully concluded, and she had done her work

317

well. She prided herself on such things. As no one was about, she began singing softly. After a minute, and while her back was turned, she heard a noise — alerting her to the fact that someone might be standing in the doorway. Turning, with a teacup in her hand, she found an aide staring at her. She was taken aback at being so caught unawares.

"You won't leave this house alive." He spoke with menace while glaring at Ada as if he hated and despised her. "Talk, and you'll receive money. But if you continue playing games, Carmichael, you'll have a *nasty* accident." With a sneering look, he nodded solemnly. "To save yourself, give up the others. That's all you need to do. Think about what I've said and be *very* careful what you do next. We're watching you. We're always watching you."

The aide continued staring for some seconds. Then he left. Ada's face had become a mask of shock and distress. She put the teacup down and her inattention caused her to set it on the edge of the table. The cup fell and broke.

"Oh, no!" The accident stunned her. She had never done such a thing before. In a hollow silence of disbelief, she bent down to pick up the colourful fragments. Tears came to her eyes — tears of shame and fear.

---

After five, the house quietened. The servants' dinner would be ready soon, as the bulk of the day's work had been done. All the cleaning and bed-making was always completed in the morning, which meant some of the maids would soon be finished for the day. Those who had still to serve guests were now in a twilight period of anticipation. They ate their own meal hurriedly or without relish because of the looming dinner to come. This approaching duty of service to the earl and his guests was the mountain's pinnacle of all the work they did. Servants must make no lapse in etiquette, nor delay in serving, and never intrude into the guests' society. Servants must hover silently, almost invisible, around those seated — beings bringing food as angels from heaven who require no thanks for themselves. With this duty still ahead, some servants could not relax and enjoy their own food, which was a shame because Mrs Potter's cooking had vastly, almost miraculously, improved. The staff of Chertsey Park, who would serve at dinner, saw it as a job to be done, and the sooner it was over, the better it would be. The servants on loan from Lyall Place were accustomed to such work, and knew what to do — please Mr Dalgleish, the butler. If they did that, then Lord Stokely would be pleased. They were not as anxious as those belonging to Chertsey Park.

For the six members of Burgoyne's Agency, the coming dinner presented to their minds all the qualities of a nightmare. Besides their regular duties, they were to eavesdrop without being detected, while being aware that Dawkins, the former intelligence officer, now knew them to be agents. So, apparently, did all of Stokely's aides, whom, they believed, were also armed. Mr Dalgleish had informed Sophie that, for tonight, Miss Walton would serve Lord Stokely. He had added no comment of his own. The agents all understood what that meant for Flora when they discussed it afterwards. Then, an aide had threatened Ada with violence unless she betrayed her friends. Sophie had immediately noticed the quieter-than-usual Ada, and her heart sank when she had learned the cause of it. She, herself, had made it known that she was willing to change sides for money, and Sophie now felt horribly embarrassed. In fact, she wanted to go home, go to bed, and stay under the covers.

Alfie and Broadbent-Wicks were gloomy, too. They all sat at the end of a table, separated from the others, picking at their food, and speaking in lowered voices. The agents looked like they were waiting for the next available tumbril to the guillotine.

"Miss," said Fern. "Is it all right if I go to a party later?"

Sophie did not at first grasp what she was saying. "A party?"

"Yes. John, he's ever so nice. He asked me special if I'd like to go. There's only a few who'll be there, and I promise I won't stay long. But I'd like to go, miss."

"John's the fella who hangs about with Kemp," said Alfie.

Sophie looked at Fern. "Absolutely not. He's tricking you somehow."

"I don't think so, miss."

"Oh, yes, he is," said Ada. "He'll get you drunk, and then what'll 'appen?"

"No, that's not true," said Fern, who, nonetheless, believed them.

"We're under attack," said Flora. "They're trying to get one of us to talk, so the fellow was probably sent to work on you."

"But, Miss Glad, he wouldn't do that, would he?"

Flora raised her eyebrows. "We're all in the soup, and they're employing different tactics with each of us, attempting to break us down."

"The rotten pig," said Fern. "So, while he had a smile all over his mush, he was lying to me? I'll *never* forgive him for that."

"And I must face an equally insincere Stokely tonight," said Flora. "They're really the same, aren't they?"

"Yes, I suppose there's no difference between them," agreed Sophie. "How I wish we could leave now."

"Tut, what a bother it all is," continued Flora. "I suppose I can put up with him through dinner. I know. I'll pretend it's an awful scene in a play, only redeemed by my killing the wicked earl in the third act. Yes, I can face his twaddle if I carry that thought in mind."

"Miss Walton," said Broadbent-Wicks. "Tell me if he bothers you. I'll make sure he *doesn't* do it again."

Flora smiled. "You are most gallant, sir." She bowed. "I thank you."

"My chief concern," said Sophie, "is that we still don't have sufficient evidence and now, it appears, we have no alternative but to turn tail and run. What we *do* have, I've hidden, so I must retrieve it before we go."

"I noticed a bloke outside with a big dog," said Alfie. "He had a shotgun. 'Course, they all carry shotguns, but this one wasn't hunting, and didn't seem to be going anywhere. I'll keep an eye out, but it might be difficult to meet Miss Elizabeth if men and dogs are out and about."

"My goodness, what on earth will happen next? Yes, please watch to see if they are maintaining a guard." Sophie suddenly laughed. "It's ridiculous. We can't get away without breaking the law. I can't warn Elizabeth not to come, nor can I reach Inspector Morton. We're just stuck here, and we're about to serve dinner as though there's nothing wrong in the world. All the while, those scoundrels are pulling the country to pieces. They have something big planned for tonight, but I can't tell what it is. Any ideas?"

The others shook their heads, except for Broadbent-Wicks.

"I don't know what it is, either. But I know this much. Those aides look rather excited, and I think they're scared of Stokely."

"Whatever makes you say that?"

"Ah, well, having worked for the jolly old government, I recognize when the man in charge wants something done immediately. Anyone caught slacking is for the chopping block. Usually, I'd swan around the office, having a chat with the fellows or the typists. Obviously, I'd shuffle a few papers when necessary, going over submitted forms, writing notes, and all that good stuff. However, when the boss was on the warpath because someone had asked him to do something, then we'd all jump to it. I remember thinking how everyone at those times looked worried... About their jobs, I suppose. Then, after the required work was done, and the boss had gone away muttering (he often muttered), we'd all breathe a sigh of relief and go back to business as usual. So, today, those chaps are running about in a lather — and it's not because of us. Stokely's their boss and they're afraid of him. There's one fellow who really should try out for walking races. His whole body moves like a piece of elastic."

"I saw him, an' all," said Alfie. "Odd-looking sort of bloke, but he's fast, that he is. He passed us half a dozen times. Like I said to Dan here, he should be in the Olympics."

Sophie regarded the men. "Do you speak to each other when outside a room?"

"Oh, yes," said Broadbent-Wicks.

"You're not supposed to... Make sure you don't get caught."

"We won't, Miss King," said Alfie. "We're always careful and extra quiet."

"Absolutely, we are," said Broadbent-Wicks. "We're like a pair of Roman statues in livery."

As they finished eating, Kemp's men, including John, came in.

"Pretend you're 'appy to see the mug," whispered Ada to Fern. "String him along like a good un'."

Fern smiled at John, who returned a furtive yet unmistakable dumb show of being pleased to see her. She waved, and then caught up with the other agents as they left the room. Outside in the corridor, Sophie took Ada to one side.

"Are you feeling any better now?" she asked.

"A little. I can't 'elp it, but he frightened me, that he did, miss. And I'm that upset about breaking the teacup."

"That was *his* fault, not yours, because he's a swine and a bully. We're leaving tonight — just remember that."

"I know, but what's going to 'appen to us afterwards, miss? That's what's worrying me now."

"I have a few ideas that we can discuss, and I'm sure the police will also have some. So, try to put it out of mind. As soon as dinner's finished, we'll stay together, get our things, and take the car."

"Very good, miss. I'll try to buck up."

Sophie fretted about the others, hating that these various

attacks upon them were happening. She could see that it was all her fault, though. If she had not brought in the box of food, then Dawkins might not have noticed her. Perhaps he would have seen her anyway, because how else, but by sneaking out to meet Elizabeth, was she to deliver timely reports to those who needed them? That was a question that came too late for consideration, and now they were all stuck, because she had not been careful enough. She was sure that Dawkins would not do anything that might ruin dinner, but afterwards he would make his move. Then, she imagined, he would try to settle matters to his satisfaction. Already there was a man and a dog patrolling outside; a man guarded the telephones, while the aides were continually prowling about the house — Dawkins, it appeared, had 'taken steps', and would not let the agents escape without trouble. Ill at ease, she went to find Mr Dalgleish to get instruction, hoping they all could get through the coming hours without incident.

# Chapter 25

# Courses

In Chertsey Park's two dining rooms, there was space enough to seat a hundred guests in comfort. The Grand Dining Room could accommodate forty and, tonight, thirty-four would be at table. The Second Dining Room was at capacity with sixty guests, all men. Fern, who worked in the Second Dining Room, told Sophie they were in a good mood and quite noisy. Sophie presumed that, now their work was over, they were letting off steam. Fern also said that three of the aides were watching the proceedings, including *her* proceedings.

Unlike previous meals, Sophie had no opportunity to get the newly arrived guests' names from their place cards. The only two she knew for certain were Charlotte Terrence and Uncle Teddy, or Edward Fielding. The rest of the guests appeared to be friends or family, and the estimation of the other agents confirmed this. When serving the first course, soup, she felt awful on Flora's behalf. Although busy herself at the other end of the table, Sophie was aware of the earl speaking to her friend.

The dinner commenced. Thirty-four spoons tinkled when touching the ringing Meissen porcelain soup bowls, part-filled with consommé. Charlotte Terrence, in a sensational burgundy evening gown, sat some distance from Stokely. The seating had been arranged in such a way that she was surrounded by men, while the other women were more equally distributed to the ends of the table. Charlotte was receiving a lot of attention, and was mindful of the fact that those about her were ones whom Stokely wished to test. There were probably others in the Second Dining Room, but here were the important men, and probably the richest. She should have been angry with Stokely for throwing her to the wolves but, as she was a tigress herself, there really was no danger.

However, being used annoyed her, although she kept it well hidden. Charlotte calculated that at least she was in the same room as her Roderick again, within striking distance, so to speak. While the consommé was being served, she first noticed the beautiful maid setting a bowl down in front of Lord Stokely, and remembered her from before. They had spoken at length, and Charlotte recalled all the lies the woman had told her while pretending to be a lady. If Flora had not been serving Lord Stokely, Charlotte might have found the memory amusing. But she *was* serving Stokely and, by necessity, was very close to him. She saw the earl speak to the so-called maid. Charlotte turned her face away to hide and then suppress a spasm of jealousy.

An aide had slipped into the room quietly to stand near Mr Dalgleish. The butler, intent upon the dinner being served correctly, disregarded the aide. These two sets of eyes made it impossible for the agents to do anything but their serving duties, nor could they communicate with one another. As Sophie took away the soup bowls, she knew the aide was watching her, which she found very irritating when *she* was supposed to be watching *him*. She removed Dawkins' bowl and, in that second, became alive to an odd sensation. Here she was, closely watched by a Stokely subordinate, ignored by his right-hand man as she took his bowl, while Stokely was unaware that police agents were all about him. Going a step further, and if the signs Sophie had witnessed so far supported her supposition, the earl would soon make advances to one of those very agents. It was obvious; Stokely had not the slightest idea what was going on around him, and Dawkins meant to keep it that way. The reason for this then hit her forcibly. Dawkins had allowed police agents to operate inside the earl's house at a critical moment when there was a need for secrecy. He was afraid to admit his mistake to his master. Sophie surmised Dawkins had blundered, and that he intended to keep quiet about the incursion.

Ada served fish to Uncle Teddy, who was engaged in conversation with Morris Wilberforce, Stokely's man in charge of finance.

"...The one stamp that would truly round out my collection is a Queen Victoria 1877 Penny Red in mint condition and perfectly centred."

"So, if you had that one, you'd finish with collecting?" asked Wilberforce.

"Dear me, *no*. Never. I would concentrate on my colonial stamp collection."

Ada retired deferentially and served the guest next to him.

Later, when she returned to retrieve the fish plates and cutlery, the conversation had shifted.

"I understand that all is proceeding according to schedule." Uncle Teddy was again talking to Wilberforce.

"It is, indeed." Wilberforce glanced at Ada who, with downcast eyes, removed Uncle Teddy's plate. When he thought she was out of earshot, he added in a quieter voice, "Tonight is pivotal."

"Let us *hope* that's the case," said Uncle Teddy, "and that the end result is what we desire."

Ada subsequently met Sophie outside the kitchen.

"Miss King," she whispered more furtively than usual. "What does pivotal mean?"

"Um, something vitally important that can affect the outcome of a matter. A policeman's signals at a crossroads are pivotal in assuring traffic runs smoothly rather than chaotically."

"Oh, I thought it 'ad to be something like that. You know we've all been thinking they're up to something special tonight? Well, Uncle Teddy knows about it an' all."

"He *does*? Good grief... I imagined he had nothing to do with Stokely's plans."

"So did I. He looks like a nice old duffer, but he ain't. Not only that, he wants whatever it is to come off perfect... Though he don't sound like he knows *all* that's going on."

"Then he's aware of the overall plan, but not the details?"

"Er... Yes, that's about it, miss, as it seems to me."

Sophie sighed. "Uncle Teddy *is* Stokely's father. Perhaps he's peculiar, too, and that's from where Stokely gets his warped view of the world."

"And a warped view of 'isself as well, miss."

"Yes. Let's return, shall we...? I've been meaning to ask you. That man there, watching us — was he the one who threatened you?"

"No, I ain't seen him since."

"Such a pity. I was thinking about how to spill something over him."

Ada laughed.

Flora served chicken cordon bleu to Lord Stokely.

"This looks good, Gladys," said Lord Stokely. "It's a pity you can't join me. Another time, perhaps?"

"I hardly like to say, my Lord," replied Flora.

"I'm being too forward, aren't I?" He smiled and looked up at her.

Flora thought he was revoltingly presumptuous, but said,

"I couldn't possibly answer such a question, my Lord,"

"How charming," said Stokely.

Flora bobbed and retired. Along the table, Charlotte could see all too well what was going on between the earl and the maid.

Part way through the course, an aide first approached Dawkins with a message. Dawkins signalled that the man give the message to Lord Stokely, which he then did. With the message received, Stokely underwent a change. He had one of his beatific moments, sitting still and looking into the distance, peaceful and content.

Charlotte saw him, as did Sophie, Flora, and several others. Those that knew him well also knew he had received good news according to his plans. Those who knew him less well wondered if the earl was a deeply spiritual man, in addition to all his other accomplishments.

Sophie's reaction to Stokely's beaming face was one of bleak dismay. She knew the man had triumphed again — that the Red Fist had struck somewhere in Britain. She went through the motions of serving food, while her mind raced everywhere, searching for a clue, a word, or at least an indication of how the earl could be brought to justice.

She was standing nearby when she heard the man next to Dawkins say,

"Ever been to Brooklands?"

"Yes, I went in September," said Dawkins. "There was a very large turnout."

"Yes, there was. I was there, too. It's a pity we didn't know each other then... Very entertaining, except for the accident. You couldn't get me in one of those machines for love nor money."

"The idea of driving flat out appeals to me," said Dawkins, "but not, as you suggest, under such competitive conditions."

"True. The accident happened right where we were. Saw the whole thing. The chap behind Blenkinsop didn't bump him, as some say. Blenkinsop's steering went, and he was wobbling all over the place until the rear of his car knocked into the chap behind. That's what caused Blenkinsop to spin off the track. He was lucky he only broke a leg."

"At that speed, yes."

Sophie had never been to Brooklands to watch the races.

Before the advent of Rabbit, she had never been interested in cars. Now, she thought, she might like to go, but not if there were going to be accidents. *That would be too ghoulish for words*, she thought. She stood for a moment longer as a new thought took shape in her mind. She gradually became more and more excited to the point where she had to leave the room and go for a walk to calm down. Near the kitchen, she met Flora.

"I'm a *complete* idiot," said Sophie.

"I shan't disagree," said Flora, "but what's disturbing you?"

"While in the garage looking for a suitable car to purloin, I found a damaged Rolls-Royce under a dust sheet. Gladys, I'm sure they used it to push Mr Auckland's car off the road. Gladys, all the damage fits with it having collided with another vehicle from behind. I saw deep, fresh scratches on the part that sticks out at the front."

"That *sounds* feasible. How can you be sure?"

"I don't think I can be, but the police *must* examine it. The car's in Stokely's garage, and Mr Auckland died on his way home... You know that man who threatened Nancy? He said she would have a nasty accident unless she betrayed us. It seems to me he has the habit of creating accidents."

"You mean he drove the car?"

"It's possible, isn't it?"

"Well, yes."

"We have to get Nancy away as soon as this blasted dinner is over... How's it going with Stokely?"

"The Lothario of Chertsey Park is making his intentions more and more obvious every time I bring him food. What the others around must think, I can't imagine. I've never come across such a detestable breach in manners."

"I'm sorry you're being put through this, and by him, of all people."

"Oh, well. What makes it worse is that Charlotte Terrence is staring daggers at me. Why is she blaming *me*? He's the one causing the trouble."

"She's still in love with Stokely, although he dropped her about three years ago. What a fine, upstanding fellow he is."

"How can she be still in love with him?"

"Don't ask me. I've never been in love."

"Ooh, Sophie-wophie..."

"Don't you *dare* use that name. I detested it at school."

"I won't, but what about Mr Yardley, hmm?"

"I like him," said Sophie in a matter-of-fact way.

"You can't deceive me. I think you're somewhere beyond liking, but short of being swept off your feet. Tell me, how often do you think about him?"

"Mr Yardley is a friend of mine. That's all there is to it. Now, let's get back to work."

"Ha-ha, I don't believe you."

Sophie turned slightly pink, laughed, then pulled her friend's arm. "Come along. We have work to do."

Alfie and Broadbent-Wicks were also present in the Grand Dining Room. Halfway through the dinner, and when their duties permitted, they took to standing behind the aide for the sole purpose of annoying him.

"Dalgleish has gone," whispered Alfie to Broadbent-Wicks.

The aide turned with a vicious look on his face, although he had not heard what Alfie had said.

"Yes, sir?" asked Alfie. "Is there anything you want?"

Several guests stared in their direction. Stokely looked up, to see what the noise was about. All any of them could see were two silent, motionless footmen, presumably being addressed by an aide who had his back to the table.

"You there!" Stokely called to the aide, who spun around to face the irritated earl. "Leave the room at once."

The man wanted to explain, but he did as he was told, much to the inward satisfaction of Alfie and Broadbent-Wicks.

The staff served desserts of several kinds from M Fournier's kitchen — crêpes, chocolate pots de crème, and profiteroles.

By this time, the guests, replete with dinner, wished to linger at the table, continuing their relaxed conversation with old or newfound friends. It happened that Lord Stokely received yet another message — his third during the meal. He arose from his place.

"I've been called away," he said. "Please, continue where you are for as long as you like, but I believe dinner is also now over in The Second Dining Room. Port can be served here and coffee in the ballroom. Dalgleish, take care of my guests."

"Yes, my Lord."

"I understand there will be several card games, so be careful." Stokely smiled. As he left the room, he stopped to talk to Charlotte.

"Dawkins can answer your questions about the other players," he said quietly. "We'll meet later."

A thrill went through her as he spoke, but this excitement was soon tempered by the sight of Flora clearing away the earl's dish.

---

The empty first floor corridor between The Grand Dining Room and the office was a familiar walk for Lord Stokely. He was absorbed — completely wrapped up in all the plans he had set in motion. Each step along this way would have made a visitor stop to admire and exclaim at the elegance and refined dignity of the surroundings, but Stokely did not see them for two reasons. The first was that this was his childhood home, and he was long accustomed to it, almost to the point of indifference. The paintings, carpets, and decoration only blended together to form a pattern and, as he walked, he accepted the pattern as a whole that required no analysis. Had one painting been removed — that he would have noticed. None were missing and so he did not see any paintings.

The second reason why no part of his surroundings intruded into his conscious thought was that he was no longer moving in a physical realm. His mind was locked in an abstract one. For Stokely, life, particularly the direction he had chosen for his life, was not made up of a series of ideas to implement, challenges to meet, and difficulties to surmount. It was much simpler than that; it was as if he were only making a cup of tea for himself. He had a boiling kettle — the people of the nation to whom he had applied heat. A warmed pot — A government on the verge of crisis. The tea of his choice — a special blend of ideas taken from others and then uniquely formulated by him to suit the British palate. His cup and saucer awaited, and he needed only to put the water on the tea, let it steep in the pot, and then pour it out.

He knew himself to be the right man for the job and he considered it inevitable that he should have it. From his childhood he had been pampered and the centre of almost everyone's attention. It was true that his father, the earl, had virtually ignored him, but his mother, Lady Georgiana, and Uncle Teddy had more than compensated for that lack of affection. Stokely had noticed early on that Uncle Teddy was more like a father to him than his own parent. Stokely was glad his ailing father had died when he was a boy. For one thing, it cleared the way for him to inherit the title while still a minor, but it also removed the one powerful person who disapproved of him. The old earl had never taken an interest in him.

Stokely bought his first newspaper when he was nineteen. It was a provincial paper with a declining circulation, but Stokely had turned it around and the newspaper was soon profitable. It had been so ever since. Other business ventures and acquisitions followed. Often, he discovered, his partners lacked vision or somehow stood in his way. It was then he learned that, to make a success of a business, the first requirement was to remove those who prevented it from achieving its full potential. He would buy his partners out when able and if it could be done cheaply. Soon he discovered that it was easier to blackmail them and, in the last resort, ensure they met with an accident. For Stokely, it was a simple balancing of economics and risks to achieve his goal. When younger and at the beginning of his career, there was less money at his disposal. The relatively inexpensive use of agents, usually criminals, to remove obstacles helped him enormously. Stokely also enjoyed the planning of a partner's downfall because, to him, it seemed just. Anyone who withstood him must pay dearly for their effrontery. *Numquam dimitte aut oblivisci* - 'Never forgive or forget' should have been his motto when he began using agents to do his bidding. It did not take long for this mode of operation to become as second nature to him.

He neared the office. Stokely was confident that his current plans would soon bear their long-awaited fruit. It was more than confidence in his abilities, though. Such confidence can be shaken. In recent years, he had enjoyed many successes. Even when there was a setback or a check to his progress, the solution was usually better than the original plan he had formulated. Stokely had moved past simple confidence. He believed he was infallible and that he could do no wrong; his destiny demanded fulfilment and nothing could be allowed to stand in its way.

"What's the news?" he asked upon entering the office.

The aide stood up. "My Lord, the Liverpool unit has completed its tasks, and did so by ten o'clock."

"Which were...? Remind me."

"Set a warehouse ablaze, fire-bomb three pubs, and detonate a bomb to destroy the bridge at Kirkland Station. Apparently, they destroyed the track and it will prevent freight being moved to and from the docks for several days."

"Excellent. And the other units?"

"They have all begun operations, but have yet to report."

"Inform me as soon as you have anything. The time is now..." Stokely looked at his watch, "... ten-fifteen. Get the National Chronicle on the phone. Tell them to run the front page with only the Liverpool story and nothing more. We cannot report the news before it happens." Stokely smiled.

Dawkins entered the room.

"The Liverpool operation has been successfully completed," said Stokely.

"Has it, my Lord?" replied Dawkins. "That's good."

"What is it?" asked Stokely, noticing Dawkins had something to say.

"I haven't mentioned this before, but we have police agents in the house."

"Here?" Stokely pointed to the floor of his ancestral home.

"Yes, although they haven't discovered anything, because we've limited their activities. We've searched their belongings and checked up on them as far as we can. These agents are masquerading as servants from the London agency. They're using false names."

"What do you propose to be done?"

"I'm undecided, my Lord. I will interview them further to make sure they know nothing. Based on the results, I will either let them go, which is preferable, or they'll meet with an accident. I was thinking a Red Fist incident would cover the matter."

"Hmm... How about a bomb? I've been meaning to remodel Chertsey for some time, and an attack on my house would raise a great deal of sympathy for the cause."

"Yes, it would, my Lord. However, if only police agents are killed in the blast, the detectives might view it suspiciously. It would also mean an investigation and unwanted attention, which we should avoid if we can. A car bomb far from the house would be more suitable."

"I suppose you're right. Still, a lot can be made of an outside attack."

"That's true, my Lord. There are six individuals from the

agency, although it may not be all of them who are informants."

"Does this include Gladys Walton?"

Dawkins nodded.

"That's a pity. See to it, Dawkins, and make sure it doesn't become a problem. I must return to my guests."

"I will deal with them shortly, my Lord."

# Chapter 26

# Time to leave

The Secret Agency intended to leave as soon after ten as was possible for them. Nestled among Sophie's calculations was a reliance upon her staff completing all known duties before then. That left the unknown duties — those sudden calls from guests for this or that thing, which they had no choice but to answer. Sophie allowed a quarter of an hour for them all to have finished their duties, assemble, and get to the garage. Then they would take the car, and intercept Elizabeth either on the road to Ottershaw or before she had left the Gardeners Arms. Once they had rendezvoused, they would all drive to the village hall in Sunningdale. There, they would give Inspector Morton the evidence, the latest report, and the keys to Stokely's limousine. That was the plan. The part that Sophie felt truly guilty about was leaving Mr Dalgleish without a word of warning — not that she could explain the reasons for the Burgoyne Agency's hasty, late-night departure.

The agents cleared away and cleaned up and then scurried about the house as they had never scurried before. Passing in front of a clock was the same as passing a sadistic, whip-wielding taskmaster. If the minute hand moved, it lashed the maid or footman on, and the time was always later than they thought it should rightfully be.

"I'm goin' to be sick," said Ada, rushing into the kitchen, returning the last of the last things she could find left in The Grand Dining Room.

"You're not allowed," said Flora, as they left the kitchen. "Nine fifty-eight. Where are the others?"

"No idea, but I saw Alfie going downstairs to the entrance about ten minutes ago."

"A late arrival or departure, probably."

"Might be. Anyway, even if it is, it shouldn't take him long. We're finished, and I 'ope the others are an' all, 'cause we don't want to get caught now."

"Let's keep out of sight so that Mr Dalgleish doesn't find us," said Flora.

They turned a corner and waited quietly.

"Someone's coming," mouthed Ada, barely making a sound.

They listened, following the footsteps that went into the kitchen. A few moments later, Sophie appeared suddenly, and they all jumped.

"Here you are," said Sophie. She joined them around the corner. "Where are the others?"

"We don't know, miss," said Ada. "We think Alfie might be seeing a guest off the premises."

"Oh. I've packed our cases. They've searched our belongings, by the way. What a blasted cheek they have."

"They better not 'ave taken nothing," said Ada.

"I doubt it. They were looking for something incriminating, so it's a good job I hid the evidence we've collected and my notebook. Now that's all safe in my pocket. I also sent Alfie to pack his and Mr Ely's cases. You won't believe this. As soon as I got our coats and cases packed and arranged and left the dormitory, Miss Beech went in. She's bound to notice."

"Do you think she'll tell Mr Dalgleish if she realizes?" asked Flora.

"Absolutely, she will." Sophie looked at her watch. "Two minutes past... Where are they?"

Alfie came around the corner, and they all jumped, which, in turn, made Alfie jump.

"I heard you speaking, miss," whispered Alfie.

"Did you?" asked Sophie, also in a whisper.

He nodded.

"Where's Mr Ely?"

"About twenty minutes ago, he was talking to that bloke Miller."

"Oh, my goodness," said Sophie.

"They were gettin' on like the best of mates."

"I don't know how he does it," said Flora.

"Nobody does, except him," said Alfie philosophically.

"Do you have your suitcase ready?" asked Sophie.

"Yes, miss. So is Dan's. They're both in my room."

They waited a minute and then Broadbent-Wicks hoved into view.

"Hello, all! Well, nearly all."

"Shh," they answered in unison.

"There's no point in whispering. Absolutely none. I'm here to bring you to the office. You know, the one where all the efficient chaps hang about. Dawkins wants to see all of us. Miss Datchet is already on the carpet and looking jolly miserable. Actually, just miserable, and not at all jolly."

"He's captured Dora!" exclaimed Sophie.

"Yes, that's about the size of it. Captured me, too. Sent two aides, and one of them started waving a pistol about in my face after I said I was busy. Naturally, I changed my mind, and thought I might as well go for a stroll with them, because they seemed so earnest. Come to think of it, they're very earnest *all* the time... Ha! That reminds me of that old Oscar Wilde play, and the importance of being Earnest. Now he *was* a clever chappy with words. I remember..."

"Stop speaking," said Sophie.

"Of course, Miss King."

"Are we going to see Dawkins?" asked Flora.

"I think we must, for Dora's sake. I don't like this business with guns. What do they think they're doing?"

"Intimidating us, and it's working rather well," said Flora.

"Let's just get Dora and go," said Ada.

"They won't do anything right now," said Alfie, "but I reckon Dawkins has it in for us."

"You mean he'll act after we leave?" asked Sophie

"Oh, yes. He'll want to protect Stokely's reputation so he won't go shooting anyone here. That was all show with the pistol."

Sophie puffed out her cheeks and blew heavily. "We'll talk to Dawkins and get Dora. Let's be quick, or we'll miss Elizabeth."

They began heading to the office. Flora called out,

"Remember what I said about the play?"

"Yes, but I'm not sure I can get away with it."

"Of course, you can. When in doubt, bluff your way out."

"I say, Miss Walton, that rhymes," said Broadbent-Wicks.

"Indeed. Are you any good at bluffing, Mr Ely?"

"Not at all. I'm positively hopeless."

"I beg to differ," said Sophie. "You've bluffed Miller."

They started climbing the servants' staircase.

"Without meaning to. And then I just kept quiet about you know what."

"What was that?" asked Ada.

"That he is a k-i-l-l-e-r," he replied, spelling it out.

"I hope he didn't cotton on to your b-l-u-f-f," said Flora.

"I don't think he d-i-d," replied Broadbent-Wicks.

"We sound like c-h-i-l-d-r-e-n," said Ada.

"Who are about to meet the headmaster, so we'd best be q-u-i-e-t now," said Sophie.

"Did you say *quite*?" asked Ada. "Quite what?"

"No, I spelled quiet. At least I think I did."

"You did," said Flora.

They arrived at the door to the office. Sophie organized them into a line with Alfie leading. She inspected their uniforms and made a quick adjustment to Broadbent-Wicks' small bow tie knot so that it lay perfectly straight. She opened the door, and the procession marched in and formed a line facing Dawkins' desk. Sophie closed the door and went to Dora, who was standing immediately in front of the desk. She smiled at her and showed where she should join the others. Sophie stood in front of the line of her employees.

Dawkins watched the proceedings. Behind him were two aides — one standing, while the other was seated at a second desk with the telephone. The latter was the one who had threatened Ada.

"You wished to see us," said Sophie.

"Thank you for coming." Dawkins got up and began slowly pacing. Although he seemed nonchalant, he rarely took his eyes off them. "I am informed by Dalgleish that your work is excellent... As we all know, that is not *why* you are here. You are police informants. Although I have asked who it is you work for and why you are present at Chertsey Park and previously at Lyall Place, you have yet to say anything. This is a private residence. That the police have sent spies here is intolerable. The matter shall be taken up with the highest authorities and not one of you will work again as an informant, perhaps not even as a servant. I will make sure that you all lose your jobs. It's as simple as that. Lord Stokely has newspapers. Your names will appear in them. Doors that were hitherto open to you shall soon be shut in your faces. Let that sink in for a moment."

"It has sunk in," said Sophie. "Is there anything else?"

"Yes, there is, Miss King." He moved a brass calendar to one side to sit on the edge of the desk. "Tell me who it is who sent you and your reason for being here, and I can save you a lot of trouble. Then, I can promise that you will not suffer the notoriety I mentioned."

"On what authority are you quizzing us?" asked Sophie.

"On Lord Stokely's authority."

"Ah, good. And what work do you do for Lord Stokely?"

"You are here to answer my questions, so save your breath."

"Will that be your answer when the police arrest you?"

"Don't play games, Miss King."

"You're playing games. I can, too."

Dawkins gave her a weary look. Sophie spoke again.

"You have bullied and berated us. You have used all manner of cowardly devices against us, but they are useless, because *you* are useless. Mr Dawkins, you are nothing but a broken reed."

Flora nearly smiled, despite the situation, because Sophie was using modified lines from the play they had discussed. The effect on Dawkins was much different. He stood up.

"You dare to insult me!?"

"It's no insult. The police will arrest you. They know every single thing you've done, and you will pay the price."

"You're bluffing. If you think the likes of Penrose and Laneford have anything, you're sadly mistaken, because there is nothing for them to have."

Flora started laughing. Sophie turned towards her and realized what she was doing — referring to a scene in the play again.

"Stop that at once," said Dawkins to Flora.

"Let her laugh. It is all rather amusing," said Sophie, who could barely believe she was saying such words. "Are those the only people you know? My, my, you are behind the times."

Dawkins fiddled with the calendar while deep in thought. He then approached the aide and whispered something to him. The aide left the room. Sophie waited a moment, then turned around to speak to the Burgoyne's staff.

"Come along. We have to be up early."

"I can't permit you to leave," said Dawkins, striding towards her. The aide at the other desk got up to join Dawkins.

"Why ever not?"

"You're nothing but a troublemaker and a liar..."

"Steady on, there," said Broadbent-Wicks. "Miss King is a lady."

"You'll keep quiet if you know what's good for you," said the aide, who moved in front of him.

"As I said," continued Dawkins to Sophie, "it's all a pretense. We shall certainly find out what you know." He gave her a wan and wicked smile.

"I thought you were a gentleman," said Broadbent-Wicks. "Obviously, you're not. You're a bounder."

Dawkins ignored him. He gripped Sophie roughly by the arm and drew her closer to him.

"I say!" said Broadbent-Wicks. He violently pushed the aide in front of him, turned in a swift movement, and delivered a hard blow on Dawkins' cheekbone. Dawkins staggered, yet did not let go of Sophie until she tripped him. Lying on the floor, his jacket fell open and before he could reach his automatic, Sophie had got to it first. The rest of the line had exploded into action. Fern held Dawkins' legs so he could not get up, while Alfie pounced on the aide. Ada took out her blackjack and started hitting the aide, who kept twisting about to avoid her blows.

"Frighten me, would you!?!" she shouted at him. "Come 'ere. I'll give *you* a nasty accident."

She kept swinging and eventually got his neck with the cosh, which ended the tussle.

"For goodness' sake! Don't kill him," said Alfie.

"I won't," said Ada, who looked like she might as she stared at the man sprawled on the floor.

"I don't believe it," said Flora, after the battle had ended. "I didn't get the chance to hit anyone." She put her cosh back in her pocket.

"Well done, matey," said Alfie to Broadbent-Wicks. "Let's get 'em tied up. The curtain cords should do the trick."

Sophie, holding a massive Webley semi-automatic with two hands, was trying to point it steadily at Dawkins, who glowered back at her.

"This thing weighs a ton. Now. You're under arrest, Dawkins. I suppose you have rights, but I don't have a clue what they are, so we won't bother with them. However, if you try to get up, I will shoot you. That's the only right you're getting from me."

"Will you really miss?" asked Fern.

"Oh, yes. You'd better believe I'll shoot... Search the room while I guard this traitor."

"Why don't you try this one," said Alfie, holding out a much smaller automatic he had removed from the aide's holster. "I've set it up, ready to fire. Just pull the trigger."

"That's much more like it," said Sophie, as they exchanged pistols. "It's so much lighter. Just pull the trigger?"

"That's right. See, with this one, you didn't have a round in the chamber and the safety was on."

"Oh. So, it wouldn't have fired?"

"No. And he knew that."

"He was obviously planning to attack me! How dreadfully devious of him." She then addressed Dawkins. "You are more loathsome than I could have believed possible."

While Alfie and Broadbent-Wicks tied up Dawkins and the aide, Flora, Ada, and Fern ransacked the office. Flora found a locked cabinet. Rather than search for the key, Ada picked the lock, and inside discovered a few documents and a locked attaché case.

"Take everything, and hurry," said Sophie.

"We should gag them," said Alfie.

"Good idea. Would handkerchiefs do?" she suggested.

"Yes."

"How about using socks?" asked Flora, who was searching through desk drawers.

"We haven't enough time," said Sophie.

"That's a shame. Putting a sock in it would have been perfect. Eh, Mr Dawkins?"

"Ready, miss," said Ada, who held the case and an armful of papers.

By the telephone, Fern was trying to take a mental photograph of a notepad. Unable to do so, she stuck it in her pocket. Alfie was busy gagging Dawkins when the telephone rang.

"You answer it," said Sophie to Broadbent-Wicks. "Pretend you're Dawkins. Try to spoil whatever it is they have planned for tonight."

"Righty-ho," said Broadbent-Wicks. "That's a clever idea, Miss King. I'd just have ignored it."

He picked up the receiver. "Dawkins here... Yes... Right... Who's this...? Ah, is it? I'm glad you telephoned, because I have something to tell you. It's all off for tonight... What? Yes, *off*, I said. Cancelled, scrubbed, and an absolute no go... Why? Well, don't let this go any further just yet. The very important person we both work for has had some of sort of fit. It's such a dreadful business. Rolling on the carpet, frothing at the mouth, and biting people, no less. All of us here discussed it and are in agreement that he's insane. Absolutely bonkers. He's going to the asylum first thing Monday morning.... What? No, the doctors are with him as we speak, and they're looking very depressed. It's a pity, but the show's over for all of us. And you know what that means. I doubt he'll be writing any cheques for some considerable length of time." Sophie frantically waved at him to be quicker. "Someone wants me, so I'll ring off now... Yes, we're all cut up about it. Is there any message I can send to him on your behalf...? You hope he gets well soon. Don't we all, old thing? Goodbye."

He replaced the receiver. "How'd I do?"

"I don't know," said Sophie. "Fine, I think. Who was it?"

"A chap calling himself Bristol Unit. There are obviously more of them, otherwise he'd come across as very odd. Who goes round calling themselves a unit? At least, I've never heard of anyone doing it. Although it might be his surname, of course. Do you know, he was near to tears at the end? I could hear it in his voice."

"Good," said Sophie, picking up the telephone. "Everyone leave, except one of you stay to watch the door. I won't be a moment."

Ada remained. She had the door cracked open to observe the hall in case someone came to the office. Sophie tried telephoning Inspector Morton, but the operator informed her the line was engaged. Next, Sophie telephoned Elizabeth.

---

"There she goes... Off a-gallivanting again." Agnes peered through a narrow gap in the curtains of the empty saloon bar, watching Elizabeth get into the car. "Where's she goin'? That's what I'd loike to know."

"To find owls," said her husband, reading a newspaper that was laid out on the counter.

"I don't believe her. I'm not that simple."

"No, you're not. But you're gettin' on the nosey side. That's because it were slow for a Saturday night."

"I've a right to look out my window when I please. And you watch what you say. I reckon she's up to no good."

"What? Meetin' a chap in the woods in winter at her age? Come off it, Aggie. That don't make no sense."

"Then what's she doing? No, it's not owls. She said she's a naturalist. I can't believe they get on loike she do. Always goin' to town and rushing about. Hardly spends any toime in the woods — except at noight, and that's not natural."

"No, it's not. You wouldn't catch me out on a cold night for no good reason. However, she loikes it and she pays what she owes, and I say good luck to her. She moight be off her head, but she's harmless and pleasant."

"She moight be a criminal... or a witch."

Her husband laughed. "No, not her."

"Then where's she going? I'll foind out if it kills me."

The telephone rang.

"That'll be her accomplice, no doubt." Agnes hastened to beat her husband to the call.

Elizabeth drove away, aware she was being observed. It

irked her but, once out of sight of the pub, she forgot about it. Her thoughts soon came around to dwell on the fact that she had not received a telephone message from Miss King. She hoped everything was all right, although she found the silence worrying. Still, she was on her way and would soon meet the lady herself in person.

# Chapter 27

# The best laid plans of mice and maids...

The ballroom had been restored to order after the work accomplished there earlier in the day, and it now functioned as a reception room. It was not particularly comfortable as such, as there were too few seats for the number of guests present. Those in attendance ignored the deficiency because a drinks table had been set up. The quantity and variety of wine, spirits, and beer were all a guest could desire. Lord Stokely set the mood for the rest of the evening with a short, genial speech, followed by a Champagne toast.

The servants had put three card tables in a quieter corner of the ballroom. Two of them were in use with newly started games. Charlotte was already busy at one of them. It was easy for her to pick out a serious gambler in the crowd — he took on a preoccupied air as soon as he saw the decks of cards. She had approached a table and sat down to play a game of patience, knowing they would come to her; and they did.

Soon, more serious card games commenced.

Charlotte concentrated on the cards and the people she played against. It was now she would learn their characteristics and habits, the ones that would betray them later. If they were good, and revealed very little about themselves, she would sacrifice a hand in an early round to see how they reacted. One man was a fool and should never gamble. He would lose later, unless dealt exceptional hands. Even then, he would signal how strong his cards were. The second man stared at his cards for too long. They all waited for him to decide what to do. This man was a calculator, weighing the odds and waiting for his moment when he had a really strong hand. In the meantime, he would lose steadily, but would become exultant when he thought he was winning. The third was unexpressive of anything. Charlotte received a message from an aide that he had ten thousand a year and did not like to lose. This was the one for her to study carefully. She noticed that *he* was also surreptitiously studying *her*.

While waiting for the slow cardplayer to take his turn, Charlotte studied another man. Lord Stokely, whom she observed in a mirror, had entered the room. Instantly, he was politely mobbed by people wishing to speak to him. They hovered about, hoping to catch his eye, or they spoke to an aide to arrange for an audience. She noticed how the aides functioned more like bodyguards than office assistants. To her, they looked like capable young men, too fit and active to be clerks. She wondered why Stokely needed three of them close by at all times. Was he worried? she asked herself. The slow cardplayer finally picked up a card from the deck. Her attention returned to the game only for a moment, because another aide approached Lord Stokely in haste. She saw Stokely's face flush and noticed an abrupt change in his manner. He was angry and, as she knew all too well, he was best avoided until his mood improved. The messenger stepped back to wait while Stokely magically reacquired a veneer of bonhomie to talk to someone. As she resumed play, she became conscious of being glad Flora was absent. How she detested her.

Mr Dalgleish surveyed the ballroom. Several nagging thoughts troubled him but, excellent servant that he was, he kept them hidden. His most recent and really the least of his concerns was where had the Burgoyne's agency servants gone? They were not needed at present, but he had become accustomed to Miss King's assiduous attention to his wishes, and she had not sought him out today as she had done on previous days. This was his minor worry. Heading the list of his major concerns was Lord Stokely himself. He had always been wilful, which Dalgleish had historically put down to overindulgence by his family. As a young footman, he had heard the rumours that the former earl was not Roderick Fielding's father, but that Uncle Edward was. When the old cook was dying, he had gone to see her. He thought her to be delirious when she mistook him for another footman who had died years earlier. She spoke familiarly and, in a dreadful rasping breath, had stated that Lady Georgiana had married Edward, and not his brother Robert, the eleventh earl. Dalgleish could see for himself that this repressed secret, now hatched out in delirium, was burdensome to the sick woman. She surprised him when she said she had been a witness at the ceremony. Despite her sincerity, Dalgleish had not believed her. However, he kept his own counsel on the matter. Over the years, he gradually saw that it was quite likely to be true after all, simply because of the way Georgiana, Edward, and Robert behaved towards one another, and towards the boy, Roderick. It was no business of his. He would never harm Lady Georgiana because of his devotion to her. Of the two men in the arrangement, he was sympathetic towards the old earl, who suffered over the years. Dalgleish was indifferent to Edward, believing him to be somehow responsible for the whole charade. Concerning the twelfth earl, Lord Roderick, Dalgleish found he could never warm to the selfish boy, the headstrong young man, or the manipulative adult.

"How is Mama managing in your absence?" asked Stokely, stopping to speak to Dalgleish on his way out of the ballroom.

"My Lord, I have telephoned Lyall Place daily, and am informed that the household is running smoothly."

"I spoke to Mama earlier, and she wants you back promptly. So, Dalgleish, you are missed." He spoke with a touch of irony. "Look after her."

"I will endeavour to do my utmost, my Lord."

"Yes, I'm sure you will."

Stokely left the ballroom, followed by the aide who had brought him the message. Afterwards, Dalgleish idly wondered what it was Lord Stokely was trying to accomplish at present. This large assembly puzzled him, for he could not see the point of it. Also, there was the continuing concern regarding Lord Stokely's acquaintances, some of whom were very low in Dalgleish's estimation. Kemp, for example, as well as several others. And, until recently, there was Ferrers who had often been to Lyall Place when Lord Stokely was present. The man, a criminal, seemed almost like a wild beast to Dalgleish. He had been afraid of Ferrers and was relieved that the man was now in prison. But what had Lord Stokely to do with men of that type? This habit of his, of surrounding himself with dubious characters, must have a foundation and a raison d'être. It was not Dalgleish's place to say anything, but he found Lord Stokely's behaviour unsettling.

Jeremy Rushton was alone in a room full of people. The only thing he wanted was to be at home with his wife. He loathed Chertsey Park and the circus within it. He loathed Stokely's ambition and continually smiling face. Most of all, he loathed himself for having set aside his better judgment for the sake of more money. Rushton liked Jack Long, but the man was now too much for him to take. Long always excused Stokely's behaviour or dismissed it as inconsequential or made it out to be oh, so reasonable. What had previously allayed and soothed Rushton's suspicions now appeared little better than a sweet, sickly opiate.

At a party, irritation and dissatisfaction do not commend the bearer to the host nor yet to other guests. Rushton could not help it, even though he knew he was being watched. This surveillance played on his nerves and made him think about how dangerous Stokely might be. Why was he being he watched? All Rushton could assume was that his reserve and his sometimes pointed questioning had attracted the wrong type of attention. Gently baulking at what amounted to a shadow government had isolated him. Dawkins, Cobden, and the omnipresent aides had noticed him for the wrong reasons. He had counted nine aides, although several looked so bland and so similar that he might have counted the same person twice. They reminded him of junior officers, ready to carry out regimental orders at a moment's notice, without question, and with great efficiency.

Rushton sipped at his glass of Champagne, but he had held it for so long it had become warm and rather flat. He likened it to the weekend he was enduring. He wondered what he should do. Go home? That's what he wanted to do, but he was leaving in the morning, anyway. He had decided that, on Monday morning, he would resign. Would it be that easy? All the gossip he had heard about Stokely over the years began nagging at him. Vindictive — people had said he was, although nothing had ever been brought home to him. There he was now — Stokely in the middle of the inevitable large group and, as always, the focus of attention. Rushton saw the aide whisper to Stokely, saw the earl's face change, saw and understood that he was, for a split second, uncharacteristically angry.

Rushton asked himself who, then, was Stokely? Dismayed at not having recognized the answer before, his time at Chertsey Park had made it clear. The man was an actor and organizer, one who was power hungry. Stokely was playing a stealthy game behind the veil of his public persona. He

351

was equal parts subtle and bold, and already he had gone very far in his schemes. Stokely wanted to run the country. The newspaperman suddenly felt out of his depth. He had a story that he could not print, neither could he take it to anyone without them laughing at him all the way down Fleet Street. Rushton thought of the police, but realized that they, too, would not listen to him. Now he was a man who knew the truth — knew it in his heart — without another soul to whom to tell it. He was left feeling lost, and feeling as though there were no point in doing anything. As all of society was flocking after the earl, he saw Stokely's accession to power to be inevitable. Rushton got himself a drink, avoiding Jack Long on the way to the table.

---

Sophie retrieved her reports and the drawings, and the four women agents entered the dormitory to get the hats, coats, and suitcases. There, they met Miss Beech and two other maids from Lyall Place.

"Where have you been, Miss King...?" asked Miss Beech, who was sitting up in bed.

"Sorry, we can't stop to chat," replied Sophie.

The Lyall Place maids stared in bewilderment as the agents picked up their belongings and put on their coats.

"Are you leaving?"

"Yes. We can't stay or they'll shoot us," said Sophie.

"I beg your pardon?"

"We're police informants. Stokely is trying to start a revolution. We must leave in order to stop him. Goodbye... Oh, and please give my apologies to Mr Dalgleish for abandoning our posts. And you'd better not say you know anything about any of us to anyone. That will be much safer for you."

The others said goodbye to the shocked audience. Then the agents bustled out of the dormitory.

By means of unfrequented passages in the attics and on the second floor, the women cautiously threaded their way unseen through the house. Their immediate objective was to rendezvous with Alfie and Broadbent-Wicks. When this was accomplished, they were at the top of the servants' stairs in the east wing, and close to the garage.

"Cuttin' it a bit fine, miss," whispered Alfie. "Let's go. There's no one on the stairs."

With Alfie in the lead, the agents, as quietly as six people on a creaking staircase could, began the slow descent. The sound of every bump, and every squeaking tread, seemed magnified tenfold.

"Sorry, miss," whispered Fern, when her case bumped against the newel post on a landing.

"I think we should make a run for it," whispered Flora.

"Not yet."

"Time is of the essence," whispered Flora.

"Fools rush in where angels fear to tread," whispered Sophie.

"A stitch in time saves nine," countered Flora.

"Slow but steady wins the race."

"Um, I can't think of anything... Too many cooks spoil the broth?"

"That doesn't make sense," whispered Sophie. "I won."

They got to the bottom and crept along the passage.

The aide silently accompanied Stokely to the first floor office. Dawkins had asked the earl to come in the hope that Stokely's presence might loosen the agents' tongues. Stokely, irritated with Dawkins because of his failure to deal with the matter, paused for the aide to open the door for him. The earl stopped on the threshold upon seeing the two bound men.

"What has happened?" he sneered. "So. You let a few servants get the jump on you, Dawkins?" He motioned to the aide to release them. "Is that one dead?"

"No, my Lord — he's only unconscious," replied the aide, who shook the prone figure gently. "Ah, he's coming round now."

Stokely ungagged Dawkins.

"Well?" he asked.

"They attacked us, my Lord."

"You were armed, weren't you?"

"Yes, my Lord. They are some type of special agent. They let slip they work for a hidden organization."

"I don't care about that. Where are they, and what do they know?"

"They must still be in the house, but they've taken papers."

Stokely strode to the cabinet and took a key from his pocket while one aide untied Dawkins, and the other sat on the carpet, rubbing his neck. Stokely opened the cabinet and screamed.

"Argh!" He sounded like a wild animal. "They've taken my manuscript...! My diary! They've *got my diary*!" He began kicking and punching the cabinet, then he pulled it over and stamped on it until the wood splintered. He spun around. "Pull yourself together, Dawkins. Find them at once. Bring them to me." The open-mouthed aide who had witnessed the earl's fit of rage had to suppress a guffaw and look away at the irony of Stokely telling Dawkins to pull himself together.

Elizabeth arrived at the end of Chertsey Park's drive a few minutes early. She got out and began looking high into the trees. A waning half moon was out, and she scanned the interlaced bare branches for signs of an owl. She took a few steps nearer to the entrance.

"Where do you think you're going?" said a low male voice from the darkness under the trees.

"Ah!" Elizabeth could not have been more shocked by the voice that came out of nowhere.

"I asked you a question." The voice had come closer. The

man fumbled in the dark to switch on a lantern. He shone it in Elizabeth's face, dazzling her.

"Take that thing away." She shielded her eyes from the glare.

"You're trespassing."

"Don't be absurd. I'm not on your property. I'm parked on the King's Highway. Put the lantern down. I can't see anything."

"I have a shotgun pointed at you, so don't go moving off that spot." He put down the lantern, then whistled sharply. From somewhere near the house came an answering whistle. A dog started to bark.

"Ready?" asked Sophie. They were at the exit of the house nearest to the garage. The others replied that they were. "If we're stopped, we say they've sent us home because, as staff, we're surplus to requirements, and we're to meet the driver here. What happens after that is anyone's guess."

She opened the door, and they began to file out. When halfway to the garage, they heard a car coming up the driveway.

"Quick," said Sophie, and they beat a hasty retreat back into the house. No sooner were they inside, the door to the Gun Room opened and they heard voices. They hurried back upstairs.

From two flights above, they listened in the stairwell to the sounds of Kemp's men moving about, and then going out of the side door.

"Do you think they're after us?" asked Flora.

"Sounds like it," said Sophie.

"What shall we do, miss?" asked Ada.

"All suggestions are welcome. We must get to the garage." She looked at her watch. "Oh, dear. We're going to miss Elizabeth... I'm sure she'll go to Inspector Morton and tell him something's gone wrong."

"That'll be all right, then. When the Old Bill shows up, we're safe."

"True. I just wish we were out of it first."

"Miss," said Alfie. "If we can't get to the garage, we need to hide somewhere, and sharpish."

"Yes... But they'll eventually find us if we remain in the house."

"They'll find us in the garage or other outbuildings, too," said Flora.

"And if we scarper across that 'eath," said Ada, "they'll find us stone cold dead in the morning."

"We *could* cross the heath," said Sophie, "but they have dogs, so they'll catch us."

"Why don't we seize the Gun Room?" said Broadbent-Wicks. "Then you can call Inspector Morton from there and they won't dare come near us since we'll all be armed to the teeth!"

"What a good idea," said Sophie.

"I thought you were joking," said Flora.

"It does sound rather drastic," agreed Sophie. "If I could only ring the Inspector and be certain that help is on the way, they won't dare do anything to us, even if we're not occupying the Gun Room."

"I ain't so sure about that either way," said Alfie. "These men might get desperate. What's in this?" He held up the attaché case. "It's bound to be state secrets, or they wouldn't have locked it away like it was."

"What are you saying?"

"We're on our own, and should expect the worse. Us getting out of here is the best plan. I think we should make a dash for the garage, and the sooner the better, because they'll think of it as well."

"We vote with a show of hands," said Sophie. "Who's for the Gun Room?" Broadbent-Wicks put his hand up. "Dash for the garage?" The rest raised their hands. "I'm sorry. It was a good idea, Mr Ely, but not the preferred one."

"I'm not put out, Miss King. I have many ideas and no one

ever seems to think very much of them."

"Let me tell you this, then. I think your idea of punching Dawkins was a rather splendid one. It certainly got us out of a desperate situation."

"Oh, I say, Miss King."

"It's gone quiet down there," said Fern. "Shall we give it a go?"

"Yes, we'd best be moving or they'll catch us right here."

They repeated their descent. Sophie looked through a window and the coast was clear as far as she could see. Alfie opened the door and peered out, then quickly shut it. "Your car's an Austin Twenty, ain't it?"

"Yes, I call it Rabbit because of the number plate. Why do you ask?"

"It's parked right outside."

"It can't be."

Before Alfie answered, they heard a commotion and Elizabeth's faint voice. "You ruffian! Let go of me!"

## Chapter 28

# Running with the hare & hunting with the hounds

After calming down, Lord Stokely instructed Dawkins to inform him as soon as he had captured the spies. In a vicious frame of mind, he returned to the ballroom. Once more, as soon as he was in the room, guests made their way towards him. Charlotte saw his reflection in a mirror; saw the irritation that was barely kept in check. Watching, as people clustered around Stokely, she recalled when she had been the flame and he the moth. The roles were now reversed, but she could never get close to him again. This evening was as much as she could ever hope for. There were so many others nearer to him now. She played cards and won the hand and a sizable pot. One player dropped out as the stakes increased. Another, willing to try his luck, immediately took his seat at the table.

"A word with you in private, if I may," said Uncle Teddy. He took Lord Stokely by the arm and led him several steps away from the group. He asked quietly, "What's happened?"

Stokely answered in a low voice. "There are police spies in the house who are masquerading as servants. Dawkins had them in the office for questioning, but they overpowered him and an aide. They're still somewhere on the estate. It's unbelievable. They've taken sensitive documents."

"Why are they here?"

"I don't know. Probably a Scotland Yard blunder. Perhaps a junior officer got a tip and acted on it. No one contacted me to say anything was planned."

"Telephone at once and have the operation called off. That'll get your documents returned."

"I shall. I wish to catch them first. This action of theirs must not go unpunished. Dawkins recommends having them killed in a Red Fist incident."

"Such a step is totally unnecessary, when a telephone call to the right person will settle things without any fuss... What the blazes is the matter with Dawkins? You should think about replacing him if he can't do his job."

"He's usually very good. I will consider what you say."

"Do so. My boy, if you need help, I'm ready. Although I say it myself, I was a good administrator in Jo'burg, where I often dealt with unpleasant situations which London never heard about."

Stokely smiled at his uncle. He patted him affectionately on the arm. "Come, let's return."

"In a moment. Are you taking up with Charlotte again?"

"No, not in any permanent sense.... You'll laugh at this one. As you well know, Mama is most insistent I marry. What do you think? A young maid here caught my eye. A real beauty, healthy looking, and well spoken, so I thought I might marry her to fulfil my obligations. It turns out she's a police spy. What do you think of that?" Stokely first smiled, and then laughed.

"You nearly came a cropper there," said Uncle Teddy, also laughing. "You can't just pick a wife at random. It's not done."

"Next time, I will first have my future bride investigated."

Uncle Teddy half-heartedly smiled at the remark. His expression gave away that his mind had wandered elsewhere.

---

During their flight, the secret agents avoided Kemp's men who brought Elizabeth into the house. They were armed with shotguns and were too many to be confronted. The man with the mastiff was among them. The group proceeded to the Gun Room to report to Kemp.

The secret agents crept down the stairs again. This time, they got out of the door and reached the garage unopposed.

"There's no key in your car," said Alfie, after checking the Austin.

"Blast them. They must have taken it," said Sophie.

Upon entering the garage, Sophie went to the board to find the right key for Stokely's Rolls-Royce. "Here's my key!" she said. It was easily recognizable. Attached to the key was a red ribbon from which hung Sophie's school punctual attendance medal for 1913-14.

"I'll take your car, shall I?" asked Alfie.

"No. Take Stokely's limousine. Here's the key for it. If all else fails, at least we will have annoyed him."

"I think we've done that all right," said Ada.

"When you get to Sunningdale, give everything to Inspector Morton or Sergeant Gowers, and, of course, tell them to come here as soon as possible."

"I know you're not coming with us, but would you like me to stay with you?" asked Flora.

"That's kind, but it won't help... Oh, take my case. And don't surrender this pistol to the police." Sophie raised her eyebrows meaningfully and handed Flora the automatic.

"Understood," said Flora.

"It was made in Belgium, so I'm calling it Le Belge."

Flora smiled. "Be careful."

"You, too... All of you."

They climbed into the limousine. When Alfie started the engine, Sophie opened the doors. As the long car passed by, they waved to her. She smiled and waved back, then shut the garage doors.

After a brief search, Sophie found a screwdriver and went to the damaged Rolls-Royce. She pulled the dustsheet back and unlatched and lifted the bonnet. It surprised her to find the engine compartment layout quite different from her own car. She found the distributor cap, undid it, and removed the rotor arm. Hurriedly, she put everything else back as she had found it. Next, she went to the board and took all the car keys. This was a delaying tactic she had decided upon, in case the inhabitants of Chertsey Park escaped by car before or when the police arrived. Sophie well knew that some of Kemp's men would know how to start a car without a key. The one vehicle she wanted to stay put under any circumstances was the car used in the murder of Mr Auckland. The vehicle was evidence that must remain where it was.

Outside, Sophie threw the keys into some bushes. After wiping grease from her fingers with a rag, she used the cloth to wrap the rotor arm. This little bundle she put under one of the remaining piles of snow near to the entrance. She would have re-entered the house immediately, but someone was talking just inside the door. Instead, she headed to the back to find another way in. Her hands were cold from the work and especially from handling the snow.

Now that her friends had gone, many things started preying upon her mind, threatening to overwhelm her. They had all said they wanted to rescue Elizabeth, and could not bear the thought of leaving her alone to face Dawkins and Stokely. They had all said, in their different ways, they must do something, but Sophie had seen their anxious faces. Escape was near, and to turn from it to go back to the very thing being evaded was too much to ask of her friends. Also, it made no sense. The mission had to be completed, and that meant the evidence must reach Inspector Morton. They only had the one chance to escape. She dearly hoped they were successful. If an armed patrol of Stokely's intercepted the car... She did not like to contemplate what would happen then.

Sophie had stayed behind because she could not leave Elizabeth. She stayed, because it was she whom Dawkins had caught returning to the house. The main underlying reason was that it was her evident duty to stay. She had the responsibility for and care of the others. At the corner of the house, she looked back. There was Rabbit, lit by a lamp. Her cold fingers touched the key in her pocket. She hesitated... No... She must clean her now dirty and frigid hands — frigid because she had been unwilling to ruin her lovely gloves because of *him*!

As Sophie went inside, wondering where she should put her hat and coat, the aides and some of Kemp's men started a systematic search of the house. They began in the attics, to the great horror of Miss Beech. She screamed when two men entered the dormitory, asking after the Burgoyne's staff. She said she knew nothing at all about them, and the two other maids were also quick to claim ignorance.

Dawkins had been looking out of the window, and wondered where Lord Stokely or, at least, where his car was going at this time of night. He now sat alone in the office, waiting for the spies to be brought back or the telephone to ring. He considered his options. Stokely would discover that an idiotic footman had tricked the Bristol unit into inaction. The blame for that would fall upon him. The blame for *everything* would fall upon him. Dawkins had two choices. The first was to cut and run, and he had a forged passport for just such a purpose. He would have to leave the estate immediately, and then spend the rest of his life looking over his shoulder.

Dawkins had done enough dirty work for Stokely to know what his prospects were. The second choice was to murder Stokely. There could be no witnesses. Whatever he chose, he must act quickly. Dawkins did not care about Stokely's manuscript, but that diary, he was sure, had to be dynamite... with a lit fuse.

There came a knock. Kemp's man, John, entered.

"Excuse me, Mr Dawkins. They've done a runner..."

"Stokely's limousine," said Dawkins, immediately perceiving what had happened. "Was anyone at the gate?"

"Yes, but he thought it was his lordship inside, so he saluted the car. It was dark, you see. We only found out because someone's taken all the car keys."

Dawkins sighed wearily. He waved the young man from the room so that he could return to his now even gloomier speculations.

Charlotte was finding the play at the table predictable. Although she had yet to hold an excellent hand herself, she was ahead by fifteen pounds. The man with ten thousand a year was also ahead. The others players had no stomach for large stakes and were losing steadily. She thought her findings that everyone was playing within their means would please Lord Stokely.

With little else to occupy him, Jeremy Rushton drifted towards the card tables. He had no taste for gambling, and did not understand those who did. Despite this, he soon recognized that among the three small groups, there were only two serious players present. He knew Miss Terence's reputation. The wealthy man, whom he did not know, handled his cards confidently. He also refrained from commenting on the play as others were apt to do, their hoping to contribute to a convivial atmosphere.

It was bad form to look over a shoulder at anyone's cards, but he would have liked to do so. Rushton felt more relaxed than he had all evening. The aides had vanished, and the weight of their gaze had, therefore, gone, too. With this relaxation of surveillance, he began to believe he may have been overreacting — assuming things as fact, when he had no proof. However, he remembered the cautioning words of the maid — not for the first time — *Get out while you can.* As luck would have it, he had not seen her since, which was unsurprising in the great barn of a house.

Watching others play cards, a dissatisfying pastime, began to bore Rushton. He looked about, intending to speak to Jack Long, so that it did not appear as if he were avoiding him. It was then he saw the maid. She was crossing the ballroom carrying her hat and coat. Rushton realized she must have come in from outside through one of the French windows. This was odd behaviour for a servant — unconscionable, in some quarters. With a reporter's eye, he scanned the room to see if anyone else had noticed her. The maid passed by Lord Stokely, who did not see her, although his uncle did. As Edward Fielding made no comment, Rushton looked at others. No one seemed to remark her presence. The maid left the room. He turned back to the card table. Instantly he saw that of all people, Miss Terrence must have been watching the maid in the mirror. Inadvertently, their eyes met. Miss Terrence smiled and so did Rushton, who also nodded. He left the area a moment later, trying to piece together why Miss Terrence would still be watching the doorway after the mysterious maid had gone through it. He sensed a story there — another one.

Being no longer a servant in the house, Sophie determined she would stop pretending to be one. As a consequence, she hung her hat and coat in the guests' cloakroom. In the nearby guests' lavatory, she washed her hands and tidied herself, chiefly by re-arranging her hair. Without the cap and apron, she might pass as a housekeeper, but not as a guest. When she emerged, an aide hurried past her. So intent was he upon finding a group of escaping servants, he overlooked the possibility that a solitary one of them was right in front of him. This lack of recognition surprised her.

She set off to find Elizabeth. Her hands were still pink with cold. At least they were now clean. Sophie assumed Elizabeth was being held by Kemp in the Gun Room. If that assumption was incorrect, Elizabeth surely must then be in the office under interrogation by Dawkins. Sophie discovered her nerves were trying to turn her into a weeping, fearful wreck. On the way to the Gun Room, she struggled to dismiss this question: *What will they do to me?* Instead, she thought of what she would say and how to conduct herself. Boldness was her best policy. Putting all thoughts of Dawkins and Stokely from her mind, she thought of Kemp first. What type of man is he? She asked herself this and considered her answers. There lay the trick of it all — to deal with the man in terms he could appreciate. She walked on, reluctantly but doggedly.

Secretary Cobden, a diffident man, preferred not to socialize with those over whom he had control. When not engaged in actual work, he spent a lot of his time making himself available in case Lord Stokely needed him. He studied the earl during these periods and, over time, had come to understand his subject's moods better than anyone else. In the ballroom, Cobden engaged in a few desultory and unsatisfactory conversations when necessary. For much of the time since dinner, he had, in the role of spectator, attached himself to a group that was having lively discussions. Cobden's principal reason for doing so was that the group lay within Lord Stokely's proximity and therefore allowed Cobden to attend his lordship if the latter needed him. He was standing there, not really listening to the debate going on around him, when someone tapped him on the arm.

"Mr Wilberforce. Is anything wrong?" asked Cobden.

"I came to ask you the same thing," said Wilberforce in a low voice. "His lordship looks angry."

"I'm sure it will pass quickly. It always does."

"I thought it was in connection with tonight's operations. As far as I know, everything's running smoothly. I wondered if something else has happened."

"Nothing of which I'm aware. Although Dawkins has been missing since dinner."

"Ah... Then, a visit to the office is in order. I'll let you know what I find out."

Cobden glanced towards Stokely. "I'll come with you."

At that same moment, Sophie descended to the ground floor and headed to the Gun Room. Her lips were compressed in a line while thinking over how she would deal with Kemp. Ahead of her, two men were lounging in the corridor. They saw her approach.

"Here, ain't she one of them?"

"Can't be. They've all cleared out."

"I'm sure she is."

"If she was, she wouldn't be comin' down here. Why would she?"

"No... S'pose you're right."

Sophie arrived at the closed door and asked,

"Is Mr Kemp inside?"

"He is, miss."

"Open the door, please."

The man hastened to do as asked. Sophie entered the Gun Room and shut the door.

"She looks like a right Tartar."

"Yes. Here, she might be a new housekeeper. Pretty, though."

"Forget about her. Bossy women are a pain in the neck."

# Chapter 29

# Sunningdale

The village of Sunningdale (Ascot 2 miles, Waterloo Station 27 miles) used to be a part of 'Old' Windsor, until it was suddenly 'created' in 1894. Sunningdale's birth was a stormy affair, with many coming forward to claim parenthood of the child. The County of Surrey said, 'It's ours, and should be called Broomhall.' The County of Berkshire said, 'Don't be ridiculous.' The conflict spread and the battle of the two counties was joined by three borough councils and four parish councils. By counting on its infant fingers, Sunningdale decided that nine councils were eight too many. So the village said, 'You lot sort it out, I'm off to play golf,' which was rather forward of the youngster.

Since then, Sunningdale has continued playing golf and avoids all controversy. On Monday morning, the village goes to the city, at which time it is reminded to buy and sell its properties through Messrs Giddy & Giddy while waiting on the platform for the train. Sunningdale enjoys its meals at set times and likes to go to bed early. It thoroughly detests having its sleep disturbed.

At eleven o'clock on Saturday night in Sunningdale's village hall, the special detachment of hand-picked men had been on high alert for what seemed like a month of Sundays. The officers' zealous attitude of 'Any moment now, and we're going in,' had plummeted to 'What a waste of time it all is.'

Inspector Morton felt jumpy. As the hours went by without hearing anything, his concern increased for Miss Burgoyne's welfare. As a policeman, he was concerned for all the Burgoyne's staff but, as a man, he was most anxious for Sophie.

"Miss Elizabeth should have been here by now," said Morton.

"She's probably got stuck up a tree looking for owls," said Sergeant Gowers, wryly.

"That isn't funny. This is a serious situation."

"We all know it is, sir. But we haven't been called in and might never be. Miller's at Chertsey Park, and we're sitting here twiddling our thumbs. What did Superintendent Penrose say about the situation earlier?"

"For us to continue being patient. He said there was nothing doing his end, either... Penrose sounded as bloody cheerful as ever."

"Cheerful or not, I never thought I'd see the day when the Yard allowed a murderer to walk around freely and yet do nothing about it."

"I know. It goes against the grain, but we'll have him and Stokely, don't you worry."

"*If* we get the call. And that's another thing. What's happened to Miss Burgoyne? Why hasn't she rung us to give her report?"

"She's in contact with Miss Elizabeth. It can't be easy for her to use a telephone when she's supposed to be a servant."

"She could manage it, if anyone can... I don't like this, sir. Not knowing anything makes me imagine all sorts of things."

"Doesn't it just?" Morton got up. "We can't bloody well make a move until we're called in... Streuth! My nerves will be shot by the time this is all over."

"It's aggravating, but then today's that type of day. Fulham only managed a draw against Lincoln City when they should have won."

"What? How can you possibly compare the two?"

"Well, Fulham didn't win and didn't lose. We're ready to go, but haven't been sent. It's like treading water, where you're swimming but making no progress."

"I'm sorry I asked. I don't quite catch your meaning. Fulham's still got a chance to go through to the next round — they get another crack at it in the replay."

"That's one way of viewing it. What I'm saying is..."

The sudden and repeated hooting from a car right outside the hall destroyed the pristine, almost holy silence of Sunningdale. The racket galvanized the police. Arising as one man, they hurried to arrest the motorist for disturbing the peace.

Morton nearly collided with a very excited Flora on the step. The hooter still sounded.

"It's you," he said, surprised at seeing her.

"Yes. You must come at once! They've taken Elizabeth prisoner!"

"Ah... Have they?"

Gowers pushed past them, shouting, "You there! Stop that row!"

"Righty-ho," called Broadbent-Wicks, who left off squeezing the bulb. Lights were being switched on in the surrounding houses.

"Who's taken her prisoner?" asked Morton, taking Flora by the arm, and moving to one side to allow others to pass.

"*Them*, of course. Don't just stand there!"

"Calm yourself... Miss Elizabeth is a prisoner, you say. Why is that?"

"Um,... Dawkins suspected we were up to something, and was playing all manner of low tricks on us, so we decided to leave with the evidence tonight. Only we couldn't, because they captured Dora and Dan. Oh, you know who I mean. They're safe and in the car, by the way, with the evidence. So, later on, Dawkins was giving us the third degree. Only Sophie, I mean Phoebe, put him in his place. Oh, she was absolutely *marvellous!* You should have seen her. She really could have gone straight to the opening night. Then I laughed, with perfect timing. That was in the play, too. Then Dawkins started getting rough with Sophie. He was really quite nasty to her."

"Was he?" said Morton.

"Yes. Then Mr Ely pushed the aide out of the way and punched Dawkins. Then it all went mad. Absolute mayhem broke out. There were coshes and guns everywhere! We won, but I'm very put out because I didn't really do anything. It was a super bundle, though. So we tied up Dawkins and the aide, and played hide and seek throughout the house, avoiding all henchman. Then Elizabeth got caught by some guards waving shotguns and with fearsome dogs. We got past them, took the car, and came over here to get you."

"Where is Miss King?" asked Morton.

"Somewhere in Chertsey Park. We couldn't all just *leave* Elizabeth. Anyway, you must rescue them. We have tons of evidence, although we haven't looked at it yet. There has to be some lurid bits in it."

"Er, who does the Rolls-Royce belong to?" asked Gowers.

"It's Stokely's. It's not stolen, though. We've brought it to you for safekeeping."

"Miss Walton," said Morton. "I must tread carefully here. Are you calling us in to Chertsey Park because a crime has been committed on the premises?"

"Haven't you been listening!? There's kidnapping, treason, murder, the food provided was awful, *and* they've been abominably rude. Sophie and Elizabeth are still in danger. Inspector, you must do something!"

Morton was about to bellow an order when a man with a military bearing approached. Wearing a scarf against the chill, and a hat covering his white head of hair, he still wore his pyjamas under his overcoat. He held a pad and pencil in his gloved hands.

"I hope you're arresting these drunkards," he said to Morton, before scowling at Flora. "We do not tolerate loutish behaviour in Sunningdale. What's the meaning of it, and who the devil *are* these people?"

"One moment, please... Get the rifles! We're going in!" He turned back to the man. "May I suggest you return home, sir? All this annoyance will soon be over."

"Rifles? Surely you won't shoot them? I'm a magistrate. Charges of drunk and disorderly or disturbing the peace only require a summons to appear in court."

"I haven't decided *if* I'll charge them yet, sir."

"Not charge them! That's tantamount to dereliction of duty. However, you have rifles, so perhaps you're busy with something else. I'll tell you what — I'll swear out the complaint. Do you have their names?"

"Not yet. Excuse me a moment," said Morton, who was quick to depart.

"What's your name?" the irate man asked Flora.

"I'm so blotto, I've forgotten. Good night, Mr Magistrate." Flora returned to the car.

"Here... Come back! I've got your car's registration number, so you shan't get away, young lady! You'll be up before *me*, in my *court*!"

The police scattered to retrieve their equipment. Morton telephoned Penrose to apprise him of the events. Penrose sounded gruff but wished Morton good luck.

---

Sophie was in the Gun Room. There she found Elizabeth, looking forlorn, with her head bowed, sitting in a chair. Kemp was behind the desk and had evidently been examining the contents of her handbag. The young man, John, his feet resting on a box, was rocking back and forth on the back legs of his chair.

371

"Well, well," said Kemp, looking up at Sophie, a leering smile on his face. "I thought you'd be long gone." He pointed a shotgun at Sophie.

"I'm not armed, so you can put that thing down. I'm only here to watch everyone get arrested. It should be quite fun."

Elizabeth looked up sharply.

"Oh, Miss Burgoyne! I'm ever so sorry, but a man jumped out at me in the dark. I couldn't get away from him because he had a gun." Elizabeth stood up, a lost, bewildered figure. Sophie put her arm around her.

"It doesn't matter," she said softly. "It's all over now."

Elizabeth began crying. She took out her handkerchief. "I'm so sorry."

"Ah, breaks your heart, doesn't it?" said Kemp to John.

"Mr Kemp, instead of mocking others' feelings, you would be better employed considering what to do when the police arrive."

"They won't be coming here. Your friend might get charged with trespassing, though." He pointed at Elizabeth. "But that's not my decision to make. Go on, John. Take these two up to Dawkins."

"John, stay where you are. I fully intend speaking to Dawkins again, but I shall explain a matter first."

"O-ho. I think you've got the wrong end of the stick." Kemp smiled.

"There is no stick. Do you think Stokely can get away with whatever he likes? You believe he can do anything he wants to, and the police won't touch him? You're wrong, Kemp, and have never made a bigger mistake in your entire life. Stokely's agents are all known. We know who he pays and the influence he's purchased. But it is not those paid police who are coming. It's not the bribed officials who are involved in tonight's affairs. You've forgotten, haven't you? There are other police and other officials. It is they who will arrive to lay charges, and none of you shall escape. Not even Stokely. When you're in prison alongside your employer, you'll have plenty of time for regret. Elizabeth, get your things. We'll see Dawkins now. I've a few words to say to him. Some intelligence officer he's turned out to be."

Elizabeth put her possessions back in her handbag while Kemp watched her. He had stopped smiling. "What are you going to say to Dawkins?" he asked.

"He said he wanted to turn King's evidence on Stokely. I'm going to inform him the police have refused such an arrangement. He's on his own, like the rest of you."

The room was silent. John had stopped rocking his chair. Kemp put the shotgun down.

When Elizabeth was ready, she and Sophie left the room.

"Send the two men outside with them. Make sure those women get to Dawkins and don't run off somewhere."

"All right."

John stepped into the corridor to speak to the two men and then returned.

"She sounds like she knows what she's talking about."

Kemp hesitated before replying. "Yes... And it's not just her who knows, is it?"

"What do we do?"

"I think we'd best see how this situation plays out. First sign of it turning stinky, then it'll be every man for himself."

"Yes... Fancy Dawkins wanting to rat on his lordship. I'd never have thought he'd do anything like that."

"Don't forget, and Dawkins knows this as well, Stokely reckons we're all expendable. We're like nothing to him. Stokely has a lot of money, and he's free with it for the type of work we can do. But if anything goes wrong or you don't do your job proper... He won't forgive or help a soul. Never has, and never will."

"I know it... This whole business is making me jumpy. How about you?"

"Oh, yes." Kemp got up. "I've got a few things to look after. I'm sure you have an' all."

The two men trailed behind Sophie and Elizabeth, which left the women free to talk in whispers.

"So the police are coming? I'm relieved to hear they are," said Elizabeth.

"They should be here soon. The others have gone to fetch them. At least, I imagine they got there all right."

"Oh. But you sounded so positive back there."

"We're in a fight, and we cannot let them see we're weak. There's no escape for us until the police come, and they shall. So, rather than be at our enemy's mercy, where we're always defending ourselves, we may as well go on the offensive." Sophie smiled at Elizabeth. "We're going to be as offensive as possible."

"I'll try to be offensive, too, but I doubt I'll be of much help, Miss King… I feel dreadful. I used your real name just now without thinking. Will that cause any trouble?"

"Don't worry. It was just a slip. We're all well past the point of no return, so it won't matter now."

"You're too kind."

"Not at all. Anyway, chin up. We'll beat them yet. What we'll do is sow seeds of discord. Hopefully, that will help the police when they arrive." She did not add — and help *us* survive. Although Sophie *hoped* the police would arrive soon, she was far from being as sure as she sounded. Her chief worry was in not understanding how far Stokely's network of influence extended. That he had not made a personal appearance in the night's proceedings gave her the slippery feeling that he was certain he would get away with everything and anything. Stokely would not act so confidently unless his assurance was based on a robust certainty. What, or who, that certainty was she did not know.

Dawkins betrayed no emotion when he looked up and found Sophie and Elizabeth in the office. He stared at Sophie. Then told the two men to stand outside.

"I want my pistol back," he said when they had left.

"I don't have it, I'm afraid. Besides, if I gave it to you, I believe you would shoot me."

"The thought would never enter my mind... Why didn't you leave?"

"I'm waiting for the police to arrive to watch them arrest you all. I'm surprised *you're* still here."

"I have work to do... Take a seat. And who are you?" He addressed Elizabeth.

"Ophelia Woodhouse."

"I presume you're the messenger between Miss King and Scotland Yard."

"I'm sure I cannot say."

"No matter. Miss King, where are the documents now?"

"In safe hands."

"Hmm... I hate to spoil your moment of triumph, but all your efforts will fail to achieve the results you desire. Lord Stokely will not be arrested, whereas you will be."

"Ah! That is such a familiar refrain. No one can touch Lord Stokely, because he has thoroughly corrupted the minds of so many, even the laws of the land are being perverted. Good is now evil, and evil good... He is untouchable... And you, of course, are equally untouchable. Not this time, however. Also, let me remind *you*, we can do great harm to Stokely's reputation."

"This is a tedious exchange," said Dawkins. "When the night's over, we will discover one of us is correct, and the other mistaken. We may as well wait for the denouement."

"Does that mean you're choosing to stay put despite the personal risk? You will not try to escape?"

"I don't follow you," said Dawkins.

"One thing we can both agree upon is Lord Stokely's vindictive nature. I'm not concerned about it, because he will soon be in handcuffs. You, however, should hope he is, too."

"Now I'm not following," said Elizabeth. "Why would Mr Dawkins want Lord Stokely arrested?"

"So that Stokely doesn't have him murdered for failing at

his job," answered Sophie.

"Oh... I know you're the enemy," said Elizabeth to Dawkins, "but, if it's not precipitate, you have my deepest sympathy... And may you rest in peace."

"This is quite droll, really," said Dawkins, who reluctantly smiled. "You have such a warped view of how things really stand."

"That is because we have a better grasp of the situation than you do. As for Lord Stokely? If you knew the truth about him, you would cut him dead in a second. In fact, you never would have had anything to do with him. Stokely has deceived you, Mr Dawkins."

"This is outlandish... In what way am I deceived?"

"Bring Stokely here, and you'll find out."

Dawkins sighed. "You're trying my patience."

"You're afraid of him, aren't you?"

"Enough."

"He'll kill you after tonight."

"*Enough*, I said."

"We're going to the kitchen to find food. If you want us, we'll be in the servants' hall."

"Before you go, who is it who's supposedly arriving to arrest Lord Stokely?"

"Let's wait for the denouement, shall we?"

Sophie and Elizabeth got up. Dawkins got up, not out of good manners, but to tell the two men outside to guard them.

"Don't let them escape," he said. "Use force if necessary."

"As it stands," said Sophie, addressing the two men, "when the police arrive, and because of your reasonable behaviour, I will put in a good word for you. However, should you do *anything* untoward, I shall make sure they throw the book at you. Kidnapping, for starters."

"Take this *bloody* woman away," said Dawkins. He shut the door with a bang.

Almost as soon as they had gone, Dawkins answered the telephone to receive a final report on an operation. He received two more final reports in quick succession. The report from the Bristol unit, he knew, was never coming. Armed with some good news to temper the bad, Dawkins believed it now expedient to see Stokely and bring him up to date on the state of affairs. Mentioning the loss of car keys, the limousine, and failing to retrieve the missing diary and manuscript would not be easy. He decided never to mention the trick played on the Bristol unit. Even as it stood without that, Stokely would make caustic comments at Dawkins' expense. While he was preparing to leave, an aide entered the room.

"Ah. We're just waiting on Bristol now," lied Dawkins, knowing that the call was never going to come. "You take over... And I'll borrow your pistol for a while. I must interview a prisoner."

"Yes, sir... Which prisoner might that be?"

"King. I captured her, and Kemp's men brought in a messenger. The messenger doesn't know anything."

"Oh, I see, sir. You'll use the messenger as leverage during interrogation."

The aide, delighted at this prospect, gave his pistol to Dawkins.

"Something like that. I'll see Lord Stokely first, though. Is he in the ballroom?"

"As far as I know, he is, sir."

# Chapter 30

# Enemy at the gates

The two women sat in the servants' hall. As she picked at her food, Sophie could not shake off an uneasy feeling, as though she were not remembering something important she had to do. Time weighed upon her. The waiting was becoming almost too much to endure.

"Is anything wrong, Miss King?" asked Elizabeth.

"No." Sophie smiled brightly. "How are your nature studies coming along?"

Elizabeth laughed shyly. "I've always liked animals, but I've *never* thought of studying them. Obviously, this is not the best time of year, but a nature study is such a good excuse to be outdoors in the country. Being out and about is much better than huddling by the fire at home and hoping for summer to come."

Sophie was relieved Elizabeth was recovering from her ordeal, and found her resilience surprising.

"I observed some fallow deer," continued Elizabeth eagerly. "One buck had a very thick coat, which was positively chocolate brown. When you see deer in the clearings, they stand out against the snow. But as soon as they're among the trees, they disappear, like ghosts."

"I'm sorry I missed them... Are you all right?"

"Now, I am, but I wasn't. When alone, I was frightened. I couldn't... I couldn't understand what was happening, you see. They wouldn't tell me *anything*. And those men... Why do people behave so badly?"

"I wish I knew the answer... I'm sorry they treated you so abominably. I never meant to put you in harm's way. Not all my plans are good ones."

"Please, don't reproach yourself. I knew it might be dangerous, and that made me feel audacious. It was stirring. And for that to happen, the danger has to be real, doesn't it?"

"I suppose so." Sophie smiled. "No harm done, then?"

"No, not at all, although I would like to leave soon."

"We shall."

As Sophie answered, she felt fear in the pit of her stomach.

---

The police convoy left Sunningdale for Chertsey Park. Following it was the Rolls-Royce. Alfie drove, and Broadbent-Wicks accompanied him up front, and said,

"Must be dashed awkward for the police wallahs — not being able to arrest a chap, while knowing he's a blaggard."

"As Miss King says," replied Alfie. "They need evidence to get a conviction."

"Yes... Something I've been meaning to ask you. I thought you were an ambulance driver in the war. How'd you get to be so handy with pistols?"

"Remember me telling you when my ambulance got blown up? That happened at the start of the German Spring Offensive in eighteen. That barrage was huge. It knocked the Fifth Army to pieces, so it did. As soon as it stopped, the whole German army came at us. They overran everything pretty much. So there's me, cut off, no ambulance, and no idea what to do with myself. One thing I was certain of, I wasn't going to be taken prisoner. Oh, no, matey, not me.

"While the Germans are attacking and I'm hiding in a trench, this sergeant comes along. His whole company's dead, wounded, or taken prisoner, and he's hopping mad. What a *nasty* bit of work he was but, blimey, he knew how to fight the Germans, and he would *not* give up. This sergeant sticks a rifle in my hand and says I'm infantry from then on. So I was. I can tell you some stories that'd turn your hair white. For ten days, me and a dozen blokes from different regiments are following this mad sergeant and fighting Germans. We're running, then fighting, running, and fighting. We had little sleep, and no supplies except what we picked up on the way. That's when I learned about pistols and a blooming sight more than that, me old fruit."

"That sounds horrific. I'm so glad you survived."

Alfie laughed. "So am I, mate. And I put my survival down to that cunning sergeant." The front was silent for a few moments. "You know, we didn't go through all that, and many blokes had it a lot worse than me, only to give the country to a barmy earl just because he wants it. He makes me sick. I hope tonight's the end of him."

In the back of the Rolls, Flora and Ada sat on the rear seat, while Fern sat on a folding one.

"Do you think they're all right?" asked Ada.

"I'm sure they must be," said Flora.

"I didn't like leaving them. I 'ate to think what's been going on."

"Very worrying," said Fern. "Was Miss King really going to shoot Mr Dawkins?"

"That's a difficult one," said Ada.

"I think she said it only to scare Dawkins," said Flora.

"That's probably it," said Ada. "If she shot someone, she'd be so upset afterwards. Glad, you should really have a word with her about it."

"As soon as this is over, I will. We can't let her go around shooting people."

"I got an idea!" said Fern. "That pistol she gave you — give it to the police."

"Yes, that's good," added Ada.

"She'll be ever so annoyed, if I do... How about this? I'll return the pistol to her right in front of Inspector Morton."

"That'll be perfect," said Ada. "You give it her back, and they take it away."

"I'm glad that's settled. Ain't it funny?" said Fern. "We're riding in a Rolls-Royce. I never thought I'd be doing such a thing in a million years."

"Me an' all. Talk about nice and comfy, though... Fern, do you know that's a drinks cabinet next to you?"

"What, this here?"

Fern groped in the dark until Ada switched on her torch to guide her. She pulled the flap out, which then formed a table. Inside was a tantalus containing two nearly full decanters.

"So Stokely's a boozer, is he?" said Fern, who then read the silver nameplates. "Brandy and whisky."

"If only I had known," said Flora. "I'd have brought cold tea to put in the decanters."

Ada and Fern giggled.

"I'd like to watch when he drank that," said Fern.

The convoy arrived at the closed gates of Chertsey Park. The police would have opened them and driven in, but entrance was denied — a body of men, some holding lanterns, had gathered on the other side of the gates.

"What's all this?" said Morton, who jumped out as soon as the car came to a halt.

"Here we go," said Gowers, joining him. "It's going to be a long night," he said gloomily.

They walked towards the group, several uniformed officers with them.

Morton addressed the shadowy mob. "In the name of the law, open these gates! I'm a Scotland Yard Detective Inspector, and I have a warrant to search these premises. Anyone hindering an officer in the course of his duties will be charged with obstruction, the penalty for which is very severe."

"No one wishes to obstruct you, Inspector." The educated voice of one of the aides sounded forth from about the middle of the group. "Your search warrant is invalid. It has already been countermanded by an authority higher than yours."

"So you say. Do you have this in writing, sir?"

"Not yet, but it's on its way as we speak, so be patient. It's coming by special messenger. Inspector, it might be a smart move for you to telephone your superior officer. Who is he, by the way?"

"That's no concern of yours. Now here's the difficulty. I have a valid warrant, and you can't present an authorization to prove your statements. Open the gates, sir, if you please."

"No. You're wasting your time and, I might add, your career. If you force an entry, you'll probably face charges of criminal mischief as well as being sued personally for damages."

"Blimey, what a mess," said Morton under his breath. He called out, "What's your name?"

"You don't need it, Inspector Morton."

"How does he know who you are?" asked Gowers in a whisper. "You never gave him your name."

"Stokely, of course. He's getting help from his highly placed friends. I hope Penrose has got this right."

"I trust Penrose, though he's often tight-lipped. If this is not a bluff, we have to act fast."

"This chap's a smooth blighter." Morton called out again, "This is your last chance. Open the gates, and allow us to do our lawful duty."

"Sorry, Inspector. In half an hour, this whole mistake will be cleared up to everyone's satisfaction. Best not make a rash decision now."

Sophie and Elizabeth had finished their snack in the servants' hall. Sophie looked at her watch again and said,

"They should be here any minute." Elizabeth did not answer. "Let's go for a walk, shall we? There are some interesting statues in a splendid entrance hall. I don't think you've seen them yet."

"Yes, I would like that. I haven't seen the hall."

They left with the two guards following them along the corridor.

"It's very elegant," said Elizabeth. "I must revise my figures for the building to include the furnishings, which must have cost far more than the house."

"You have the researcher's eye for such things. It had slipped my mind."

"Do you think Lord Stokely will interview us?"

"I don't believe he will... I hope he doesn't. I don't like scenes and I have the feeling he will make one. So, I'd rather not meet him."

"If you don't mind my saying, Miss King, you seem to be in a lot of *scenes*, even though you don't want them."

"I do, rather. To be honest, I've simply had enough of them for today, and seeing Stokely would likely be the worst of all... It's his title, I suppose... Being in his house, of course. I just want the police to take him away so he can do no more harm."

"Yes... Are we safe, do you think?"

"Up to a point. They might bully us again, but no more than that."

"No, I don't mean now. It's after we leave, isn't it, that there's likely to be repercussions?"

"Yes, Elizabeth, I'm afraid so."

"Oh, well. Not to worry, Miss King. As my mother used to

say, sufficient unto the day is the evil thereof."

"My father often quotes that — usually when a talkative parishioner, there's one in particular, is standing on the vicarage doorstep... Here's the entrance hall. What do you think?"

"How spectacular, and so very surprising... And they're original statues, not casts."

While Sophie and Elizabeth were quietly examining statues, the two guards hung back near to the Grand Salon entrance. An aide came up to them and, by the trick of the marble hall, the two women could plainly hear what they said. The aide spoke first.

"The police have arrived. Go to the gates to see if you're needed there. I'll watch these two."

"Yes, sir. Will the police come into the house?"

"Of course, they won't. A stupid CID inspector has got above his station, and he'll be sorry he ever tried."

"That's a relief. We don't like nosey rozzers."

"Off you go."

The aide took over their position. Elizabeth, dismayed, was about to speak, but Sophie, putting a finger to her lips, cautioned her to say nothing. Instead, they continued examining statues, and then slowly moved away from the hall towards the ballroom. They noticed the aide followed them much more closely than their two former companions, making private speech impossible.

"They say," began Sophie in a clear voice, "it is always darkest before dawn. But that's rubbish. The most profound darkness is that of an Englishman who would betray his country, to give it to a tyrant. That is a darkness with no dawn."

"Oh, you mean a traitor, do you, Miss King? Yes, a traitor is so thoroughly unpleasant. It makes one wonder what sort of upbringing he or she has had."

Elizabeth's response, and how she had instantly caught on, startled Sophie.

"Er, yes, yes. Take Stokely, for instance. He won't get anywhere. His sins will catch up with him, and all the lackeys who depend upon him will end up in prison or on the gallows."

"I don't agree with the death penalty as a rule. But what else can be done with such fools?"

A few guests had drifted from the ballroom ahead and were chatting in the corridor.

"Stokely is so short-sighted, he also qualifies as a fool. And, naturally, being superficial, he attracts the gullible and the subservient."

The aide grabbed Sophie's arm and wheeled her about to face him, angrily saying, "Shut up!" In the same instant, the cosh flew from her pocket and connected with his head. The aide slumped to the ground and did not move.

"Are you all right?" asked Elizabeth of the man.

"He's not dead. We must get out of here at once." As Sophie took the man's automatic, he groaned. "Come on!"

"Here! What's going on!" shouted another man from outside the ballroom.

Sophie grabbed Elizabeth's arm, and they ran towards the entrance hall.

"My coat!" said Sophie.

"Yes! You'll catch cold, Miss King. You must wear a coat in this weather."

"It's in here."

She darted towards the cloakroom to retrieve it. A man came running towards Elizabeth as she waited outside.

"Hurry, Miss King! There's a man coming."

Sophie leaped from the cloakroom, her coat half on, hat awry, holding gloves in one hand and the pistol in the other.

"Stop where you are! I'm a crack shot!"

She aimed the pistol, and the man turned about and ran off.

"I didn't know you were proficient with firearms," said Elizabeth.

"I'm not... Look at that. I forgot the safety catch again."

They hurried to the main staircase.

"Where are we going?" asked Elizabeth.

"Not sure yet. To get Rabbit or go on foot to the gates — which would be best, do you think?"

They clattered down the steps.

"Oh, ah, Rabbit, if may be so bold." Elizabeth was panting. "I don't like leaving the car to the mercies of these people."

"Quite right, too. Neither do I."

They were through the door and out into the frosty night air. Dashing at Elizabeth's best pace, they made for the garage where the car had been parked.

"I can't drive," said Elizabeth. "I'm too puffed out."

"Then you'll take the gun," said Sophie. "The engine should still be warm, so we'll have it started in no time."

They went around the corner of the house and, in a few seconds, reached the car.

"Thank goodness all the men are down at the gate or else they'd have caught us by now," said Sophie. She got in the driver's side while Elizabeth sat in the front passenger seat.

"But Miss King, how will we get through them?"

"We'll soon find out. The police are there... Here's the gun." She handed it to Elizabeth.

"Do you know if there's a cartridge in the chamber?" asked Elizabeth.

"No. I don't know how it works," admitted Sophie sheepishly.

Sophie pressed the self-starter button on the car. The engine sprang to life.

"I know they work on a slide mechanism," said Elizabeth, examining the pistol, her hands trembling from her exertions. "It's difficult to tell in the dark. Where did I put my torch...? Ah, here it is... Could you hold it a moment, please?"

Sophie held the torch.

"Ah, yes. This is how it works... See? Pull this big top part all the way back."

"Oh, yes. And now the bullet is in the barrel."

"Forgive me, but it's a cartridge or round, Miss King. The bullet is only the rounded part protruding from the brass casing."

"Yes, it would be. I can see that now. We'll try the gates."

"Am I to shoot people?"

"I hope not."

"Because I don't think I can bring myself to do it, Miss King. I really can't. I will point the pistol at them, though."

"That should be sufficient. Don't forget to tell them you're a crack shot."

"No, I shan't. I thought your ruse worked excellently well."

Sophie put the car in gear, and they set off.

---

Near to the police in the road, a car drew up. In the distance could be heard the distinctive rumble of approaching lorries.

"Who the blazes is this?" said Morton. "Ah, come *on*! It's bound to be the messenger *and* reinforcements of the wrong kind. What a nightmare."

Footsteps came towards him and Sergeant Gowers.

"Don't come any closer!" called Morton. "Who might you be?"

"Hello, old boy. Having a spot of bother?"

It was Sinjin Yardley, and Morton breathed the biggest sigh of relief in his career.

"You might say that."

"I've brought some help with me, so let's have a chinwag in private, shall we?"

"Who just arrived?" called the aide from behind the gates. "If it's the messenger, you're to come to me at once."

"Whoever you are!" shouted back one of the new arrivals, a Yorkshireman. "Shut yer gob!"

This made the police officers laugh.

"That has got to be Len Feather," said Gowers, smiling to

himself.

Two lorries arrived and parked, but left their engines running and lights on. Separated from the rest, Morton and Yardley had a conversation.

"You'll have to clue me in. Is the army taking over?" asked Morton, nodding towards the lorries.

Morton could now see Yardley outlined in the lights. He was carrying a rifle and wearing a hotch-potch of military garb, including a Russian-style insulated hat with earflaps.

"Not at all. This is your show. We've been staying at Blackdown Camp in Pirbright. A short while ago, we received a message to come over to Chertsey Park. So, here we are. We're on hand just in case Stokely's boys get a bit frisky, otherwise we'll stay out of it."

"Ah. So a lot more's going on than I've been told?"

"Than any of us have been told," said Sinjin. "Stokely's going root and branch, if possible. You need to know that all the fellows with me are working strictly off the record, you understand. No matter what happens here, we're all *actually* still in Blackdown Camp having a reunion. However, I definitely do not recommend Blackdown as a place to hold a reunion. The food is atrocious, but that's beside the point."

"What is it you'll do, then?" asked Morton.

"Make it noisy. Shake things up. Disarm the beggars, that sort of thing."

"Ah... I can't, um... I'm a police officer, you understand?"

"Yes, perfectly. You tell me what your plans are, and I'll make suggestions. How does that sound?"

"Very well. Because they're holding the gate, I didn't want to get into a shoving match before we reached the house. We were going to go over the wall to avoid them, *then* get control of the house. My men are armed. Do you know anything about the messenger with orders rescinding the search warrant I have?"

"No. But, um, we'll block the road both ways to make sure those orders can't arrive until you've done everything you want. How does that sound?"

"Bloody marvellous."

# Chapter 31

# The Grand Salon

The rumour spread in Chertsey Park. From ballroom to servants' hall, they all knew — a maid had attacked an aide. They were saying it was no less than attempted murder.

Charlotte Terrence became thoughtful upon hearing the news. Although the card games were ongoing, both she and the wealthy man were having a drink after dropping out of the play. The other gamblers were not in their league monetarily nor in skills. The wealthy man suggested several reasons for the incident, the report of which he considered overblown. Charlotte excused herself. She went to find out what had happened. Intrigued, she believed such a thing could not occur in such a house as Chertsey Park — unless, of course, Miss King was involved.

Jeremy Rushton considered the story of the attack. It was worth his while to find out more, to see if it was newsworthy. If so, would Stokely mind him publishing it? He noticed Charlotte get up and walk with alacrity. This suggested to him something was amiss, because she previously moved with the relaxed attitude of a person at a party. He followed her, believing she knew the truth of what was going on.

Separately, Charlotte and Rushton entered the Grand Salon a moment after Dawkins left. Lord Stokely was present but, instead of the usual cluster of diverse people around him, this time there was only Cobden, Wilberforce, and an aide. By their looks, it was obvious their discussion concerned some unpleasantness. Stokely looked up and saw Charlotte, but made no sign of greeting.

Charlotte hesitated, then stopped, unsure as to what to do. Rushton caught up with her.

"Hello, you're Charlotte Terrence. We haven't been introduced, but my name's Rushton. I run one of Lord Stokely's papers. I'm very pleased to meet you."

"Hello... A newspaperman? You must be after the story about the maid."

"I am. Who is she, exactly?"

Charlotte paused, was about to say something, then obviously changed her mind. "I don't really know. I've seen her about, of course."

"Ah," said Rushton, aware that Charlotte was concealing information. They continued talking, unable to approach Stokely without butting into his private deliberations, also not wishing to leave and look awkward doing so.

Dawkins retrieved his coat from the cloakroom. His intention was to discover for himself what was occurring at the gates. Considering how the evening had gone, he deemed it better that he should be away from Stokely. That Miss King should escape from the house not once, but twice, had made Dawkins' position quite clear. He was out of favour with the earl and was likely to remain so forever. He exited through the front doors and into the headlight beams of an accelerating car. Dawkins stepped into the car's path while drawing his gun. He aimed at the windscreen.

"Blast the man!" said Sophie, upon seeing him. She applied the brakes.

"How terribly unfortunate," said Elizabeth in resignation. "I'll hide the pistol under the seat, shall I?"

"What...? Yes, please, do."

The car slowed to a halt right at the front doors.

Dawkins, keeping his gun aimed at Sophie, came to the driver's side of the car. She lowered the window.

"A wise decision, Miss King. I'm an excellent shot with a pistol, and you wouldn't have got away... Both of you step out slowly. Put your hands in the air."

They obeyed him. Sophie, with her arms up, said,

"You shall not harm us, because we have plenty of evidence that can destroy Stokely." She doubted the drawings, letter, and research were up to the task, but she pressed on. "Its publication is dependent upon our well-being. Keep us safe, and I'll consider returning it."

"Inside," said Dawkins.

He kept them covered and signalled with the pistol for them to enter the house. Sophie and Elizabeth were mounting the front step when the unmistakable rat-a-tat-tat of a machine gun smashed the quiet of the heath. The sound came from the open space in front of the house. They turned to see tracer bullets streaking in a straight line across the open land and into the night.

Dawkins immediately took cover behind the car. Sophie stared, open-mouthed. Elizabeth was equally stunned. Realizing they could escape, Sophie grabbed Elizabeth's hand and pulled her inside the house. Then she bolted the doors on Dawkins. The firing stopped.

"Hide in the attics?" said Elizabeth.

"Yes!" said Sophie, who had not thought ahead that far.

"Who is attacking the house?" asked Elizabeth, as they began climbing the marble stairs.

"Well, it's not Stokely attacking himself. It can't be the police, can it?"

"No... Oh, *no*. Not again," exclaimed Elizabeth in dismay.

An aide had appeared at the top of the staircase. He was the one from the office, whose neck was now bandaged, and was openly pointing a pistol at them.

"You won't escape this time. Come here."

There was nothing for it. Caught, Sophie and Elizabeth

trudged up the remaining stairs. While doing so, Cobden came out of the Grand Salon.

"Are these the miscreants?" he asked the aide.

"Yes, Secretary Cobden."

"Take them at once to his lordship. I know he will want to interview them."

"What was that gunfire, sir?"

"Nothing to fear, as it was not unexpected. A show of strength by reactionary forces, that's all it was. They and the police obviously control things outside, so we must expect an investigation in the house soon. Do what you need to do as soon as you have delivered these two."

"Yes, sir."

"Oh, by the way. Should you see Mr Dawkins, send him here at once."

The aide gave a salute. He then turned to speak to Sophie with an ugly leer on his face. "You're for it now."

Ushered in at gunpoint, Sophie and Elizabeth entered to silent stares. Uncle Teddy had joined the group.

"Is a pistol necessary?" asked Rushton, shocked. His question went unanswered.

"Roderick?" said Charlotte.

"We can dispense with the pistol," said Stokely.

The aide pocketed his gun and, just as he was closing the doors, Wilberforce came in, followed by Kemp.

"What's happening, my Lord?" asked Wilberforce.

"Ask Kemp."

The gamekeeper became awkward — his world was below stairs or about the estate, not in the Grand Salon. "Uh, the police are approaching the house. There's an army detachment, or something, spread out about the grounds. About fifty of them. We were forced to let them in the gates. They were pointing Lewis guns and rifles at us... not the police, the others."

"They're not from the army, then?" asked Stokely.

"No, my Lord. They're not in uniform, and they're ready to

shoot. They got behind us, gave a machine gun demonstration, and then twenty seconds to open the gates."

Unremarked by the others, Uncle Teddy leaned towards Stokely to whisper intensely, "It doesn't matter. Remember, regardless of whatever may happen, *be* the statesman you are."

"Ring the bell for drinks," said Stokely a moment later. "We may as well make ourselves comfortable while we wait. Cobden, tell the guests in the ballroom that everything is under control and the police have arrived."

Stokely approached Sophie. "Miss King and Miss Woodhouse? Welcome to my home. Several unfortunate events have occurred — misunderstandings — but we shall soon clear them up. Please, be seated."

Sophie and Elizabeth sat down at a nearby table. Dawkins came into the room and immediately bestowed an evil look upon the two women.

While drinks were being served, the police arrived in force at the front door. Dalgleish entered to inform Lord Stokely of this unparalleled event at Chertsey Park. Becoming the focus of the room's attention, he crossed the red carpet to deliver the message.

"My Lord," said Dalgleish. "The police are outside and wishing to speak to you."

"Send them in," replied Stokely.

Dalgleish bowed and stepped away to open the doors. Inspector Morton, Sergeant Gowers, and three constables entered the Salon. They looked prosaic, as if they had no right to be in such a sumptuous reception room.

"Lord Stokely," said Inspector Morton. "I'm Inspector Morton of the Criminal Investigation Department, Scotland Yard. I have here a warrant to search the premises..."

"Even though it is invalid, you may as well go ahead," said Lord Stokely.

"We've already started."

"You've done *what*?" He was tense, on the verge of anger.

Uncle Teddy quietly cleared his throat.

"Then, carry on. You won't find anything. What *is* important is that there are some documents which have been stolen. They must be returned immediately."

"I have them here," said Morton.

"Do you? Excellent. Now, these women." Stokely pointed to Sophie and Elizabeth without looking at them. "They stole the documents and passed them to their confederates. The younger one assaulted one of my employees and then tried to murder another. There was a third assault by others, which resulted in this gentleman's neck wound. Be so kind as to arrest these violent criminals and remove them from my sight."

"I'll attend to them once I've finished executing the warrant." Morton did not look at Sophie. Instead, he took an attaché case, some papers, and a notebook from a constable. "Would these be your items and missing documents, your lordship?"

"I really couldn't say. You'll have to ask my aides."

"Sir?" asked Morton, addressing the aide. "Are these the items that were taken?"

"Yes, they are."

"Ah, good." Inspector Morton handed over the case and notebook to him. The aide examined the attaché case and found it locked.

"May I say something?" asked Sophie.

"Not at the moment, miss," said Morton. "*If* you don't mind."

Sophie did mind, but was in no position to do anything — having been accused of attempted murder. What stunned her into complete disbelief was Inspector Morton's behaviour. Her heart sank, because she now suspected he was working for Stokely. Three aides and four of Kemp's men, including Miller, came into the room. Their sudden appearance alarmed her even further.

"Is there anything else I can do for you?" asked Stokely of Morton.

"No. We'll just wait here until they've finished searching the house."

"I think not, because I have guests. Go to the office and wait there. I'll send food and drink to you if you wish. Ah, here's Cobden returned. He'll show you the way."

Morton did not move or reply. In the stony, tense silence that followed, Kemp slipped out of the Salon.

Avoiding the police, who were searching rooms, Kemp got out of a window on the ground-floor and in the darkness crept to the kennels. There, he hurriedly let out the little cocker spaniel to the barking chorus of the other dogs. He left the kennels to enter the nearby woods. He retrieved a knapsack and his shotgun that he had left hidden behind a tree. Then, with a pocketful of shells and his favourite dog at his heels, he passed quietly, poacher-like, through the woods. Soon he was out on the heath and disappeared into the night.

In the Grand Salon, Wilberforce said to Morton,

"You've blundered badly. Talk about the incompetence of the police."

"There's no point, Wilberforce," said Stokely. "He'll soon learn the error of his ways. It will be a pleasure to see him disgraced."

Discovering, in this turn of events, that Morton did *not* work for Stokely brought Sophie immense relief, yet she could not understand what he was doing. A police whistle blew outside.

Stokely became agitated and had difficulty with his temper. "Do you realize the insult you've offered me, a peer of the realm?" He paced while addressing Morton. "I can't understand you, man. You're acting illegally, on your own authority. Are you insane!"

"I'm acting within the law," said Morton, whose colour heightened at being berated.

"Where is that damned messenger? He should have been here by now... Unless your men have prevented him getting through."

"They may have done, although I'm not aware of it, your lordship."

"Yes," said Stokely in a knowing tone.

The doors burst open and eight men wearing balaclavas and carrying pistols and rifles came in. Dawkins attempted to leave, but a man trained a rifle on him, which persuaded him to stay.

"Ey up!" said a giant of a man carrying a Lewis gun in a sling so that he could walk and shoot at the same time. "Members of the public here to assist the police in the apprehension of criminals." Sophie knew at once it was Len beneath the balaclava.

"Thank you for the help," said Morton. "Don't let anyone leave. Those fellows over there are probably carrying firearms. Could you see to them, please?"

"Yes." He swung the machine gun towards them. "I hear you're not being sociable. We can't have that, now. So don't move and pass us your guns. Do it slowly, like."

Several of the newcomers began searching the aides and removing their pistols.

"Go on," said Gowers to a constable. "You saw Miller first, so nick him."

"Right, I'll do it, sarge." The constable stepped forward and put a hand on the now disarmed Miller's shoulder. "Albert Miller. I arrest you for the murder of…"

The room listened, astonished the police were arresting the Fleet Street murderer right in front of them. Miller could not escape. He sagged and was compliant, becoming resigned to his capture and probable fate.

"Lord Stokely," asked Morton, "what can you tell me about Albert Miller?"

"I've never seen him before and don't know the name."

"Come, come, Lord Stokely. He lives on your estate."

"Then he must be one of Kemp's men… Where is Kemp? He was here a moment ago."

"He left the room, my Lord," said Cobden.

"There you are. Find Kemp. Talk to *him* about this fellow. Now attend to me, Morton. I want these women arrested at once."

"I think not," said Sophie, to both Stokely and Morton. "That man with the bandage is quite possibly the murderer of Mr Auckland of the Times. There's a Rolls-Royce in the garages and it was used to push his car off the road. I know this aide was involved, because he threatened a member of my staff with a similar fate to that of Mr Auckland. Said there would be a nasty accident. Obviously, since he works for Stokely, it was Stokely who wanted Mr Auckland killed and sent this brute to do it. The damage to the car makes it very apparent what happened."

"The woman's a lunatic," said Stokely.

"She sounds sensible enough to me," said Morton. He nodded to Gowers, who approached the aide to arrest him.

"I arrest you for the wilful murder of Mr James Auckland..."

Gowers relieved the aide of the attaché case and notebook. A constable handcuffed him.

"Would there be any more murderers?" asked Morton of Sophie.

"Well him, of course." Sophie pointed at Stokely.

Uncle Teddy suddenly intervened. "Nothing you do here tonight concerning Lord Stokely shall come to fruition. This woman's calumny need not even be refuted, as it is patently false. But you, sir, are acting illegally, without authority, and shall pay dearly. This matter has already been referred to the highest authorities in the land. You won't have a leg to stand on when it all comes out."

"It's all right, Uncle Teddy. He's looking for a promotion, and she's nothing — an ignorant witch who has a hidden agenda for revolution. I don't doubt she belongs to the Red Fist."

"Ignorant witch! You're not even an earl. You're Edward Fielding, *esquire*, that's all, and you're unfit for even that courtesy. *He's* Lord Stokely!" She pointed to Uncle Teddy.

"Don't be so stupid," said Stokely.

"No, she's quite correct," said Elizabeth. "You see, in eighteen-seventy-eight... Oh, I'm terribly sorry. I didn't mean to presume."

"Fancy that," said Len, laughing. "You're not an earl after all. How funny can this get?"

"What's funny?" asked Sinjin Yardley, hearing the tail-end of the conversation upon entering the Salon. He was wearing a balaclava and carrying a revolver. Walking in front of him was a woebegone aide with a bruised face. "Arrest this fellow," he said to the nearest constable. "He came at me with a knife. Can't give you my name and all that at the moment." Having deposited his prisoner, he approached the main party.

"We just found out," said Len. "Stokely here is only a pretend earl."

"Is that so...? How'd he pull it off?"

"This is preposterous. Absolutely beyond words." Stokely turned to Uncle Teddy. "Have you ever heard of such a stupid thing?"

Uncle Teddy could not reply. He was stricken, white-faced — unseeing and unhearing. The last few seconds had wrought the change, converting a lively gentleman into a bewildered invalid. Stokely saw this, and he changed, too. Slowly, his confidence gave way, and he smiled vacantly, waiting for his uncle's denial to come, and realized it would not. Stokely and his uncle had never looked more alike.

"Uncle Teddy?" Stokely queried his relative, as if searching for an answer from someone not present.

"Excuse me," the uncle replied at last, putting a hand to his forehead. "Tonight's been a little too much for me. Sorry to be a bore. If I sit down for a moment, I'll feel better."

The significance of this exchange — not the words but that which the words cloaked — had not been lost upon those present. All the proceedings, but the last especially, had caught Charlotte unawares. Her reasoning drifted. She suddenly laughed, not from any comedy she had found, but from a reaction to the breakdown of Stokely's world. He was a pitiable figure to her and, although a wish to comfort him arose, Charlotte could not see how that was possible. He was too remote from her to be reached.

"What's the matter with Charlotte? Why is she laughing?" Stokely asked Wilberforce.

"Roderick. Is it true?" Charlotte called out.

"Of course, not. It's a grotesque game these fools are playing, nothing more."

"Roderick Fielding," began Morton, "I arrest you for the crime of treason. Anything…"

Cobden and Wilberforce interrupted him with their vigorous protests.

"Mr Cobden and, ah, Mr Wilberforce, I am placing you both under arrest for obstruction. Handcuffs on both of them, please. In fact, cuff the lot and we'll sort it all out later."

"We're running short on handcuffs here," said Gowers.

"I've got some rope," said Len. "In me haversack. S'pose, I can put this down now." He set aside the machine gun to find the rope.

"Now, let's try again," said Morton. "Roderick Fielding…"

After Morton had finished speaking and handcuffing Stokely, the erstwhile earl said,

"You'll regret this. I shan't be held for long, then *you'll* be in jail. Dull-witted men shall not interfere with my plans. My friends are too powerful and will move heaven and earth to have me released. You common, jumped-up little person. Make the most of your pathetic moment of glory. It won't last long."

Sophie watched as Inspector Morton struggled to maintain his composure.

"In the black maria with them."

"Roderick," said Charlotte. "Shall I come with you?"

"Oh, go away."

As the constable was marching Stokely from the room, they met a man in the doorway, which caused some hesitation.

"Are you the messenger?" asked Stokely eagerly.

The man paused, considering his answer. "I am a messenger of sorts, Lord Stokely."

"Good. Take these handcuffs off me at once!"

"What's all this?" Morton came over to see what the hold-up was and found it was Archie Drysdale.

"Hello. Apologies for not arriving sooner, but the fellows on the road wouldn't believe me when I said I was friendly."

"Sorry about that, old man," said Sinjin. "Didn't know you were coming."

"Not to worry. Completely sensible and as it should be. Someone vouched for me in the end. Looks like you have a decent catch here. Busy night, eh, Inspector?"

"Rather, sir."

"I say, can we have Stokely hear the latest? He'll be dashed interested."

"Er, I don't see why not. Bring him back, constable. We don't want this gentleman having to bellow."

"Very considerate of you," said Archie. They walked further into the Salon. "Do I espy a couple of non-combatants?"

"Yes. That's Miss Terrence and Mr Rushton... What's he doing still here? He's a newspaperman."

"Let me talk to him first."

Archie approached Jeremy Rushton.

"Good evening, Mr Rushton," said Archie. He leaned towards him and whispered, "I don't believe you're one of Stokely's boys. If we find out you are, you had better start praying."

"I'm not... I've resigned, effective immediately."

"Glad to hear it. You have a story that you'll want to peddle along Fleet Street, and I don't blame you in the slightest. However, whatever story you publish, those men in black masks do not exist. I do not exist. You may think you know something about those two ladies." Archie pointed to Sophie and Elizabeth. "They do not exist, either. Give me your word that they will not appear in print, and you're free to go. And for goodness' sake, man, don't make me come after you with charges of treason. Understood?"

"Perfectly, Mr…?"

"Nobody."

"I give you my word that I'll do as you recommend. I'll leave at once, if I may."

"Is it all right if Mr Rushton leaves?" asked Archie.

"Yes… I don't believe we have anything against him," said Morton.

"Excellent. Off you go, Rushton."

After he had gone, Archie said,

"Gather around, friend and foe alike."

"Who the devil do you think you are?" said Stokely. "How dare you order me about in my own house?"

"Pipe down, Stokely. You're in police custody and should be careful what you say." He turned to the others. "I understand a messenger was expected. He was nabbed an hour ago. Also nabbed, some of you will be happy to hear, were a permanent under-secretary, two generals, two judges, and a Scotland Yard Assistant Commissioner. Yours, I'm afraid, Morton. Smaller fry have been caught or are being pursued. Stokely, your treacherous network is effectively dismantled, *never* to rise again."

"You have nothing against *me*, whoever you are," said Stokely.

"Now, there, you're wrong. Superintendent Penrose orchestrated raids on your newspaper offices and printing presses. Just imagine, he found tomorrow's front page all typeset and ready to be printed. The headline, as I'm sure you're aware, denounced tonight's Red Fist outrages of riot, arson, and bombings. The problem is, your front page contained news that had only just come in, and yet it would take at least an hour to write the reports and set up the page. You're sunk, good and proper. Prior knowledge of Red Fist activities can only mean you control them. They shut your papers down, by the way. With all the arrests there and elsewhere, the jail cells are doing a roaring trade tonight. Not quite the message you were hoping for, I think. You can take him away now, if you'd be so kind."

# Chapter 32

# Reunion

The uniformed police and the men wearing balaclavas removed all the prisoners from the Grand Salon.

"Splendid job, Morton." Archie shook the inspector's hand. "Well done, Gowers." He shook his hand, too. "Can't have been easy."

"It *was* touch and go for a while," said Morton.

"One thing. Do you have solid evidence on Stokely? I ask because, despite everything pointing to him, I've seen nothing yet that absolutely connects with his being the mastermind of it all."

"Don't you worry, sir," said Morton. He held up the attaché case. "Sergeant Gowers picked the lock before we got here. Stokely's diary was inside. It lays out everything, the whole blooming lot. He's done for, on that alone."

"I have it in my pocket," said Gowers. "Also, there's a notebook which has references to tonight's Red Fist operations — although you have to read it carefully to work it out. Did they do much damage?"

"That's good news about the diary and notebook," said Archie. "As for damage, sadly, they did much too much. Besides Liverpool, which was the newspaper story that already damns Stokely, there were attacks, riots, and bombings in three other cities. One person killed and deliberately targeted, it seems. I'm so relieved this has ended."

"So are we all," said Morton.

"Yes, indeed. Excuse me a moment."

Archie went over to see Sophie and Elizabeth.

"Good evening, Miss King and Miss...?" Archie knew her real name, but not her pseudonym.

"Miss Woodhouse. Good evening."

"Good evening, Archie."

"How are you both? Comfortable? Can I get you anything?"

"We're both worn out," said Sophie. "Shall we get some tea going?"

"Good idea," said Archie. "I'll ring the bell for that."

"Oh, yes. I'm forgetting that I'm not a servant at present. I suppose we've been fired."

"I should think well and truly fired, Miss King," said Elizabeth.

"Don't take it to heart," said Archie.

"There's something I must tell you," said Sophie. "I never meant to say he wasn't the earl. I was going to keep that quiet."

"So that was you who discovered it?" asked Archie.

"Actually, it was Elizabeth and Auntie Bessie who did. I so wish I hadn't spoken... Look."

Sitting by himself, Uncle Teddy had in the last hour acquired that fragility of age which states, 'You can see for yourself, I have very little time left to me.'

"I've done that to him," said Sophie. "I betrayed his secret. I should have kept quiet!"

"Perhaps. I don't know the ins and outs of it," said Archie, "but I know this much. He's also up to his neck in this business. Fielding has been an advisor to Stokely to the extent the police may decide to bring charges against him. So bear that in mind."

"Really? And what about Lady Georgiana?"

"Not involved, although she must have known of Stokely's aims and ambition."

"Despite that, I can't help feeling sorry for both Uncle Teddy and Lady Georgiana."

"His not being an earl may have come out at the trial, so don't go blaming yourself. It couldn't be helped... Hmm, no one's answering the bell. Not surprising, really."

"We'll go to the kitchen," said Sophie. "I must first tell the police where I've hidden things."

"Do that, but don't be anxious, and take good care of yourselves. I'm sorry, I must leave. There's an endless list of things to do, and I want to hear your reports, but they can wait a while. Before I go, I want to thank you both, with all my heart, for doing such tremendous work. Tonight's success would not have come off without you. What you probably don't realize is that it was all down to the timing of the thing. Unless we could seize all the controlling parts of the network simultaneously, our plans would have been thwarted. The starting gun, so to speak, was the call for Morton to come to Chertsey Park. There had to be a valid reason for him to do that, and Burgoyne's provided it. Two murderers arrested — and all thanks to you. The evidence — absolutely superb. With Morton's arrival here, we launched operations at other places. Stokely's reaction was to telephone high-ranking officials in his pay, which was his call for help to get him out of the jam. We knew he would do that, and so we arrested the officials he contacted before they could create a fuss. With his network of agents now leaderless, we can attend to the rank and file over the coming days."

"How marvellous. You go, Archie. Don't worry about us."

"Toodle-pip."

"You mustn't speak like that when not wearing your monocle."

"Of all things to happen, I broke the dratted object this morning. Now I have nothing to twirl."

"It's ridiculous. You don't even need one."

"Perhaps not, but I use a monocle for my impenetrable disguise. Honestly, I become a completely different person

when I wear it."
   Sophie laughed.
   "Good night, Archie."
   "Good night, Soap. Good night, Miss Woodhouse."
   "Good night, Mr Drysdale."

---

Edward Fielding watched as they took his son away, and now he sat staring at nothing.
   "May I join you?" asked Charlotte.
   He looked up and struggled to recognize her. "Yes."
   They sat in silence; she observing the conquerors in possession of the Grand Salon, and he not seeing them.
   Charlotte wanted to talk, and Uncle Teddy was the only person present who was not against Stokely. She was empty and could not understand her loss. He was gone, yes, but had he ever existed? 'Go away' were his last words to her. Go away. Yet he had already gone from her, long before tonight. There was a time, even more remote and uncertain now, when they had been close. She trod again the well-worn track that led her nowhere, but now, rather than arriving at a destination, her familiar sequence of thoughts simply stopped. What had she lost? She concluded it was only her hope.
   "What will you do?" she asked.
   Edward was quiet for a long time, during which he searched for an answer. All he knew was that the woman who asked him the question had loved his son.
   "I shan't be earl... Can't... Years ago, I killed a man. Here, in England... It was an accident... if drunkenness is an excuse. Hushed it up." He sighed. "That's why I went overseas. I knew that, if I became earl, the incident would come back to haunt me... There's more to it, but it's unimportant... I'll refuse. The

titles will go to my nephew, Charles Fielding."

Charlotte was unprepared for this extraordinary confidence, and had not been thinking about titles. "I don't understand why they said he wasn't the earl."

"He's my son, you see, so he shouldn't have the title at present. I married Georgie, but the marriage was entered in the registry as though my brother Humphrey had married her. He was failing and could not have children. The title would come to me after his death. I didn't want it, as I mentioned, and so we planned for Roderick to have it, and to leave me out of the picture. Easy enough with a tame minister from another county officiating... Now it will all come out."

She considered what she heard. Before she could ask a question, Uncle Teddy continued.

"There's nothing left for me. Georgie prefers living alone, my other children are dead... What will you do, Charlotte?"

She shrugged her shoulders. "I don't know... He's too great a man. Does he have no chance?"

"No. You heard what they said. They've also captured those who would have helped him. Perhaps, in a year's time, he would have ruled Britain, but his opportunity has gone for good. I asked him, repeatedly, not to resort to violence, but he wouldn't listen... What could I do?"

"I don't know... Prison and the trial will destroy him... I wish... There's no point in wishing."

"I'm sorry, Charlotte... You're right, though, about Roderick. He will suffer through this."

---

Sinjin Yardley re-entered the Grand Salon, still wearing his balaclava. He walked quickly past Morton and Gowers, heading towards Sophie and Elizabeth.

"Dear ladies, I humbly apologize for being so inattentive, but there was a lot going on, as you witnessed *and* took part in yourselves."

"Most certainly there was, and we forgive you. This is Miss Ophelia Woodhouse."

"Absolutely charmed to make your acquaintance, Miss Woodhouse. I understand you have been doing such sterling work, which we all *much* appreciate."

"You're too kind, Mr — Oh, that's right. No names. But I know who you are." Elizabeth became almost roguish.

"Rather awkward, isn't it? However, what a tremendously successful night it's been, and a long time coming. It was worth all the setbacks and frustration in the end."

"Yes. I feel relieved rather than triumphant," said Sophie. "It's a pity we couldn't have acted sooner for the sake of all those innocent people."

"Quite so, and it is regrettable that anyone had to suffer. The blighter's gone now... Look, I'm rather in a rush, so please excuse my precipitate behaviour. Miss King. A friend of mine has a box at the Albert Hall. He and his wife are awfully nice, and he's invited me and a friend to a Dame Clara Butt Concert. Would you be interested in accompanying me? It's a Saturday afternoon, February nineteenth. He's given me first dibs, but I have to give him my answer very soon."

"I would very much like to hear Dame Clara, and would be delighted to accompany you, but I absolutely refuse to accept an invitation from a man wearing a balaclava. It's *not* the done thing."

"Ha! Of course, it isn't. I can't take it off, because I'm not supposed to be here. May I telephone you tomorrow?"

"Yes, you may. Only promise me you won't still be wearing that thing when you do."

Sinjin roared with laughter. "I promise. Good night, Miss Woodhouse. Miss King, I will count the minutes until we speak again."

"Good night, Mr Balaclava."

409

"Very good," said Sinjin, wagging a finger and smiling as he left.

"Did you see that?" asked Morton. He had been watching Yardley speak to Sophie.

"Couldn't miss him," said Gowers. "I think I must be blunt, sir. You need to get a move on, otherwise you won't stand a chance."

"But I've not the foggiest how to approach her."

"Just go up to her now, right now, and say, would you like to go to... Where is it you want to go?"

"Er, I thought about a restaurant, but I could never keep chatting away for hours. So I settled on Kew Gardens."

"Well, that's nice. She'll probably like that. Take her for tea, afterwards, right?"

"Oh, yes, yes... That's a good idea."

"You all set, then?"

"Not really. Supposing she doesn't like Kew Gardens?"

"No, everyone does... Um, you could always take her to a football match."

"Football? Oh, come off it. This is no time for joking and she wouldn't like it."

"I'm only doing my best to help, sir."

"I know you are. All right. I'm ready. Let's see how it goes."

"A pint says..."

"Don't you dare."

Morton felt more fear and embarrassment in crossing the broad red carpet this time than when first entering the Grand Salon to arrest Stokely. He made it, somehow.

"Good evening, Miss King and Miss Elizabeth."

They greeted him.

"I'm ever so sorry for cutting you off earlier. I didn't mean to be rude."

"We quite understand, Inspector. They were very difficult circumstances and a terrible ordeal for you."

"Not the easiest arrest of my career, I have to say. Although you endured the ordeal, too. When he insulted you, I felt like clocking him one."

"So did I. Anger is not always helpful, is it? I regret having answered how I did. Still, it's done now, and I can't undo it."

"You were in the right, Miss King. Miss Woodhouse, I wonder if you could explain the circumstances of Roderick Fielding's birth when it's convenient. I doubt it will affect the case, but there will be a lot of questions raised."

"Certainly, Inspector Morton," said Elizabeth. "I'll write it down for you."

"That will be perfect, thank you very much. I have to leave shortly — we have more or less finished here." Morton cleared his throat. "I was wondering, Miss King, if you would do me the honour of accompanying me to Kew Gardens?"

The unexpected request staggered Sophie. It took her a moment to understand what he had said.

"Ah, Kew Gardens?"

"Yes. I was thinking of a Saturday afternoon, work permitting, of course. Yours and mine." He smiled. "I thought of Kew Gardens because everyone likes it there, and it doesn't matter about the weather, so much of it being inside, you see."

"Yes, that's true." Sophie briefly glanced at Elizabeth, who was trying not to exist by staring at a painting across the room. "I think Kew would be very enjoyable," said Sophie, feeling more trapped than otherwise.

"You do? Oh, that's wonderful. Would this coming Saturday afternoon at two o'clock be convenient?"

"Ah... Yes, at the moment it is, work permitting."

"I could meet you at your home. White Lyon Yard, isn't it?"

Sophie was aghast. She decided that Inspector Morton should not meet Auntie Bessie unless fully prepared for an onslaught. "We could meet at Kew Gardens Station instead."

"We can do that. Afterwards, we'll have tea, shall we?"

"Yes, that would be pleasant."

"Do you know something?" He became relaxed and smiled. "I had a very odd idea. Silly, really. I was going to suggest we go to a football match."

"A football match! What a splendid idea. I've never been to one and I've always wanted to go."

"You have? Oh, oh, I see. Would you like to see Chelsea play?"

"Absolutely!"

"Very good. That's settled then, except we'll meet at West Brompton at two. Afterwards, we'll still have tea, but at my mother's house. It's where I live, actually, and it's very near the football grounds. It's a big building, and mother runs it as a boarding house. She has help, of course. When I have the time, I do a few repairs about the place. What I'm trying to say is, there's a private sitting room where we can have our tea, only I have to book it off. We wouldn't want to share the room with the other boarders, would we? It's very nice, and you'll be able to meet mother. I think that's all for now. Good night. I have to see about the people in the ballroom. They're getting a bit bolshie."

Sophie and Elizabeth barely had time to say goodbye before Morton rushed away. Sophie turned to Elizabeth and said in a quiet, disbelieving way, "His mother?"

"How'd it go, sir?" asked Gowers when the conquering hero returned.

"It was much easier than I thought. I don't know *why* I was so anxious. On a whim, I thought I'd mention a football match to her, and she went for it like mad. I'm so relieved it's all arranged. The nice thing is, she's coming round to the house for tea and she'll meet mother. I'm sure they'll get on." There was a long pause. "What?"

"You might not know this, sir," said Gowers in a gentle, weary voice, "so I'll come to the point. A fella goes to see his girl's parents — mother, father, what have you — so that they can see what he's like, and warn him off if he's no good. Fair enough. When a girl goes to meet her fella's parents, it only means one thing. He's about to propose or has done so already, as in, they are affianced or on the verge thereof. Did you happen to discuss anything like that first with Miss King?"

"No."

"Ah, I see."

"Should I go back and explain it to her?"

"You've dug a hole. You're in it. Don't make it any deeper, sir. Use the telephone, and change the plan another day, after due consideration. She's seeing *you*, not your mother, lovely woman that she is. Give her my regards, by the way."

"Blimey... Let's go the ballroom."

"Yes, sir."

---

"They shouldn't 'ave kept us in that cold car. I'm freezing, I am an' all." Ada opened the servants' door, and the five agents entered the house.

"I can't believe we missed the last act," said Flora.

"That would have been so nice to see, but right now, I'm starving," said Fern.

"We can put that right," said Alfie.

"I've been thinking," said Broadbent-Wicks. "We should keep Stokely's Rolls-Royce for the agency. He doesn't need it now."

"No, he don't," said Ada, "'cause he's got a black maria. Do you think that was him looking out the little square window at the back?"

"If it was, he wouldn't have appreciated us waving to him," said Flora.

Ada laughed. "We gave whoever it was a nice send-off, though."

Inside the servants' entrance, a constable with a rifle approached them.

"Where do you think you're going?" he asked.

"It's all right, we've got clearance," answered Flora. "We're the ones who came to Sunningdale."

"I know that, miss. Who gave you clearance to come in?"

"Inspector Morton."

"He can't have, because he's been inside the whole time."

"Ah, a mere technicality, officer. At the gates, he categorically stated that we could come in after it was all over."

"No one's said it's all over, so you can't come in."

"But we saw them getting carted away," said Ada.

"I can't help that, miss."

"I say, why don't you arrest us and then escort us to Inspector Morton?" asked Broadbent-Wicks.

"Because you haven't broken a law, sir. Not yet, anyway."

"That's a shame. It would have solved the bally problem."

"We used to work here," said Fern, "and we only want something to eat."

"Yes!" exclaimed Flora. "We're cold and hungry, tired, and, with great sacrifice, we passed through dreadful terrors, pursued by a legion of enemies, so that you could come and save the day. Have a *heart*, constable." Flora employed the same imploring expression she used when beseeching a stubborn father in a play. In that instance, she reduced many in the audience to tears, although the beseeched parent remained intractable, and refused to let her marry the man she loved.

"All right. Go to the kitchen and stay put. I'll get word to Inspector Morton that I've let you in. But don't go making a monkey out of me."

"We shan't do that, constable," said Flora. "You have a beautiful and compassionate soul."

"That's right, and I give it a polish every day. So move along before I change my mind."

They found Sophie and Elizabeth at a table, and there followed a reunion made noisy for several reasons. The first was that rejoicing broke out because everyone was safe. The second was Stokely being in custody. Last, which severely distracted the secret agents' attention from the first two, was the mountain of abandoned food in M Fournier's kitchen.

"They just left it all here?" asked Flora.

"There was supposed to be a supper," said Sophie. "Then the police arrived. We've been told that M Fournier was, at first, up in arms at being questioned in his kitchen. He had a tantrum but afterwards consented to answer questions. Since then, he and his staff haven't been seen, but it's believed by the other servants that they're getting drunk somewhere. With all the upset, the guests in the ballroom lost their appetites. Obviously, they didn't like the gunfire and masked men running about the place. Therefore, all this has been left."

"Is it all right if we stuff ourselves silly?" asked Fern. "It was ever so cold hanging about outside and I'm so hungry."

"Don't restrain yourself. We haven't. Can't have such excellent food going to waste. The kettle's hot, but you'll need to add more water." Sophie then bit into a vol-au-vent.

The five newcomers went to work in piling up their plates.

"This all looks jolly good. I say, the police missed taking this as evidence, what?" Broadbent-Wicks laughed as he heaped his plate higher. "I'd have taken it if I were a policeman... That's a good idea. I'll become a policeman."

"You'd be out in all weathers," said Ada.

"I don't mind that. They have capes, coats and helmets."

"There's a lot of walking, mate," said Alfie.

"As a footman, I've learned to stand. As a policeman, I shall learn to walk. What do you think, Miss King? Am I bobby material?"

"No, I can't say you are. You'd have to take a lot of orders without commenting."

"Ah! That's very observant. I chatter on sometimes. How about a fireman? Hosing down the fire and up the ladder rescuing people?"

"How about a window cleaner? We use ladders," said Alfie.

"Come out with me on my rounds."

"Oh, right! We discussed that, didn't we? I'll be a window cleaner, then."

"Is there good money in that?" asked Fern.

"Yes, if you're quick and line up the jobs proper," said Alfie. "Don't get much from each customer, but it soon adds up."

"Miss? Where are we all sleeping tonight?" asked Ada.

"Blast it!" said Elizabeth. "I'm locked out of the Gardeners Arms!"

Frozen motionless, they all stared blankly at Elizabeth, who promptly turned crimson.

"Dear me. I'm so dreadfully sorry. What must you think of me? I've never, in my *life*, expressed myself with such vehemence. I do beg your pardons."

"Not to worry," said Sophie. "You've been through very trying times, and it's quite understandable."

"I wonder where you got it from?" said Flora, with an impish air.

"Please, don't," said Elizabeth.

"Sorry if it sounded like it, but I wasn't teasing *you*," said Flora, who turned an innocent face towards Sophie.

"To answer Nancy's... I think we may as well drop the pseudonyms. To answer Ada's question, we shall stay here. We'll go to our old rooms for the night and leave tomorrow."

"I don't have any of my things, Miss Burgoyne," said Elizabeth.

"I'm sure we can lend or find what you need. We're in a dormitory with the Lyall Place maids, and there's a spare bed."

"That's such a relief."

"I've got an extra night dress," said Ada. "It's brand new."

"Thank you. You are most kind."

"Use my hand cream, if you like," said Fern.

"Thank you."

"You can borrow my hairbrush," said Flora.

"Very thoughtful of you."

"I can find you a new toothbrush from the supplies," said

Sophie.

"Too kind."

"I have a clean pair of socks you can use," said Broadbent-Wicks. "They're good woollen ones, a bit on the large size for you, though. I received them at Christmas, so they've had very little wear. You could wear 'em in bed or... I'll tell you what they *are* good for. If you take a run, and then slide along a smooth floor — they're perfect for that sort of thing."

"I don't know what to say."

"Oh, no need to thank me. We're all mucking in together... Please don't get the wrong idea, though. I'm not staying in the ladies' dormitory. That's an absolutely absurd notion, don't you know. What I mean to say is, we're all pals taking the rough with the smooth."

"How is your food, Mr Broadbent-Wicks?"

"Absolutely scrumptious. You must hand it to the Froggies; they have a way with food that beggars belief. Old M Fournier is a veritable wizard."

"Don't forget to eat," said Sophie.

"Of course not, Miss... Ha! I nearly said King when I should now say Burgoyne... Are you a Froggie, I mean, a French person, Miss Burgoyne?"

"Long ago, my family originated in France. We are thoroughly English now. The French do not think of themselves by that name, however. It's rather rude."

"I suppose it is. But then the French must have a nickname for us, surely?"

"Yes. Les Rosbifs."

"You mean Roast Beefs?" asked Ada. "When you think of it, that's not too bad."

Sophie nodded.

"Surprisingly, it isn't," agreed Broadbent-Wicks. "You're right, Miss McMahon. They could have thought of something much, much worse. Anyway, despite all of that, M Fournier is a pukka sahib who knows how to whack up a mess of pottage."

"Yes, he is," said Flora. "However, he failed in one respect this weekend. He didn't make rum baba, and I'm sure it would have been superb if he had."

"I love rum baba," said Ada.

"I've never had it. What's it like?" asked Fern.

"It's a dessert — a small cake, soaked in this rum syrup, and served with clotted cream. I can't describe the taste, only I know you'd love it."

"Excuse me," said Sophie. "How about this? We shall all go to an expensive restaurant tomorrow night, and for dessert eat rum baba. I'm rather partial to it, too. That will be our celebratory dinner. Fern has to return to Lady Holme soon, hence the haste."

"That will be beautiful, miss. Who does the best rum baba? Anyone know?" Ada looked at the others.

"Claridge's, by a mile," said Flora.

"Claridge's it is," said Sophie. "You're coming, aren't you, Elizabeth?"

"May I?"

"It won't be the same if you don't! Everyone, do you know, Elizabeth is a marvellous ally in a tight corner? Thoroughly dependable in the face of danger. And she's an ace researcher."

"We should have a toast with Champagne," said Flora.

"Tomorrow night," said Sophie.

"You're all so kind," said Elizabeth. "It was such tremendous fun... I can say that, now that we're all safe."

"Hear, hear," said Alfie.

Inspector Morton entered the kitchen wearing an overly bright expression, and avoiding, as much as he could, looking at Sophie.

"Er, yes, thank you for showing us where you threw the car keys and hid the rotor arm, Miss King. A couple of chaps tried to get away in the Rolls, and, er, it makes us suspicious of their being complicit in Mr Auckland's death. And we have the man you pointed out earlier. They certainly didn't get anywhere, did they? Not after you saw to things in the engine." He laughed, and then pulled at his collar as if it constricted him.

"It's funny, I thought I might find you all here... If I had known there was all this food, I'd have come earlier, because now I can't stop. I've just come to say goodbye, and thank you for the solid work that each of you has done. The police very much value your efforts. We'll have to, um, talk next week, Miss King, to clear up a few matters. Er, you should know that we've released them from the ballroom, so you'll probably have company in a minute or two. I believe that's everything."

Sophie said, "I think Burgoyne's Agency should give a round of applause in appreciation for Inspector Morton and his men. They all did exceptional work tonight."

They clapped and commented.

"That's very nice of you. Very nice, indeed. I'll tell the lads; it'll please them no end."

"I nearly forgot something," said Flora, addressing Sophie. "You asked me to look after this for you." Flora produced the automatic pistol and gave it to her.

"Yes, I did." Sophie received the pistol flat in both hands and held it there. She looked at Inspector Morton and saw an officious look descend upon his features. "Do you want this?" she asked.

"I should take that, yes. Evidence, you understand."

Sophie offered the pistol, and he took it.

"Thank you, Flora," said Sophie, who smiled sweetly.

"I'll be off then," said Morton. "Good night."

They all bid him a good night. Elizabeth smiled, remembering the identical pistol lying underneath Rabbit's front passenger seat.

"I'm sorry to do that to you," said Flora. "You'll only get into trouble if you're running around with a pistol."

"It's for your own good, miss," said Ada.

"You are both probably correct, and I'm not upset with you, so not to worry."

There followed a small silence. In it, Flora suspected Sophie was up to something.

"I'll be glad to leave 'ere," said Ada. "What with all that's gone on, it's put me right off statues."

"They're ancient ones," said Elizabeth. "Quite valuable, too."

"They might be, Miss Elizabeth, but I've taken against 'em, and I don't know why that is."

"S'posing you had a nightmare where they all came to life?"

"Thank you very much, Fern. I'll probably *will* dream about them now."

"I think such a dream would be interesting. I like that sort of thing."

"Not for me. Statues look cold. And the clothes they wear aren't proper for this country. Them Romans would all have died of pneumonia, walking about like that."

"But they *were* here," said Sophie.

"I know that much, miss. But all their stuff's gone, ain't it? Just bits of broken wall left."

"We should go to Bath," suggested Sophie. "It's named after the Roman baths there. They are quite a sight, *and* they're still standing."

"Yes, I'd like to see that."

"They also founded Londinium," said Flora. "Those bits of broken walls you've seen about — they were part of their city. In fact, what we call 'The City' is approximately the same area as Londinium."

"I didn't know that... Why'd they call it Londinium when it's London?"

"It's the other way around," said Sophie. "We get the name London from Londinium."

"Well, I never. Did you know this?"

"No, it's news to me," said Fern.

"Alfie?"

"Um... No, I don't think I've heard of that."

"I bet *you* knew."

"Actually, I did," said Broadbent-Wicks.

"And Miss Elizabeth knows, I can tell. You know why that is? You've all 'ad a proper education, and we ain't."

"Ada? Might I suggest something?" said Elizabeth, with some awkwardness.

"What's that?"

"It's not too late to learn. It never is... I'm sorry if this is forward of me, but could I teach you a few subjects? All of you?"

Ada was thoughtful. "I think I'd like that very much, Miss Elizabeth."

"Thank you, Miss Elizabeth. I'd go for that," said Alfie.

"Fern, we could correspond. Like they do for correspondence courses."

"Wouldn't it be a lot of trouble for you?"

"Not at all. I'd enjoy it immensely."

"Oh... That's *really* nice of you."

Elizabeth smiled.

# Chapter 33

# Aftermath

The sun rose on stricken Chertsey Park. Most of its inhabitants awoke unrefreshed and worried. By contrast, those of Burgoyne's Agency had slept the sleep of the just and got up with lighter hearts. Unburdened of their responsibilities, they were more akin to cheerful sprites who might enjoy running about indoors, while everyone else plodded.

Miss Beech and the other Lyall Place maids had received more scares in a single night than ever before in all their lives combined. The horrors had begun with Sophie's sensational declaration that she and her staff were police agents and that there might be shootings. Afterwards, aides and Kemp's men visited the dormitory several times, with each visit being ruder and louder than the last. Then it went quiet for a while, until the machine gun started to fire outside. A man came and hid in the dormitory, but then ran away. Someone ran past the dormitory door. Then two polite men wearing balaclavas apologized for intruding, but asked if any men were hiding under the beds, and had they seen anyone trying to escape? The police came and asked similar questions. Another long, quiet period followed. Finally, as a gathering of spectres in a cemetery, the ladies of Burgoyne's Agency returned in the middle of the night, with Miss King softly whispering,

"Hello, it's only us. We're truly sorry to disturb you, but we have decided to stay after all. I hope you don't mind that we've brought a friend. Miss Woodhouse got locked out of her place and needs somewhere to sleep. Were you disturbed at all earlier?"

Yes, Miss Beech had been disturbed. Although she now feared Sophie as a harbinger of great doom and a menace in her own right, Miss Beech vented some annoyance at the frightfulness of everything since last they met. She demanded answers. Sophie briefly explained what had happened to Lord Stokely and why he was on his way to prison. Miss Beech wished she had not asked. She believed she would never sleep again, but she did, within a few minutes of all the lights being switched off.

Breakfast they had to get for themselves, because Mrs Potter, the incumbent cook, had disappeared. A little before, Sophie hunted about for Mr Dalgleish, who was not in his room. She found him in the Grand Salon sitting by himself, looking not too dissimilar to Uncle Teddy the night before.

"Miss King." He stood up. "I thought you had left."

"I've come to apologize for behaving so shabbily towards you."

He nodded in agreement as she spoke.

"The police asked me to do some special work, and part of it was to deceive. You neither deserved such treatment, nor should you suffer the results of the work. Sad to say, you have been treated poorly by me, and the results, I don't doubt, are devastating to your position."

"I cannot forgive you, Miss King. You broke a sacred trust. Entering a house, an earl's house, by subterfuge... I have no words for such outrageous behaviour. I could understand it better if you were a common thief, but you're not... I trusted you."

"I'm so sorry. I felt it had to be done."

"And I feel, I *know*, it should not have been done."

"I agree. Betraying your trust was wrong."

Dalgleish looked away. "Are the charges against Lord Stokely true?"

"Yes."

"And all that went on here was part of his plan to overthrow the government? The Red Fist and all those things?"

"Yes."

"That's very bad of him... Very bad."

She could see he was in conflict. On one side was his long life of duty to a family. On the other was disgust that the earl was a traitor to his country.

"I overhead someone say that Lord Stokely is illegitimate, and should not be an earl... I always wondered... Is this true?"

"I understand it to be so. I don't know if any admission has been made but, as far as I know, Uncle Teddy is his father. It was he who married Lady Georgiana, only it was represented in the documents that the old earl married her. I suppose, legally speaking, because Roderick was not an heir of the body of the old earl, he was not the next in line for the earldom, and should never have received the titles."

"Yes... Yes, I was told something about this by a former cook. She was dying and, as I thought then, delirious. She mistook me for another person long since gone. So, it is true... Ah, then, Mr Edward is the earl... Dear, dear... I must attend to him." He took two paces towards the door and stopped. "Should I refer to him as Lord Stokely?"

"I'm unsure. Would it not be best to ask him first?"

"That would be proper... I am sorry, Miss King, that we are parting on such terms. I cannot forgive."

"I know you can't, Mr Dalgleish."

She watched him leave the Grand Salon, then left herself. Outside, she met Mrs Newnham, the housekeeper. Sophie had seen her so seldom that she had almost forgotten about her.

"Miss King, have you seen Kemp?"

"No, I haven't. I understand he escaped last night. The police want to speak to him."

"That's what I've been told. So he's really gone, has he?"

"There's nothing for him to come back to, really. Yes, I would say he's gone for good."

"Nothing to come back to. That's so true." She began to laugh.

"Are you all right?"

"I don't know... They say that some prisoners don't want to leave the cell when their time's up... I have to leave. It's all smashed, isn't it?"

"I'm going to eat some breakfast. Why don't you come with me?"

"I've eaten already, thank you, Miss King."

"You could come anyway. Have some tea and we can talk."

"That's kind, but no, thank you... I must find another position. I can't stay here any longer. They'll make changes, sure enough, and they won't want me."

"Ah... You could try Burgoyne's Agency. I'm sure they can find something suitable for you."

"Do you think they would? I haven't done a very good job here, have I? I used to, years ago. I was very good and had the charge of a fine house. Then... then I came here."

"Is there something you should tell me?" Sophie spoke in a softer voice.

"I haven't told anyone. They don't know."

"Would you tell me?"

"He told me not to."

"Kemp?"

"Yes."

"He's your husband?"

"Yes..." She sighed deeply. "For years, in name only. Newnham is my maiden name. But please, don't tell anyone."

"I promise I won't. Come along with me. You're having tea, and that's final. Everything will get better."

They walked together. Sophie puzzled over whether she should be Burgoyne or King.

"I'm Sophie. If you don't mind my asking, what's your Chris-

425

tian name?"

"Marion."

"Marion. I had a friend at school named Marion, and I've always liked that name."

"It's been years since anyone's called me by it."

"Well, everything's changing. Why not for the best? Perhaps you'll hear your name more often from now on."

---

It was necessary that they should leave Chertsey Park in batches. Elizabeth took Flora, Ada, Alfie, and Broadbent-Wicks in Rabbit to the station first, and then returned. The second contingent had to stop at the Gardeners Arms in Ottershaw to retrieve Elizabeth's luggage. Despite yesterday's heroics, Elizabeth could not face Agnes after being locked out for the night.

Marion accompanied Sophie, Fern, and Elizabeth. Sophie had learned that Kemp had left Marion destitute, having controlled her wages for years. Their marriage was only a secret because Kemp wished not to be encumbered by an acknowledged wife. Sophie had tried to speak to Edward Fielding about the matter, but he refused to see her. Without revealing Marion's secret, she consulted Mr Dalgleish, but he was in no position to act, and stated that he had learned from Mr Fielding that he would refuse the earldom, but gave no reason. Sophie could not just leave Marion, so they took her with them. She and Fern would stay at Lady Shelling's for the night — there was room enough for both of them.

Sophie entered the Gardeners Arms. Agnes was busy behind the bar, but turned a face to Sophie, full of horrified apprehension.

"May I speak to you privately?" asked Sophie.

"Yes. Whatever's happened to Miss Woodhouse? Nothing bad, I hope. I've been that worried about her."

"I will reveal all in a moment."

"Will you? Come through here, miss." Agnes lunged at the counter flap and lifted it for Sophie. "Go to the back, first on your roight."

They settled in a small room.

"Would you like some tea?" Agnes did not want tea. She wanted to *know*.

"Thank you, but I can't stop. Here's the money in full for the room."

Sophie proffered an unsealed envelope. Agnes took it and peered inside.

"Thank you very much." She shifted her chair a little closer and stared at Sophie. "So what happened to Miss Woodhouse?"

"You know how she's a naturalist and likes to study owls?"

"Yes."

"And you know how she was so late last night?"

"Yes."

"Well, she went to Chertsey Park."

"Did she now? And what happened?"

"She was instrumental in having Lord Stokely arrested for treason."

"No!"

"Yes!"

"I've got so many questions. They're all a-tumblin' in my moind. I don't know what to ax."

"She's a police spy."

"Never…! You wouldn't think that to look at her, now would you?"

"No, you wouldn't. And that's why she's so good. She got evidence against Lord Stokely, and that was how the police could raid Chertsey Park last night."

"Just shows you, don't it? You never know about people. Him so famous, but then I don't really care about him. I'm interested in Miss Woodhouse, I am. 'Cause she stayed roight here, she did. Now, let me tell you what I know. We heard a lot about last noight one way or t'other. There were men in balaclavas, there were machine guns, and black marias. Is that all true?"

"Yes."

"Oh, lovely... And you're saying Miss Woodhouse is responsible for it all?"

"Not all of it, but a big important part."

"There... Tut, fancy that. A police spy at her age... And him up on treason charges... Is she all roight?"

"Yes. She's out in the car, and very tired."

"The poor soul, she would be... Oh, I wish you'd stay for another half hour."

"I'm so sorry. I must get her luggage and leave."

"Of course. I won't hold you up. Tell Miss Woodhouse she's welcome back any time she loikes, an' I'll give her something off the room if she stays... Fancy all that happening here." Agnes shook her head.

They said goodbye, and Sophie took away Elizabeth's luggage. The moment the door closed behind her and while the bell still jangled, Agnes was on the telephone ringing a friend.

"Joan, it's me, Agnes. Come round roight away. I've got summat to tell that you won't believe. No, you *won't* believe it, and I can't say it on the phone... Then turn the roast beef down, and have it late. Don't worry about him grumbling; they only ever go to sleep afterwards, so what's the difference?"

---

The sun also rose over Chertsey Station. There waited Detective Sergeant Gowers and a dozen constables. From the 10:14, the police intercepted eleven union members travelling independently of one another. These men, from different parts of the country, heading for Chertsey Park, were unaware of the previous night's events. They took the news of Stokely's arrest badly. Without exception, it produced disbelief, followed by a persecuted look when each man considered his own involvement in Stokely's schemes. They gave their names and addresses, and Gowers struck them off a list he had. One tried to flee, but was arrested and charged with trespassing on railway property after he had made the mistake of running along the tracks.

Gowers had slept for three hours. Among the documents retained by Vincent Cobden, secretary, he had found a list of names of the union men who would arrive on Sunday. There were thirty-six names on his copy of the list and, he supposed, they were each to receive a share of the £20,000 in cash contained in two strong boxes. Gowers had found the boxes in the Chertsey Park office.

Once, between train arrivals, Gowers crossed to the other platform to say goodbye to those from Burgoyne's Agency who were travelling back to London by train.

The 11:08 brought four more into the net, but there were none on the 12:02. Sergeant Gowers assumed someone had tipped off the other Stokely agents that the police were waiting for them. The others could be traced and, for all of them, once the charges to be laid were determined dependent upon the evidence, they could be brought to trial.

---

In Stepney, by standing on the doorstep of 143 Barnes Street, a glimpse might be had of a tiny portion of tiny York Square Gardens. Elizabeth had to be satisfied with that glimpse because, although she would have liked to live right on the square, the rent was far cheaper for her downstairs flat on Barnes Street.

It was almost three when she put the key in the lock to her flat. She was glad to be home, but excited about going to, of all places, Claridge's. What a whirlwind of activity it had been in the last few days, and tomorrow, she would receive £40! At present, though, she must get ready for the celebration.

She closed the door. "Desdemona…! There you are, my darling."

A fluffy black cat trotted eagerly towards her. Elizabeth stroked, and the cat purred.

"Now where is naughty Mr Falstaff, hmm?"

She quickly inspected her two rooms, the small bathroom, and the tiny kitchen. In looking for the errant cat, while followed by Desdemona, Elizabeth found her place in order.

"He's outside, I suppose."

She opened the back door to find Nick dangling a piece of string for Falstaff, a tabby, to catch at.

"Miss Elizabeth!" Nick stood up straight. "I wasn't expecting you back until tomorrow."

"It all ended early."

"What happened?"

"They arrested Stokely for treason. I saw them do it."

"Did you really? I wish I'd been there. What else happened?"

"Oh. I'm not sure if Miss Burgoyne would like me discussing the matter."

"Probably not, but I always find out stuff, anyway. Go on, miss, you can tell us a bit."

"It was extraordinary, really. There's one part I can tell you. Ruffians took me prisoner at Chertsey Park."

"No… Did they hurt you?"

"I can't say they did, but it was most upsetting at the time."

"Who are these blokes? I'll punch 'em for you."

"Nicholas, mind your temper. They're all under arrest."

"That's all right, then. But I don't like the idea of them upsetting you. Who do they think they are?"

"They were big men, and you're fourteen."

"I'm quick on me feet. Anyway, forget about them... Your cats are funny. You can do anything you like with Desdemona. You can pick her up and she's like a baby in your arms. But him..." Nick dangled the string for the cat. "Falstaff's artful. He's always up to something he shouldn't be."

"Don't I know it? But he's a lovely boy."

"One thing, miss. You won't tell me mates I've been playing with cats, will you?"

"I don't even know your friends, but why should it be a secret?"

"Yes, well. You see, fellas get on a certain way when they're together, and I'd never hear the last of it."

"Teasing, you mean. I shan't tell anyone. I'd ask you to stay for tea, but I have to go out soon... Nicholas, you have done very well looking after my home and my cats. It's been a great relief for me to know you were here taking care. I want you to have this."

She offered him half-a-crown, a stupendous amount within her economy.

"No, miss. That's very kind of you, but I can't accept. Miss Burgoyne's looked after all that."

"I know, but I want you to have it."

"I'm sorry, I have to say no... You're my friend. I can't take money from you."

"Ah, is that so? What a nice boy you are."

Nick became embarrassed. "Shall I come round tomorrow evening like I was supposed to?"

"You don't need to now."

"No, I don't mind. We can have a natter."

Elizabeth thought of how long it had been since she had entertained anyone. She had the idea of getting cakes from the bakery.

"I look forward to seeing you, Nicholas."

The meeting of Burgoyne's Secret Agency at Claridge's in Mayfair was a huge, exuberant, belt-loosening success. It was also attended by a mystery that had the agents wildly speculating. An unknown person sent and paid for a magnum of Champagne for their table. The cork flew, bubbles fizzed, and they laughed, but they never found out who had been their benefactor.

Archie Drysdale and Victoria Redfern sat in a secluded part of the same restaurant. They had arrived earlier than Burgoyne's Agency, and so noticed them enter. They also left earlier, and the agents were too engrossed in conversation to witness their rather stealthy departure. Archie knew it was an important celebration for them, and Victoria, now much more knowledgeable about Archie's work, had insisted upon sending the Champagne to Burgoyne's table. It was sent without a message to, as she said in her own words, 'Give them something to think about while they're laughing their heads off.'

---

Marion Newnham, lately the housekeeper at Chertsey Park, was already asleep when Sophie and Fern returned to White Lyon Yard at eleven. Fern, who would be travelling the next day, went to her bed. Sophie, still treading the heights of giddy euphoria, although the descent had begun, was ambushed upon her return by Aunt Bessie.

"I think I'm a wee bit tipsy," said Sophie, who lounged in her beautiful mauve evening gown, her head resting on the back of the armchair.

"So, I see," said Aunt Bessie.

"Some *wonderful* person sent us Champagne, and I don't know who it was."

"Probably a scientist conducting an experiment to see how quickly young women lose their wits."

"Ha. That's funny. You're always so amusing."

Aunt Bessie got up and rang the bell.

"How many glasses did you have?"

"Ooh... Four, five... No idea, really."

"In future, you shall have two and no more."

"But it's so very drinkable."

"So is coffee. Hawkins shall bring us a pot and that you will drink."

"It will keep me awake... I have work tomorrow."

"You're going in late. Do you honestly think, for one moment, that I'm going to let you sleep without first learning what happened? I shall not!"

"Of course, Auntie. I'm not sleepy."

"Sit up properly, then. You look like a drunken sailor."

"I don't!"

"There. Now you're sitting as a lady should... Ah, Hawkins."

"Yes, my Lady?"

"A pot of coffee and make it strong."

"At once, my Lady."

"Sophie, tell me everything down to the minutest detail. Omit nothing, otherwise I shan't sleep."

Aunt and restored niece talked until one in the morning, which was when Aunt Bessie ran out of questions and Sophie had no more to tell.

"Now I shall tell you something," said Aunt Bessie. "While you were stirring up the nest of vipers at Chertsey Park, I was conducting research in Fortnum and Mason's tea rooms. It appears that Edward Fielding killed a man, whether by accident or design — my informant did not know. It was something she heard from her mother, and goodness only knows where *she* got it from. Nevertheless, because of the death, Uncle Teddy wanted nothing to do with the title, and it was why he went overseas. What do you think of that, my dear? It's the basis for the whole charade and the half-baked reason to have his monstrous son inherit the title in such an imbecilic fashion!"

Sophie laughed. "Well done, Auntie! You've just fitted the last piece of the puzzle in its place. So *that* was the reason for the subterfuge!"

They chatted a little longer. At the very end, Sophie had a question.

"Auntie... Remember I received all that money to fight Stokely?"

"Yes, dear. Twenty-five hundred pounds, wasn't it?"

"That's right. I've spent three hundred for the wages and some incidentals on this last mission. I still have the rest, and I don't know what to do with it now that Stokely is defeated."

"An interesting problem... Save it to fight the next wicked villain who happens along?"

"There shan't be any more like him."

"Use it for other, more minor, cases?"

"That doesn't seem right to me. I try to think what Sir Ephraim would want me to do with it. I could return it to him, I suppose, but I don't think he would accept it. He said it was to carry on the fight. The fight's over. I always imagined the money would go to lawyers. It all would have gone to bring a suit against Stokely."

"Yes... Stokely hurt many people." Aunt Bessie raised her eyebrows.

"He did... What a good idea... A fund! People were injured and died. Some had their homes burnt. The money could help them... How would I go about administering it?"

"That takes some experience, which you do not possess. See Blackstone, my lawyer. He's a clever fellow, and I'm sure he could administer such a fund or knows of someone trustworthy who can."

"That's marvellous, and what a relief. I think it will please Sir Ephraim when I tell him... You're so clever."

"As well as amusing?"

"I'm sorry about that."

"I shan't mention it again... Would you be offended if I contributed to your fund?"

"You will? Oh, you are such a dear."

Sophie went over to kiss her aunt. Aunt Bessie patted her arm affectionately.

"Go to bed now, Sophie. You've had enough excitement for a long while to come."

# Chapter 34

# Epilogue

Stokely's reputation of having Britain's best interests at heart was so firmly entrenched in the public's mind that, rather than believe he was a traitor under arrest, the public preferred the idea that some horrible mistake had been made. With this as the starting point, acceptance that Stokely was a traitor was slow to take hold. The newspapers generally supported the same view, because Stokely was, after all, one of their own. They sought to question motives, rather than seek out facts. Stokely's own papers limped on but circulation dropped, because they published no private revelations about the earl's conduct nor gave explanation for the basis for the treason charges.

If the public thought the charge of treason was probably a mistake, it considered the murder, fraud, and conspiracy charges to be a sick joke, allowing them to disbelieve them until the trial would settle matters. Some anti-Stokely opinion did surface. Rambling and confused as to fact, epistolic exchanges appeared in several papers. The opposition put questions to the government, who replied it was in the hands of the police, or the legal process must run its course, so they were unable to comment fully. Actually, the government wished it would all go away, because the breadth and depth of

Stokely's network of infiltration was an acute embarrassment to them. The plan, more of a hope, was to let it all come out in dribs and drabs, making everyone tired of the story to the point where they might just forget about it.

Beyond the realms of newspapers, public opinion, and government silence, in the real centres of power and influence, such details as were circulated were sufficient to convince the hearer that Stokely was guilty of absolutely everything. This conviction was also widely held among his former closest supporters who now distanced themselves from the pariah. Added to facts were rumours and, if half of these had any truth to them, it was a surprise that Stokely had not been in the dock years ago.

Supporting Stokely had been an organization. He had lavished his care and money upon it. Without those attentions, it quickly fell to pieces. The destruction was hastened by more than a hundred arrests, additional to those made at Chertsey Park. The Red Fist disappeared immediately, and all the vital work Secretary Cobden had collected in the ballroom was in boxes, which rested on old shelves in a dingy locked room at Scotland Yard.

Roderick Fielding had to enter a plea. Knowing he could not win, he hoped to salvage something of his reputation. He would plead guilty to treason and not guilty to everything else. His intention was to speak at the coming trial, not in his defence, because he had none, but to justify himself. He would show them all that, while he may be technically guilty, his intentions and goals were loftier and more sublime than his enemies could appreciate. Pages littered his cell as he drafted and redrafted his speech. There was little else to do as few people visited him. When Lady Georgiana came, the meeting was raw and difficult and ended with her in tears. Stokely said it did him no good to see her behave this way, and told her that next time she came she was forbidden to cry.

The only twinge of conscience Stokely felt was when Edward Fielding came. He looked so old and beaten; it startled the prisoner. The twinge proved momentary. How could his father have so mismanaged his birth as to do him out of the titles? Stokely now considered Edward to be neither his uncle nor his father. After a brief, unsatisfactory interview, Stokely asked him not to visit again.

Mr Johnston, former Conservative but now independent MP for Walthamstow North, felt lonely sitting by himself in the House of Commons after having left the coalition government. The police had told him little about the blackmail case. They had been almost as reticent about the matter as he had. After all, he had not *known* he was a shareholder in a company that employed underage workers. Nobody had told *him*. And it would be *awful* if it *all* came out. Selling the shares had not made him feel any better.

He thought it funny, though, that about the time of Stokely's arrest, the blackmailer had stopped contacting him. Johnston hoped he had gone for good, but did not know for certain, and that worried him. As the blackmailer had not contacted him in the last week, Johnston was feeling a wave of relief in hoping and half believing it was 'all over'. He decided he would try to rejoin the government.

Politicians never suffer from embarrassment unless the newspapers get hold of something. Johnston had left the government, and now he would seek to return to it. What was embarrassing about that? Nothing. So he had a private word with an influential person. Johnston whispered in the influential ear. From the influential mouth came the words, "I'll see what can be done." And, within the hour, it *was* done.

The government firmly believed a vote was a vote, no matter who cast it. Johnston said to a reporter that it had all been a 'Misunderstanding', which had been 'Resolved', and that was the 'End of the Matter'. The newspapers which had printed the report of Johnston's dramatic departure, now stated that all previously irreconcilable differences had, indeed, been reconciled by the disputants who now waved olive branches, wore broad smiles, and gave hearty handshakes.

---

Late Thursday morning, Flora climbed the stairs of Marble Arch Underground Station. Next week, she had two auditions which, if her success rate held true, would mean she would land one of the parts. At present, with time on her hands and money in her purse, she was going to Selfridges. She had persuaded herself to buy several necessities at the department store, but also reasoned that there must be one or two frivolities she needed even more.

Driving westward along Oxford Street, Mr Philpott steered the car carefully around obstacles and at a cautious speed because of the pedestrians who wilfully launched themselves from the pavement without warning to cross the road. In the rear sat Lord Sidney Laneford, reading a newspaper. He put it down at Oxford Circus and looked about the street.

"Traffic's very slow today."

"It is, my Lord," said Philpott.

Lord Laneford looked at his watch. Flora was crossing Old Quebec Street.

"Why they choose the Great Western for the annual meeting, I'll never know."

"Tradition, my Lord?"

"One that needs throwing overboard. The place has a peculiar smell. Have you noticed it?"

Philpott worked the gears. "I believe it's the wax polish they use on the floors, my Lord."

"Ah... Better step on it or we'll be late."

"I will endeavour to arrive on time, my Lord."

They passed Harewood Place. Flora gazed at items displayed in a shop window.

Lord Laneford worked for the Home Office, nominally in the capacity of a financial advisor, but in reality overseeing a secretive branch of HO spies.

"This commitment takes me away from attending to the fallout of the Stokely affair... Very inconvenient."

"Indeed, it is, my Lord."

A policeman on point duty waved the car through the New Bond Street crossroad. Flora crossed Portman Street.

After Orchard Street, Flora slowed to look in Selfridges' windows. She found they always had such nice displays.

"The lunch will be over by two," said Laneford. "I'll meet you outside no later than a quarter past."

"Understood, my Lord."

The car was stopped by a policeman at Duke Street. Lord Laneford pursed his lips and stared up at the façade of the Selfridges building across the street. They waited. Flora drifted to another window. The car began moving again. Flora quickened her pace towards the entrance.

"Stop the car!"

"Where, my Lord?"

"Right here, man, right here!"

"Yes, my Lord."

The car blocked traffic as Laneford got out.

"You can't park on the road," said Laneford. "I don't know, um, just take the rest of the day off."

"Oh, my Lord? What about the luncheon?"

"I'm not going. Use your discretion to get me out of it. Don't you understand? It's Flora Dane!"

"Is it, my Lord?"

"Yes. Oh, my hat." He retrieved his hat and umbrella from the back, then shot into Selfridges' entrance.

He started off in pursuit of the woman who had once pretended to be his wife — an arrangement falling well outside of standard Home Office procedures. As soon as he was inside, he moderated his speed while still looking for

Flora. Laneford was tall, in his thirties, and very well dressed. With a slightly old-fashioned air, he gave the impression of being dependable and kind, although at the moment he was glancing feverishly and hawk-like along aisles and at different counters.

He saw her waiting at the lifts and raced over despite the trepidation he felt at the coming meeting. He slowed to a walk, trying to hide a thumping heart.

"Hello," he said pleasantly as he raised his hat. "Fancy meeting you here."

"Sidney! How *lovely* to see you!"

She was so delighted, all his doubts melted away.

"You're here shopping, I take it?" he asked.

"Naturally. Just for a few things I need. What are you here for?"

"I've no idea."

"Really? But I know you to be a very busy gentleman."

"Not today. I'm just mooching about to pass the time. I thought I'd see if they had anything here that interests me. What a happy coincidence, though. Will you have lunch at the restaurant upstairs?"

"I hadn't planned to."

"Well, you are going to now. I positively insist."

"Do you? That's very bold, but I accept." She laughed.

The lift arrived, and the uniformed woman operator greeted them brightly. They entered with several others. When they got off at the floor Flora wanted, Laneford took her to one side, out of the way of other passengers.

"I must say this first... I've missed you."

Flora smiled. "Have you...? I didn't believe all that rot about killing time for a second."

"It was rather thin, but all I could think of in the moment. I happened to see you from my car while passing. You came in here... And I followed."

"Ah, so that's it... Fate has smiled for once." She put her arm through his. "See, we needn't miss each other again. Let's go to the restaurant. My shopping can wait."

She turned him about and pressed the button for the lift.

"Do I continue calling you Gladys?"

"The name's Flora. But you're such a clever spy, Sidney, I'm sure you knew it already."

---

Early Friday morning, Sophie was in her office, Elizabeth was at her desk, Nick and another messenger were on their bicycles picking up work, and Miss Jones' typing department was busy. Three applicants had been dealt with and one placement made. Then someone began noisily climbing the stairs.

"Hello. You're new since I was here last," said the woman dressed in black.

"Good morning. I must be, because we haven't met before," said Elizabeth.

Sophie flung open her door. "Mrs Barker! I *knew* I recognized the voice... No... Did he die?"

"Yes, sadly he's gone," said Mrs Barker.

"Do come and sit in here... Elizabeth, would you make some tea, please?"

"Yes, Miss Burgoyne."

With the door closed and tea in front of them, Mrs Barker explained matters to Sophie.

"Sir Ephraim took a turn for the worse, let me see, on a Wednesday, that'd be January the twelfth. Yes, that's it. He went right off his food and I knew then, that he'd be not much longer for this world. It's always the same. They don't touch their food and they drop off like flies."

"Didn't he eat anything?"

"Not proper food. Toast or thin gruel towards the end. A

body can't live on that. I tried my best to tempt, but no, he wouldn't touch any more than a mouthful or two. And I think he did that just to say he'd eaten. But at the end, not a *morsel* was passing his lips."

"When did he die, exactly?"

"Monday night, seven o'clock, and he was buried yesterday. And do you know, the family dismissed me immediately afterwards. It's disgusting. Not even a day to gather my wits. But then it's all about money with them. They dismissed some others at the same time."

"That's really too bad of them."

"Having said that, Sir Ephraim was very generous towards me. Two hundred pounds. How about that? You could have knocked me down with a feather. To tell the truth, I wasn't expecting anything... Well, one hopes, of course. His secretary, Mr Reese, give it me, because I wasn't in the will. Mrs Fisher was, and she was looking so anxious, poor thing. Then after the will was read, you could see the relief in her face. She didn't say anything, but I knew then that he'd done right by her... It's *very* difficult when grief and a want for money are mixed up."

"I completely understand that. Did, by any chance, Sir Ephraim hear of Lord Stokely's arrest?"

"I'm not sure." Mrs Barker looked puzzled. "His valet, Mr Fenton, read the papers to him religiously, but I don't know if he was taking it in. He'd sunk very low, you see... Wait. I tried him with an egg Monday morning, and Mr Fenton took the papers up on the tray, and the story was in them then... Oh. Was *he* behind that business at Abinger Mansion? Stokely?"

"Yes."

"That's dreadful. How *wicked* of him... I suppose Sir Ephraim knew Lord Stokely had done him wrong, and you want to know if Mr Fenton read him the story? Then, let me see. I do believe... Nurse Gleason said Sir Ephraim had a crying fit Monday morning when Mr Fenton was with him. There you are. That *has* to be it."

443

"It sounds like it, doesn't it? Then Sir Ephraim died knowing that Stokely had been charged... I imagine he cried because it opened old wounds. Oh dear, I feel so sorry for him... How about you. Are you keeping well?"

"A bit sad and quiet at the moment, as is to be expected. But I'm as fit as anything and ready to work, that I am. I knew you'd be interested in the goings-on at Abinger Mansion, so I'd have come anyway, but I'd like to go back on your books, if you'll take me."

"There's *no* question about that, Mrs Barker. What type of position are you looking for?"

"Permanent, but not for an invalid near the end. It's very trying. I'll do temporary in the meantime."

"I'll make a note." Sophie took Mrs Barker's card from a drawer. "Where are you living now?"

"With my sister, until I'm settled."

"I have her address here."

"That's good. Now, Miss Burgoyne." Mrs Barker glanced at the door to see if anyone was listening and then spoke very low. "If you get one of those funny jobs from the police, and a cook's wanted, then you need look no further than here." She put her hand flat on the desk and nodded emphatically.

Sophie leaned forward and spoke in an equally low and serious voice. "I shall file *that* information in a safe place." She pointed to the side of her head.

Mrs Barker smiled. "I'd best be going. I know how busy you get, and I don't want to wear out my welcome. Say hello to Ada, and Miss Flora for me." She stood up. "Thank you for the tea. It was very nice meeting you again, Miss Burgoyne, that it was."

"And I'm glad to see you, too, even under such sad circumstances."

Superintendent Percival Penrose, Special Duties, Scotland Yard, had had a long and eventful career as a policeman. His most enjoyable years had been as an inspector, so he preferred being called 'Inspector', the name with which he felt most comfortable. In his present position, as superintendent of special duties, the work put him under continual strain. This pressure allowed little time for those small interactions with other officers and the public that made life pleasant for him — interactions outside of an actual arrest, that is. Because of this noticeable lack, a brief excursion away from the Yard was like a restorative for Penrose. Going to Burgoyne's Agency admirably filled the bill. It was not too far, and the visit was just long enough to serve its purpose. He could talk about cases and find diversion at the same time.

On Tuesday morning, the eighth of February, 1921, Penrose climbed the agency's stairs.

"Good morning, Miss Elizabeth," said Penrose.

"Good morning, Inspector Penrose," she replied.

"You remembered, that's nice... Here's a thing I've turned over in my mind. Why do people call you Miss Elizabeth? Everyone does it."

"I don't know, I'm sure. I've always wondered about the phenomenon." Elizabeth summoned up her courage. "Why are you called, 'Inspector'?"

"I prefer it. A foible of mine, but it takes a sight of training with some." He smiled. "I know Miss Burgoyne is always busy. Do you think I could be squeezed in for a few minutes? That's all I need."

Elizabeth stared for a moment. Penrose, a big man, looked about as unsqueezable as they came. "I'm sure she will make time for you, Inspector."

A minute later, Penrose sat across the desk from Sophie. She got up and opened the window a little.

"That will save you asking," said Sophie.

"Aren't you the thoughtful one," said Penrose, who took out his pipe and pouch, and slowly attended to them while speaking. "You're probably wondering why I'm here."

"Absolutely. Your visits always have a surprise attached to them. Is it about Stokely?"

Penrose smiled. "I'll tell you summat. I'm that sick of hearing the fella's name, I don't mind never hearing it again. No, he's in the past now, and good riddance."

"That must make it much quieter for you, then."

"Ha...! I wish. You should see my desk. There are more files on it than there are in the records room... That's a slight exaggeration, but I'm as swamped as ever I was."

"Is that so? No putting your feet up on the desk?"

"There's no room for 'em. Can't moan to the other officers. We're all in the same boat." He finished packing his pipe and held it ready in his hand. "The reason for my visit is this. We have a lot of minor cases on the go. Until now, when the Yard's employed Burgoyne's, we've asked for a team. For some cases I have, it only requires a servant slipping in quiet like. Other cases need one person staying for a longer period. It could be a matter of weeks or even months. I'm not suggesting you do that work, because I'm sure you have your hands full. You must have a few sensible people who can keep their eyes and ears open. A person like that would come in quite handy."

"I have people on the books who can fulfil your requirements. Several have worked at dinners in the past when I've needed to make up the numbers for a police operation."

"Arh, that's good. Some houses will be more middle class than what's gone before. The type where it's just a couple of maids doing the housework, and one needs to be on our side."

"I'm sure I can find suitable candidates. Getting them into the household will be difficult."

"I was thinking about that. If the party we're interested

in should advertise for help, your maid answers the advertisement. Also, a Burgoyne's circular could be popped in the letter box. That's all a bit hit and miss, though. The key is to have the party find Burgoyne's for themselves. Any ideas?"

"Yes."

"What?"

"Knock on the door and ask for work with valid references in hand."

"I knew I came to the right place... Can't make the party suspicious, though."

"It won't. I'll train my candidates thoroughly."

Penrose and Sophie discussed it further and ended by haggling over the compensation for such services. Penrose had yet to light his pipe.

"Now there's one thing that's been a-nagging at me for a very long time. It's a peculiar set-up if I'm reading it right."

"I'm all agog, Inspector."

"You'd think feuding was a thing of the past. There are these two families that live cheek by jowl in a certain county, and they hate one another. Have done for two hundred years, so I'm told. Back then, there were fights and murders, arson, and general nastiness on both sides. Don't know who started it because there are two versions of the story. That don't matter. It all died down, with only a tamer outbreak now and again. Well, as of today, there have been two murders in the past year — one in each family. Both are unsolved, and pretty near everyone's a suspect. Can you imagine it? Magically, both families are struck dumb. They don't so much as blame each other."

"I've never heard of anything like it," said Sophie.

"It gets stranger still. There's an annual ball in that part of the county. It's an important affair and everyone attends from miles around. The two families alternate in hosting this ball. One feuding family has it in their house, and the other feuding family attends. Apparently, missing the ball is just not done. There. What do you think of that?"

"They are completely ridiculous."

"Arh, but it's what they do." He looked at his pipe for a moment. "I can get Burgoyne's in working the ball, because I know which family is holding it this year. They'll need extra staff, four servants for certain. They've yet to announce the date. Probably late June or it might be July. Would you have any interest? I believe we've established the rates between us now."

Sophie considered the matter. "If I consent to this, will you tell me more? Right away?"

"Miss Burgoyne, you only need to say yes."

"Yes."

Penrose lit his pipe.

# Also By

**If you have enjoyed this book, please help by leaving a good review. It is greatly appreciated.**

### SOPHIE BURGOYNE SERIES
Secret Agency
Lady Holme
Dredemere Castle
Chertsey Park
Primrose Hill (coming soon)

### BRENT UMBER SERIES
Death between the Vines
Death in a Restaurant
Death of a Detective
Death at Hill Hall
Death on the Slopes
Death of a Narcissist

Printed in Great Britain
by Amazon